TALES OF MAJIPOOR

D0530288

TALES OF MAJIPOOR

ROBERT SILVERBERG

Copyright © Agberg, Ltd 2013

The right of Robert Silverberg to be identified as the
author of this work has been asserted by him in accordance
with the Copyright, Designs and Patents Act 1988.

First published in Great Britain in 2013
by Gollancz
An imprint of the Orion Publishing Group
Orion House, 5 Upper St Martin's Lane, London wc2h 9ea
An Hachette UK Company

This edition published in Great Britain in 2013 by Gollancz

1 3 5 7 9 10 8 6 4 2

A CIP catalogue record for this book
is available from the British Library

isbn 978 0 575 13007 4

Typeset by Deltatype Ltd, Birkenhead, Merseyside

Printed by CPI Group (UK) Ltd, Croydon, cro 4yy

The Orion Publishing Group's policy is to use papers that
are natural, renewable and recyclable products and made
from wood grown in sustainable forests. The logging and
manufacturing processes are expected to conform to the
environmental regulations of the country of origin.

www.orionbooks.co.uk
www.gollancz.co.uk

FOR WOJTEK

Who thought of this book before I did

Acknowledgments

"The End of the Line," copyright © 2011 by Agberg, Ltd. First published in *Asimov's Science Fiction*.

"The Book of Changes," copyright © 2003 by Agberg, Ltd. First published in *Legends Two*.

"The Tomb of the Pontifex Dvorn," copyright © 2011 by Agberg, Ltd. First published in *Subterranean*.

"The Sorcerer's Apprentice," copyright © 2004 by Agberg, Ltd. First published in *Flights*.

"Dark Times at the Midnight Market," copyright © 2010 by Agberg, Ltd. First published in *Swords and Dark Magic*.

"The Way They Wove the Spells in Sippulgar," copyright © 2009 by Agberg, Ltd. First published in *Fantasy & Science Fiction*.

"The Seventh Shrine," copyright © 1998 by Agberg, Ltd. First published in *Legends*.

Tales of Majipoor, copyright © 2013 by Agberg, Ltd.

Contents

Prologue

They came from Old Earth. They found an enormous planet, a gigantic world which, huge as it was, was suitable for human settlement because of its low gravitational pull. Life abounded there, life of all sorts, including a sparse population of aboriginal humanoids, mysterious shapeshifting forest-dwellers. To the settlers from Old Earth, those natives – the Piurivars, they called themselves, but the Earthmen called them Shapeshifters or Metamorphs – did not seem important. Surely there was room among them on this vast planet for colonists from another world.

And so the colony was planted. Settlements sprouted and grew, first on the continent called Alhanroel, then on the wild secondary continent of Zimroel, and even some on the desert continent of Suvrael in the sun-blasted south. Life was easy on fertile Majipoor. In the kindly tropical and subtropical climates, the human population grew and grew and grew, and over the course of time other settlers from different worlds came, the reptilian Ghayrogs and the burly four-armed Skandars and the small many-tentacled Vroons, and others besides. What had become a population of thousands expanded to millions – to billions—

As their little towns grew into large cities and the cities into vast metropolises, the settlers felt the need of a worldwide governmental system. They devised one: a double monarchy, the Pontifex and the Coronal, an emperor and a king, with each Pontifex choosing his successor when his turn came to ascend to the senior title. The Pontifex reigned from a subterranean Labyrinth and rarely was seen by ordinary mortals. His younger colleague, the Coronal, was the public face of the monarchy, eventually coming to establish his court at a sprawling castle atop the colossal peak known as Castle Mount. Somehow the system worked, mostly.

The years passed. Thousands of years. A civilization of unique complexity evolved on Majipoor.

There were problems, of course—

1

The End of the Line

"If you really want to learn something about the Shapeshifters," the District Resident said, "you ought to talk to Mundiveen. He lived among them for about a dozen years, you know."

"And where do I find this Mundiveen?" Stiamot asked.

"Oh, you'll see him around. Crazy old doctor with a limp. Eccentric, annoying, a mean little man – he stands right out."

It was Stiamot's second day in Domgrave, the largest city – an overgrown town, really – in this obscure corner of northwestern Alhanroel. He had never been in this part of the continent before. No one he knew ever had, either. This was agricultural country, a fertile land of odd greenish soil where a widely spaced series of little settlements, mere scattered specks amidst zones of densely forested wilderness, lay strung out along the saddle that separated massive Mount Haimon from its almost identical twin, the equally imposing Zygnor Peak. The planters here ruled their isolated estates as petty potentates, pretty much doing as they pleased. The region was in its dry time of the year here, when everything that was not irrigated was parched, and the wind out of the west carried the faint salt tang of the distant sea. The only official representative of the government was the District Resident, a fussy, soft-faced man named Kalban Vond, who had been stationed out here for many years, filing all the proper reports on time and stamping all the necessary bureaucratic forms but performing no other significant function.

But now the Coronal Lord Strelkimar, who had grown

increasingly strange and unpredictable in his middle years, had taken into his head to set forth on a grand processional, only the second one of his reign, that would take him on a great loop, starting from the capital city of Stee that sprawled halfway up the slope of the great central Mount and descending into the western lowlands beyond, and through these northwestern provinces, out to the sea via Sintalmond and Michimang, down the coast to the big port of Alaisor, and inland again via a zigzag route through Mesilor and Thilambaluc and Sisivondal back up the flank of the Mount to Stee. It was traditional for the Coronal to get himself out of the capital and display himself to the people of the provinces every few years, Majipoor being so huge that the only way to sustain the plausibility of the world government was to give the populace of each far-flung district the occasional chance to behold the actual person of their king.

To Stiamot, though, this particular journey was an absurd one. Why, he wondered, bother with these small agricultural settlements, so far apart, ten thousand people here, twenty thousand there, where the government's writ was so very lightly observed? This was mainly a wilderness territory, after all, with only this handful of plantations interrupting the thick texture of the forests. The Coronal, Stiamot thought, would do better directing his attention to the major cities, and the cities of the other continent, at that, where he had never been. Over there in distant, largely undeveloped Zimroel, in such remote, practically mythical places as Ni-moya and Pidruid and Til-omon, was the Coronal Lord Strelkimar anything more than a name? And what concern did their people have, really, with the decrees and regulations that came forth from Stee? He needed to make his presence felt there, where a huge population gave no more than lip service to the central government. Here, there was little to gain from a visit by the Coronal.

The chosen route was not without its dangers. The valley towns, Domgrave and Bizfern and Kattikawn and the rest, were mere islands in a trackless realm of forests, and through those forests flitted mysterious bands of aboriginal Metamorphs, still unpacified, who posed a frequent threat to the nearby human settlements. The Metamorphs constituted a great political problem for the rulers of Majipoor, for in all the thousands of years of human settlement here they had never fully reconciled themselves to the existence of the intruders among them, and now seemed to be growing increasingly restive. There were constant rumors that some great Metamorph insurrection was being planned; and, if that was so, this would be the place to launch it. Nowhere else on the continent of Alhanroel were humans and Metamorphs so closely interwoven. It was not impossible that the Coronal's life would be at risk here.

But it was not Stiamot's place to set royal policy, or even to quarrel with it, only to see that it was carried out. He was one of the most trusted members of the Coronal's inner circle, which was not saying much, for Strelkimar had never been an extraordinarily trusting man and had grown more and more secretive as time went along. Possibly the irregular way he had come to the throne had something to do with that, the setting aside of his kindly, foolish, ineffectual cousin Lord Thrykeld, a virtual coup d'etat. In any case, a counsellor who contradicted the Coronal was not likely to remain a counsellor very long; and so, when Strelkimar said, "I will go to Alaisor by way of Zygnor Peak and Mount Haimon, and you will precede me and prepare the way," Stiamot did not presume to question the wisdom of the route. He was not a weak or a passive man, but he was a loyal one, and he was the Coronal's right hand, who would never even consider rising up in opposition to his master.

And the journey had a special appeal for Stiamot. He was among those at court who had begun to give careful thought to the need for a new policy toward the aboriginal folk. A good first step would be to learn more about them, and he hoped to do that by coming here.

They had always fascinated him, anyway: their silent, stealthy ways, their aloof and unreadable natures, their customs and religious ideas, and, above all, their biologically baffling gift of shapeshifting. He had spent the past several years gathering whatever information he could about them, striving to know them, to get inside their minds. Without that, what sort of settling of accounts with them could be achieved? But he had never managed any real understanding of them. He knew some words of their language, he had collected a few of their paintings and carvings, he had read what he could find of what had been written about them, and still he stood entirely outside them. They remained as alien to him as they had been when, as a small boy, he had first heard that there existed on Majipoor a race of strange beings that once had had exclusive possession of the vast planet, long before the first humans had ever come to it.

There were no Metamorphs in Stee or any of the other cities in the capital territory, of course, but Stiamot, traveling through the land on this or that mission for the Coronal, had had a few brief glimpses of them. And once, when the Coronal had journeyed down to the Labyrinth to confer with the senior monarch, the Pontifex Gherivale, Stiamot had taken the opportunity to visit the nearby ruins of the ancient Metamorph capital of Velalisier, and quite a wondrous time he had had among those stone temples and pyramids and sacrificial altars. Out here in the hinterlands he hoped for a chance to experience the Metamorph culture at close range. And perhaps the eccentric Dr. Mundiveen would consent to serve as his guide.

Stiamot's first few days in Domgrave were spent arranging for the Coronal's arrival, checking out the route he would travel for places of possible risk and seeing to it that the Coronal's lodgings would be not only secure but appropriately comfortable. It was too much to expect luxury in these parts, but a certain degree of magnificence was necessary to remind the local grandees that the ruler of the world was among them. Kalban Vond, the District Resident, offered his own house for the Coronal's use – no palace, but the closest thing to a stately house that Domgrave could provide, a many-balconied building three stories high with ornate moldings and handsome inlays of decorative woods – and Stiamot set about having it bedecked with such tapestries and carpets and draperies as this very provincial province could supply. He himself commandeered a smaller but nevertheless pleasant house not far from the main highway as his own headquarters. He met with wine-merchants and providers of meat and game. He sent messengers to the prime landholders of the territory, inviting them to the great banquet that the Coronal would hold. In the evenings he dined with the Resident, who managed to produce reasonable fare, if nothing on a par with what Stiamot had become accustomed to at court, and plied him with questions about the region, the climate, the predominant crops, the personalities of the heads of the leading families, and – eventually – about the Metamorph tribes of the forests.

The Resident, plump and slow-moving and at least twenty years older than Stiamot, was a conventional, cautious man, and beneath his caution Stiamot thought he could detect a weariness, a bleakness of spirit, a thwarted sense that he had hoped for more out of life than a career as District Resident in an unimportant and backward rural district. But he did not seem unintelligent. He listened carefully to Stiamot's questions and responded in abundant detail, and when Stiamot had returned once too often to the subject of the Metamorphs Kalban Vond said, "You keep coming back to them, don't you? They must interest you very much."

"They do. It's nothing of an official nature, you understand. Just my own curiosity. We could say that I'm something of a student of them."

The Resident's sleepy blue eyes turned suddenly bright. "A student? What interests you, may I ask, about those sneaky, nasty savages?"

Stiamot, startled, caught his breath. But he showed his

displeasure only by the slightest quirk of his lips. "Is that how you see them?"

"Most of us do, out here."

"Be that as it may, we have to consider that we share the planet with them. They were here first. We thrust ourselves down among them and shoved them aside."

"So to speak," said Kalban Vond primly. "Majipoor's a big place. There's plenty of room for both races, wouldn't you say?"

Stiamot managed a faint smile. "I wonder if they see it that way. But in any case, problems are brewing, and it's necessary to give some thought to them. Our population is growing very rapidly, and I don't just mean the human population. Ghayrogs – Hjorts –the other non-human groups also—"

"Room for all," Kalban Vond said, sounding a little nettled. "A very big world. We've lived side by side with them fairly peacefully for thousands of years."

"Side by side, yes. And fairly peacefully, I suppose. But, as I say, there are more of us than ever before. The world is big, but it isn't infinite. And those thousands of years have gone by, and have they become our friends? Are we heading toward any sort of real rapport with them? You know as well as I do that there have been some very unpleasant incidents, and it's my impression that those incidents are becoming more frequent. They hate us, don't they? And we fear them. They put up with our settling on their world because they have no choice, and here in this valley you live next door to them wondering how long they'll continue to maintain the peace. That's so, isn't it?"

"Perhaps you put it a bit extremely," the Resident said. "Hate – fear—"

"A moment ago you called them 'sneaky, nasty savages.' Which one of us is being extreme? Is that how you usually speak of your friends, Resident?"

"I never claimed they were my friends, you know," said Kalban Vond. 'You're the one who used the word."

Stiamot could make no response to that. In the chilly silence that followed the Resident turned aside to open a second bottle of wine and refill their bowls. Something of a confrontational tone was creeping into the conversation, and perhaps this was meant as a calming gesture. They were drinking a surprisingly fine wine, a blue one from Stoienzar in the south. Stiamot had never expected to be offered anything so good here, or to have the Resident be so generous with it.

After a moment he said, a little more gently, "I think we both agree, at any rate, that we're not making much progress toward developing a more harmonious relationship with them. Not making any at all, in fact. But we need to. As our population grows, so does their resentment of our presence here. If we don't come to some sort of understanding with them soon, we'll find ourselves in a state of constant collision with them. Warfare, in fact. I've heard the rumors."

"Well, Prince Stiamot, at least here we agree."

"It can't be allowed to happen. We need to head it off."

"And do you have a plan? Does Lord Strelkimar?"

"It's not something his lordship has spoken of with me. But I assure you the Council has been discussing it."

Kalman Vond sat up alertly, and his eyes were once again gleaming. All that weariness and self-pitying sadness had fallen from him in a moment. Stiamot saw the man's unabashed eager excitement: it must seem to him that he was about to be made privy to intimate details of the deliberations of the Council. Sitting here sipping wine with one of the Coronal's close advisors was surely the biggest thing that had happened to him in all the years since he had been posted to this dreary province, and the thought that he would very shortly be playing host to the Coronal himself in his very own home must be dizzying.

But no revelations of court deliberations were going to be forthcoming tonight. Stiamot said, "We've been speaking about the Metamorphs only in the most general way, so far. Everyone agrees that we need to examine the whole problem much more thoroughly than ever before. And, as I said, my interest in them is a matter of mere personal curiosity. They fascinate me. Now that I find myself in a district where Metamorphs actually live, I hope to get a chance to learn something more about them – some details of their culture, their governmental structure, their religious beliefs, their art—"

"You ought to talk to Dr. Mundiveen about all that," said Kalban Vond.

Of course Stiamot's interest in the Metamorphs was much more than a matter of mere personal curiosity, but there was no reason why he had to explain that to the District Resident. The Metamorph problem had been central to Council discussions for the past several years, and, though nothing whatever had been heard from the Coronal on the topic, it surely had to be on his mind as well.

By and large, the Metamorphs kept to their secluded forest homes and the people of the cities and farming districts of Majipoor to the territories they occupied, and each group did its best to pretend that the other was not there, or was, at least, invisible. But there had been a good many ugly incidents. Wherever Metamorph and human interests overlapped, difficulties arose. The Metamorphs held certain places sacred, but who knew which ones they were, until a trespass had occurred? The ever-expanding human population of Majipoor, and its constantly increasing non-human adjuncts, kept pushing outward into new lands where the Metamorphs would abide no intrusion. Reports trickled to the capital of occasional outbreaks of conflict, of kidnappings and killings, of skirmishes, of massacres, even. Information took so long to reach Stee from outlying regions, and arrived in such uncertain form, that no one at the capital could be completely certain of what was taking place; but plainly there was friction, there was violence, and neither side was wholly without blame. Now and again Metamorphs, erupting out of nowhere in the night, had slaughtered human settlers venturing into places that should not have been ventured into. Humans, coming upon some tempting locality that invited settlement, had driven its Metamorph population out by force, or simply destroyed them. There had, of course, been such incidents throughout all the thousands of years since the first emigrants from Old Earth had come to this world. But as the cities spread outward and the agricultural settlements that supported them multiplied, they appeared to be increasing in number, and there were those at court who felt that sooner or later some great precipitating event would touch off an all-out war between the Metamorphs and the humans of Majipoor, and that event could not be many years away.

The court was broken into various factions. Some members of the Coronal's inner circle, a majority, perhaps, felt that a time was coming when complete separation of the races would have to be enforced, with the Metamorphs packed off into reservations of their own, possibly on the relatively lightly inhabited continent of Zimroel, and permitted there to live as they had always lived, but without access to the territories occupied by humans. An opposing group – not very numerous, but they were exceedingly vocal – regarded that as a futile notion, and were ready to launch an all-out war of extermination, arguing that the Metamorphs could never be confined in that way and such a plan was simply a prescription for an eternity of guerilla warfare.

Stiamot himself, who was by nature a mediator, a peacemaker, had emerged as the leader of a moderate central faction, one that saw great practical difficulties in the separationist scheme and looked upon the idea of a war of extermination as barbaric and repellent. It was Stiamot's hope that through sympathetic meetings of the minds, a determined attempt by each species to understand the needs and goals of the other, a permanent detente could be established, with clear lines of territorial delineation for each race and complete freedom of travel across those boundaries. In Council he had argued as persuasively as he knew how for such a policy. But Stiamot had not been able to make much headway with that over the extremists to either side of him. So little was known of the real nature of the Metamorphs, and so little had been done to reach out to them, that most council-members looked upon his position as hopelessly idealistic. As for the Coronal, he had stayed aloof from the discussions thus far, lost as he was in what seemed to be some inner anguish that had no connection to any of the governmental issues of the day. But he could not remain aloof forever.

The Coronal's arrival in Domgrave was still at least a week away when Stiamot saw his first Shapeshifter. It was the quiet time of the morning midway between breakfast and lunch, when the air was dry and still and the sun, climbing toward noon height, held everything in the grip of its insistent force. Stiamot was returning to his lodgings from a meeting with the head of the municipal police, going on foot down a sleepy street of small white-fronted houses flanked by rows of dusty-leaved matabango trees. A tall, *very* tall, figure wrapped in a flimsy, loosely fitting green robe emerged from an alley fifty feet in front of him, began to cross the street, saw him, halted, turned to face him, stared.

Stiamot halted as well. He knew at once that the man – *was* it a man? – was a Metamorph, and he was astonished to encounter one right here in town. The few others that he had seen before had been like wraiths, flitting through the edge of some forest glade and vanishing into the underbrush as soon as they were aware that they were being perceived. But here was this one right in downtown Domgrave, unmistakably a Metamorph, tall, thin, sallow-skinned, sharp of cheekbone, with long nar-row eyes that sloped inward toward the place where its nose would be if there were anything more than a minuscule bump where a nose ought to be. It seemed as curious about him as he was about it, pausing, standing in that odd stance of theirs, one long leg wrapped around the shin of the other so that it stood with utter and total dignity while balanced on its left foot alone. Its stare was calm and chilly. Stiamot wondered what, if anything, he could do to capitalize on the opportunity that had been so unexpectedly presented to him. "I greet you in the name of the Coronal Lord Strelkimar, whose counsellor I am?" No. Ridiculous. "I am Prince Stiamot of Stee, and I have come here to learn something about –" No. No. "I am a newcomer in Domgrave, and I wonder whether you and I—"

Impossible. There was nothing he could say that would be appropriate. The Shapeshifter clearly did not want anything to do with him. Those cold downsloping eyes left no doubt of that. The purpose of that icy glare was to establish a boundary, not to build a bridge. Stiamot and the Metamorph were separated not only by fifty feet of space but by an infinitely greater gulf of difference, and there was no way to breach that barrier. All Stiamot could do was stand, and stare, and curse himself for a blithering feckless fool, hopelessly unprepared for this meeting with one of the beings he had come here to make contact with.

Then for a single strange moment the outlines of the Shapeshifter's body seemed to blur and flicker, and Stiamot realized he was watching some kind of brief, barely perceptible metamorphosis take place, a loosening and transmogrification of form that ended as quickly as it had begun, as though the Shapeshifter were saying, mockingly, *I can do this and you cannot*. And then the Metamorph swung around and continued on its way across the street, disappearing from view in a dozen long-legged strides, leaving Stiamot standing stunned and bewildered in the mid-morning stillness.

There was a second significant encounter much later that same day. Stiamot had fallen into the habit of going at the end of the day with some of the younger staff aides to an inn just off the main square that was frequented by the town's wealthier planters and any visitor from the outlying plantations who happened to be in Domgrave on business. Since these people were going to bear most of the not inconsiderable expense of playing host to a Coronal making the grand processional, it seemed like a wise tactic for Stiamot to go among them, share a couple of flasks of wine with them in their cramped, dreary little tavern, reassure them that they would find the visit of the Coronal Lord very much to their benefit.

"He wouldn't have bitten you, you know," a dry, flat-toned voice said as Stiamot entered.

He turned. "Pardon me?"

"The Piurivar. They're a damned shy bunch, most of them. If you actually want to get anywhere with them, you've got to open your mouth, not just stand there like a gaffed gromwark waiting for them to say something. I'm Mundiveen, by the way."

Stiamot had already figured that much out. *Crazy old doctor with a limp*, Kalban Vond had said. *Eccentric, annoying. Stands right out*. That much was easy. The man who stood before him, one elbow hooked lazily over the counter of the bar, was old, small, lean almost to the point of fleshlessness, a short, compact figure with piercingly intense gray eyes and a long, wild shock of coarse, unkempt white hair. Stiamot, who was only of medium height himself, towered over him. Mundiveen held his head at an odd angle to his neck and his body pivoted strangely at the middle, as though there might be some sort of a twist in his spine. It was not hard to imagine that he would walk with a limp.

"Stiamot," he said uncomfortably. "Of Stee."

"Yes. Yes, of course. The Coronal's advance man. Everybody in town knows who you are."

"And what I've been doing, also, I guess. You saw me talking to the – Piurivar, you called it?"

"That's what they call themselves. I like to use the term too. Metamorph, Shapeshifter, Piurivar, whatever you like. No, I didn't see you with him. What would I be doing awake at that hour? But he told me about it. He said you looked at him as though he were a creature from some other world. What do you like to drink, eh, Stiamot? First one's on me."

Stiamot shot a quick glance at the two aides with whom he

had entered the inn, wordlessly telling them to fade away, and said to Mundiveen, "Let's start with gray wine, shall we? And then, when I'm paying, we can go on to the blue."

It was strange how quickly Stiamot began to feel at ease with this quirky little man. They would never be friends, Stiamot saw at once: the doctor was all sharp edges, prickly as a zelzifor, and Stiamot doubted that "friendship" was a word in his working vocabulary. The harsh, hopeless laugh with which he punctuated his sentences betrayed a profound mistrust of humanity. But Mundiveen seemed to be willing enough to accept a little companionship from Stiamot, at least. They crossed the room together – he did have a distinct limp, Stiamot saw – and settled at a corner table, and a zone of privacy appeared to take form around them, an invisible wall that set the two of them off from the crowd of noisy, boisterous planters who filled the room.

Mundiveen let him know right away that he was just about the only man in town who understood anything about the Shapeshifters. "Spent a lot of time with them, you know. Right there in their own forest. Helped one mend a badly broken arm – they do have bones, by the way, nothing like yours or mine but bones all the same, and they can break – and he took a kind of liking to me, and that was the beginning. One outcast to another, you might say."

"That's how you see yourself, an outcast?"

"That's what I am," said Mundiveen, laughing his hopeless little laugh, and bent low over his wine-bowl to forestall further inquiry.

"The District Resident said you'd lived among them for a dozen years."

"I still do live among them. If I can be said to live among anybody, that is."

"You live in the forest?

"I have a place in town, and one in the forest. I move from

15

one to the other as the spirit takes me. We need another flask of wine. You pay, this time."

"Of course." Stiamot signalled to the barmaid. "Where were you from, originally?"

"Stee, same as you."

"Stee? Really?"

"You seem surprised. No reason to be. Stee's a big city; nobody can know everybody. It was a long time ago, anyway. You were probably just a boy when I left there. Your Coronal, Lord Strelkimar. How is he?"

That was an odd phrase, Stiamot thought: *your* Coronal. He was everybody's Coronal. "His health, you mean?"

"His health, his state of well-being, his inner equilibrium, whatever you want to call it."

Stiamot hesitated. His eyes met the little man's – they were very pale eyes, not gray, as Stiamot had first thought, but a sort of washed-out yellowish-green, and one seemed imperfectly aligned with the other – and they revealed nothing, absolutely nothing. It would be improper, of course, for him to discuss the Coronal's state of well-being, of inner equilibrium, with any stranger he happened to meet in a tavern, even if the Coronal were in a perfect state of well-being, but especially because he was not. He paused just long enough and said, "He's fine, of course."

"I knew him," said Mundiveen. "In my days at court. Before he became Coronal. And for a short while after."

"You were at court?"

"Of course," Mundiveen said, and took refuge once more in his wine-bowl.

The conversation, when it resumed, centered on the Shape-shifters. Mundiveen seemed to know – how? From the Resident, no doubt – that Stiamot had some special interest in them, and asked him what that was about. Stiamot attempted to explain, as he had to Kalban Vond, that it was primarily a matter of intellectual curiosity, a private hobby: he was, he said, fascinated by their folkways, their religious beliefs, their art, their language. But the fact that he was a member of the Coronal's staff, and not just that but an actual member of his Council, obviously made all that ring false to Mundiveen, who listened with as much patience as he seemed able to muster and finally said, "I'm sure you find them very interesting. So do I. Well, is some sort of policy shift in the making?"

"Policy of what sort?"

"You know what I'm saying. Policy toward the Piurivars."

Stiamot smiled. "Even if there were, I'd hardly be likely to want to discuss it, would I?"

"Even if there were, I suppose you wouldn't," said Mundiveen.

Beyond any doubt Mundiveen was the man to cultivate here. He was unlikely to learn anything valuable about the Metamorphs from the planters, all of whom appeared to regard them with contempt or loathing, if not complete indifference, mere impediments to their intended expansion of their plantations. But Stiamot knew he had to go slowly with this sardonic, bitter little cripple. There was something dark and angry in Mundiveen that had to be approached with caution: one could not be too open with him until one had some idea of the forces that drove that anger and that bitterness, and it was too soon to start probing for that now.

Besides, he had plenty of other things to do. Couriers brought him daily bulletins on the progress of the Coronal and his traveling companions: he was in Byelk, he was in Bizfern, he was in Milimorn, he was in Singaserin, he was moving steadily westward. He would stay the night in Kattikawn and in three days he would arrive in Domgrave. Stiamot spent the three days going over the final invitation list for the state banquet they would hold here, working out the formal program of speeches, conferring with the purveyors of meats and wines. And there were security issues to address. The Metamorphs came and went as they chose in the dark, sinister forests that surrounded these valley towns, and, as Stiamot could testify from personal experience, they seemed able to materialize and disappear like phantoms. If they had it in mind to assassinate a Coronal, madness though that would be, they would never have a better opportunity than this. Strelkimar was coming with his own guard, of course, but Stiamot thought it wise to enlist local peacekeepers in his service as well, and did.

On the second of those three busy days he went to the tavern again in the afternoon and found Mundiveen there once more, and had the same sort of uneasy arm's-length conversation with him over a couple of expensive flasks of wine, centering mostly on Mundiveen's years in the forest with the Shapeshifters. He wasn't actually a doctor, Mundiveen admitted: in the days of the former Coronal Lord Thrykeld he had been a mining engineer, whose special responsibility in the government was supervision of the sparse mineral resources that the giant but metal-poor world of Majipoor had to offer. Once his days at court had ended – and he offered no information about that – he had lived in retirement in Deepenhow Vale, farther down the Mount from Stee, where somehow he had picked up a few medical skills, and then he had found it best to leave the Mount entirely and wander off toward the west, coming eventually to the forests of this northwestern region. There, as he put it, he "made himself useful as a physician to the Piurivars."

Carefully, during the course of the evening, Stiamot nudged Mundiveen into telling him some tales of life in the Shapeshifter encampments in the forests surrounding Domgrave. He learned something about their tribal arrangements – they had a single monarch, he said, the Danipiur, who in some fashion ruled over all the scattered bands of Piurivars everywhere in the world – and a little, though it was not very articulately expounded, about their religious beliefs. In a muddled, sketchy way Mundiveen related also a Piurivar myth, the legend of some dreadful ancient sin they had committed at the old Shapeshifter capital of Velalisier long before the first human settlers had arrived, a sin so grievous that it had brought a curse down on them and led directly to the downfall of the race.

Stiamot supposed that someone who had as little liking for mankind as Mundiveen apparently did would have made a compensating shift in the other direction, taking refuge among the Metamorphs as he had because he saw them as the only beings on the planet worth living among, pure and true and noble, altogether undeserving of having lost their planet to the human oppressors who had settled among them six thousand years before. But it was not like that at all. Mundiveen never spoke of the Metamorphs with the sort of scorn that the District Resident had expressed – "sneaky, nasty savages" – but he seemed to have no more fondness for then than he did for humanity, letting slip between the lines, as he told Stiamot one story and another that night, that he found them a difficult, quarrelsome, even treacherous race – "a slippery crew" was the phrase he used – and that much of his medical work consisted of repairing damage that one Metamorph had done to another.

The legend of that ancient sin and the curse evidently had something to do with his attitude toward the Piurivars – the unspeakably evil thing that they had done twenty thousand years ago that had crushed them under the vengeance of their own gods. Whatever that had been, and Mundiveen could not or would not say what it was, the tale seemed to have revealed something about their basic nature to him and mark them in Mundiveen's eyes as a dark, troublesome lot. But perhaps, Stiamot thought, Mundiveen was inherently incapable of liking anyone at all, and chose to live among the Shapeshifters only because he preferred them, for all their faults, to his own species. Despite his manifold shortcomings, though, Mundiveen had had more first-hand experience of Shapeshifter life than anyone else Stiamot had ever encountered, and in the remainder of his time in Domgrave he intended to learn all that he could about them from the sharp-edged little man.

News of the Coronal's imminent arrival reached Stiamot two

days later. He gathered a troop of peacekeepers and rode out to meet him east of town and escort his party into the city.

Strelkimar, wrapped in that dark cloud that seemed to go with him everywhere, greeted Stiamot in a perfunctory way, acknowledging him curtly with a quick, minimal movement of his hand. The Coronal was a commanding figure of a man, tall and powerfully built, but today he looked tired. That unfathomable darkness that lay at the core of his soul showed through plainly to the surface. Everything about Lord Strelkimar was dark: his eyes, his beard, the black doublet and leggings that he almost always wore, and, thought Stiamot, his soul itself. Stiamot suspected that the strange chain of events that had brought Strelkimar to the summit of power, the abrupt abdication and disappearance of his predecessor and all the whispered gossip that had surrounded the change of rule, had left some indelible mark on him. But all of that had happened before Stiamot's own time at court; he had heard the stories, of course, but had no hard knowledge of what had really taken place.

"Has your journey been a good one, my lord?" Stiamot asked.

The question was mere routine courtesy, the obligatory sort of thing that a courtier would ask his arriving master. But it seemed to anger the Coronal: Lord Strelkimar's obsidian eyes flared for a moment, and he scowled as though Stiamot had said something offensive. Then he softened. Stiamot was one of his favorites, after all, though it had appeared to take a moment or two for him to remember that. "These towns are all alike," he said gruffly. "I'll be glad to move along through here to Alaisor."

"I'm sure you will," said Stiamot. "The sea air will do you good, my lord. But I have a fine lodging waiting for you, and there will be an audience of notables tonight, and a state banquet tomorrow evening."

"An audience, yes. A banquet. Very good." The Coronal seemed ten thousand miles away. Stiamot conducted him into town – the whole population had turned out, lining the one main street on both sides – and took him to the Residency, where

Kalban Vond greeted him with embarrassing obsequiousness. The Coronal asked to be left alone in his chambers for an hour or two. Stiamot obliged. He was glad to be free of the Coronal's oppressive presence for a little while. When he returned in late afternoon, Strelkimar seemed refreshed – he had had a bath and changed his clothes, a different black doublet, different black leggings, and he had even donned his crown, that slender shining circlet that was his badge of office and which most of the time he disdained to wear. But his lips were clamped, as ever, in that brooding scowl that he seemed never to shed.

"Well, Stiamot, have you been keeping yourself amused here?"

"This is hardly an amusing place, sir."

"I suppose not. Seen any Shapeshifters, have you?"

Was that some sort of mocking jab? There was a strange glint in the Coronal's dark eyes. Stiamot had been a member of the Coronal's council the past seven years, and was as close to him, quite likely, as anyone. But he never could tell, even after so much time, quite where he stood with Lord Strelkimar. He came from a good family though not one of the great ones, and had risen very swiftly at court through diligence, loyalty, intelligence, and – to some degree – luck, a matter of being in the right place at the right time. Still, the Coronal was a mystery to him. Much of the time he still found Strelkimar an enigma, baffling, opaque, impenetrable. He said warily, "As a matter of fact, I have, my lord. One. Right in the center of town, crossing a street. We stopped and stared at each other for a moment or two. He did a quick little shapeshifting trick, or so I thought. And then he went walking away."

"Right out in the open," the Coronal said. "So there are some actually living in this town?"

"I don't think so. But they're in the forests all around, and I guess one of them comes drifting through, occasionally."

"And why is that?" said the Coronal, toying with the starburst decoration on the breast of his doublet.

"I have no idea, sir. But I can try to find out. I've met a man here who knows a great deal about them – has lived with them, even, in the forests – and he's been telling me something about them. I hope to learn more from him."

"Yes. Yes." The Coronal peered at his knuckles as though he had never seen his hands before. "The Shapeshifters," he murmured, after a time. "What an enigma they are, Stiamot. What a puzzle. I will never understand them."

Stiamot said nothing. An enigma contemplating an enigma was too much for him to deal with.

Brusquely, in an entirely different tone of voice, the Coronal said, "And what time is this audience I'm holding supposed to happen?"

"In two hours, my lord."

"Can you manage to make it any sooner? I'd like to get it over with."

"That would be difficult, sir. Some of the planters live a considerable distance from town. I don't see any way we could—"

"All right. All right, Stiamot." There was another long pause. Then, suddenly, unexpectedly: "Tomorrow morning, bring me this forest-dweller of yours, this Shapeshifter expert. Maybe he can teach me a thing or two about them."

Getting Mundiveen to come to a private morning interview with the Coronal was not so easy to accomplish. The little man had already made it clear to Stiamot that he was anything but an early riser; and simply to locate him was a problem. But with the District Resident's help he tracked Mundiveen to his lair, a little ramshackle cottage in a dreary corner of town, and sent one of his aides in to ascertain whether he was awake. He was, though not happy about it. Fortunately, the Coronal was no early riser either, and his idea of "morning" was more like early afternoon.

Mundiveen seemed taken aback by this summons to the Coronal's chambers. "Why does he want to see me?"

"I told him you knew a great deal about the Piurivars. He's

interested in them, all of a sudden. At court he hasn't wanted to talk about them or, maybe, even to think about them, but now, for some reason – please, Mundiveen. You have to come."

"Do I?"

"He is the Coronal."

"And he can call me to his side just like that, with a snap of his fingers?"

"Please, Mundiveen. Don't be difficult."

"Difficult is what I am, my friend."

"For me. A favor. Let him ask you a few questions. This is more important than you can possibly know. The future of Majipoor may depend on it."

"I doubt that. But for me my *not* seeing him is more important than *you* can possibly know. Let me be, Stiamot."

"A few questions, only. I've promised him I'll bring you. Come. Come, Mundiveen."

"Well—"

Stiamot saw him weakening. Some powerful inner struggle was going on; but as the moments passed Mundiveen's resistance appeared to be diminishing. Refusing a royal command was evidently something that even the crusty, acerbic Mundiveen was unwilling to do. Or perhaps it was merely the fierce lofty indifference that seemed to underlie everything he said or did, that cosmic shrug with which he faced the world, that led him ultimately to yield.

"Give me half an hour to get myself ready," Mundiveen said.

But the meeting was a brief and unhappy one. Mundiveen was strangely tense and withdrawn during the journey to the Residency, saying almost nothing. He came limping into the Coronal's chamber with Stiamot beside him, and when he saw Strelkimar he shot a look of such coruscating hatred at him as Stiamot had never seen in human eyes. Strelkimar, who was poring over a sheaf of newly arrived dispatches, took no notice. He barely looked up, greeting Mundiveen with no more than a grunt and a casual glance, and signalled that he wanted to continue reading for a moment. One had to grant a Coronal such whims, but Stiamot knew that Mundiveen was no man to honor even a Coronal's whim, and half expected him to turn indignantly and leave. Surprisingly, though, he simply stood and waited, a tightly controlled figure, practically motionless, his breath coming in a harsh rasp, and at last the Coronal looked up again. This time, when his eyes met Mundiveen's, some violent unreadable emotion – shock, anger, despair? – swirled for an instant across Lord Strelkimar's face. Then it vanished, and was replaced by a steely fixed stare. He stared at Mundiveen with a terrible piercing force that reminded Stiamot of the look that that Metamorph had given him in the street. But despite the grim power of that stare Strelkimar seemed somehow unnerved by Mundiveen's presence, confounded, dazed.

"You are the expert on Shapeshifters?" the Coronal asked finally, in a low, husky voice.

"If that is what your man tells you, my lord, I will not deny it."

"Ah. Ah." A long silence. He was still staring. Another string of unfathomable emotions played across his features, a twitching of his lip, a clenching of his jaw. He was holding some inward debate with himself. Then the Coronal shook his head, slowly, the way a man at the last extremity of exhaustion might shake it. He was barely audible as he said, not to Mundiveen but to Stiamot, "It was a mistake to call him here. This is not a good moment for a meeting. I find myself very weary, this morning."

"If you say so, my lord."

"Very weary indeed. The man can go. Perhaps another time, then."

He made a gesture of dismissal.

Stiamot was dumfounded. To ask that Mundiveen be brought, and then to react like this, and send him away so hastily—!

But Mundiveen did not seem troubled by the discourtesy. If anything, he appeared to be relieved to take his leave of the

Coronal. Stiamot saluted and they went from the room, and, outside, Mundiveen said, "I wondered how he'd react when he saw me. Took him a moment to recognize me, I suppose. How awful he looked. By the Divine, what a haunted look there is in that man's eyes! And for good reason, let me tell you."

"I can't begin to tell you how sorry I am that—" Stiamot paused. "He recognized you, you say? He's seen you before?"

Acidly Mundiveen said, "I told you I was at court, in the time before he was Coronal. And for a little while afterward. You don't remember my saying that?"

"Yes. Yes, of course. I must have forgotten it."

"I wish I could. We go a long way back, your Coronal and I."

Stiamot passed his hand across his forehead as though to clear it from cobwebs. "You need to tell me what this is all about."

"I do? I *need* to? The same way I needed to go and see Lord Strelkimar?"

"For the love of the Divine, Mundiveen—"

Mundiveen let his eyes slip closed for an instant. "All right. Let's go have a bowl or two of wine, then, and I'll tell you."

"Wine? This early in the day?"

"Wine, Prince Stiamot. Or no story."

"All right," Stiamot said. "Wine."

Mundiveen said, "I wasn't always twisted up like this, you know. In the days when Lord Thrykeld was Coronal I was quite an athlete, as a matter of fact. And when I was on a surveying trip I could walk miles and miles without the slightest fatigue."

"Back when you were a mining engineer."

"When I was a mining engineer, yes. At least you remembered that much. I was going to find the world's biggest iron mine, I thought. Not that Lord Thrykeld cared very much about that. All he cared about, really, was poetry and singing and his Ghayrog favorite. Do you know about that, the Ghayrog? Before your time, I suppose. But no matter. Thrykeld was the Coronal Lord, and I served him as loyally as you seem to serve

Strelkimar, and I was going to present him with more iron than had ever been discovered before."

Mundiveen helped himself liberally to the wine. He seemed calm, icily controlled, betraying no sign of the ferocious rage that had come over him in his first moment in the Coronal's presence. Stiamot waited, saying nothing.

"The former Coronal, Lord Thrykeld," Mundiveen said at last. "I suppose history will call him a great fool. You probably know very little about him."

"Not much, really," said Stiamot. "Only the standard information."

"Then you must think he was a great fool. Most people do. Well, probably he was. But he was a gentle, sweet man, with a considerable gift for poetry and music. The people loved him. Everyone loved him. You must have loved him yourself, when you were a boy. But in the third or fourth year of his reign something began to change in him. There was this Ghayrog at court, a certain Valdakko, some sort of conjurer, I think. The Coronal spent more and more time with him, and then he brought him into the Council. Well, that was a little unusual, a Ghayrog in the Council. There never had been one before. They have equality under the law, of course, but they are reptilian, you know. Their metabolisms aren't like ours and neither are their minds. Thrykeld's cousin Strelkimar was High Counsellor then, and I can tell you, he wasn't pleased when the Coronal began to jump this Valdakko up like that. He took it as well as anyone could, though. But when Thrykeld decided that he wanted the Ghayrog to be High Counsellor in Strelkimar's place, things got, shall we say, a little tense."

"I heard about that," Stiamot said. "The Ghayrog as High Counsellor."

Mundiveen had finished his first bowl of wine, though Stiamot had had only a few sips of his. He went to work on a second one, savoring the wine, pondering it, seemingly lost in recollection of a far-off time. At length he began to speak again. "Strelkimar was very diplomatic about it all, at least outwardly. He behaved as though his cousin was just going through a phase. He loved Thrykeld, you know – as I said, we all loved him; a kind, good man – but gradually it became clear that the Coronal had become unstable, was slipping over, in fact, into a kind of megalomania."

Mundiveen went on to describe how, urged on by his Ghayrog counsellor, Lord Thrykeld had promulgated a law giving him the power to annul any previous statute without consent of the Council. This was absolutism; it was something entirely new in the history of the world. Strelkimar and a few of the other counsellors then made their objections known, objected very strongly, Mundiveen said, and Thrykeld – a Thrykeld none of them had ever known before – retaliated immediately, dismissing the entire Council except for the Ghayrog. He intended to rule, he announced, by personal decree.

"Strelkimar confronted him on that, of course," Mundiveen said. "Thrykeld flew into a rage. No one had ever seen him even mildly angry before. He ordered Strelkimar banished to Suvrael and all his possessions confiscated."

Astounded, Stiamot said, "I never heard a thing about that. It was never made public, was it?"

"Of course not. No one beyond the Council ever knew anything about it. Except me."

"You weren't a Council member."

"No. But I was very close to the Coronal. To his cousin, too. And I was stupid enough to try to intervene in the crisis. I got between them: I told Lord Thrykeld that it was very dangerous to try to strip a great prince like Strelkimar of his estates, and I went to Strelkimar and begged him to be patient, to wait his cousin's madness out, even to go into exile for a time until things calmed down. I was the very soul of moderation and conciliation. So of course they both turned on me."

Stiamot signalled for another flask of wine. The little man seemed to have an infinite capacity.

"It was impossible to reason with the Coronal," Mundiveen

said, when he was sated for the moment. "He was far gone in his lunacy and the only person he would listen to was the Ghayrog. He drove me from his side. Strelkimar now let it be known that he felt the Coronal would have to be set aside, for the good of the whole commonwealth. I opposed him on that. I felt I had no choice about it. I went to him and said that Thrykeld was undoubtedly behaving very strangely, but no Coronal had ever been removed from office in all the history of the world; that to depose one would be an offense against the Divine; that all of this would surely blow over in a little while. No, said Strelkimar, his cousin was hopelessly mad. He intended to push him aside. I made the error of getting very excited. I swore great purple oaths that I would stand beside the anointed Coronal no matter what Strelkimar did. I threatened to go to the people with word that Strelkimar was planning to overthrow their monarch. I vowed to fight him every step of the way. My behavior was extremely rash. I *forbade* him to depose Thrykeld. Imagine that! Saying a thing like that to a man like Strelkimar. I became as crazy as Thrykeld himself was, I suppose."

He fell silent. The silence stretched for a minute or more. When it began to seem as though he did not intend to resume at all, Stiamot prodded him:

"And—?"

"And that evening three hired thugs wearing masks came for me and took me from Stee to someplace far downslope, Furible or Stipool or one of those cities, and there they beat me until both they and I were sure that I was at the edge of death, and then they left me. But I didn't die. They badly damaged me, but I lived. All they did was cripple me, as you see. Or did you think I was born with my backbone all askew like this?"

"Strelkimar's men, were they?"

"They didn't go to the trouble of telling me that. Make your own guesses."

"And the next thing to do was killing Lord Thrykeld, I

suppose," said Stiamot, wondering whether he had fallen into some dream.

"Oh, no, nothing like that. They killed the Ghayrog, yes, but the Coronal was persuaded to sign a document of abdication. I can just imagine how he was persuaded, too. In his statement he declared that his health had unfortunately become too poor to permit him to continue to meet his royal responsibilities, and so he was withdrawing from the throne and going off to live in Suvrael. He sent a separate message to the Pontifex Gherivale, urging him most strongly to appoint Strelkimar as the new Coronal. So it was done; and Thrykeld left the palace; and then we heard the regrettable news that Thrykeld's ship had been sunk by a sea-dragon en route to Suvrael, as you probably remember, and that was that. As for me, I suspected that it would not be a smart idea to return to the capital. In fact I discovered, when I had begun to recover from what your Coronal's men had done to me, that I had lost all interest in the company of my own species, and I was years in recovering even a little of it. So I floated off quietly into the forests and took up my new career as a doctor to the Piurivars." He paused again a moment and stared thoughtfully into his wine bowl. Then, looking up, he gave Stiamot a sharp sidelong glance. "Is there anything else you'd like to know, now?"

"No," Stiamot said. "I think I've heard too much already."

These revelations had rocked him like an earthquake.

He had known, of course, that Lord Thrykeld had given up his throne, pleading incapacity to serve, and that soon afterward he had been lost at sea. He had suspected, as many people did, that there probably had been more to the change of monarchs than that, that the forceful and charismatic Lord Strelkimar very likely had been instrumental in his cousin's decision to abdicate, though he had taken the tale of Thrykeld's deteriorating health at face value. But Mundiveen's tale of strife at court, of ultimatum and counter-ultimatum between the cousins, of the forcible overthrow of a king – and of Mundiveen's own near-fatal beating – gave the history of the years just before his own arrival at court a darker hue than he ever could have imagined. It all fit together now, Mundiveen's sour cynicism, Strelkimar's haunted, guilt-stricken eyes, the awkwardness and strangeness of the meeting of the two men this morning, so many years after all those terrible events. Lord Strelkimar lived daily with the knowledge that he had stolen the throne; Mundiveen lived daily with his fury and pain. And Stiamot had stupidly brought the two of them face to face.

"Now," Mundiveen said, "tell me what your Lord Strelkimar wants to know about the Piurivars."

"We want to find a solution to the problem of how we are going to live with them in the years to come, how we are going to share the planet. The Council is split in various ways, putting forth all sorts of ideas ranging from a geographical separation of the races to an all-out war of extermination. I myself hope to find some middle course. The Coronal hasn't been taking part in our discussions up to now, but he seems to have come around to an awareness that we need to deal with the issue. And so, in my innocence, I told him that I had encountered someone who had intimate knowledge of the Piurivar way of life, and he asked me to bring you to speak with him. Not knowing, of course, that that man was you."

"The truth must have come as a great surprise to him."

"Something of a shock, I would say."

Mundiveen smiled balefully. "Well, so be it. If he had allowed me to tell him anything, I would have said that there's no good solution to be found. Humans and Piurivars are never going to get along, my friend. Believe me. Never. *Never.*"

The formal state banquet was held as scheduled that evening, in the municipal festival hall, a lofty wooden structure with an arching roof far above. Planters had come in from all about, drawn by the novelty of a Coronal in their midst. A high table had been set up where the Coronal, in full royal regalia, sat flanked by members of his entourage, a duke or two, a couple of Council members, a sprinkling of Pontifical officials. District Resident Kalban Vond sat at the Coronal's right hand – the greatest honor ever accorded him, Stiamot supposed.

Just as the first course was being served Stiamot heard the sounds of a commotion outside, shouts, angry cries. Alarmed, he rushed to the window.

A struggle of some kind was going on right outside the hall. Stiamot saw bursts of flame limned against the night, shadowy figures running about. Looking back at the high table, he saw the Coronal sitting altogether motionless, frowning, lost once again in the darkness of his own thoughts. He seemed entirely unaware that anything unusual might be taking place. But the District Resident beside him looked stricken and aghast. His mouth was agape; his soft, fleshy face seemed to be sagging.

Then, unexpectedly, astonishingly, a side door that Stiamot had not noticed before opened and Mundiveen came limping in. After what had passed between the Coronal and him this morning, he was the last person, perhaps, whom Stiamot expected to see in the banqueting hall tonight. Flushed, panting, he made his way laboriously to Stiamot's side at the window.

"Metamorphs," he said hoarsely. "Disguised as townsfolk. Knives under their cloaks. They're throwing firebrands."

Stiamot looked out again. In the chaos beyond the window he was able to make out the guards attempting to form a phalanx. They were surrounded on three sides by a host of cloaked figures in rapid motion, flickering, changing dizzyingly from one shape to another as they moved.

He seized Mundiveen by the shoulder. "What is this?"

"The beginning of the insurrection, I think. They want to burn the building down."

"The Coronal—!"

"Yes, the Coronal."

"I'm going out there," said Stiamot. "I have to do something."

"No one can do anything. Especially not you."

Hesitating only a moment, Stiamot said, "Well, then, what about you? Even in the darkness, they'll recognize you. And you could talk to them. They trust you if they trust anybody. You've done so many things for them. Explain to them now that this is insane, that they have to withdraw or they'll all die, that the Coronal is too well guarded."

Mundiveen glared at him scornfully. "Why would they care about that? They're beyond all caring about anything. Don't you see, Stiamot, there's no hope? This is a war to the death, beginning right now, right here, and it will never end, at least not until you people recognize that you have no choice but to eradicate them altogether."

His words hit Stiamot with the force of a punch. *You people?* Did Mundiveen, then, think that he stood outside the human race? *You have to eradicate them altogether?* This, from a man who had spent so many years living among them? Stiamot faltered, speechless.

But then, abruptly, between one instant and the next, Mundiveen's expression changed. A flash of something new came into his eyes, a wild, almost gleeful look, something Stiamot had never seen in them before. "All right," he said, with a savage, twisted grin. "As you wish, my friend. I'll go to them. I'll talk to them."

"But – wait – wait a moment, Mundiveen—"

Mundiveen broke free of Stiamot's grasp and ran from the hall.

By now the Coronal seemed to have realized that there was trouble of some sort; he had half-risen from his seat and was looking questioningly toward Stiamot. Stiamot beckoned urgently to him to sit down. His figure would be too conspicuous this way if the Metamorphs succeeded in breaking into the hall.

Then he returned his attention to the window. Mundiveen had somehow succeeded in getting through the line of guards. Stiamot could see his small, angular form, moving clumsily and with great difficulty but even so at remarkable speed into the midst of the attackers. He was visible for a moment, his hands lifted high as though he were calling for their attention. Then the Shapeshifters swarmed in around him, surrounding him, yelling so loudly that their fierce incomprehensible cries penetrated the walls of the building. Stiamot had a fragmentary glimpse or two of Mundiveen tottering about at the center of their group, and then, as Stiamot watched in horror, they closed their circle tightly about him and Mundiveen seemed to melt, to vanish, to disappear entirely from view.

In the morning, after order had been restored and the bodies cleared away, and while the preparations for the Coronal's departure from Domgrave were being made, Lord Strelkimar called Stiamot to his side.

The Coronal was so pale that the blackness of his beard seemed to have doubled and redoubled in the night. His hands were shaking. He had not dressed; he wore only a casual robe loosely girt, and a flask of wine stood before him on the table.

Stiamot said at once, "My lord, the Shapeshifters—"

Strelkimar waved him to silence with an impatient gesture. "Forget the Shapeshifters for a moment, Stiamot, and listen to me. There's news from the Labyrinth." Lord Strelkimar's voice was a ragged thread, the merest fragment of sound. Stiamot had to strain to hear him. "A message came to me in the afternoon, just as I was getting dressed for the banquet. The Pontifex Gherivale has died. It was a peaceful end, I am told. This has been a day of great surprises, and they are not yet over, my lord."

My lord? My lord? Had he lost his mind?

Blinking in confusion, Stiamot said, "What are you saying, my lord?"

"Don't call me 'my lord.' That's you, Stiamot. I am Pontifex, now."

"And I am—?" The startling implications began to sink in,

and his mind swirled in a jumble of wonder and disbelief. This was unthinkable. "Do I understand you correctly, my lord? How can this be? You are asking me – me—"

"We are in need of a new Coronal. There's a vacancy in the position. The succession must be maintained."

"Yes, of course. But – Coronal – me? Surely you aren't serious. Consider how young I am!" He felt as though he were moving in a dream. "There are counsellors much senior to me. What about Faninal? What about Kreistand?"

"They'll be disappointed, I suppose. But we need a Coronal, right away, and we need a young one. You'll be fighting the war against the Shapeshifters for the rest of your life."

"The war?" said Stiamot leadenly.

"Yes, of course, the war. *Your* war. The war that we pretended for so long wasn't coming, and which has now arrived. And happy I am to be able to hand it to you and hide myself away in the Labyrinth. I have enough sins on my soul for one lifetime." Strelkimar rose. He loomed over Stiamot, a big man, heavy-muscled, deep-chested, still young himself. His face was bloodless with fatigue. Stiamot saw what might have been tears glistening at the corners of Strelkimar's eyes. "Come, man. Let's go out to the others and give them the news."

Stiamot nodded like one who moves in a trance. As it all sank in, the meaning of the bloody events of the night before, the change of government at the Labyrinth, his own precipitous rise to the Coronal's throne, he knew that Strelkimar was right about the coming of the war. He had known that it was coming from the moment of Mundiveen's death, or even a little earlier. There is no hope, the little man had said, before running from the banquet hall to yield himself up to his doom. This was something new, an attack on the Coronal himself, and it would not stop there. This is a war to the death. The uneasy peace that had obtained so long between human and Metamorph was at its end. And this was the end of the line, too, for Stiamot's own dreams of a moderate middle course, of some peaceful resolution of the

Metamorph problem. The races must be separated, he thought, or else one of them must be exterminated; and now that high power had been thrust upon him, he would choose the lesser of the two evils.

"Come," Strelkimar said again. "I have to introduce the new Coronal to them. Come with me, Lord Stiamot."

The war began in earnest in the spring. It ended in victory in the thirtieth year of Lord Stiamot's reign.

2

The Book of Changes

~~~

Standing at the narrow window of his bedchamber early on the morning of the second day of his new life as a captive, looking out at the blood-red waters of the Sea of Barbirike far below, Aithin Furvain heard the bolt that sealed his apartment from the outside being thrown back. He glanced quickly around and saw the lithe catlike form of his captor, the bandit chief Kasinibon, come sidling in. Furvain turned toward the window again.

"As I was saying last night, it truly is a beautiful view, isn't it?" Kasinibon said. "There's nothing like that scarlet lake anywhere else in all Majipoor."

"Lovely, yes," said Furvain, in a remote, affectless way.

With the same relentless good cheer Kasinibon went on, addressing himself to Furvain's back, "I do hope you slept well, and that in general you're finding your lodgings here comfortable, Prince Aithin."

Out of some vestigial sense of courtesy – courtesy, even to a bandit! – Furvain turned to face the other man. "I don't ordinarily use my title," he said, stiffly, coolly.

"Of course. Neither do I, as a matter of fact. I come from a long line of east-country nobility, you know. Minor nobility, perhaps, yet nobility never the less. But they are such archaic things, titles!" Kasinibon grinned. It was a sly grin, almost conspiratorial, a mingling of mockery and charm. Despite everything Furvain found it impossible to dislike the man. "You haven't answered my question, though. Are you comfortable here, Furvain?"

"Oh, yes. Quite. It's absolutely the most elegant of prisons."

"I do wish to point out that this is not actually a prison but merely a private residence."

"I suppose. Even so, I'm a prisoner here, is that not true?"

"I concede the point. You are indeed a prisoner, for the time being. My prisoner."

"Thank you," said Furvain. "I appreciate your straight-forwardness." He returned his attention to Barbirike Sea, which stretched, long and slender as a spear, for fifty miles or so through the valley below the gray cliff on which Kasinibon's fortress-like retreat was perched. Long rows of tall sharp-tipped crescent dunes, soft as clouds from this distance, bordered its shores. They too were red. Even the air here had a red reflected shimmer. The sun itself seemed to have taken on a tinge of it. Kasinibon had explained yesterday, though Furvain had not been particularly interested in hearing it at the time, that the Sea of Barbirike was home to untold billions of tiny crustaceans whose fragile bright-colored shells, decomposing over the mil-lennia, had imparted that bloody hue to the sea's waters and given rise also to the red sands of the adjacent dunes. Furvain wondered whether his royal father, who had such an obsessive interest in intense color effects, had ever made the journey out here to see this place. Surely he had. Surely.

Kasinibon said, "I've brought you some pens and a supply of paper." He laid them neatly out on the little table beside Furvain's bed. "As I said earlier, this view is bound to inspire poetry in you, that I know."

"No doubt it will," said Furvain, still speaking in that same distant, uninflected tone.

"Shall we take a closer look at the lake this afternoon, you and I?"

"So you don't intend to keep me penned up all the time in these three rooms?"

"Of course I don't. Why would I be so cruel?"

"Well, then. I'll be pleased to be taken on a tour of the lake," Furvain said, as indifferently as before. "Its beauty may indeed stir a poem or two in me."

Kasinibon gave the stack of paper an amiable tap. "You also may wish to use these sheets to begin drafting your ransom request."

Furvain narrowed his eyes. "Tomorrow, perhaps, for that. Or the day after."

"As you wish. There's no hurry, you know. You are my guest here for as long as you care to stay."

"Your prisoner, actually."

"That too," Kasinibon said. "My guest, but also my prisoner, though I hope you will see yourself rather more as guest than prisoner. You will excuse me now. I have my dreary administrative duties to deal with. Until this afternoon, then." And grinned once more, and bowed and took his leave.

Furvain was the fifth son of the former Coronal Lord Sangamor, whose best-known achievement had been the construction of the remarkable tunnels on Castle Mount that bore his name. Lord Sangamor was a man of a strong artistic bent, and the tunnels, whose walls were fashioned from a kind of artificial stone that blazed with inherent radiant color, were considered by connoisseurs to be a supreme work of art. Furvain had inherited his father's aestheticism but very little of his strength of character: in the eyes of many at the Mount he was nothing more than a wastrel, an idler, even a rogue. His own friends, and he had many of them, were hard pressed to find any great degree of significant merit in him. He was an unusually skillful writer of light verse, yes; and a genial companion on a journey or in a tavern, yes; and a clever hand with a quip or a riddle or a paradox, yes; and otherwise – otherwise—

A Coronal's son has no significant future in the administration of Majipoor, by ancient constitutional tradition. No function is set aside for him. He can never rise to the throne himself, for the crown is always adoptive, never hereditary. The Coronal's eldest son would usually establish himself on a fine estate in one of the Fifty Cities of the Mount and live the good life of a provincial duke. A second son, or even a third, might remain at the Castle and become a councillor of the realm, if he showed any aptitude for the intricacies of government. But a fifth son, born late in his father's reign and thereby shouldered out of the inner circle by all those who had arrived before him, would usually face no better destiny than a drifting existence of irresponsible pleasure and ease. There is no role in public life for him to play. He is his father's son, but he is nothing at all in his own right. No one is likely to think of him as qualified for any kind of serious duties, nor even to have any interest in such things. Such princes are entitled by birth to a permanent suite of rooms at the Castle and a generous and irrevocable pension, and it is assumed of them that they will contentedly devote themselves to idle amusements until the end of their days.

Furvain, unlike some princes of a more restless nature, had adapted very well to that prospect. Since no one expected very much of him, he demanded very little of himself. Nature had favored him with good looks: he was tall and slender, a graceful, elegant man with wavy golden hair and finely chiseled features. He was an admirable dancer, sang quite well in a clear, light tenor voice, excelled at most sports that did not require brute physical force, and was a capable hand at swordsmanship and chariot-racing. But above all else he excelled at the making of verse. Poetry flowed from him in torrents, as rain falls from the sky. At any moment of the day or night, whether he had just been awakened after a long evening of drunken carousing or was in the midst of that carousing itself, he could take pen in hand and compose, almost extemporaneously, a ballad or a sonnet or a villanelle or a jolly rhyming epigram, or quick thumping short-legged doggerel, or even a long skein of heroic couplets, on any sort of theme. There was no profundity to such hastily dashed-off stuff, of course. It was not in his nature to probe the depths of the human soul, let alone to want to set out his findings in the form of poetry. But everyone knew that Aithin Furvain had no master when it came to the making of easy, playful verse, minor verse that celebrated the joys of the moment, the pleasures of the bed or of the bottle, verse that poked fun without ever edging into sour malicious satire, or that demonstrated a quick verbal interplay of rhythm and sound without actually being about anything at all.

"Make a poem for us, Aithin," someone of his circle would call out, as they sat at their wine in one of the brick-walled taverns of the Castle. "Yes!" the others would cry. "A poem, a poem!"

"Give me a word, someone," Furvain would say.

And someone, his current lover, perhaps, would say at random, "Sausage."

"Splendid. And you, give me another, now. The first that comes to mind."

"Pontifex," someone else would say.

"One more," Furvain would beg. "You, back there."

"Steetmoy," the reply would come, from someone at the back of the group.

And Furvain, glancing for just a moment into his wine-bowl as though some poem might be lurking there, would draw a deep breath and instantaneously begin to recite a mock epic, in neatly balanced hexameter and the most elaborate of anapestic rhythms, about the desperate craving of a Pontifex for sausage made of steetmoy meat, and the sending of the laziest and most cowardly of the royal courtiers on a hunting expedition to the snowbound lair of that ferocious white-furred creature of northern Zimroel. Without pausing he would chant for eight or ten minutes, perhaps, until the task was done, and the tale, improvised though it was, would have a beginning and a middle and an uproariously funny end, bringing him a shower of enthusiastic applause and a fresh flask of wine.

The collected works of Aithin Furvain, had he ever bothered

to collect them, would have filled many volumes; but it was his custom to toss his poems aside as quickly as he had scribbled them, nor were many of them ever written down in the first place, and it was only through the prudence of his friends that some of them had been saved and copied and circulated through the land. But that was of no importance to him. Making poetry was as easy for him as drawing breath, and he saw no reason why his quick improvisations should be saved and treasured. It was not, after all, as though they had been intended as enduring works of art, such as his royal father's tunnels had been meant to be.

The Coronal Lord Sangamor had reigned long and generally successfully as Majipoor's junior monarch for nearly thirty years under the Pontifex Pelxinai, until at last the venerable Pelxinai had been gathered to the Source by the Divine and Sangamor had ascended to the Pontificate himself. As Pontifex it was mandatory for him to leave Castle Mount and relocate himself in the subterranean Labyrinth, far to the south, that was the constitutional home of the elder ruler. For the remainder of his life he would rarely be seen in the outside world. Aithin Furvain had dutifully visited his father at the Labyrinth not long after his investiture as Pontifex, as he and his brothers were supposed to do now and then, but he doubted that he would ever make another such journey. The Labyrinth was a dark and gloomy place, very little to his liking. It could not be very pleasing for old Sangamor either, Furvain suspected; but, like all Coronals, Sangamor had known from the start that the Labyrinth was where he must finish his days. Furvain was under no such obligation to reside there, nor even to go there at all if he chose not to. And so Furvain, who had never known his father particularly well, did not see any reason why the two of them would ever meet again.

He had effectively separated himself from the Castle as well by then, too. Even while Lord Sangamor still reigned there, Furvain had set up a second residence for himself at Dundilmir, one of the Slope Cities far down toward the base of the gigantic upthrusting fang of rock that was Castle Mount. A schoolmate and close friend of his named Tanigel had now come into his inheritance as Duke of Dundilmir, and had offered Furvain some property there, a relatively modest estate overlooking the volcanic region known as the Fiery Valley. Furvain would in essence be Duke Tanigel's court jester, a boon companion and maker of comic verse on demand. It was mildly irregular for a Coronal's son to accept a gift of land from a mere duke, but Tanigel understood that fifth sons of Coronals rarely were men of independent wealth, and he knew also that Furvain had grown weary of his listless life at the Castle and was looking to shift the scene of his idleness elsewhere. Furvain, who was not one to stand overmuch on dignity, had gladly acceded to Tanigel's suggestion, and spent most of the next few years at his Dundilmir estate, enjoying raucous times amongst Tanigel and his prosperous hard-drinking friends and going up to the great Castle at the summit of the Mount only on the most formal of occasions, such as his father's birthday, but scarcely returning to it at all after his father had become Pontifex and moved along to the Labyrinth.

Even the good life at Dundilmir had palled after a time, however. Furvain was entering his middle years, now, and he had begun to feel something that he had never experienced before, a vague gnawing dissatisfaction of some unspecifiable kind. Certainly he had nothing specific to complain about. He lived well, surrounded by amusing and enjoyable friends who admired him for the one minor skill that he practiced so well; his health was sound; he had sufficient funds to meet the ordinary expenses of his life, which were basically reasonable ones; he was rarely bored and never lacked for companions or lovers. And yet there was that odd ache in his soul from time to time, now, that inexplicable and unwarranted pang of malaise. It was a new kind of mood for him, disturbing, incomprehensible.

Perhaps the answer lay in travel, Furvain thought. He was a

citizen of the largest and grandest and most beautiful world in all the universe, and yet he had seen very little of it: only Castle Mount, and no more than a dozen or so of the Mount's Fifty Cities at that, and the pleasant but not very interesting Glayge Valley through which he had passed on his one journey to his father's new home in the Labyrinth. There was so much more out there to visit: the legendary cities of the south, places like Sippulgar and golden Arvyanda and many-spircd Kcrthcron, and the stilt-legged villages around silvery Lake Roghoiz, and hundreds, even thousands of others spread like jewels across this enormous continent of Alhanroel, and then there was the other major continent too, fabulous Zimroel, about which he knew practically nothing, far across the sea, abounding in marvelous attractions that sounded like places out of fable. It would be the task of several lifetimes to travel to all of those places.

But in the end he went in a different direction entirely. Duke Tanigel, who was fond of travel, had begun speaking of making a journey to the east-country, that empty and virtually unknown territory that lay between Castle Mount and the shores of the unexplored Great Sea. It was ten thousand years, now, since the first human settlers had come to dwell on Majipoor, which would have been time enough for filling up any world of normal size; but so large was Majipoor that even a hundred centuries of steady population growth had not been sufficient for the settlers to establish footholds in all its far-flung territories. The path of development had led steadily westward from the heart of Alhanroel, and then across the Inner Sea that separated Alhanroel from Zimroel to the other two. Scarcely anyone but a few inveterate wanderers had ever bothered to go east. There was a scruffy little farming town out there, Vrambikat, in a misty valley lying practically in the shadow of the Mount, and beyond Vrambikat there were, apparently, no settlements whatever, or at least none that could be found in the roster of the Pontifical tax-collectors. Perhaps an occasional tiny settlement existed out there; perhaps not. In that sparsely populated region, though, lay an assortment of natural wonders known only from the memoirs of bold explorers. The scarlet Sea of Barbirike – the group of lakes known as the Thousand Eyes – the huge serpentine chasm called the Viper Rift, three thousand miles or more long and of immeasurable depth; and ever so much more – the Wall of Flame, the Web of Jewels, the Fountain of Wine, the Dancing Hills – much of it, perhaps, purely mythical, the inventions of imaginative but untrustworthy adventurers. Duke Tanigel proposed an expedition into these mysterious realms. "On and on, even to the Great Sea itself!" he cried. "We'll take the whole court with us. Who knows what we'll find? And you, Furvain – you'll write an account of everything we see, setting it all down in an unforgettable epic, a classic for the ages!"

But Duke Tanigel, though he was good at devising grand projects and planning them down to the finest detail, was less diligent in the matter of bringing them into the realm of actuality. For months the Duke and his courtiers pored over maps and explorers' narratives, hundreds and even thousands of years old, and laid out grandiose charts of their own intended route through what was, in fact, a trackless wilderness. Furvain found himself completely caught up in the enterprise, and in his dreams often imagined himself hovering like a great bird over some yet-to-be-discovered landscape of inconceivable beauty and strangeness. He yearned for the day of departure. The journey to the east-country, he came to realize, met some inner need of his that he had not previously known existed. The Duke continued planning endlessly for the trip, but never actually announced a date for setting forth, and finally Furvain came to see that no such expedition ever would take place. The Duke had no need actually to go, only to plan. And so one day Furvain, who had never gone any large distance by himself and usually found the whole idea of solitary travel a bit unpleasant, resolved to set out alone into the east-country.

*

Even so, he needed one last push, and it came to him from an unexpected quarter.

During the tense and bothersome period of hesitation and uncertainty that preceded his departure he paid a visit to the Castle, on the pretext of consulting certain explorers' charts said to be on deposit at the royal library. But once at the Castle he found himself unwilling to approach the library's unthinkable, almost infinite vastness, and instead paid a call on his father's famous tunnels, over on the western face of the Mount within a slim rocky spire that jutted hundreds of feet upward from the Mount's own bulk.

Lord Sangamor had caused his tunnels to be constructed in a long coiling ramp that wound upward through the interior of that elongated stony spire. In the forges of the secret chambers of the royal artisans, deep beneath the Castle of the Coronal, Sangamor's workmen had devised the radiant synthetic stone out of which the tunnels were to be built, and smelted it into big dazzling slabs; then, under the Coronal's personal direction, teams of masons had shaped those raw slabs of glowing matter into rectangular paving-blocks of uniform size, which they fastidiously mortared into the walls and roofs of each chamber according to a carefully graded sequence of colors. As one walked along, one's eyes were bombarded with throbbing, pulsing emanations: sulphur-yellow in this room, saffron in the next, topaz in the one after that, emerald, maroon, and then a sudden staggering burst of urgent red, with quieter tones beyond, mauve, aquamarine, a soft chartreuse. It was a symphony of colors, an unfailing outpouring of glowing light every moment of the day. Furvain spent two hours there, moving from room to room in mounting fascination and pleasure, until suddenly he could take no more. Some unexpected eruption was taking place within him. Sensations of vertigo and nausea swept through him. His mind felt numbed by the tremendous power and intensity of the display. He began to tremble, and there was a pounding in his chest. Obviously a quick retreat was necessary.

He rushed toward the exit. Another half-minute within those tunnels, Furvain realized, and he would have been forced to his knees.

Once outside, Furvain clung to a parapet, sweating, dazed, until in a little while something like calmness returned. The strength of his reaction perplexed him. The physical distress was over, but something else still remained, some sort of free-floating disquiet, at first hard to comprehend, but which he came quickly to understand for what it was: the splendor of the tunnels had kindled in him at first a sense of admiration verging on awe, but that had gone moving swiftly onward through his soul to become a crushing, devastating sensation of personal inadequacy.

He had always regarded this thing that the old man had built as nothing much other than a pleasant curiosity. But today, apparently having entered once more into that strangely over-sensitized, almost neurasthenic state that had been typical of his recent moods, he had been overwhelmed by a new awareness of the greatness of his father's work. Through Furvain now was running a surge of something he was forced to recognize as humility, an emotion with which he had never been particularly well acquainted. And why should he not feel humble? His father had achieved something rare and wonderful here. Amidst all the exhausting cares and distractions of state, Lord Sangamor had found the strength and inspiration to create a masterpiece of art.

Whereas he himself – whereas he—

The impact of the tunnels was still reverberating in him that evening. Rather than going on to the library afterward he arranged to dine with an old lover, the Lady Dolitha, in the airy restaurant that hung just above the Grand Melikand Court. She was a delicate-looking woman, very beautiful, dark-haired, olive-skinned, keen-witted. They had had a tempestuous affair for six months, ten years before. Eventually a certain unfettered sharpness about her, an excessive willingness to utter truths that one did not ordinarily utter, an overly sardonic way in which she sometimes chose to express her opinions, had cooled his desire for her. But Furvain had always prized the companionship of intelligent women, and the very quality of terrifying truthfulness that had driven him from her bed had made her appealing to him as a friend. So he had taken pains to preserve the friendship he had enjoyed with Dolitha even after the other sort of intimacy had been severed. She was as close as a sister to him now.

He told her of his experience in the tunnels. "Who would have expected such a thing?" he asked her. "A Coronal who's also a great artist!"

The Lady Dolitha's eyes sparkled with the ironic amusement that was her specialty. "Why do you think the one should exclude the other? The artistic gift's something an artist is born with. Later, perhaps, one can also choose the path that leads toward the throne. But the gift remains."

"I suppose."

"Your father sought power, and that can absorb one's entire energies. But he also chose to exercise his gift."

"The mark of his greatness, that he had breadth enough of soul to do both."

"Or confidence enough in himself. Of course, other people make different choices. Not always the right ones."

Furvain forced himself to meet her gaze directly, though he would rather have looked away. "What are you saying, Dolitha? That it was wrong of me not to go into the government?"

She put the back of her small hand to her lips to conceal, only partly, her wry smile.

"Hardly, Aithin."

"Then what? Come on. Spell it out! It isn't much of a secret, you know, even to me. I've fallen short somewhere, haven't I? You think I've misused my gift, is that it? That I've frittered away my talents drinking and gambling and amusing people with trivial little jingling rhymes, when I should have been closeted away somewhere writing some vast, profound philosophical masterpiece, something somber and heavy and pretentious that everybody would praise but no one would want to read?"

"Oh, Aithin, Aithin—"

"Am I wrong?"

"How can I tell you what you should have been writing? All I can tell you is that I see how unhappy you are, Aithin. I've seen it for a long time. Something's wrong within you – even you've finally come to recognize that, haven't you? – and my guess it must have something to do with your art, your poetry, since what else is there that's important to you, really?"

He stared at her. How very characteristic of her it was to say a thing like that.

"Go on."

"There's very little more to say."

"But there's something, eh? Say it, then."

"It's nothing that I haven't said before."

"Well, say it again. I can be very obtuse, Dolitha."

He saw the little quiver of her nostrils that he had been expecting, the tiny movement of the tip of her tongue between her closed lips. It was clear to him from that that he could expect no mercy from her now. But mercy was not the commodity for which he had come to her this evening.

Quietly she said, "The path you've taken isn't the right path. I don't know what the right path would be, but it's clear that you aren't on it. You need to reshape your life, Aithin. To make something new and different out of it for yourself. That's all. You've gone along this path as far as you can, and now you need to change. I knew ten years ago, even if you didn't, that something like this was going to come. Well, now it has. As you finally have come to realize yourself."

"I suppose I have, yes."

"It's time to stop hiding."

"Hiding?"

"From yourself. From your destiny, from whatever that may be. From your true essence. You can hide from all those, Aithin,

48

but you can't hide from the Divine. So far as the Divine is concerned, there's no place where you can't be seen. Change your life, Aithin. I can't tell you how."

He looked at her, stunned.

"No. Of course you can't." He was silent a moment. "I'll start by taking a trip," he said. "Alone. To some distant place where there'll be no one but myself, and I can meet myself face to face. And then we'll see."

In the morning, dismissing all thought of the royal library and whatever maps it might or might not contain – the time for planning was over; it was the time simply to go – he returned to Dundilmir and spent a week putting his house in order and arranging for the provisions he would need for his journey into the east-country. Then he set out, unaccompanied, saying nothing to anyone about where he was going. He had no idea what he would find, but he knew he would find something, and that he would be the better for it. This would be, he thought, a serious venture, a quest, even: a search for the interior life of Aithin Furvain, which somehow he had misplaced long ago. *You have to change your life*, Dolitha had said, and, yes, yes, that was what he would do. It would be a new thing for him. He had never embarked on anything serious before. He set out now in a strangely optimistic mood, alert to all vibrations of his consciousness. And was barely a week beyond the small dusty town of Vrambikat when he was captured by a party of roving outlaws and taken to Kasinibon's hilltop stronghold.

That there should be anarchy of this sort in an outlying district like the east-country was something that had never occurred to him, but it was no major surprise. Majipoor was, by and large, a peaceful place, where the rulers had for thousands of years ruled by the freely given consent of the governed; but the distances were so vast, the writ of the Pontifex and Coronal so tenuous in places, that quite probably there were many districts where the central government existed only in name. When it took months for news to travel between the centers of the administration and remote Zimroel or sun-blasted Suvrael in the south, was it proper to say that the arm of the government actually reached those places? Who could know, up there at the summit of Castle Mount, or in the depths of the Labyrinth, what really went on in those distant lands? Everyone generally obeyed the law, yes, because the alternative was chaos: but it was quite conceivable that in many districts the citizens did more or less as they pleased most of the time, while maintaining staunchly that they were faithful in their obedience to the commandments of the central government.

And out here, where no one dwelled anyway, or hardly anyone, and the government did not so much as attempt to maintain a presence – what need was there for a government at all, or even the pretense of one?

Since leaving Vrambikat Furvain had been riding quietly along through the quiet countryside, with titanic Castle Mount still a mighty landmark behind him in the west but now beginning to dwindle a little, and a dark range of hills starting to come into view ahead of him. Every prospect before him appeared to go on for a million miles. He had never seen open space such as this, with no hint anywhere that human life might be present on this world. The air was clear as glass here, the sky cloudless, the weather gentle, springlike. Broad rolling meadows of bright golden grass, short-leaved, fleshy-stemmed, dense as a tightly woven carpet, stretched off before him. Here and there some beast of a sort unknown to Furvain browsed on the grass, paying no heed to him. This was the ninth day of his journey. The solitude was refreshing. It cleansed the soul. The deeper he went into this silent land, the greater was his sense of inner healing, of purification.

He paused at noon at a place where little rocky hills jutted from the blunt-stalked yellow grass to rest his mount and allow it to graze. He had brought an elegant beast with him, high-spirited and beautiful, a racing-mount, really, not perfectly suited for long plodding marches. It was necessary to halt frequently while the animal gathered its strength.

Furvain did not mind that. With no special destination in mind, there was no reason to adopt a hurried pace.

His mind roved ahead into the emptiness and tried to envision the marvels that awaited him. The Viper Rift, for example: what would that be like, that colossal cleft in the bosom of the world? Vertical walls that gleamed like gold, so steep that one could not even think of descending to the rift floor, where a swift green river, a serpent that seemed to have neither head nor tail, flowed toward the sea. The Great Sickle, said to be a slender, curving mass of shining white marble, a sculpture fashioned by the hand of the Divine, rising in superb isolation to a height of hundreds of feet above a tawny expanse of flat desert, a fragile arc that sighed and twanged like a harp when strong winds blew across its edge: an account dating from Lord Stiamot's time, four thousand years before, said that the sight of it, limned against the night sky with a moon or two glistening near its tip, was so beautiful it would make a Skandar drayman weep. The Fountains of Embolain, where thunderous geysers of fragrant pink water smooth as silk went rushing upward every fifty minutes, day and night – and then, a year's journey away, or perhaps two or three, the towering cliffs of black stone, riven by dazzling veins of white quartz, that guarded the shore of the Great Sea, the unbroken and unnavigable expanse of water that covered nearly half of the giant planet—

"Stand," a harsh voice suddenly said. "You are trespassing here. Identify yourself."

Furvain had been alone in this silent wilderness for so long that the grating sound ripped across his awareness like a blazing meteor's jagged path across a starless sky. Turning, he saw two glowering men, stocky and roughly dressed, standing atop a low outcropping of rock just a few yards behind him. They were armed. A third and a fourth, farther away, guarded a string of a dozen or so mounts roped together with coarse yellow cord.

He remained calm. "A trespasser, you say? But this place belongs to no one, my friend! Or else to everyone."

"This place belongs to Master Kasinibon," said the shorter and surlier-looking of the two, whose eyebrows formed a single straight black line across his furrowed forehead. He spoke in a coarse, thick-tongued way, with an unfamiliar accent that muffled all his consonants. "You'll need his permission to travel here. What is your name?"

"Aithin Furvain of Dundilmir," answered Furvain mildly. "I'll thank you to tell your master, whose name is unknown to me, that I mean no harm to his lands or property, that I'm a solitary traveler passing quickly through, who intends nothing more than—"

"Dundilmir?" the other man muttered. The thick eyebrow rose. "That's a city of the Mount, if I'm not mistaken. What's a man of Castle Mount doing wandering around in these parts? This is no place for you." And, with a guffaw: "Who are you, anyway, the Coronal's son?"

Furvain smiled. "As long as you ask," he said, "I might as well inform you that in point of fact I *am* the Coronal's son. Or I was, anyway, until the death of the Pontifex Pelxinai. My father's name is—"

A quick backhand blow across the face sent Furvain sprawling to the ground. He blinked in amazement. The blow had been a light one, merely a slap; it was the utter surprise of it that had cost him his balance. He could not remember any occasion in his life when someone had struck him, even when he was a boy.

"—Sangamor," he went on, more or less automatically, since the words were already in his mouth. "Who was Coronal under Pelxinai, and now is Pontifex himself—"

"Do you value your teeth, man? I'll hit you again if you keep on mocking me!"

In a wondering tone Furvain said, "I told you nothing but the simple truth, friend. I am Aithin of Dundilmir, the son of Sangamor. My papers will confirm it." It was beginning to dawn on him now that announcing his royal pedigree to these men like this might not have taken the most intelligent possible course to take, but he had never given any thought before this to the possibility that there might be places in the world where revealing such a thing would be unwise. In any case it was too late now for him to take it back. He had no way of preventing them from examining his papers; they plainly stated who he was; it was best to assume that no one, even out here, would presume to interfere with the movements of a son of the Pontifex, mere fifth son though he might be. "I forgive you for that blow," he said to the one who had struck him. "You had no idea of my identity. I'll see that no harm comes to you for it. And now, if you please, with all respect to your Master Kasinibon, the time has come for me to continue on my way."

"Your way, at the moment, leads you to Master Kasinibon," replied the man who had knocked him down. "You can pay your respects to him yourself."

They prodded him roughly to his feet and indicated with a gesture that he was to get astride his mount, which the other two – grooms, evidently – tied to the last of the string of mounts that they had been leading. Furvain saw now what he had not noticed earlier, that what he had taken for a small hummock at the highest ridge of the hill just before him was actually a low structure of some sort; and as they went upward, following a steep path that was hardly a path at all, a mere thin scuffing of hoofprints through the grass, all but invisible at times, it became clear to him that the structure was in fact a substantial hilltop redoubt, virtually a fortress, fashioned from the same glossy gray stone as the hill itself. Though apparently only two stories high, it spread on and on for a surprising distance along the ridge, and, as the path they were following began to curve around to the side, giving Furvain a better view, he saw that the structure extended down the eastern front of the hill for several additional levels facing into the valley beyond. He saw, too, the red shimmer of the sky above the valley, and then, as they attained the crest, the startling red slash of a long narrow lake that could only be the famed Sea of Barbirike, flanked by parallel rows of dunes whose sand was of the same brilliant red hue. Master Kasinibon, whoever he might be, this outlaw chieftain, had seized for the site of his citadel one of the most spectacular vantage-points in all of Majipoor, a site of almost unworldly splendor. One had to admire the audacity of that, Furvain thought. The man might be an outlaw, yes, a bandit, even, but he must also be something of an artist.

The building, when they finally came over the top of the hill and around to its front, turned out to be a massive thing, square-edged and heavy-set, designed for solidity rather than elegance, but not without a certain rustic power and presence. It had two long wings, radiating from a squat central quadrangle, that bent forward to reach a considerable way down the Barbirike Valley side of the hill. Its designer must have had impregnability in mind more than anything else. There was no plausible way to penetrate its defenses. The building could not be approached at all from its western side, because the final stretch of the hillside up which Furvain and his captors had just come was wholly vertical, a bare rock face impossible to ascend, and the building itself showed only a forbidding windowless facade on that side. The path from below, once it had brought them to that point of no ascent, made a wide swing off to the right, taking them over the ridge at the hill's summit and around to the front of the building, where any wayfarer would be fully exposed to the weaponry of the fortress above. Here it was guarded by watchtowers. It was protected also by a stockade, a portcullis, a formidable rampart. The building had only one entrance, not a large one. All its windows were constricted vertical slits, invulnerable to attack but useful to the defenders in case attack should come.

Furvain was conducted unceremoniously within. There was no shoving or pushing; no one actually touched him at all; but the effect was one of being hustled along by Kasinibon's men, who doubtless would shove him quite unhesitatingly if he made it necessary for them to do so. He found himself being marched down a long corridor in the left-hand wing, and then up a single flight of stairs and into a small suite of rooms, a bedroom and a sitting-room and a room containing a tub and a washstand. It was a stark place. The walls were of the same blank gray stone as the exterior of the fortress, without decoration of any kind. The windows of all three rooms, like all those in the rest of the building, were mere narrow slits, facing out toward the lake. The place was furnished simply, a couple of spare utilitarian tables and chairs and a small, uninviting bed, a cupboard, a set of empty shelves, a brick-lined fireplace. They deposited his baggage with him and left him alone, and when he tried the door he discovered that it was bolted from without. So, then, it was a suite maintained for the housing of unwilling guests, Furvain thought. And doubtless he was not the first.

Not for many hours did he have the pleasure of meeting the master of this place. Furvain spent the time pacing from room to room, surveying his new domain until he had seen it all, which did not take very long. Then he stared out at the lake for a while, but its loveliness, remarkable though it was, eventually began to pall. Then he constructed three quick verse epigrams that made ironic fun of his new predicament, but in all three instances he was oddly unable to find an adequate closing line, and he eradicated all three from his memory without completing them.

He felt no particular annoyance at having been captured like this. At this point he saw it as nothing more than an interesting novelty, a curious incident of his journey into the east-country, an episode with which to amuse his friends after his return. There was no reason to feel apprehensive. This Master Kasinibon was, most likely, some petty lordling of the Mount who had grown tired of his coddled, stable life in Banglecode or Stee or Bibiroon, or wherever it was he came from, and had struck out for himself into this wild region to carve out a little principality of his own. Or perhaps he had been guilty of some minor infraction of the law, or had given offense to a powerful kinsman, and had chosen to remove himself from the world of conventional society. Either way, Furvain saw no reason why he should come to harm at Kasinibon's hands. No doubt Kasinibon wanted merely to impress him with his own authority as master of this territory, and to storm and bluster a bit at Furvain's temerity in entering the district without the permission of its self-appointed overlord, and then he would be released.

The shadows over the red lake were lengthening now as the sun proceeded on in its journey toward Zimroel. Restlessness began to grow in Furvain with the coming of the day's end. Eventually a servant appeared, an expressionless puffy-faced Hjort with great staring batrachian eyes, who set before him a tray of food and departed without saying a word. Furvain inspected his meal: a flask of pink wine, a plate of some pallid soft meat, a bowl filled with what looked like unopened flower-buds. Simple fare for rustic folk, he thought. But the wine was supple and pleasant, the meat was tender and bathed in a subtle aromatic sauce, and the flower-buds, if that was what they were, released an agreeable sweetness when he bit into them, and left an interesting subtaste of sharp spiciness behind.

Not long after he was done, the door opened again and a small, almost elfin man of about fifty, grey-eyed and thin-lipped, garbed in a green leather jerkin and yellow tights, came in. From his swagger and stance it was plain that he was a person of consequence. He affected a clipped mustache and a short, pointed beard and wore his long hair, which was a deep black liberally streaked with strands of white, pulled tightly back and knotted behind. There was a look of slyness about him, of a playful slipperiness, that Furvain found pleasing and appealing.

"I am Kasinibon," he announced. His voice was soft and light but had the ring of authority to it nevertheless. "I apologize for any deficiencies in our hospitality thus far."

"I have noticed none," said Furvain coolly. "Thus far."

"But surely you must be accustomed to finer fare than I'm able to offer here. My men tell me you are the son of Lord Sangamor." Kasinibon offered Furvain a quick cool flicker of a smile, but nothing that could be interpreted as any sort of gesture of respect, let alone obeisance. "Or did they misunderstand something you said?"

"There was no misunderstanding. I'm indeed one of Sangamor's sons. The youngest one. I am called Aithin Furvain. If you'd like to see my papers—"

"That's scarcely necessary. Your bearing alone reveals you for whom and what you are."

"And if I may ask—" Furvain began.

But Kasinibon spoke right over Furvain's words, doing it so smoothly that it seemed almost not to be discourteous. "Do you, then, have an important role in His Majesty's government?"

"I have no role at all. You are aware, I think, that high office is never awarded on the basis of one's ancestry. A Coronal's sons do the best they can for themselves, but nothing is guaranteed to them. As I was growing up I discovered that my brothers had already taken advantage of most of the available opportunities. I live on my pension. A modest one," Furvain added, because it was beginning to occur to him that Kasinibon might have a ransom in mind.

"You hold no official post whatever, is that what you're saying?"

"None."

"What is it that you do, then? Nothing?"

"Nothing that could be considered work, I suppose. I spend my days as companion to my friend, the Duke of Dundilmir. My role is to provide amusement for the Duke and his court circle. I have a certain minor gift for poetry."

"Poetry!" Kasinibon exclaimed. "You are a poet? How splendid!" A new light came into his eyes, a look of eager interest that had the unexpected effect of transforming his features in such a way as to strip him of all his slyness for a moment, leaving him look strangely youthful and vulnerable. "Poetry is my great passion," Kasinibon said, in an almost confessional tone. "My comfort and my joy, living out here as I do on the edge of nowhere, so far from civilized pursuits. Tuminok Laskil! Vornifon! Dammiunde! Do you know how much of their work I've committed to memory?" And he struck a schoolboy pose and began to recite something of Dammiunde's, one of his most turgid pieces, a deadly earnest piece of romantic fustian about star-crossed lovers that Furvain, even as a boy, had always found wildly ludicrous. He struggled now to maintain a straight face as Kasinibon quoted an extract from one of its most preposterous sequences, the wild chase through the swamps of Kajith Kabulon. Perhaps Kasinibon came to suspect, in time, that his guest did not have the highest respect for Dammiunde's famous work, because a glow of embarrassment spread across his cheeks, and he broke the recitation off abruptly, saying, "A little old-fashioned, perhaps. But I've loved it since my boyhood."

"It's not one of my favorites," Furvain conceded. "But Tuminok Laskil, now—"

"Ah, yes. Tuminok Laskil!" At once Kasinibon treated Furvain to one of Laskil's soppiest lyrics, a work of the Ni-moyan poet's extreme youth for which Furvain could not even pretend to hide his contempt, and then, reddening once again and again leaving the poem unfinished, switched hastily to a much later verse, the third of the dark *Sonnets of Reconciliation*, which he spoke with surprising eloquence and depth of emotion. Furvain knew the poem well and cherished it, and recited it silently along with Kasinibon to the finish, and found himself unexpectedly moved at the end, not only by the poem itself but by the force of Kasinibon's admiration for it and the deftness of his reading.

"That one is much more to my taste than the first two," said Furvain after a moment, feeling that something had to be said to break the awkward stillness that the poem's beauty had created in the room.

Kasinibon seemed pleased. "I see: you prefer the deeper,

more somber work, is that it? Perhaps those first two misled you, then. Let me not do that: please understand that for me as it is for you, late Laskil is much to be preferred. I won't deny that I have a hearty appreciation for plenty of simple stuff, but I hope you'll believe me when I say that I turn to poetry for wisdom, for consolation, for instruction, even, far more often than I do for light entertainment. Your own work, I take it, is of the serious kind? A man of your obvious intelligence must be well worth reading. How strange that I don't know your name."

"I said I had a minor gift," Furvain replied, "and minor is what it is, and my verse as well. Light entertainment is the best I can do. And I've published none of it. My friends think that I should, but such trifling pieces as I produce hardly seem worth the trouble."

"Would you favor me by quoting one?"

This seemed entirely absurd, to be standing here discussing the art of poetry with a bandit chieftain whose minions had seized him without warrant and who now had locked him up in this grim frontier fortress, for what Furvain just now was beginning to suspect might be an extended imprisonment. And at the moment nothing would come to mind, anyway, except some of his silliest piffle, the trivial lyrics of a trivial-minded courtier. He could not bear, suddenly, to reveal himself to this strange man as the empty, dissolute spinner of idle verse that he knew he was. And so he begged off, claiming that the fatigue of his day's adventures had left him too weary to be able to do a proper recitation.

"Tomorrow, then, I hope," Kasinibon said. "And it would give me much pleasure not only if you would allow me to hear some of your finest work, but also for you to compose some memorable new poems during your stay under my roof."

Ah," said Furvain. He gave Kasinibon a long, piercing look. "And just how long, do you think, is that stay likely to be?"

"That will depend," Kasinibon said, and the slippery glint of slyness, not so pleasing now, was back in his eyes, "on the generosity of your family and friends. But we can talk more about that tomorrow, Prince Aithin." Then he gestured toward the window. Moonlight now glittered on the breast of the scarlet lake, carving a long ruby track running off toward the east. "That view, Prince Aithin: it certainly must be inspiring to a man of your poetic nature." Furvain did not reply. Kasinibon, undeterred, spoke briefly of the origin of the lake, the multitude of small organisms whose decaying shells had given it its extraordinary color, like any proud host explaining a famed local wonder to an interested guest. But Furvain had little interest, just now, in the beauty of the lake or the role its inhabitants had played in its appearance. Kasinibon seemed to perceive that, after a bit. "Well," he said, finally. "I bid you goodnight, and a good night's rest."

So he was indeed a prisoner, being held here for ransom. What a lovely, farcical touch! And how appropriate that a man who could in his middle years still love that childish, idiotic romantic epic of Dammiunde's would come up with the fanciful idea, straight out of Dammiunde, of demanding a ransom for his release!

But for the first time since being brought here Furvain felt some uneasiness. This was a serious business. Kasinibon might be a romantic, but he was no fool. His impregnable stone fortress alone testified to that. Somehow he had managed to set himself up as the independent ruler of a private domain, less than two weeks' journey from Castle Mount itself, and very probably he ruled that domain as its absolute master, beholden to no one in the world, a law unto himself. Obviously his men had had no idea that they would be kidnapping a Coronal's son when they had come upon a lone wayfarer in that meadow of golden grass, but all the same they had not hesitated to take him to Kasinibon after Furvain had revealed his identity to them, and Kasinibon himself did not seem to regard himself as running any serious risk by making Lord Sangamor's youngest son his prisoner.

A prisoner held for ransom, then.

And who was going to pay that ransom? Furvain had no significant assets himself. Duke Tanigel did, of course. But Tanigel, most likely, would think the ransom note was one of Furvain's pleasant jests, and would chuckle and throw it away. A second, more urgent request would in all probability meet the same fate, especially if Kasinibon asked some ridiculous sum as the price of Furvain's freedom. The Duke was a wealthy man, but would he deem it worth, say, ten thousand royals to have Furvain back at his court again? That was a very high price to pay for a spinner of idle verse.

To whom, then, could Furvain turn? His brothers? Hardly. They were, all four of them, mean-souled, purse-pinching men who clutched tight at every coin. And in their eyes he was only a useless, frivolous nullity. They'd leave him to gather dust here forever rather than put up half a crown to rescue him. And his father the Pontifex? Money would not be an issue for him. But Furvain could easily imagine his father shrugging and saying, "This will do Aithin some good, I think. He's had an easy ride through life: let him endure a little hardship, now."

On the other hand, the Pontifex could scarcely condone Kasinibon's lawlessness. Seizing innocent travelers and holding them for ransom? It was a deed that struck at the very core of the social contract that allowed a civilization so far-flung as Majipoor's to hold together. But a military scout would come out and see that the citadel was unassailable, and they would decide not to waste lives in the attempt. A stern decree would be issued, ordering Kasinibon to release his captive and desist from taking others, but nothing would be done by way of enforcing it. I will stay here the rest of my life, Furvain concluded gloomily. I will finish my days as a prisoner in this stone fortress, endlessly pacing these echoing halls. Master Kasinibon will award me the post of court poet and we will recite the collected works of Tuminok Laskil to each other until I lose my mind.

A bleak prospect. But there was no point in fretting further over it tonight, at any rate. Forvain forced himself to push all these dark thoughts aside and made himself ready for bed.

The bed, meager and unresilient, was less comfortable than the one he had left behind in Dundilmir, but was, at least, to be preferred to the simple bedroll laid out on the ground under a canopy of stars that he had used these past ten days of his journey through the east-country. As he dropped toward sleep, Furvain felt a sensation he knew well, that of a poem knocking at the gates of his mind, beckoning to him to allow it to be born. He saw it only dimly, a vague thing without form, but even in that dimness he was aware that it would be something unusual, at least for him. More than unusual, in fact: something unique. It would be, he sensed, a prodigious work, unprecedented, a poem that would somehow be of far greater scope and depth than anything he had ever produced, though what its subject was was something he could not yet tell. Something magnificent, of that he felt certain, as the knocking continued and became more insistent. Something mighty. Something to touch the soul and heart and mind: something that would transform all who approached it. He was a little frightened of the size of it. He scarcely knew what to make of it, that something like this had come into his mind. There was great power to it, and soaring music, somber and jubilant all at once. But of course the poem had *not* come into his mind – only its dimensions, not the thing itself. The actual poem would not come into clear view at all, at least not of its own accord, and when he reached through to seize it, it eluded him with the swiftness of a skittish bilantoon, dancing back beyond his reach, vanishing finally into the well of darkness that lay beneath his consciousness, nor would it return even though he lay awake a long while awaiting it.

At last he abandoned the effort and tried to compose himself for sleep once again. Poems must never be seized, he knew; they came only when they were willing to come, and it was futile to try to coerce them. Furvain could not help wondering, though, about its theme. He had no idea of what the poem had been about, nor, he suspected, had he been aware of it even in the instant of the dream. There was no specificity to it, no tangible substance. All he could say was that the poem had been some kind of mighty thing, a work of significant breadth and meaning, and a kind of majesty. Of that he was sure, or reasonably sure, anyway: it had been the major poem of which everyone but he himself was certain he was capable, offering itself to his mind at last. Teasing him, tempting him. But never showing anything more of itself to him than its aura, its outward gleam, and then dancing away, as though to mock him for the laziness of all his past years. An ironic tragedy: the great lost poem of Aithin Furvain. The world would never know, and he would mourn its loss forever.

Then he decided that he was simply being foolish. What had he lost? His drowsy mind had been playing with him. A poem that is only a shadow of a shadow is no poem at all. To think that he had lost a masterpiece was pure idiocy. How did he know how good the poem, had he been granted any clear sight of it, would have been? What means did he have to judge the quality of a poem that had refused to come into being? He was flattering himself to think that there had been any substance there. The Divine, he knew, had not chosen to give him the equipment that was necessary for the forging of major poems. He was a shallow, idle man, meant to be the maker of little jingling rhymes, of light-hearted playful verse, not of masterpieces. That beckoning poem had been a mere phantom, he thought, the delusion of a weary mind at the edge of sleep, the phantasmagoric aftermath of his bizarre conversation with Master Kasinibon. Furvain let himself drift downward again into slumber, and slipped away quickly this time.

When he woke, with vague fugitive memories of the lost poem still troubling his mind like a dream that will not let go, he had no idea at first where he was. Bare stone walls, a hard narrow bed, a mere slit of a window through which the morning sun was pouring with merciless power? Then he remembered. He was a prisoner in the fortress of Master Kasinibon. He was angry, at first, that what he had intended as a journey of private discovery, the purifying voyage of a troubled soul, had been interrupted by a band of marauding ruffians; then he was once more amused at the novelty of having been seized in such a fashion; and then he became angry again over the intrusion on his life. But anger, Furvain knew, would serve no useful purpose. He must remain calm, and look upon this purely as an adventure, the raw material for anecdotes and poems with which to regale his friends when he was home at last in Dundilmir.

He bathed and dressed and spent some time studying the effects of morning light on the still surface of the lake, which at this early hour seemed crimson rather than scarlet, and then grew irritable again, and was pacing from room to room once more when the Hjort appeared with his breakfast. In mid-morning Kasinibon paid his second visit to him, but only for a few minutes, and then the morning stretched on interminably until the Hjort came by to bring him lunch. For a time he plumbed his consciousness for some vestige of that lost poem, but the attempt was hopeless, and only instilled in him pangs of regret for he knew not what. Which left him with nothing to do but stare at the lake; and though the lake was indeed exquisite, and of the sort of beauty that changed from hour to hour with the changing angles of the sunlight, Furvain could study those changes only so long before even such beauty as this ceased to stir a response in him.

He had brought some books with him on this journey, but he found that he had no interest in reading now. The words seemed mere meaningless marks on the page. Nor could was he able to find distraction in poetry of his own making. It was as if the vanishing of that imaginary masterpiece of the night had taken the ability even to write light verse from him. The fountain that had flowed in a copious gush all his life had gone mysteriously dry: just now he was as empty of poetry as the walls of these rooms were of ornament. So there he was without solace for his solitude. Solitude had never been this much of a problem for him before. Not that he had ever had to put up with any great deal of it, but he had always been able to divert himself with versifying or word-games when he did, and that, for some reason he failed to comprehend, was cut off from him now. While he was still traveling on his own through the east-country he had found being alone to be no burden at all, in fact an interesting and stimulating and instructive new experience; but out there he had had the strangeness of the landscape to appreciate, the unusual new flora and fauna that each day brought, and also he had been much absorbed by the whole challenge of solitary travel, the need to manage his own meals, to find an adequate place to make camp at night, a suitable source of water, and all that. Here, though, locked up in these barren little rooms, he was thrown back on his own resources, and the only resource he had, really, was the boundless fertility of his poetic imagination; and, although he had no idea why, he seemed no longer to have any access to that.

Kasinibon returned for him not long after lunch.

"To the lake, then?" he asked.

"To the lake, yes."

The outlaw chieftain led him grandly through the clattering stone hallways of the fortress, down and down and down, and ultimately to a corridor on the lowest level, through which they emerged onto a little winding path covered with tawny gravel that curved off in a series of gentle switchbacks to the red lake far below. To Furvain's surprise Kasinibon was unaccompanied by any of his men: the party consisted only of the two of them. Kasinibon walked in front, completely untroubled, apparently, by the possibility that Furvain might choose to attack him.

I could snatch his knife from its scabbard and put it to his throat, Furvain thought, and make him swear to release me. Or I could simply knock him down and club his head against the ground a few times, and run off into the wilderness. Or I could—

It was all too inane to contemplate. Kasinibon was a man of small stature but he looked quick and strong. Doubtless he would instantly make Furvain regret any sort of physical attack. Probably he had bodyguards lurking in the bushes, besides. And even if Furvain did somehow succeed in overpowering him and getting away, what good would it do? Kasinibon's men would hunt him down and take him prisoner again within an hour.

I am his guest, Furvain told himself. He is my host. Let us leave it at that, at least for now.

Two mounts were waiting for them at the edge of the lake. One was the fine, high-spirited creature, with fiery red eyes and flanks of a deep maroon, that Furvain had brought with him from Dundilmir; the other, a short-legged, yellowish beast, looked like a peasant's dray-mount. Kasinibon vaulted up into its saddle and gestured to Furvain to follow suit.

"Barbirike Sea," said Kasinibon, in a tour-guide's mechanical voice, as they started forward, "is close to three hundred miles long, but no more than two thousand feet across at its widest point. It is closed at each end by virtually unscalable cliffs. We have never been able to find any spring that flows into it: it replenishes itself entirely through rainfall." Seen at close range, the lake seemed more than ever like a great pool of blood. So dense was the red hue that the water had no transparency whatever. From shore to shore it presented itself as an impenetrable sheet of redness, with no features visible below the surface. The reflected face of the sun burned like a sphere of flame on the still waters.

"Can anything live in it?" Furvain asked. "Other than the crustaceans that give it its color?"

"Oh, yes," said Kasinibon. "It's only water, you know. We fish it every day. The yield is quite heavy."

A path barely wide enough for their two mounts side by side separated the lake's edge from the towering dunes of red sand that ran alongside it. As they rode eastward along the lake, Kasinibon, still playing the guide, pointed out tidbits of natural history to Furvain: a plant with short, purplish, plumply succulent finger-shaped leaves that was capable of flourishing in the nearly sterile sand of the dunes and dangled down over the crescent slopes in long ropy strands, and a yellow-necked beady-eyed predatory bird that hovered overhead, now and again plunging with frightful force to snatch some denizen of the water out of the lake, and furry little round-bodied crabs that scuttered around like mice along the shore, digging in the scarlet mud for hidden worms. He told Furvain the scientific name of each one, but the names went out of his mind almost at once. Furvain had never troubled to learn very much about the creatures of the wild, although he found these creatures interesting enough, in their way. But Kasinibon, who seemed to be in love with this place, evidently knew everything there was to know about each one. Furvain, though he listened politely enough to his disquisitions, found them distracting and bothersome.

For Furvain the overwhelming redness of the Barbirike Valley was the thing that affected him most deeply. This was beauty of an astounding sort. It seemed to him that all the world had turned scarlet: there was no way to see over the tops of the dunes, so that the view to his left consisted entirely of the red lake itself and the red dunes beyond it, with nothing else visible, and on his right side everything was walled in by the lofty red barrier of the dunes that rose just beside their riding-track, and the sky overhead, drawing reflected color from what lay below it, was a shimmering dome of a slightly paler red. Red, red, and red: Furvain felt cloaked in it, contained in it, sealed tight in a realm of redness. He gave himself up to it entirely. He let it engulf and possess him.

Kasinibon seemed to take notice of Furvain's long silence, his air of deepening concentration. "What we see here is the pure stuff of poetry, is it not?" Kasinibon said proudly, making a sweeping gesture that encompassed both shore and sky and the distant dark hulk of his own fortress, looming at the top of the cliff that lay at their backs. They had come to a halt half a league up the valley. It looked much the same here as at the place where they had begun their ride: red everywhere, before and behind, an unchanging scarlet world. "I draw constant inspiration from it, and surely you will as well. You will write your masterpiece here. That much I know."

The sincerity in his voice was unmistakable. He wants that poem very much, Furvain realized. But he resented the little man's jarring invasion of his thoughts and he winced at that reference to a "masterpiece." Furvain had no wish to hear anything further about masterpieces, not after last night's painful quasi-dream, in which his own mind seemed to have been mocking him for the deficiencies of his ambitions, pretending to lead him toward some noble work that was not within his soul to create.

Curtly he said, "Poetry seems to have deserted me for the moment, I'm afraid."

"It will return. From what you've told me, I know that making poems is something that's innate to your nature. Have you ever gone very long without producing something? As much as a week, say?"

"Probably not. I couldn't really say. The poems happen when they happen, according to some rhythm of their own. It's not something I've paid much conscious attention to."

"A week, ten days, two weeks – the words will come," said Kasinibon. "I know they will." He seemed strangely excited. "Aithin Furvain's great poem, written while he is the guest of Master Kasinibon of Barbirike! I might even dare to hope for a dedication, perhaps. Or is that too bold of me?"

This was becoming intolerable. Would it never end, the world's insistence that he must pull some major enterprise from his unwilling mind?

Furvain said, "Shall I correct you yet again? I am your prisoner, Kasinibon, not your guest."

"At least you say that, I think, without rancor."

"What good is rancor, eh? But when one is being held for ransom—"

"Ransom is such an ugly word, Furvain. All that I require is that your family pay the fee I charge for crossing my territory, since you appear to be unable to pay it yourself. Call it ransom, if you like. But the term does offend me."

"Then I withdraw it," said Furvain, still concealing his irritation as well as he could beneath a forced lightness of tone. "I am a man of breeding, Kasinibon. Far be it from me to offend my host."

In the evening they dined together, just the two of them, in a great echoing candlelit hall where a platoon of silent Hjorts in gaudy livery did the serving, stalking in and out with the absurd grandeur that the people of that unattractive race liked to affect. The banquet was a rich one, first a compote of fruits of some kind unknown to Furvain, then a poached fish of the most delicate flavor, nestling in a dark sauce that must have been based in honey, and then several sorts of grilled meats on a bed of stewed vegetables. The wines for each course were impeccably chosen. Occasionally Furvain caught sight of some of the other outlaws moving about in the corridor at the lower end of the hall, shadowy figures far away, but none entered the room.

Flushed with drink, Kasinibon spoke freely of himself. He seemed very eager, almost pathetically so, to win his captive's friendship. He was, he said, a younger son himself, third son of the Count of Kekkinork. Kekkinork was not a place known to Furvain. "It lies two hours' march from the shores of the Great Sea," Kasinibon explained. "My ancestors came there to mine the handsome blue stone known as seaspar, which the Coronal Lord Pinitor of ancient times used in decorating the walls of the city of Bombifale. When the work was done some of the miners chose not to return to Castle Mount. And there at Kekkinork they have lived ever since, in a village at the edge of the Great Sea, a free people, beyond the ken of Pontifex and Coronal. My father, the Count, was the sixteenth holder of that title in the direct line of succession."

"A title conferred by Lord Pinitor?"

"A title conferred by the first Count upon himself," said Kasinibon. "We are the descendants of humble miners and stonemasons, Furvain. But, of course, if one only goes back far enough, which of the lords of Castle Mount would be seen to be free of the blood of commoners?"

"Indeed," Furvain said. That part was unimportant. What he was struggling to assimilate was the knowledge that this small bearded man sitting elbow to elbow with him had beheld the Great Sea with his own eyes, had grown to manhood in a remote part of Majipoor that was widely looked upon as the next thing to mythical. The notion of the existence of an actual town of some sort out there, a town unknown to geographers and census-keepers, situated in an obscure location at Alhanroel's easternmost point many thousands of miles from Castle Mount, strained credibility. And that this place had a separate aristocracy of its own creation, counts and marquises and ladies and all the rest, which had endured for sixteen generations there – that, too, was hard to believe.

Kasinibon refilled their wine-bowls. Furvain had been drinking as sparingly as he could all evening, but Kasinibon was merciless in his generosity, and Furvain felt flushed, now, and a little dizzy. Kasinibon had taken on the glossy-eyed look of full drunkenness.

He had begun to speak, in a rambling, circuitous way that Furvain found difficult to follow, of some bitter family quarrel, a dispute with one of his older brothers over a woman, the great love of his life, perhaps, and an appeal laid before their father in which the father had taken the brother's side. It sounded familiar enough to Furvain: the grasping brother, the distant and indifferent noble father, the younger son treated with offhand disdain. But Furvain, perhaps because he had never been a man of much ambition or drive, had not allowed the disappointments of his early life ever to stir much umbrage in his mind. He had always felt that he was more or less invisible to his dynamic father and his rapacious, aggressive brothers. He expected indifference from them, at best, and was not surprised when that was what he got, and had gone on to construct a reasonably satisfactory life for himself even so, founded on the belief that the less one expected out of life, the less one was likely to feel dissatisfied with what came one's way.

Kasinibon, though, was of another kind, hot-blooded and determined, and his dispute with his brother had mounted to something of shattering acrimony, leading finally to an actual violent assault by Kasinibon on – whom? – his brother? – his father? – Furvain was not entirely sure which. It finally came to pass that Kasinibon had found it advisable to flee from Kekkinork, or perhaps had been exiled from it – again, Furvain did not know which – and had gone roaming for many years from one sector of the east-country to another until, here at Barbirike, he had found a place where he could fortify himself against anyone who might attempt to offer a challenge to his truculent independence. "And here I am to this day," he concluded. "I have no dealings with my family, nor any with Pontifex or Coronal, either. I am my own master, and the master of my little kingdom. And those who wander across my territory must pay the price. More wine, Furvain?"

"Thank you, no."

He poured, as though he had not heard. Furvain began to brush his hand aside, then halted and let Kasinibon fill the bowl.

"I like you, you know, Furvain. I hardly know you, but I'm as good a judge of men as you'll ever find, and I see the depth of you, the greatness in you."

And I see the drunkenness in you, Furvain thought, but he said nothing.

"If they pay the fee, I'll have to let you go, I suppose. I'm an honorable man. But I'd regret it. I've had very little intelligent company here. Very little company of any sort, as a matter of fact. It's the life I chose, of course. But still—"

"You must be very lonely."

It occurred to Furvain that he had not seen any women at the fortress, nor even any sign of a female presence: only the Hjort servants, and the occasional glimpse of some of Kasinibon's followers, all of them men. Was Kasinibon that rarity, the one-woman man? And had that woman of Kekkinork, the one his brother had taken from him, been that woman? It must be a grim existence for him, then, in this desolate keep. No wonder he sought the consolations of poetry; no wonder he was still capable, at this advanced age, of finding so much to admire in the nonsensical puerile effusions of Dammiunde or Tuminok Laskil.

"Lonely, yes. I can't deny that. Lonely – lonely—" Kasinibon turned a bloodshot gaze on Furvain. His eyes had taken on a glint as red as the waters of the Barbirike Sea. "But one learns to live with loneliness. One makes one's choices in life, does one not, and although they are never perfect choices, they are, after all, one's own, eh? Ultimately, we choose what we choose because – we choose – because – because—"

Kasinibon's voice grew less distinct and trailed off into incoherence. Furvain thought he might have fallen asleep; but no, no, Kasinibon's eyes were open, his lips were slowly moving, he was searching still for the precise phrase to explain whatever it was he was trying to explain. Furvain waited until it became clear that the bandit chieftain was never going to find that phrase. Then he touched Kasinibon lightly on the arm. "You must forgive me," he said. "The hour is very late." Kasinibon nodded vaguely. A Hjort in livery showed Furvain to his rooms.

In the night Furvain dreamed a dream of such power and lucidity that he thought, even as he was experiencing it, that it must be a sending of the Lady of the Isle, who visits millions of the sleepers of Majipoor each night to bring them guidance and comfort. If indeed it were a sending, it would be his first: the Lady did not often visit the minds of the princes of the Castle, and in any case she would not have been likely to visit that of Furvain, for it was the ancient custom for the mother of the current Coronal to be chosen as Lady of the Isle, and thus, for most of Furvain's life, the reigning Lady had been his own grandmother. She would not enter the mind of a member of her own family except at some moment of high urgency. Now, of course, with Lord Sangamor having moved on to become Sangamor Pontifex, there was a new Coronal at the Castle and a new Lady at the helm of the Isle of Sleep. But even so – a sending? For *him?* Here? Why?

As he was drifting back into sleep once the dream had left him, he decided that it had not been a sending at all, but merely the workings of his own agitated mind, stirred to frantic excitation by his evening with Master Kasinibon. It had been too personal, too intimate a vision to have been the work of the stranger who now was Lady of the Isle. Yet Furvain knew it to have been no ordinary dream, but rather one of those strange dreams by which one's whole future life is determined.

For in it his sleeping mind had been lifted up out of Kasinibon's stark sanctuary and carried from it over the night-shrouded plains of the east-country, off to the other side of the blue cliffs of Kekkinork where the Great Sea began, stretching forth into the immeasurable and incomprehensible distances that separated Alhanroel from the continent of Zimroel half a world away. Here, far to the east of any place he had ever known, he could see the light of the dawning day gleaming on the breast of the ocean, which was a gentle pink in color at the sandy shore, then pale green, and a deeper green farther out, and then deepening by steady gradation to the azure gray of the unfathomable depths.

The Spirit of the Divine lingered high above that mighty ocean, Furvain perceived: impersonal, unknowable, infinite, all-seeing. Though the Spirit was without form or feature, Furvain recognized it for what it was, and the Spirit recognized him, touching his mind, gathering it in, linking it, for one stunning moment, to the vastness that was itself. And in that infinitely long moment the greatest of all poems was dictated to him, poured into him in one tremendous cascade, a poem that only a god could create, the poem that encompassed the meaning of life and of death, of the destiny of all worlds and all the creatures that dwelled upon them. Or so Furvain thought, later, when he had awakened and lay shivering, feverish with bewilderment, contemplating the vision that had been thrust upon him.

No shard of that vision remained, not a single detail by which he could try to reconstruct it. It had shattered like a soap-bubble and vanished into the darkness. Once again he had been brought to the presence of a sublime poem of the greatest beauty and profundity and then it had been snatched away again.

Tonight's dream, though, was different in its deepest essence from the one of the night before. That other dream had been a sad cruel joke, a bit of mere harsh mockery. It had flaunted a poem before him but had given him no access to it, only the humiliating awareness that a major poem of some sort lurked somewhere within him but would be kept forever beyond his reach. This time he had had the poem itself. He had lived it, line by line, stanza by stanza, canto by canto, through all its grand immensity. Although he had lost it upon waking, perhaps it could be found again. The first dream had told him, *Your gift is an empty one and you are capable of nothing but the making of trivialities.* The second dream had told him, *You contain godlike greatness within you and you must now strive to find a way to draw it forth.*

Though the content of that great vision was gone, Furvain realized in the morning that one aspect of it still remained, as though burned into his mind: its framework, the container for the mighty poem itself: the metric pattern, the rhyme-scheme, the method of building verses into stanzas and the grouping of stanzas into cantos. A mere empty vessel, yes. But if the container, at least, was left to him, there might be hope of rediscovering the awesome thing that it had contained.

The structural pattern was such a distinctive one that he knew he was unlikely to forget it, but even so he would not take the risk. He reached hastily for his pen and a blank sheet of paper and scribbled it down. Rather than attempting at this point to recapture even a fragment of what would be no small task to retrieve, Furvain used mere nonsense syllables to provide a shape for the vessel, meaningless dum-de-dum sounds that provided the basic rhythmic outline of one extended passage. When he was done he stared in wonder at it, murmuring it to himself over and over again, analyzing consciously now what he had set down as a sort of automatic transcription of his dream-memory. It was a remarkable structure, yes, but almost comically extreme. As he counted out its numbers he asked himself whether anything so intricate had ever been devised by poet's mind before, and whether any poet in the long history of the universe would ever have been able to carry off a long work using prosody of such an extravagant kind.

It was a marvel of complexity. It made no use of the traditional stress-patterned metrics he knew so well, the iambs and trochees and dactyls, the spondees and anapests, out of which Furvain had always built his poems with such swiftness and ease. Those traditional patterns were so deeply engrained in him that it seemed to others that he wrote without thinking, that he simply exhaled his poems rather than creating them by conscious act. But this pattern – he chanted it over and over to himself, struggling to crack its secret – was alien to all that he understood of the craft of poetry.

At first he could see no sort of regularity to the rhythms whatever, and was at a loss to explain the strangely compelling power of them. But then he realized that the metric of his dream-poem must be a quantitative one, based not on where the accents fell but on the length of syllables, a system that struck Furvain at first as disconcertingly arbitrary and irregular but which, he saw after a while, could yield a wondrously versatile line in the hands of anyone gifted enough to manipulate its intricacies properly. It would have the force almost of an incantation; those caught up in its sonorous spell would be held as if by sorcery. The rhyme-scheme too was a formidable one, with stanzas of seventeen lines that allowed of only three different rhymes, arranged in a pattern of five internal couplets split by a triolet and balanced by four seemingly unrhymed lines that actually were reaching into adjacent stanzas.

Could a poem actually be written according to such a structure? Of course, Furvain thought. But what poet could possibly have the patience to stay with it long enough to produce a work of any real scope? The Divine could, of course. By definition the Divine could do anything: what difficulties would a mere arrangement of syllables and rhymes offer to the omnipotent force that had brought into being the stars and worlds? But it was not just blasphemous for a mere mortal to set himself up in competition with the Divine, he thought, it was contemptible folly. Furvain knew he could write three or four stanzas in this kind of scheme, if he turned himself properly to the task, or perhaps seven, that made some kind of poetic sense. But a whole canto? And a series of cantos that would constitute a coherent work of epic magnitude? No, he thought. No. No. That would drive him out of his mind. No doubt of it, to undertake a task of such grandeur would be to invite madness.

Still, it had been an extraordinary dream. The other one had left him with nothing but the taste of ashes in his mouth. This one showed him that he – not the Divine, but *he*, for Furvain was not a very religious man and felt sure that it was his own dreaming mind that had invented it, without supernatural assistance – was able to conceive a stanzaic system of almost impossible difficulty. It must have been in him all along, he thought, gestating quietly, finally erupting from him as he slept. The tensions and pressures of his captivity, he decided, must have aided in the birth. No longer was he as amused as he once had been about spending his days in Kasinibon's custody. It was becoming harder to take a comic view of the affair. The rising anger he felt at being held prisoner here, the frustrations, his growing restlessness: all that must be altering the chemistry of his brain, forcing his thoughts into new channels, his inner torment bringing out new aspects of his poetic skill.

Not that he had the slightest idea of trying to make actual use of such a system as the night just past had brought him; but it was pleasing enough to know that he was capable of devising such a thing. Perhaps that portended a return of his ability to write light verse, at least. Furvain knew that he was never going to give the world the deathless masterpiece that Kasinibon was so eager to have from him, but it would be good at least to regain the pleasant minor skill that had been his until a few days before.

But the days went by and Furvain remained unaccountably unproductive. Neither Kasinibon's urgings nor Furvain's own attempts at inducing the presence of the muse were in any way helpful, and his old spontaneous facility was so far from being in evidence that he could almost persuade himself that it had never existed.

His captivity, now, was weighing on him with increasing discomfort. Accustomed as he was to a life of idleness, this kind of forced inactivity was nothing he had ever had to endure before, and he longed to be on his way. Kasinibon tried his best, of course, to play the part of the charming host. He took Furvain on daily rides through the scarlet valley, he brought forth the finest wines from his surprisingly well-stocked cellar for their nightly dinners, he provided him with whatever book he might fancy – his library was well stocked, also – and lost no opportunity to engage him in serious discussion of the literary arts.

But the fact remained that Furvain was here unwillingly, penned up in this dour, forbidding mausoleum of a place, snared midway through a crisis of his own and compelled, before he had reached any resolution of that, to live as the prisoner of another man, and a limited man at that. Kasinibon now allowed him to roam freely through the building and its grounds – if he tried to escape, where could he hope to go, after all? – but the long echoing halls and mainly empty rooms were far from congenial. There was nothing really congenial about Kasinibon's company, either, however much Furvain pretended that there was, and there was no one else here to keep company with Furvain than Kasinibon. The outlaw chieftain, walled about by his hatred for his own family and stunted by his long isolation here, was as much a prisoner at Barbirike as Furvain himself, and behind his superficial amiability, that elfin playfulness of his, some hidden fury lurked and seethed. Furvain saw that fury and feared it.

He had still done nothing about sending out a ransom request. It seemed utterly futile, and embarrassing as well: what if he asked, and no one complied? But the growing probability that he was going to remain here forever was starting to engender a sense of deep desperation in him.

What was particularly hard to bear was Kasinibon's fondness for poetry. Kasinibon seemed to want to talk about nothing else. Furvain had never cared much for conversation about poetry. He was content to leave that to the academic folk, who had no creative spark themselves but found some sort of fulfillment in endless discussions of the thing that they were themselves unable to produce, and to those persons of culture who felt that it was incumbent on them to be seen carrying some slim volume of poetry about, and even to dip into it from time to time, and to utter praise for some currently acclaimed poet's work. Furvain, from whom poems by the ream had always emerged with only the slightest of efforts and who had had no lofty view of what he had achieved, had no interest in such talk. For him poetry was something to make, not something to discuss. What a horror it was, then, to be trapped like this in the presence of the most talkative of amateur connoisseurs of the art, and an ignorant one at that!

Like most self-educated men, Kasinibon had no taste in poetry at all – he gobbled everything omnivorously, indiscriminately, and was uncritically entranced by it all. Stale images, leaden rhymes, bungled metaphors, ridiculous similes – he had no difficulty overlooking such things, perhaps did not even notice them. The one thing he demanded was a bit of emotional power in a poem, and if he could find it there, he forgave all else.

And so Furvain spent most nights in the first weeks of his stay at the outlaw's keep listening to Kasinibon's readings of his favorite poems. His extensive library, hundreds and hundreds of well-thumbed volumes, some of them practically falling apart after years of constant use, seemed to contain the work of every poet Furvain had ever heard of, and a good many that he had not. It was such a wide-ranging collection that its very range argued for its owner's lack of discernment. Kasinibon's passionate love of poetry struck Furvain as mere promiscuity. "Let me read you this!" Kasinibon would cry, eyes aglow with enthusiasm, and he would intone some incontestably great work of Gancislad or Emmengild; but then, even as the final glorious lines still were echoing in Furvain's mind, Kasinibon would say, "Do you know what it reminds me of, that poem?" And he would reach for his beloved volume of Vortrailin, and with equal enthusiasm declaim one of the tawdriest bits of sentimental trash Furvain had ever heard. He seemed unable to tell the difference.

Often he asked Furvain to choose poems that he would like to read, also, wanting to hear how a practitioner of the art handled the ebb and flow of poetic rhythms. Furvain's own tastes in poetry had always run heavily to the sort of light verse at which he excelled himself, but, like any cultivated man, he appreciated more serious work as well, and on these occasions he took a deliberate malicious pleasure in selecting for Kasinibon the knottiest, most abstruse modern works he could find on Kasinibon's shelves, poems that he himself barely understood and should have been mysteries to Kasinibon also. These, too,

Kasinibon loved. "Beautiful," he would murmur, enraptured. "Sheer music, is it not?"

I am going to go mad, Furvain thought.

At some point during nearly every one of these nightly sessions of poetic discourse Kasinibon would press Furvain to recite some of his own work. Furvain could no longer claim, as he had on the first day, that he was too tired to comply. Nor could he pretend very plausibly that he had forgotten every poem he had ever written. So in the end he yielded and offered a few. Kasinibon's applause was hearty in the extreme, and seemed unfeigned. And he spoke at great length in praise not just of Furvain's elegance of phrasing but his insight into human nature. Which was all the more embarrassing; Furvain himself was abashed by the triviality of his themes and the glibness of his technique; it took every ounce of his aristocratic breeding to hold himself back from crying out, "But don't you see, Kasinibon, what hollow word-spinning that is!" That would have been cruel, and discourteous besides. Both men now had entered into a pretense of friendship, which might not even have been a pretense on Kasinibon's part. One may not call one's friend a fool to his face, Furvain thought, and expect him to go on being your friend.

The worst part of all was Kasinibon's unfeigned eagerness to have Furvain write something new, and important, while a guest under his roof. There had been nothing playful about that wistfully expressed hope of his that Furvain would bring into being here some masterpiece that would forever link his name and Kasinibon's in the archives of poetry. Behind that wistfulness, Furvain sensed, lay ferocious need. He suspected that matters would not always remain so amiable here: that indirection would turn to blunt insistence, that Kasinibon would squeeze him and squeeze him until Furvain brought forth the major work that Kasinibon so hungrily yearned to usher into existence. Furvain replied evasively to each of Kasinibon's inquiries about new work, explaining, truthfully enough, that inspiration was still denied to him. But there was a mounting intensity to Kasinibon's demands.

The question of ransom, which Furvain had continued to push aside, needed to be squarely faced. Furvain saw that he could not remain here much longer without undergoing some kind of inner explosion. But the only way he was going to get out of this place, he knew, was with the help of someone else's money. Was there anyone in the world willing to put up money to rescue him? He suspected he knew the answer to that, but shied away from confirming his fears. Still, if he never so much as asked, he would spend the remaining days of his life listening to Master Kasinibon's solemn, worshipful readings of the worst poetry human mind had ever conceived, and fending off Kasinibon's insistence that Furvain write for him some poem of a grandeur and majesty that was not within Furvain's abilities to produce.

"How much, would you say, should I ask as the price of my freedom?" Furvain asked one day, as they rode together beside the shore of the scarlet sea.

Kasinibon told him. It was a stupendous sum, more than twice Furvain's own highest guess. But he had asked, and Kasinibon had answered, and he was in no position to haggle with the bandit over the amount.

Duke Tanigel, he supposed, was the first one he should try. Furvain knew that his brothers were unlikely to care much whether he stayed here forever or not. His father might take a gentler position, but his father was far away in the Labyrinth, and appealing to the Pontifex carried other risks, too, for if it came to pass that a Pontifical army were dispatched to Barbirike to rescue the captive prince, Kasinibon might react in some unpleasant and possibly fatal way. The same risk would apply if Furvain were to turn to the new Coronal, Lord Hunzimar. Strictly speaking, it was the Coronal's responsibility to deal with such matters as banditry in the outback. But that was exactly what Furvain was afraid of, that Hunzimar would send troops out here to teach Kasinibon a lesson, a lesson that might have ugly consequences for Kasinibon's prisoner. Even more probably, Hunzimar, who had never shown much affection for any of his predecessor's sons, would do nothing at all. No, Tanigel was his only hope, faint though that hope might be.

Furvain did have some notion of the extent of Duke Tanigel's immense wealth, and suspected that the whole gigantic amount of his ransom would be no more than the cost of one week's feasting and revelry at the court in Dundilmir. Perhaps Tanigel would deign to help, out of fond memories of happy times together. Furvain spent half a day writing and revising his note to the Duke, working hard to strike the proper tone of amused, even waggish chagrin over his plight, while at the same time letting Tanigel know that he really did have to come through with the money if ever he hoped to see his friend Furvain again. He turned the letter over to Kasinibon, who sent one of his men off to Dundilmir to deliver it.

"And now," said Kasinibon, "I propose we turn our attention this evening to the ballads of Garthain Hagavon—"

At the beginning of the fourth week of his captivity Furvain made the dream-journey to the Great Sea once again, and again took dictation from the Divine, who appeared to him in the guise of a tall, broad-shouldered, golden-haired man of cheerful mien, wearing a Coronal's silver band about his head. And when he woke it was all still in his mind, every syllable of every verse, every verse of every stanza, every stanza of what appeared to be a third of a canto, as well as he could judge the proportions of such things. But it began to fade almost at once. Out of fear that he might lose it all he set about the work of transcribing as much of it as he could, and as the lines emerged onto the paper he saw that they followed the inordinately intricate metrical pattern and rhyming scheme of the poem that had been given to him by the hand of the Divine that other time weeks before: appeared to be, indeed, a fragment of that very poem.

A fragment was all that it was. What Furvain had managed to get down began in the middle of a stanza, and ended, pages later, in the middle of another one. The subject was warfare, the campaign of the great Lord Stiamot of thousands of years before against the rebellious aboriginal people of Majipoor, the shapeshifting Metamorph race. The segment that lay before him dealt with Stiamot's famous march through the foothills of Zygnor Peak in northern Alhanroel, the climactic enterprise of that long agonizing struggle, when he had set fire to the whole district, parched by the heat of the long dry summer, in order to drive the final bands of Metamorph guerrillas from their hiding places. It broke off at the point where Lord Stiamot found himself confronting a recalcitrant landholder, a man of the ancient northern gentry who refused to pay heed to Stiamot's warning that all this territory was going to be put to the torch and that it behoved every settler to flee at once.

When it became impossible for Furvain to go any further with his transcription he read it all back, astounded, even bemused. The style and general approach, the bizarre schemes of rhyme and metric apart, were beyond any doubt his own. He recognized familiar turns of phrase, similes of a kind that had always come readily to him, choices of rhyme that declared themselves plainly as the work of Aithin Furvain. But how, if not by direct intervention of the Divine, had anything so complicated and deep sprung from his own shallow mind? This was majestic poetry. There was no other word for it. He read it aloud to himself, revelling in the sonorities, the internal assonances, the sinewy strength of the line, the inevitability of each stanza's form. He had never written anything remotely like this before. He had had the technique for it, very likely, but he could not imagine ever making so formidable a demand on that technique.

And also there were things in here about Stiamot's campaign that Furvain did not in fact believe he had ever known. He had learned about Lord Stiamot from his tutors, of course. Everyone did; Stiamot was one of the great figures of Majipoor's history.

But Furvain's schooling had taken place decades ago. Had he ever really heard the names of all these places – Domgrave, Milimorn, Hamifieu, Bizfern, Kattikawn? Were they genuine place-names, or his own inventions?

His inventions? Well, yes, anyone could make up names, he supposed. But there was too much here about military procedure, lines of supply and chains of command and order of march and such, that read like the work of some other hand, someone far more knowledgeable about such things than he had ever been. How, then, could he possibly claim this poem as his own? Yet where had it come from, if not from him? Was he truly the vehicle through which the Divine had chosen to bring this fragment into existence? Furvain found his slender fund of religious feeling seriously taxed by such a notion. And yet – and yet—

Kasinibon saw at once that something out of the ordinary had happened. "You've begun to write, haven't you?"

"I've begun a poem, yes," said Furvain uneasily.

"Wonderful! When can I see it?"

The blaze of excitement in Kasinibon's eyes was so fierce that Furvain had to back away a few steps. "Not just yet, I think. This is much too soon to be showing it to anyone. At this point it would be extremely easy for me to lose my way. A casual word from someone else might be just the one that would deflect me from my path."

"I swear that I'll offer no comment at all. I simply would like to—"

"No. Please." Furvain was surprised by the steely edge he heard in his own voice. "I'm not sure yet what this is a part of. I need to examine, to evaluate, to ponder. And that has to be done on my own. I tell you, Kasinibon, I'm afraid that I'll lose it altogether if I reveal anything of it now. Please: let me be."

Kasinibon seemed to understand that. He grew instantly solicitous. Almost unctuously he said, "Yes. Yes, of course, it would be tragic if my blundering interference harmed the flow of your creation. I withdraw my request. But you will, I hope, grant me a look at it just as soon as you feel that the time has come when you—"

"Yes. Just as soon as the time has come," said Furvain.

He retreated to his quarters and returned to work, not without trepidation. This was new to him, this business of setting down formally to work. In the past poems had always found *him* – taking a direct and immediate line from his mind to his fingertips. He had never needed to go searching for *them*. Now, though, Furvain self-consciously sat himself at his little bare table, he laid out two or three pens at his side, he tapped the edges of his stack of blank paper until every sheet was perfectly aligned, he closed his eyes and waited for the heat of inspiration.

Quickly he discovered that inspiration could not simply be invited to arrive, at least not when one was embarked on an enterprise such as this. His old methods no longer applied. For what he had to do now, one had to go out in quest of the material; one had to fix it in one's gaze and seize it firmly; one had to compel it to do one's bidding. He was writing, it seemed, a poem about Lord Stiamot. Very well: he must focus every atom of his being on that long-ago monarch, must reach out across the ages and enter into a communion of a sort with him, must touch his soul and follow his path.

That was easy enough to say, not so easy to accomplish. The inadequacies of his historical knowledge troubled him. With nothing more than a schoolboy's knowledge of Stiamot's life and career, and that knowledge, such as it ever had been, now blurred by so many years of forgetfulness, how could he presume to tell the tale of the epochal conflict that had ended for all time the aboriginal threat to the expansion of the human settlements on Majipoor?

Abashed at his own lack of learning, he prowled Kasinibon's library, hoping to come upon some works of historical scholarship. But history, it seemed, was not a subject that held any great interest for his captor. Furvain found no texts of any consequence, just a brief history of the world, which seemed to be nothing more than a child's book. From an inscription on its back cover he saw that it was in fact a relic of Kasinibon's own childhood in Kekkinork. It contained very little that was useful: just a brief, highly simplified recapitulation of Lord Stiamot's attempts to seek a negotiated peace with the Metamorphs, the failure of those attempts, and the Coronal's ultimate decision to put an end once and for all to Metamorph depredations against the cities of the human settlers by defeating them in battle, expelling them from human-occupied territories, and confining them for all time in the rain-forests of southern Zimroel. Which had, of course, entangled the world in a generation-long struggle that ended ultimately in success and made possible the explosive growth of civilization on Majipoor and prosperity everywhere on the giant world. Stiamot was one of the key figures of Majipoor's history, the builder of the Castle and the architect of the final conquest of the Metamorphs. But Kasinibon's little history-book told only the bare outlines of the story, the politics and the battles, not a word about Stiamot as a man, his inner thoughts and emotions, his physical appearance, anything of that sort.

Then Furvain realized that he had no real need to know those things. He was writing a poem, not an historical text or a work of biography. He was free to imagine any detail he liked, so long as he remained faithful to the broad outline of the tale. Whether the actual Lord Stiamot had been short or tall, plump or thin, cheerful of nature or a dyspeptic brooder, would make no serious difference to a poet intent only on recreating the Stiamot legend. Lord Stiamot, by now, had become a mythical figure. And myth, Furvain knew, has a power that transcends mere history. History could be as arbitrary as poetry, he told himself: what is history, other than a matter of choice, the picking and choosing of certain facts out of a multitude to elicit a meaningful pattern, which was not necessarily the true one?

The act of selecting facts, by definition, inherently involved discarding facts as well, often the ones most inconvenient to the pattern that the historian was trying to reveal. Truth thus became an abstract concept: three different historians, working with the same set of data, might easily come up with three different "truths". Whereas myth digs deep into the fundamental reality of the spirit, into that infinite well that is the shared consciousness of the entire race, reaching the levels where truth is not an optional matter, but the inescapable foundation of all else. In that sense myth could be truer than history; by creating imaginative episodes that clove to the essence of the Stiamot story, a poet could reveal the truth of that story in a way that no historian could claim to do. And so Furvain resolved that his poem would deal with the myth of Stiamot, not with the historical man. He was free to invent as he pleased, so long as what he invented was faithful to the inner truth of the story.

After that everything became easier, although there was never anything simple about it for him. He developed a technique of meditation that left him hovering on the border of sleep, from which he could slip readily into a kind of trance. Then – more rapidly with each passing day – Furvain's guide would come to him, the golden-haired man wearing a Coronal's silver diadem, and lead him through the scenes and events of his day's work.

His guide's name, he discovered, was Valentine: a charming man, patient, affable, sweet-tempered, always ready with an easy smile, the absolute best of guides. Furvain could not remember any Coronal named Valentine, nor did Kasinibon's boyhood history text mention one. Evidently no such person had ever existed. But that made no difference. For Furvain's purposes, it was all the same whether this Lord Valentine had been a real historical figure or was just a figment of Furvain's imagination: what he needed was someone to take him by the hand and lead him through the shadowy realms of antiquity, and that was what his golden-haired guide was doing. It was almost as though he were the manifestation in a readily perceptible form of the will of the Divine, whose vehicle Furvain had become. It is through the voice of this imaginary Lord Valentine, Furvain told himself, that the shaping spirit of the cosmos is inscribing this poem on my soul.

Under Valentine's guidance Furvain's dreaming mind traversed the deeds of Lord Stiamot, beginning with his first realization that the long poisonous struggle with the Metamorphs must be brought to a conclusive end and going on through the sequence of increasingly bloody battles that had culminated in the burning of the northlands, the surrender of the last aboriginal rebels, and the establishment of the province of Piurifayne in Zimroel as the permanent home and place of eternal confinement of the Shapeshifters of Majipoor. When Furvain emerged from his trance each day the details of what he had learned would still be with him, and had the balance and shape and the tragic rhythm that great poetry requires. He saw not only the events but the inexorable and inescapable conflicts out of which they arose, driving even a man of good will like Stiamot into the harsh necessity of making war. The pattern of the story was there; Furvain had merely to set it all down on paper: and here his innate technical skill was fully at his command, as much so as it had ever been in the old days, so that the intricate stanza and complex rhythmic scheme that he had carried back from his first dreaming encounters with the Divine soon became second nature to him, and the poem grew by a swift process of accretion.

Sometimes it came a little *too* easily. Now that Furvain had mastered that strange stanza he was able to reel off page after page with such effortless fluency that he would on occasion wander on into unexpected digressions that concealed and muddled the main thrust of his narrative. When that happened he would halt, rip the offending sections out, and go on from the point where he had begun to diverge from his proper track. He had never revised before. At first it seemed wasteful to him, since the discarded lines were every bit as eloquent, as sonorous, as the ones he kept. But then he came to see that eloquence and sonorousness were mere accessories to the main task, which was the telling of a particular tale in a way that most directly illuminated its inner meaning.

And then, when he had brought the tale of Lord Stiamot to its conclusion, Furvain was startled to find that the Divine was not yet done with him. Without pausing even to question what he was doing, he drew a line beneath the last of the Stiamot stanzas and began to inscribe a new verse – beginning, he saw, right in the middle of a stanza, with the triple-rhyme passage – that dealt with an earlier event entirely, the project of Lord Melikand to import beings of species other than human to help with the task of settling the greatly underpopulated world that was Majipoor.

He continued in that project for another few days. But then, while the Melikand canto was yet unfinished, Furvain discovered himself at work on a passage that told still another story, that of the grand assembly at Stangard Falls, on the River Glayge, where Dvorn had been hailed as Majipoor's first Pontifex. At that moment Furvain realized that he was writing not simply an account of the deeds of Lord Stiamot, but an epic poem embracing nothing less than the whole of Majipoor's history.

It was a frightening thought. He could not believe that he was the man for such a task. It was too much for a man of his limitations. He thought he saw the shape that such a poem must take, as it traversed the many thousands of years from the coming of the first settlers to the present day, and it was a mighty one. Not a single great arc, no, but a series of soaring curves and dizzying swoops, a tale of flux and transformation, of the constant synthesis of opposites, as the early idealistic colonists tumbled into the violent chaos of anarchy, were rescued from it by Dvorn the law-giver, the first Pontifex, spread out in centrifugal expansion across the huge world under the guidance of Lord Melikand, built the great cities of Castle Mount, reached across into the continents of Zimroel and Suvrael, came inevitably and tragically into collision with the Shapeshifter aboriginals, fought the necessary though appalling war against them under the leadership of Lord Stiamot, that man of peace transformed into a warrior, that defeated and contained them, and so onward to this present day, when billions of people lived in peace on the most beautiful of all worlds.

There was no more splendid story in all the universe. But was he, Aithin Furvain, such a small-souled man, a man flawed in so many ways, going to be able to encompass it? He had no illusions about himself. He saw himself as glib, lazy, dissolute, a weakling, an evader of responsibility, a man who throughout his whole life had sought the path of least resistance. How could he, of all people, having no other resource than a certain degree of cleverness and technical skill, hope to contain such a gigantic theme within the bounds of a single poem? It was too much for him. He could never do it. He doubted that anyone could. But certainly Aithin Furvain was not the one to attempt it.

And yet he seemed somehow to be writing it. Or was it writing him? No matter: the thing was taking shape, line by line, day by day. Call it divine inspiration, call it the overflowing of something that he had kept penned unknowingly within him for many years, call it whatever one wished, there was no denying that he had already written one full canto and fragments of two others, and that each day brought new verses. And there was greatness in the poem: of that he was certain. He would read through it over and over again, shaking his head in amazement at the power of his own work, the mighty music of the poetry, the irresistible sweep of the narrative. It was all so splendid that it humbled and bewildered him. He had no idea how it had been possible to achieve what he had done, and he shivered with dread at the thought that his miraculous fount of inspiration would dry up, as suddenly as it had opened, before the great task had reached its end.

The manuscript, unfinished though it was, became terribly

precious to him. He came to see it now as his claim on immortality. It troubled him that only one copy of it existed, and that one kept in a room that could only be locked from outside. Fearful now that something might happen to it, that it might be blotted into illegibility by the accidental overturning of his ink-stand, or stolen by some prying malicious denizen of the fortress jealous of the attention paid to Furvain by Master Kasinibon, or even taken out of his room as trash by some illiterate servant and destroyed, he copied it out several times over, carefully hiding the copies in different rooms of his little suite. The main draft he buried each night in the lowest drawer of the cupboard in which he kept his clothing; and, a few days later, without really knowing why, he fell into the habit of painstakingly arranging three of his pens in a star-shaped pattern on top of the pile of finished sheets so that he would know at once if anyone had been prowling in that drawer.

Three days after that he saw that the pens had been disturbed. Furvain had taken care to lay them out with meticulous care, the central pen aligned each time at the same precise angle to the other two. This day he saw that the angle was slightly off, as though someone had understood that the purpose of the arrangement was the detection of an intrusion and had replaced the pens after examining the manuscript, but had not employed the greatest possible degree of accuracy in attempting to mimic Furvain's own grouping of the pens. That night he chose a new pattern for the pens, and the next afternoon he saw that once again they had been put back almost as he had left them, but not quite. The same thing happened over the succeeding two days.

It could only have been the doing of Kasinibon himself, Furvain decided. No member of Kasinibon's outlaw band, and certainly not any servant, would have taken half so much trouble over the pens. He is sneaking in while I am elsewhere, Furvain thought. He is secretly reading my poem.

Furious, Furvain sought Kasinibon out and assailed him for violating the privacy of his quarters.

To his surprise, Kasinibon made no attempt to deny the accusation. "Ah, so you know? Well, of course. I couldn't resist." His eyes were shining with excitement. "It's marvelous, Furvain. Magnificent. I was so profoundly moved by it I can hardly begin to tell you. The episode of Lord Stiamot and the Metamorph priestess – when she comes before him, when she weeps for her people, and Stiamot weeps also—"

"You had no right to go rummaging around in my cupboard," said Furvain icily.

"Why not? I'm the master here. I do as I please. All you said was that you didn't want to have a discussion of an unfinished work. I respected that, didn't I? Did I say a word? A single word? For days, now, I've been reading what you were writing, almost since the beginning, following your daily progress, practically participating in the creation of a great poem myself, and tears came to my eyes over the beauty of it, and yet not ever once did I give you a hint – never once—"

Furvain felt mounting outrage. "You've been going into my room all along?" he sputtered, astounded.

"Every day. Since long before you started the thing with the pens. Look, Furvain, a classic poem, one of the great masterpieces of literature, is being born under my own roof by a man I feed and shelter. Am I to be denied the pleasure of watching it grow and evolve?"

"I'll burn it," Furvain said. "Rather than let you spy on me any more."

"Don't talk idiocy. Just go on writing. I'll leave it alone from now on. But you mustn't stop, if that's what you have in mind. That would be a monstrous crime against art. Finish the Melikand scene. Do the Dvorn story. And continue on to all the rest." He laughed wickedly. "You can't stop, anyway. The poem has you in its spell. It possesses you."

Glaring, Furvain said, "How would you know that?"

"I'm not as stupid as you want to think I am," said Kasinibon. But then he softened, asked for forgiveness, promised again to control his overpowering curiosity about the poem. He seemed genuinely repentant: afraid, even, that by intruding on Furvain's privacy this way he might have jeopardized the completion of the poem. He would never cease blaming himself, he said, if Furvain took this as a pretext for abandoning the project. But also he would always hold it against Furvain. And then, once more with force: "You *will* go on with it. You *will*. You could not possibly stop."

Furvain was unable to maintain his anger in the face of so shrewd an assessment of his character. It was clear that Kasinibon perceived Furvain's innate slothfulness, his fundamental desire not to involve himself in anything as ambitious and strenuous as a work on this scale. But also Kasinibon saw that the poem held him in thrall, clasping him in a grip so powerful that even an idler such as he could not shrug off the imperative command that each day was willing the poem into being. That command came from somewhere within, from a place beyond Furvain's own comprehension; but also, Furvain knew, it was reinforced by Kasinibon's fierce desire to have him bring the work to completion. Furvain could not withstand the whiplash force of Kasinibon's eagerness atop that other, interior command. There was no way to abandon the work.

Grudgingly he said, "Yes, I'll continue. You can be sure of that. But keep out of my room."

"Agreed."

As Kasinibon began to leave Furvain called him back and said, "One more thing. Has there been any news yet from Dundilmir about my ransom?"

"No. Nothing. Nothing," replied Kasinibon, and went swiftly from the room.

No news. About what I expected, Furvain thought. Tanigel has thrown the note away. Or they are laughing about it at court: can you believe it, poor silly Furvain, captured by bandits!

He felt certain that Kasinibon was never going to hear from Tanigel. It seemed appropriate, then, to draft new ransom requests – one to his father at the Labyrinth, one to Lord Hunzimar at the Castle, perhaps others to other people, if he could think of anyone who was even remotely likely to be willing to help – and have Kasinibon send his messengers forth with them.

Meanwhile Furvain continued his daily work. The trance state came ever more easily; the mysterious figure of Lord Valentine appeared whenever summoned, and gladly led him back through time into the dawn of the world. The manuscript grew. The pens were not disturbed again. After a little while Furvain ceased taking the trouble to lay them out.

Furvain saw the overall shape of the poem clearly, now.

There would be nine great sections, which in his mind had the form of an arch, with the Stiamot sequences at the highest part of the curve. The first canto would deal with the arrival of the original human settlers on Majipoor, full of the hope of leaving the sorrows of Old Earth behind and creating a paradise on this most wonderful of all worlds. He would depict their tentative early explorations of the planet and their awe at its size and beauty, and the founding of the first tiny outposts. In the second, Furvain would portray the growth of those outposts into towns and cities, the strife between the cities that arose in the next few hundred years, the spreading conflicts that caused in time the breakdown of all order, the coming of turbulence and general nihilism.

The third canto would be Dvorn's: how he had risen up out of the chaos, a provincial leader from the west-country town of Kesmakuran, to march across Alhanroel calling upon the people of every town to join with him in a stable government uniting all the world under its sway. How by force of personality as well as strength of arms he had brought that government into being – the non-hereditary monarchy under the authority of an emperor to whom he gave the ancient title of Pontifex, "bridge-builder," who would choose a royal subordinate, the Coronal

Lord, to head the executive arm of his administration and ultimately to succeed him as Pontifex. And Furvain would tell how Dvorn and his Coronal, Lord Barhold, had won the support of all Majipoor and had established for all time the system of government under which the world still thrived.

Then the fourth canto, a transitional one, depicting the emergence of something resembling modern Majipoor out of the primordial structure devised by Dvorn. The construction of the atmosphere-machines that made possible the settling of the thirty-mile-high mountain that later would be called Castle Mount, and the founding of the first cities along its lower slopes. Lord Melikand's insight that the human population alone was insufficient to sustain the growth of a world the size of Majipoor, and his importation of the Skandars, the Vroons, the Hjorts, and the other various alien races to live side by side with humankind there. The exacerbation of human–Metamorph conflicts, now, as the relatively sparse aboriginal population found itself being crowded out of its own territories by the growth of the settlements. The beginnings of war.

Lord Stiamot's canto, already completed, would be the fifth one, the keystone of the great arch. But reluctantly Furvain realized that Stiamot required more space. The canto would have to be expanded, divided perhaps into two, or more likely three, in order to do justice to the theme. It was necessary to limn Stiamot's moral anguish, the terrible ironies of his reign, the man of peace compelled for his people's sake to wage a ghastly war against the original inhabitants of the world, innocent though those inhabitants were of anything but the desire to retain possession of their own planet. Stiamot's construction of a castle for the Coronal at the highest point of the Mount, symbolizing his epic victory, would be the climax of the middle section of the poem. Then would come the final three cantos, one to show the gradual return to general tranquility, one to portray Majipoor as a fully mature world, and one, a visionary ninth one not entirely shaped yet in Furvain's mind, which would, perhaps, deal somehow with the healing of the unresolved instabilities – the *wound* – that the war against the Metamorphs had created in the fabric of the planet's life.

Furvain even had a name for the poem, now. *The Book of Changes* was what he would call it, for change was its theme, the eternal seasonal flux, the ceaseless ebb and flow of events, and in counterpoint to that the steady line of the sacred destiny of Majipoor beneath. Kings arose and flourished and died, movements rose and fell, but the commonwealth went ever onward like a great river, following the path that the Divine had ordained for it, and all its changes were but stations along that path. Which was a path marked by challenge and response, the constant collision of opposing forces to produce an inevitable synthesis: the necessary triumph of Dvorn over anarchy, the necessary triumph of Stiamot over the Metamorphs, and – someday in the future – the necessary triumph of the victors over their own victory. That was the thing he must show, he knew: the pattern that emerges from the passage of time and demonstrates that everything, even the great unavoidable sin of the suppression of the Metamorphs, is part of an unswerving design, the inevitable triumph of organization over chaos.

Whenever he was not actually working on the poem Furvain felt terrified by the immensity of the task and the insufficiency of his own qualifications for writing it. A thousand times a day he fought back the desire to walk away from it. But he could not allow that. *You have to change your life*, the Lady Dolitha had told him, back there on Castle Mount, what seemed like centuries ago. Yes. Her stern words had had the force of an order. He *had* changed his life, and his life had changed him. And so he must continue, he knew, bringing into being this great poem that he would give to the world as his atonement for all those wasted years. Kasinibon, too, goaded him mercilessly toward the same goal: no longer spying on him, never even inquiring after the poem, but forever watching him, measuring his progress by the gauntness of his features and the bleariness of his eyes, waiting, seeking, silently demanding. Against such silent pressure Furvain was helpless.

He worked on and on, cloistered now in his rooms, rarely coming forth except for meals, toiling each day to the point of exhaustion, resting briefly, plunging back into trance. It was like a journey through some infernal region of the mind. Full of misgivings, he traveled by wandering and laborious circuits through the dark. For hours at a time he was certain that he had become separated from his guide and he had no idea of his destination, and he felt terrors of every kind, shivers and trembling, sweat and turmoil. But then a wonderful light would shine upon him, and he would be admitted into pure meadow lands, where there were voices and dances, and the majesty of holy sounds and sacred visions, and the words would flow as though beyond conscious control.

The months passed. He was entering the second year of his task, now. The pile of manuscript steadily increased. He worked in no consecutive way, but turned, rather, to whichever part of the poem made the most insistent call on his attention. The only canto that he regarded as complete was the central one, the fifth, the key Stiamot section; but he had finished much of the Melikand canto, and nearly all of the Dvorn one, and big pieces of the opening sequence dealing with the initial settlement. Some of the other sections, the less dramatic ones, were mere fragments; and of the ninth canto he had set down nothing at all. And parts of the Stiamot story, the early and late phases, were still untold. It was a chaotic way to work, but he knew no other way of doing it. Everything would be handled in due time, of that he felt sure.

Now and again he would ask Kasinibon whether any replies had come to his requests for ransom money, and invariably was told, "No, no, no word from anyone." It scarcely mattered. Nothing mattered, except the work at hand.

Then, when he was no more than three stanzas into the ninth and final canto, Furvain suddenly felt as though he stood before an impassable barrier, or perhaps an infinite dark abyss: at any rate that he had come to a point in the great task beyond which he was incapable of going. There had been times in the past, many of them, when Furvain had felt that way. But this was different. Those other times what he had experienced was an *unwillingness* to go on, quickly enough conquered by summoning a feeling that he could not allow himself the shameful option of not continuing. What he felt now was the absolute *incapacity* to carry the poem any further, because he saw only blackness ahead.

Help me, he prayed, not knowing to whom. *Guide me*.

But no help came, nor any guidance. He was alone. And, alone, he had no idea how to handle the material that he had intended to use for the ninth canto. The reconciliation with the Shapeshifters – the expiation of the great unavoidable sin that humankind had committed against them on this world – the absolution, the redemption, even the amends – he had no notion whatever of how to proceed with that. For here was Majipoor, close to ten thousand years on beyond Dvorn and four thousand years beyond Stiamot, and what reconciliation, even now, had been reached with the Metamorphs? What expiation, what redemption? They were still penned up in their jungle home in Zimroel, their movements elsewhere on that continent tightly restricted, and their presence anywhere in Alhanroel forbidden entirely. The world was no closer to a solution to the problem of the Shapeshifters than it had been on the day the first settlers landed. Lord Stiamot's solution – conquer them, lock them up forever in southern Zimroel and keep the rest of the world for ourselves – was no solution at all, only a mere brutal expedient, as Stiamot himself had recognized. Stiamot had known that it was too late to turn back from the settlement of the planet. Majipoor's history could not be unhappened. And so, for the sake of Majipoor's billions of human settlers, Majipoor's millions of aborigines had had to give up their freedom.

If Stiamot could find no answer to the problem, Furvain thought, then who am I to offer one now?

In that case he could not write the ninth canto. And – worse – he began to think that he could not finish the earlier unfinished cantos, either. Now that he saw there was no hope of capping the edifice with its intended conclusion, all inspiration seemed to flee from him. If he tried to force his way onward now, he suspected that he would only ruin what he had already written, diluting its power with lesser material. And even if somehow he did manage to finish, he felt now in his hopelessness and despair that he could never reveal the poem to the world. No one would believe that he had written it. They would think that some sort of theft was involved, some fraud, and he would become a figure of scorn when he was unable to produce the real author. Better for there to be no poem at all than for that sort of disgrace to descend upon him in his final years, he reasoned.

And from that perception to the decision that he must destroy the manuscript this very day was a short journey indeed.

From the cupboards and crannies of his apartment in Kasinibon's fortress he gathered the various copies and drafts, and stacked them atop his table. They made a goodly heap. On days when he felt too tired or too stale to carry the poem onward, he had occupied his time in making additional copies of the existing texts, in order to lessen the risk that some mischance would rob him of his work. He had kept all his discarded pages, too, the deleted stanzas, the rewritten ones. It was an immense mound of paper. Burning it all would probably take hours.

Calmly he peeled an inch-thick mass of manuscript from the top of his stack and laid it on the hearth of his fireplace.

He found a match. Struck it. Stared at it for a moment, still terribly calm, and then brought it toward the corner of the stack.

"What are you doing?" Kasinibon cried, stepping swiftly into the room. Briskly the little man brought the heel of his boot down on the smouldering match and ground it out against the stone hearth. The pile of manuscript had not had time to ignite.

"What I'm doing is burning the poem," said Furvain quietly. "Or trying to."

"Doing *what*?"

"Burning it," Furvain said again.

"You've gone crazy. Your mind has snapped under the pressure of the work."

Furvain shook his head. "No, I think I'm still sane. But I can't go on with it, that I know. And once I came to that realization, I felt that it was best to destroy the incomplete poem." In a low, unemotional tone he laid out for Kasinibon all that had passed through his mind in the last half hour.

Kasinibon listened without interrupting him. He was silent for a long moment thereafter. Then he said, looking past Furvain's shoulder to the window and speaking in a strained, hollow, barely audible tone, "I have a confession to make, Furvain. Your ransom money arrived a week ago. From your friend the Duke. I was afraid to tell you, because I wanted you to finish the poem first, and I knew that you never would if I let you go back to Dundilmir. But I see that that's wrong. I have no right to hold you here any longer. Do as you please, Furvain. Go, if you like. Only – I beg you – spare what you've written. Let me keep a copy of it when you leave."

"I want to destroy it," Furvain said.

Kasinibon's eyes met Furvain's. He said, speaking more strongly now, the old whiplash voice of the bandit chieftain, "No. I forbid you. Give it to me freely, or I'll simply confiscate it."

"I'm still a prisoner, then, I see," said Furvain, smiling. "Have you really received the ransom money?"

"I swear it."

Furvain nodded. It was his time for silence, now. He turned his back on Kasinibon and stared out toward the blood-red waters of the lake beyond.

Was it really so impossible, he wondered, to finish the poem? Dizziness swept over him for an instant and he realized that some unexpected force was moving within him. Kasinibon's shamefaced confession had broken things open. No longer did he feel as though he stood before that impassable barrier. Suddenly the way was open and the ninth canto was in his grasp after all.

It did not need to contain the answer to the Shapeshifter problem. Since Stiamot's day, forty centuries of Coronals and Pontifexes had failed to solve that problem: why should a mere poet be able to do so? But questions of governance were not his responsibility. Writing poetry was. In *The Book of Changes* he had given Majipoor a mirror that would show the world its past; it was not his job to provide it with its future as well. At least not in any explicit way. Let the future discover itself as its own time unfolds.

Suppose, he thought – suppose – suppose – I end the poem with a prophecy, a cryptic vision of a tragic king of the years to come, a king who is, like Stiamot, a man of peace who must make war, and who will suffer greatly in the anguish of his kingship. Fragmentary phrases came to him: "A golden king ... a crown in the dust ... the holy embrace of sworn enemies ... " What did they mean? He had no idea. But he didn't need to know. He needed only to set them down. To offer the hope that in some century to come some unimaginable monarch, who could unite in himself the forces of war and peace in a way that would precisely balance the suffering and the achievement of Stiamot, would thereby put an end to the instability in the Common-wealth that was the inevitable consequence of the original sin of taking this planet from its native people. To end the poem with the idea that reconciliation is possible. Not to explain how it will be achieved: merely to say that achieving it is possible.

In that moment Furvain knew not only that he could go on to the finish but that he *must* go on, that it was his duty, and that this was the only place where that could be accomplished: here, under the watchful eye of his implacable captor and guardian. He would never do it back in Dundilmir, where he would inevitably retrogress into the shallowness of his old ways.

Turning, he gathered up a copy of the manuscript that included all that he had written thus far, and nudged it across the table to Kasinibon. "This is for you," he said. "Keep it. Read it, if you want to. Just don't say a word to me about it until I give you permission."

Kasinibon silently took the bundle from him, clutching the pages to his breast and folding his arms across them.

Furvain said, then, "Send the ransom money back to Tanigel. Tell the Duke he paid it too soon. I'll be staying here a little while longer. And send this with it." He pulled one of his extra copies of the finished text of the Stiamot canto from the great mound of paper on the table. "So that he can see what his old lazy friend Furvain has been up to all this time out in the east-country, eh?" Furvain smiled. "And now, Kasinibon, please – if you'll allow me to get back to work—"

3

The Tomb of the Pontifex Dvorn

In the days when Simmilgord was a wiry little boy growing up in the Vale of Gloyn he was fond of going out by himself into the broad savanna where the red gattaga-grass grew. Bare little stony hillocks rose up there like miniature mountains, eighty or ninety feet high. Clambering to the top of this one or that, he would shade his eyes against the golden-green sunlight and look far outward across that wide sea of thick copper-colored stalks. It amused him to pretend that from his lofty perch he could see the entire continent of Alhanroel from coast to coast, the great city of Alaisor in the distant west, the unthinkable height of Castle Mount rising like a colossal wall in the other direction, and, somewhere beyond that, the almost unknown eastern lands stretching on and on to the far shore of the Great Sea, marvel after marvel, miracle after miracle, and when he was up there he felt it would be no difficult thing to reach out and embrace the whole world in all its wonder.

Of course no one could actually see as far as that, or anything like it. Simply to think about such a distance made one's head spin. Alhanroel was too big to grasp, a giant continent that one could spend an entire lifetime exploring without ever fully coming to terms with the immensity of it, and Alhanroel was just one of the three continents of which the vast world of Majipoor was comprised. Beyond its shores lay the other two continents of Zimroel and Suvrael, nearly as large, and on the far side of Zimroel began the almost mythical Great Sea that no one had ever been able to cross. Simmilgord knew all that. He was a good student; he had paid attention to his geography lessons and his history books. But still it was a glorious thing to go scrambling up to the summit of some jagged little rockpile and stare out beyond the endless mats of coppery-hued gattaga, beyond the grazing herds of stupid flat-faced klimbergeysts and the snuffling pig-like vongiforin that rooted about among them digging for tasty seeds, beyond the grove of spiky gray skipje-trees and the towering gambalangas that grazed on their tender topmost leaves, and imagine that he could take in all of Alhanroel in a single swiveling glance, the bustling seaports in the west and the lush tropical forests to the south and the great Mount with its Fifty Cities to the east, and the Castle at its summit from which the Coronal Lord Henghilain ruled the world in high majesty and splendor. He wanted to swallow it all at a single gulp, woodlands and jungles, deserts and plains, rivers and seas. Mine! Mine! This whole extraordinary world – mine! For Simmilgord there was a kind of wild soaring music in that thought: the vast symphony that was Majipoor.

Even at the age of ten Simmilgord understood that he was never going to see any of those places. The world was too huge, and he was too insignificant, nothing but a farmer's son whose probable destiny it was to spend his life right here in Gloyn, growing lusavender and hingamort and never getting any farther from home than one of the market towns of west-central Alhanroel, Kessilroge, maybe, or Gannamunda, or at best Marakeeba, somewhere off to the east. What a dreary prospect! Then and there, clinging to the top of that barren little mass of granite, he vowed to transcend that vision of an empty future, to make something out of his life, to rise up out of the Vale of Gloyn and make a mark in the world that would cause others to take note of him. He would become an adventurer, a soldier of fortune, a world traveler, the confidante of dukes and princes, perhaps even a figure of some prominence at the Coronal's court. Somehow – somehow—

That romantic dream stayed with him as he grew into adolescence, though he scaled back his ambitions somewhat. He came to understand that he was better fitted by temperament to be a scholar of some sort than any kind of swashbuckling hero; but even that was far better than staying here in Gloyn and, like his father and all who had come before him for the past twenty generations, live from harvest to harvest, consuming his life in the unending cycle of planting and growing and gathering and marketing.

In Upper School he found himself drawn to the study of history. That was how he would encompass the magnificence that was Majipoor, by taking all its long past within himself, mastering its annals and archives, delving into the accounts of the first settlers to come here from Old Earth, the initial wonderstruck discoveries of strange beasts and natural wonders, the early encounters with the aboriginal Shapeshifters, the founding of the cities, the creation of its governmental structure, the reigns of the first Pontifexes and Coronals, the gradual spreading out from Alhanroel to the outer continents, the conquest of mighty Castle Mount, and all the rest. The romance of the world's long history set his soul ablaze. What fascinated him in particular was that someone, one man, the Pontifex Dvorn, had been able to make a unified and cohesive realm out of all this immensity.

What Dvorn had accomplished held a special fascination for him. It was Simmilgord's great hope to plunge into all of that and make out of Majipoor's unthinkable complexity a single coherent narrative, just as Dvorn, long ago, had made one world out of hundreds of independent city-states. He dreamed of earning admission to the Hall of Records within the enormous library Lord Stiamot had founded atop the Mount that coiled around the Castle's heart from side to side like a giant serpent, or of prowling through the dusty documents stored in the nearly as capacious archive in the depths of the Labyrinth, and bringing forth out of all that chaotic data a chronicle of

Majipoor's history that would supersede anything that had ever been written.

Simmilgord was surprised to find his father encouraging him in this dream. He had not expected that. But there were other sons to work the farm, and Simmilgord had never shown much enthusiasm for the farm chores, anyway; plainly he was meant for other things. It seemed best for him to go to the famous University at Sisivondal and work to achieve his goal. And so he did. When he was sixteen he set out down the Great Western Highway, making the long eastward trek through Hunzimar and Gannamunda and Kessilroge and Skeil into the dusty plains of central Alhanroel, coming finally to Sisivondal, the tirelessly busy mercantile center where all the main shipping routes of Alhanroel crossed.

What a drab place it was! Miles and miles of faceless flat-roofed warehouses, of long monotonous boulevards decorated only with the sort of ugly black-leaved plants, squat and tough and spiky,that could withstand the long months of rainless days and hot winds under which the city suffered, the dreariest city imaginable on a world where most places took pride in the beauty and boldness of their architecture. Day and night cara-vans thundered down its grim streets, bringing or taking every sort of merchandise the huge planet produced. In the midst of the constant hubbub was the formidable wall surrounding the great University – Sisivondal's one center of high culture, second only to the revered University of Arkilon in scholarly repute – erected by the proud and wealthy merchants of the city to mark their own worldly success. But even the University was a somber thing, one bleak red-brick pile after another, all of its buildings done in a style more appropriate to a prison than to a temple of learning. Simmilgord, who had seen nothing of the world but the pleasant pastoral groves of the Vale of Gloyn, but who knew from his books of such dazzling and amazingly beautiful far-off places as glorious Stee, the grandest of the Fifty Cities of Castle Mount, and glistening white Ni-moya, Zimroel's big river-port, and spectacular Stoien of the crystal pavilions on the tropical southern coast, was stunned by the eye-aching awfulness of it all.

He knew, though, that the University of Sisivondal was his key to the greater world beyond. He found lodgings; he enrolled in the requisite courses; he made new friends. Once he was done with the basic curriculum he moved on to serious historical study, quickly seizing upon the earliest years of the imperial government as his special area of study. The titanic first Pontifex, Dvorn – what had he been like? How had he been able to impose his ideas of government on the unruly settlers? By what miracle had he devised a scheme of rule for this gigantic planet so efficient that it had endured, virtually without change, for more than twelve thousand years now?

Simmilgord looked forward to a time when the thesis on Dvorn that he planned to write, full of unanswered questions though it was likely to be, would win him admission to the archival centers of Majipoor's two capitals, the Pontifical one in the Labyrinth and the grand sprawling one at the Castle of the Coronal, where he could delve into the ancient secrets of those early days. But for one reason and another that time never seemed to arrive. He took his degree, and wrote his thesis – painfully, pitifully short on hard information – and got his doctorate, and he was taken on as a lecturer at the University with the hope of a professorship somewhere in the future, and he published a few papers – somewhat speculative in nature – on the founding of the Pontificate, and won the admiration of a handful of other historians thereby.

But that was all. The romance, the fantasy, that he had thought his life as a scholar would provide never seemed to materialize. He had reached the age of twenty-five, an age when one's life seems to be settling into its permanent pattern, and that pattern was not an inspiring one.

He began to think that he was going to spend the rest of his days in ghastly Sisivondal, delivering the same lectures year after year to ever-changing audiences of uninterested undergraduates and writing papers that recapitulated existing knowledge or invented shaky new theories about that which was unknown. That was not the vision he had had when he had climbed those little upjutting hillocks in the Vale of Gloyn and pretended he could take in the whole continent from Alaisor to the shores of the Great Sea in a single sweeping view.

And then the chairman of his department called him and said,"We would hate to lose you, Simmilgord, but I have a query here from the city of Kesmakuran – you know the place, surely? Just a piffling little agricultural town, but one of the oldest in Alhanroel. The alleged birthplace of the Pontifex Dvorn. Thought to be the site of his tomb as well, I think."

"I know it well, yes," said Simmilgord. "Two years ago and again last year I applied for a research grant to do some work there, but so far—"

"We have more than a research grant for you, I'm glad to say. The city fathers of Kesmakuran have decided to freshen up Dvorn's burial site, and they're looking for a curator. They've read your work on Dvorn and they think you're just the man. Clean the place up a little, establish a small museum nearby, turn Kesmakuran into something of a destination for tourists. It's an extremely old place, you know – older than Alaisor, older than Stoien, older than half the cities on Castle Mount, and they're very proud of that. There's enough in their budget to let you have an archaeologist to assist you, too, and I know that you and Lutiel Vengifrons are great friends, so we thought of recommending the two of you as a team – if you're interested, that is—"

"Curator of the tomb of the Pontifex Dvorn!" Simmilgord said in wonder. "Am I interested? Am I?"

Lutiel Vengifrons said, "It's a little bit of a career detour for us, don't you think?" As usual, there was a bit of an adversarial edge in his tone. The friendship that held Simmilgord and Lutiel together was based on an attraction of opposites, Simmilgord a tall, thin, flimsily built man of mercurial temperament, Lutiel short and strong, wide-shouldered, barrel-chested, cautious and stolid by nature.

"A detour? No, I don't think so," Simmilgord replied. "It puts me right where I want to be. How can I claim to be an expert on the reign of Dvorn when I haven't even visited the city where he was born and where he's supposed to be buried? But I could never afford to make the trip, and that research grant always seemed to be dangling just out of reach – and now, to live right there, to have daily access to all the important sites of his life—"

"And to turn them into tourist attractions?"

"Are you saying you don't want to go with me?" Simmilgord asked.

"No – no, I didn't say that. Not exactly. But still – I can't help wondering whether two earnest young scholars really ought to let themselves get involved with any such scheme. 'Clean the place up a little,' the chairman said. What does that mean? Deck it out with marble and onyx? Make it into some kind of gaudy amusement-park thing?"

"Maybe have a little modern plumbing put in, at most," said Simmilgord. "And some decent lighting. Look, Lutiel, it's a brilliant opportunity. Maybe you worry too much about being an earnest young scholar, do you know what I mean? What an earnest young scholar like you needs to do is go to Kesmakuran and dig around a little and uncover a bunch of astounding arti-facts that bring Dvorn out of the realm of culture-hero myths and turn him into a real person. And here's your chance to do it. Why, right now we don't even know that he ever existed, and—"

Lutiel Vengifrons gasped. "Can you seriously mean a thing like that, Simmilgord? He *had* to exist. *Somebody* had to be the first Pontifex."

"Somebody, yes. But that's all we can say. About the actual Dvorn we know practically nothing. He's just a name. His life is an absolute mystery to us. For all we know, Furvain might have made him up out of whole cloth because he needed a vivid character to fill out that part of his poem. But now – well—"

Simmilgord paused, startled and baffled by what he had just heard himself saying.

Never before had he expressed doubts about the real existence of Dvorn. And in fact he felt none. That Aithin Furvain's famous poem of four thousand years ago was the chief source of information about Dvorn, and that Furvain had not been any sort of scholar, but simply the wastrel son of Lord Sangamor, an idler, something of a fool, a *poet*, practically a myth himself, was irrelevant. Furvain must have had some concrete source to work from. There was no reason to take his cunningly constructed verses as a work of literal history, but no reason to discard them entirely as poetic fabrications, either. And there was no arguing away the fact that the Pontificate *had* been founded, after all, that some charismatic leader had put the whole thing into shape and persuaded the squabbling peoples of Majipoor to unite behind him, and if that leader had not been the Dvorn of Furvain's poem he must have been someone very much like him, whose existence could very likely be proven by the proper sort of archaeological and historical research.

So in raising an argument that cast doubts on Dvorn's literal existence, Simmilgord realized, he was simply taking an extreme position for the sake of overcoming Lutiel's doubts about their taking the job. What he yearned for, above all else, was to get out of dusty, parched Sisivondal, away from the endless paper-shuffling and bureaucratic nonsense of university life, and plunge into some genuine historical research. And he very much wanted Lutiel to accompany him, because there definitely would be some excavating to do at the tomb site and he was no archaeologist, and Lutiel was. They would make a good team out there in Kesmakuran. But suggesting that in the present state of knowledge no one could even be sure that Dvorn had ever existed was to overstate the case. Of *course* Dvorn had existed.

That much they could take for granted. It would be their job to discover what he really had been like and how he had achieved what he had achieved. And what an exciting task it would be! To dig deep into the world's remote, almost mythical past – to make direct contact with the stuff of fantasy and romance – !

"I don't think I'm phrasing this the right way," he said finally. "What I mean is that most of what we think we know about Dvorn is derived from an epic poem of long ago, not from direct scientific research, and we're being handed an invitation to do that research and establish our scholarly reputations by bringing him out of the realm of myth and poetry into some sort of objective reality. Forget the part about setting up a tourist attraction there. That's just incidental. The chance to do important research is what matters. Come with me, Lutiel. It's a once-in-a-lifetime opportunity."

In the end, of course, Lutiel agreed. Unlike Simmilgord, he had not a shred of romance in his soul. He was no climber of hills, no dreamer of wondrous dreams. What he was was a patient plodder, a stolid sifter of sand and pebbles, as archaeologists often tend to be. But even so he could see the merits of the offer. There had never been any scientific excavations carried out at Kesmakuran: just some occasional amateur digs in the course of the past thousand years or so, turning up a few fragmentary inscriptions that appeared to date from the time of the first Pontificate, and that was all – though it had been enough for the uncritical residents of the place to seize upon as proof of the claim that Dvorn had been born and died in their ancient but otherwise unremarkable town. But beyond question there was no event more important in the long history of human settlement on Majipoor than the inspired creation of a political system that had survived in nearly its original form these twelve thousand years. Kesmakuran was generally accepted as the traditional place of the great first Pontifex's birth; it was reasonable at least to postulate that some evidence of Dvorn's existence might be found there. And the city fathers of Kesmakuran were handing the two of them the key to the site.

"Well –" said Lutiel Vengifrons.

Kesmakuran turned out to be not much more than a village, with a population of perhaps a hundred thousand at most, but it was a pretty village, and after the brutal implacability of Sisivondal and the long, wearying journey across central Alhanroel into the western provinces it seemed almost idyllic. It lay in the heart of prosperous farming country – everything from Gannamunda and Hunzimar westward was farming country, thousands of miles of it, blessed by the beneficial westerly winds that carried the rains inland from the distant coast – and Simmilgord rejoiced in the sight of broad fertile plains and cultivated fields again, so different from the interminable brick drabness of Sisivondal's innumerable warehouses and depots. He had never been this far west before, and, although Alaisor and the other coastal cities still lay many days' journey beyond here, it seemed to his eager imagination that he need only climb the nearest hill to behold the bosom of the Inner Sea shimmering in the golden-green afternoon sunlight. The air was fresh and sweet and moist out here, with a bit of the tang of a wind from the ocean. In parched, nearly rainless Sisivondal every intake of breath had been a struggle and the hot, dry air had rasped against his throat.

Simmilgord and Lutien were given a cottage to share, one of a row of nearly identical square-roofed buildings fashioned from a pinkish-gold stone that was quarried in the mountains just south of town. Their host, Kesmakuran's mayor, fluttered about them fussily as though he were welcoming some dukes or princes of Castle Mount, rather than a pair of uncertain young academics newly emerged from a sheltered scholastic existence.

Kyvole Gannivad was the mayor's name. He was a stubby, rotund man, bald except for two reddish fringes above his ears, stocky with the sort of solid stockiness that made you think that no matter how hard you pushed him you could not knock him over. He had trouble remembering their names, calling Simmigord "Lutilel" a couple of times and once transforming Lutiel's surname into "Simmifrons," which seemed odd for a politician, but otherwise he was ingratiating and solicitous to the point of absurdity, telling them again and again what an honor it was for the town of Kesmakuran to be graced by renowned scholars of their high intellect and widely acclaimed accomplishments. "We are counting on you," he said several times, "to put our city on the map. And we know that you will."

"What does he mean by that?" Lutiel asked, when they were finally alone. "Are we supposed to do real research here, or does he think we're going to act as a couple of paid publicists for them?"

Simmilgord shrugged. "It's the sort of thing that mayors like to say, that's all. He can't help being a home-town booster. He thinks that if we set up a nice little four-room museum next door to the site of the tomb and find a few interesting old inscriptions to put in it, visitors will come from thousands of miles around to gawk."

"And suppose that doesn't happen."

"Not our problem," said Simmilgord. "You know what you and I came here to do. Pulling the tourists in is his job, not ours."

"What if he tries to push us in directions that compromise the integrity of our work?"

"I don't think he will. But if he tries, we can handle him. He's nothing but a small-town mayor, remember, and not a particularly bright specimen of his species. Come on, Lutiel. Let's unpack and have a look at the famous tomb."

But that turned out not to be so simple. They needed to go with the official custodian of the tomb, and it took more than an hour to locate him. Then came the trek to the tomb itself, which was at the southern edge of town, far across from their lodgings, at the foot of the range of mountains out of which the city's building-blocks had been carved. It was late afternoon before they reached it. An ugly quarry scar formed a diagonal slash across the face of the mountain; below and to both sides of it grew a dense covering of blue-black underbrush, descending to ground level and extending almost to the outermost street of the city, and here, nearly hidden by the thick tangle of brush, was the entrance to Dvorn's tomb, or at least what was said to be Dvorn's tomb: a black hole stretching downward into the earth.

"I will go first," said their guide, Prasilet Sungavon, the local antiquarian who was the custodian of the tomb. "It's very dark down there. Even with our torches, we won't have an easy time."

"Lead on," Simmilgord said impatiently, gesturing with his hand.

Prasilet Sungavon had annoyed them both from the very start. He was a stubby little Hjort, squat and puffy-faced and bulgy-eyed, a member of a race that apparently could not help seeming officious and self-important. About a third of the population of Kesmakuram were Hjorts, evidently. By profession Prasilet Sungavon was a dealer in pharmaceutical herbs, who long ago had taken up amateur archaeology as a weekend hobby. "I've been digging down here, man and boy, for forty years," he told them proudly. "And I've found some real treasures, all right. Just about anything that anybody knows about Dvorn, they know because of the things I've found." Which would irritate Lutiel Vengifrons considerably, because, as a professionally trained archaeologist, he surely would dislike the thought that this pill-peddler had spent decades rummaging around at random with his spade and his pick in this unique and easily damaged site. Simmilgord was bothered by him too, since it was unlikely that Prasilet Sungavon had the knowledge or the wit to derive any sort of solid historical conclusions from whatever he had managed to scrape loose in the depths of the tomb.

But, whether they liked it or not, the Hjort was the official municipal custodian of the tomb, the man with the keys to the gate, and they could do nothing without his cooperation. So they lit their torches and followed him down a stretch of uneven flagstone steps to a place where a metal grillwork barred their entry, and waited while Prasilet Sungavon elaborately unlocked a series of padlocks and swung the gate aside.

A dark, muddy, musty-smelling passage, low and narrow, with a cold breeze rising up out of it, lay before them. Through swerves and curves it led onward for some unknown distance into the heart of the mountain on a gradual sloping descent. Because of his height, Simmilgord had to crouch from the start. The floor of the passage was a thick, spongy layer of muddy soil; the sides and roof of it had been carved, none too expertly, from the rock of the mountain above them. The entranceway, the Hjort told them, had now and then been blocked by the backwash from heavy storms, and had had to be cleared at least five times in the last two thousand years, most recently a century ago. When they had gone about fifteen feet in, Prasilet Sungavon indicated a crude niche cut into the tunnel wall. "I found remarkable things in there," he said, without explanation. "And there, and there," pointing at two more niches further along. "You'll see."

The air in the tunnel was cold and dank. From somewhere deeper in came the sound of steadily dripping water, and occasionally the quick clatter of wings as some cave-dwelling creature, invisible in the dimness, passed swiftly by overhead. Other than that, and the hoarse, ragged breathing of the Hjort, all was silent in here. After about ten minutes the passage expanded abruptly into a high-roofed circular chamber, lined all about by a coarse and irregular wall of badly matched blocks of gray stone, that could very readily be regarded as a place of interment. And against the left side of it sat a rectangular lidless pink-marble box, three or four feet high and about seven feet long, that was plausibly a sarcophagus.

"This is it," said the Hjort grandly. "The tomb of the Pontifex Dvorn!"

"May I?" Lutiel Vengifrons said, and, without waiting for a

reply, stepped forward and peered into the box. After a moment Simmilgord, more diffidently, went up alongside him.

The sarcophagus, if that indeed was what it was, was empty. That was no surprise. They had not expected to find Dvorn lying here with his hands crossed on his chest and a benign smile on his Pontifical features. The stone box was roughly carved, with clearly visible chisel-marks all along its bare sides. There did not seem to be any inscriptions on it or any sort of ornamentation.

"A tomb, yes, very possibly," said Lutiel Vengifrons after a while. He made the concession sound like a grudging one. "But just how, I wonder, were you able to identify this place specifically as the tomb of Dvorn?"

His tone was cool, skeptical, challenging. Unflustered, the Hjort replied, "We know that he was born in Kesmakuran, and that after his glorious century-long reign as Pontifex he died here. There is no doubt of that. It has always been understood locally that this is his tomb. That is the tradition. No one questions it. No other city in the world makes any such claim. Plainly this is an archaic site, going back to the earliest days of the settlement of Majipoor. The effort that must have been involved at that early time in digging such a long passageway indicates that this could only be the tomb of someone important. I ask you: Who else would that be, if not the first Pontifex?"

The logic did not seem entirely impeccable. Simmilgord, who had his own ideas about the unquestioning acceptance of local tradition as historical certainty, began to say something to that effect, but Lutiel nudged him ungently in the ribs before he could get out more than half a syllable. For the moment it was Lutiel who was conducting the interrogation. Prasilet Sungavon continued, still unperturbed, "Of course the body had disintegrated in the course of so long a span of time. But certain relics remained. I will show them to you when we come out of here."

"What about the lid?" Lutiel Vengifrons said. "Surely nobody would bury such an important personage in a sarcophagus that had no lid."

"There," said the Hjort, aiming his torch into a dark corner of the tomb-chamber. Against the far wall lay what must once have been a long stone slab, now cracked into three pieces and some bits of rubble.

"Tomb-robbers?" Simmilgord asked, unable to keep silent any longer.

"I think not," the Hjort said sharply. "We are not that sort of folk, here in Kesmakuran. Doubtless some visitors long ago lifted the lid to make certain that Dvorn's body really did lie here, and as they carried it to one side they dropped it and it broke."

"No doubt that is so," said Simmilgord, working hard to keep the sarcasm from his voice.

He could feel himself slipping into a profound bleakness of spirit. This dark, muddy hole in the ground – this miserable crude stone coffin with its shattered lid – these unprovable conjectures of Prasilet Sungavon – how did any of this constitute any sort of substantive information about the life of the Pontifex Dvorn? He wondered how he and Lutiel could possibly fulfill even the slightest part of the scientific mission that had taken them halfway across the continent from Sisivondal. It all seemed hopeless. There was so little to work with, and what little there was undoubtedly was contaminated by the passionate desire of the Kesmakuran folk to inflate its significance into something of major historical importance. Right here at the beginning of everything Simmilgord saw only disaster encroaching on him from all sides.

Prasilet Sungavon, though, stood before them smiling an immense Hjortish smile, a foot wide from ear to ear. Obviously he was very pleased with himself and the cavern over which he presided.

With a brisk professionalism that belied his gloom Simmigord said, "Well, now, is there anything else we should see?"

"Not here. At my house. Let us go."

One room of Prasilet Sungavon's house had been turned

into a kind of Dvorn museum. Three cases contained artifacts that had been taken from the tomb, most of them by the Hjort himself, some by the anonymous predecessors of his who had poked around in the tomb in the course of the previous thousand years. "These," he said resonantly, indicating several small yellowish objects, "are some of the Pontifex's teeth. And this is a lock of his hair."

"Still retaining some color after twelve thousand years," said Lutiel. "Remarkable!"

"Yes. Verging on the miraculous, I would say. These, I am told with good authority, are his knucklebones. Nothing else of the body remains. But how fortunate we are to have these few relics."

"Which you say can be identified as those of the Pontifex Dvorn," Simmilgord said. "May I ask, by what evidence?"

"The inscriptions from the tomb," said the Hjort. "I will show you those tomorrow."

"Why not now?"

"The hour grows late, my friend. Tomorrow."

There was no mistaking the inflexibility in his tone. Tomorrow it would have to be. The Hjort had the upper hand, and it seemed that he meant to keep it that way.

It was a depressing evening. Neither man had much to say, and little of that was optimistic. What had been put forth to them as the tomb of Dvorn was nothing much more than a muddy unadorned underground chamber that could have been built for almost any purpose at any time in the past twelve thousand years, the putative teeth and hair and bones that Prasilet Sungavon had shown them were absurdities, and the Hjort's proprietary attitude toward the site was certainly going to make any sort of real probing very difficult. There hadn't even been any Hjorts on Majipoor in the early centuries of the Pontificate – it was Lord Melikand who had brought all the non-human races here, thousands of years later, an amply chronicled fact – and yet here was this one behaving as though he owned the place. That was likely to be an ongoing problem.

The inscriptions from the tomb, at least, provided one mildly hopeful sign when Prasilet Sungavon let them see them the next day. From a locked cabinet the Hjort drew five small plaques of yellow stone. He had found them, he said, hidden away in the niches leading up to the tomb-chamber. Their surfaces appeared to have been damaged by unskillful cleaning, but nevertheless it was possible to see that they bore lettering, worn and indistinct, in some kind of barely familiar angular script that at even such brief inspection as this Simmilgord believed could be accepted – with a stretch – as an early version of the writing still in use in modern times.

A shiver of excitement ran down his spine. If these things were genuine, they could be the world's oldest surviving written artifacts. What an amazing notion that was! That romantic element in his soul that had blazed in him since his boyhood atop the hillocks of the Vale of Gloyn still lived in him: to hold these chipped and battered little slabs of stone aroused in him a feeling of being in contact with the whole vast sweep of the world's history from the beginning. And for the first time since their arrival in Kesmakuran he began to think that their long journey across the continent might yet result in something useful.

But he was no paleographer. He had never handled any documents remotely as old as these would have to be, if indeed they dated from the era of the early Pontificate, and what he saw here was altogether mysterious to him. No actual intelligible words leaped out to him from the worn surfaces of the slabs. At best he had a vague sense that faint marks that they bore *were* words, that they said something meaningful in a language that was akin, in an ancestral way, to the one that the people of Majipoor still spoke.

He looked across to Lutiel Vengifrons. "What do you think?"

"Extraordinary," Lutiel said. "They could actually be quite old, you know." The way he said it left no doubt that he too was greatly moved, even shaken, by the sight of the slabs. Simmilgord took note of that: Lutiel, steady and sober-minded and conservative, was not a man given to overstatement or bursts of wild enthusiasm. But then his innate sobriety of mind reasserted itself. "—If they're authentic, that is."

"*How* old, Lutiel?"

A shrug. "Lord Damiano's time? Stiamot's? No, older than that – Melikand, maybe."

"Not as old as the era of Dvorn, then?"

"I can't say, one way or the other, not just by one fast look. They're hard to read. I'm not very much of an expert on the most archaic scripts. And the lighting in here isn't good enough for this kind of work. I'd need to examine them under instruments – a close study of their surfaces—"

Prasilet Sungavon gathered up the slabs and said, "Let me tell you what they say. This one –" It was the largest of them. He pursed his immense lips and slowly traced a line across the surface of the slab with a thick ashen-gray forefinger. "'I, Esurimand of Kesmakuran, acting at the behest of Barhold, anointed successor to the beloved Pontifex Dvorn—'" Looking up, he said, "That's all can be read of this one. But on the next it says, 'The blessings of the Divine upon our great leader, who in the hundredth year of his reign –' Again, it's not possible to make out anything after that. But the next one says, 'For which we vow eternal gratitude –' and this one, 'May he enjoy eternal repose.' The fifth tablet is completely unintelligible."

Simmilgord and Lutiel Vengifrons exchanged glances. The look of skepticism in Lutiel's eyes was unmistakable. Simmilgord silently indicated his agreement. It was all he could do to keep himself from laughing.

But he tried to preserve some semblance of scholarly detachment. They could not afford to seem to be mocking Prasilet Sungavon to his face. "Quite fascinating," he said crisply. "Quite. And would you care to tell us how you were able to arrive at these translations?"

But he must not have been able to conceal the scorn in his voice very well, for the Hjort fixed his huge bulging eyes on him with a look that must surely be one of anger.

"Years of study," said Prasilet Sungavon. "Unremitting toil. Comparing old texts with older ones, and even older ones yet, until I had mastered the writings of the ancients. And then – long nights of candlelight – straining my eyes, struggling to comprehend these faint little scratchings in the stone—"

"He's making it all up, of course," Lutiel said, hours later, when they had returned to their own quarters. "The slabs might be real, and the inscriptions, but he invented those texts himself."

"I'm not so sure of that," said Simmilgord. He had been through a long and troubling conversation with himself since they had left the Hjort's place. "I doubted his translations as much as you did at first, when he started reeling off all that glib stuff about the beloved Pontifex Dvorn, and so forth. But you saw his library. He's done some genuine work on those inscriptions. We ought to allow for the possibility that they do say something like what he claims they say."

"But still – how pat it is, how neat, the reference to Barhold, the line about eternal repose—"

"Pat and neat if he's building support for a hoax, yes. But if that truly is Dvorn's tomb—"

Lutiel gave him an odd look. "You really want to believe that it is, don't you?"

"Yes. No question that I do. Don't you?"

"We are supposed to begin with the evidence, and work toward the hypothesis, Simmilgord. Not the other way around."

"You *would* say something like that, wouldn't you? You know that I'd never try to deny that a proper scholar ought to work from evidence to hypothesis. But there's nothing wrong with starting from a hypothesis and testing it against the evidence."

"The evidence of myth and tradition and, quite possibly, of fabricated artifacts?"

"We don't know that they're fabricated. I don't like that Hjort any more than you do, but his findings may be legitimate all the same. Look, Lutiel, I'm not saying that that *is* Dvorn's tomb. I simply answered your question. Do I *want* to believe it's Dvorn's tomb? Yes. Yes, I do. I think it would be wonderful if we could prove that it's the real thing. Whether it is or not is what we're here to find out."

It was as close as they had ever come to a real quarrel. But gradually the discussion grew less heated. They both saw that arguing with each other about the authenticity of the texts or the scholarly credentials of Prasinet Sungavon was pointless. They had come to Kesmakuran to conduct independent research and reach their own conclusions. Each of them had already let Prasilet Sungavon see that they had their doubts about the things he had shown them – they had, in fact, not been able to do a very good job of concealing their disdain for his methods and his results – and it was clear that the Hjort was annoyed by that. In his own eyes he was the leading authority on the tomb of the Pontifex Dvorn and they were merely a pair of snotty wet-behind-the-ears University boys, and indeed there was some truth to that. In the future they would have to take a less condescending approach to him, for Prasilet Sungavon held the keys to the tomb and without his cooperation they would accomplish nothing.

They tried to do just that in their next meeting with the Hjort, letting him know how excited they were by all that they had seen so far, and how eager they were to build on the splendid work he had done. He seemed mollified by that. Simmilgord asked to be allowed to take the slabs back to their house for study, and, although Prasilet Sungavon refused, he did let them make copies to work with. He also was willing to give them access to his own extensive library of paleographic texts. Lutiel said that he wanted to have lighting installed in the tomb – at the expense of the University, naturally – and the Hjort unhesitatingly agreed. Nor did he seem to be troubled by Lutiel's suggestion of extending the existing excavation deeper into the mountainside, which somehow no one had thought of doing since the cavern first had become known to the people of Kesmakuran.

The first surprise came when they began poring over the inscriptions on the tablets and comparing the characters with the examples of early Majipoori script in Prasilet Sungavon's books. In twelve thousand years one would expect any sort of alphabet to undergo some metamorphosis, but careful inspection of the tablets under adequate lighting quickly revealed that they were decipherable after all, once one made allowances for the erosion of the surface that time and careless cleaning had inflicted, and, after they had learned to make those allowances, they could see that the Hjort's readings were not very far from the mark. "See – here?" Lutiel said. "By the Divine, it *does* say 'Dvorn' – I'm certain of it!"

Simmilgord felt the shiver of discovery again. "Yes. And this – isn't it 'Barhold'?"

"With the pontifical sign next to both names!"

"E-tern-al re-pose –"

"I think so."

"Where's the part about 'the hundredth year of his reign?'"

"I don't see it."

"Neither do I. But of course Dvorn *didn't* reign a hundred years. That's culture-hero stuff – myth, fable. Just because it's in Furvain doesn't mean it's true. Nobody lives that long. The Hjort must have interpolated it to make the Kesmakurans happy. They want to believe that their great man was Pontifex for a century, just as it says in the *Book of Changes*, and so he found it on this slab for them."

"It's probably this line here," Lutiel said, pointing with his pencil. "You can make out about one letter out of every six, at best, in this section. Prasinet Sungavon would have been able to translate it any way he liked."

"But the rest of it—"

"Yes. It does all match up, more or less. We have to be nicer to him, Simmilgord. We really *do* have the tomb of Dvorn here, I think. You know how skeptical I was at first. But it gets harder and harder to argue this stuff away."

The installation of the lighting system began the next day. While that was going on, and Lutiel was purchasing the tools he would need for the dig, Simmilgord busied himself in the municipal archives, digging back through astonishingly ancient records. With the mayoral blessing of Kyvole Gannivad all doors were thrown open to him, and he roamed freely in a labyrinth of dusty shelves. The archive here was nothing like what he imagined was held in the Castle Mount library, or in the storage vaults of the Labyrinth, but it was impressive enough, particularly for so minor a town as Kesmakuran. And it appeared as though no one had looked at these things in decades, even centuries. For two days he wandered through an unfruitful host of relatively recent property deeds and tax records and city-council minutes, but then he found a staircase leading downward to a storeroom of far older documents, documents of almost unbelievable antiquity. Some of them went back six, seven, eight thousand years, to the days of Calintane and Guadeloom and the mighty Stiamot who reigned before them, and some were older than Stiamot even, bearing the seals of Coronals and Pontifexes whose names were mere shadows and whispers; and beneath these were what seemed to be transcriptions, themselves several thousand years old, of what appeared to be documents from the very earliest years of human settlement on Majipoor.

It was a wondrous thing to read these old texts. Simply to handle them was a thrill. Here – Simmilgord, still caught in the struggle between his skepticism and his eagerness to believe, could not help wondering whether it was a latter-day forgery – was a document that purported to be a copy of a decree issued by Dvorn when he was nothing more than the head of the provincial council of Kesmakuran. Here – how startling, if authentic! – was the text of Dvorn's fiery message to his fellow leaders in west-central Alhanroel, calling on them to unite and form a stable national government. Here – there seemed to be a considerable gap in time – was an edict of Dvorn's having to do with water rights along the Sefaranon River. So his regime had already extended its reach that far to the west! Whatever clerk had been responsible for making this copy of the primordial original document had drawn a replica of something very much like the Pontifical seal on it. Then there was a decree that bore not only Dvorn's name but that of Lord Barhold, the first Coronal, which indicated that Dvorn had by then devised the system of dual rule, a senior monarch who shaped policy and a junior one who saw to its execution; and after that came one that indicated that Barhold had succeeded to the title of Pontifex and had appointed a Coronal of his own.

Simmilgord felt dazed by it all. A sensation as of a great swelling chord of music came soaring up from the core of his soul, music that he had heard before, the great song of Majipoor that had resounded in his heart now and again throughout all his days. Since his boyhood he had lived with the deeds of the Pontifex Dvorn alive in his mind, the dawn of his campaign to bring the scattered cities of Majipoor together into a single realm, the first gathering of support at Kesmakuran, the arduous march to Stangard Falls, the proclamation of a royal government, the founding of the Pontificate and the struggle to win worldwide acceptance. Certainly it was the great epic of the world's history. But nearly all that Simmilgord knew of it came from Aithin Furvain's poem. Until this moment he had feared that every detail of the story, so far as anyone could say with certainty, might merely be a work of imaginative recreation.

Now, though, here in his hands, was the evidence that Furvain had told the true story. It was impossible to resist the desire to accept these documents as authentic. As he scanned through them, running his fingers over them, caressing them almost in a loving way, the whole stupendous sweep of Majipoor's history came pouring in on him like the invincible flow of a river in full spate. Simmilgord had not known any such sensations since his boyhood in the Vale of Gloyn, when he had felt the first stirrings of that hunger to comprehend this vast world that had eventually set him on the path he followed now. The documents *had* to be real. No one, not even for the sake of enhancing provincial pride, could have gone to the trouble of forging all this. Unimportant little Kesmakuran did indeed seem to be the place from which Dvorn's unification movement had sprung; and, no matter how pompous Prasilet Sungavon's manner might be, it was starting to be hard to reject the conclusion that the tomb of which he was the custodian was the actual burial-place of the first Pontifex.

Lutiel, meanwhile, had been making significant progress toward the same conclusion. He had recruited a crew of diggers from the local farms, three boys and two girls, and had given them a quick course in the technique of archaeological excavation, and – while Prasilet Sungavon stood by, watching somewhat uneasily – had begun to push the zone of exploration well beyond the tomb-chamber.

As Lutiel had begun to suspect almost from the first day, there was more to the underground structure than the entry-way and the burial chamber. Some probing on the far side of that chamber revealed that its rough-hewn wall was even more irregular than usual in certain places, and when he lifted away a little of the masonry in those places he discovered that behind the jumbled stones lay circular openings, probably plugged long ago by rockfalls. And behind those were four additional passage-ways leading off at sharp angles from the main entry tunnel. Succeeding days of excavation demonstrated that at one time the tomb-chamber had been at the center of a cluster of such tunnels, as though in ancient times solemn ceremonial processions had come to it from various directions.

Prasilet Sungavon, who made a point of being present at each day's work as if he feared that Lutiel might damage the precious tomb in some way, displayed mixed feelings as these discoveries proceeded. Plainly he was displeased as his own inadequacies as an archaeologist were made manifest: that he had never thought of digging deeper in at the site himself could only be an embarrassment to him. But his yearning for antiquarian knowledge was genuine enough, however inadequate his scientific skills might be, and he showed real excitement as Lutiel pushed his various excavations farther and farther.

Especially when more tablets turned up in these outer passages: commemorative plaques that showed an evolution in Majipoori script that had to cover several thousand years, culminating in a perfectly legible one declaring that the prodigious Stiamot, conqueror of the aboriginal Metamorphs, had come here on pilgrimage after his succession to the Pontificate and had performed a ceremony of thanksgiving at the tomb of his revered predecessor Dvorn.

Here was proof absolute of the authenticity of the site. That night Mayor Kyvole Gannivad gave a celebratory feast, and the golden wine of Alaisor flowed so freely that both Simmigord and Lutiel found it necessary to declare a holiday from their labors on the next day.

That was the first surprise: the confirmation that this was, in fact, the veritable tomb of Dvorn.

The second surprise, which came a few weeks later, was much less pleasant. They were both back at work, Simmilgord ploughing through a mountain of dusty documents, Lutiel meticulously extending his dig, when messengers came to each of them to say that the mayor wished to see them at his office immediately.

Simmilgord, arriving first, waited fifteen minutes in the office vestibule for Lutiel to get there, and ten fretful minutes more before Kyvole Gannivad appeared. The round little man came bouncing out, flushed with excitement, beckoning with both hands. "Come! Come! We have a visitor, a most important visitor!"

The huge figure of a Skandar waited within, practically filling the mayoral office: a ponderous bulky being, at least eight and a half feet tall, with four powerful arms and a thick shaggy pelt. Kyvole Hannivad said grandiloquently, "My friends, it is my great pleasure to introduce you to—"

But the Skandar needed no introduction. Simmigord knew him instantly by the two bizarre stripes of orange fur that slanted diagonally like barbaric ornaments through his dense gray-blue facial pelt, and by the fiery intensity of his eyes. This could only be Hawid Zakayil, the forceful and autocratic Superintendent of Antiquities of Alhanroel, a man who was ex officio director of half the museums of the continent, who had positioned himself as the supreme authority on all questions having to do with the past of Majipoor, who spent his days in perpetual motion, moving from one major site to another, taking command of anything that might be going on there, personally announcing all major discoveries, putting his name to innumerable books and essays that – so it was widely thought – were primarily the work of other people. He was a force of nature, a living hurricane, dynamic and irresistible. He had come once to the University when Simmilgord was there, to address the senior convocation, and the event was nothing that Simmilgord could ever forget.

It was only to be expected, Simmilgord thought dolefully, that the ubiquitous and omnipotent Hawid Zakayil would turn up here sooner or later. Confirmation of the authenticity of the tomb of Dvorn? Discovery of a Stiamot inscription? And of documents, or at least copies of documents, that cast new light on pivotal moments in the career of the first Pontifex? How, in the light of all of that, could he have stayed away? And what would happen now to the two young scholars who had made these discoveries?

Simmilgord, looking quickly toward Lutiel, had no difficulty reading the message that his friend's eyes conveyed.

We are lost, Lutiel was thinking. *We are doomed.*

Simmilgord felt very much the same way.

But for the moment all was jubilation and good cheer, at least outwardly. The towering Skandar reached out, taking both of Simmilgord's hands in his two left ones and Lutiel's in the right pair, and told them in booming tones how proud he was of the things they had achieved. "I met you both, you know, in Sisivondal, your graduation week, and I knew even then that you were destined for great things. As I told you at the time. Surely you remember!"

Surely Simmilgord did not. He had seen Hawid Zakayil then, yes, but only at a distance, simply as a member of the audience during that lengthy and vociferous harangue. Not a single word had passed between them on that occasion or at any time since. But he was not about to contradict the great man about that, or, indeed, about anything else.

They spoke with him for a long while about the work they had been doing in Kesmakuran. Then, of course, there had to be an inspection of Simmilgord's collection of archival material, and of the tablets that Lutiel had found in the newly opened tunnels, and then a tour of the tunnels themselves. At some point in the afternoon Prasilet Sungavon interpolated himself into the group, introduced himself effusively to Hawid Zakayil, and let the Skandar know, without saying so in quite those words, that Simmilgord and Lutiel would not have accomplished a thing here without his own thoughtful guidance. "You have done well," the Superintendent of Antiquities told him, and the Hjort beamed a great Hjortish grin of self-satisfaction. Simmilgord and Lutiel maintained a diplomatic silence.

Hawid Zakayil was so big that the tour of the tunnels was something of a challenge, and at one ticklish moment it seemed as if he were going to become stuck in the tightest of the passageways. But he extricated himself with the skill of one who was accustomed to life on a world where nearly everything was constructed for the benefit of much smaller beings. He moved quickly from place to place within the site, sniffing at the sarcophagus, staring into the niches where the stone tablets had been found, pushing at the chamber walls as though testing their solidity. "Wonderful," he said. "Marvelous. How thrilling it is to realize that we stand right at the birthplace of the history of Majipoor!"

Simmilgord thought he heard Lutiel snicker. This was no birthplace, for one thing: it was a tomb. And Simmilgord knew that Hawid Zakayil's appropriation to himself of the entire past of Majipoor had always bothered Lutiel. He was just a Skandar, after all, Lutiel had often said: a latecomer to the planet, like the Hjorts and Ghayrogs and all the other non-human races. Lutiel believed that the history of Majipoor was the history of the human settlement of the planet. Simmilgord had often tried to dispute that point. Majipoor had been here for millions of years before the arrival of the first intruders from space, and probably would survive their extinction as well. "We are *all* latecomers here, if you look at things from the point of view of the Metamorphs," he would say. "So what if the humans got here before the Skandars and the Hjorts? We all came from somewhere else. And all of us working together have made the place we call Majipoor what it is." But there was no appeasing Lutiel on that issue, and Simmilgord, after a time, ceased to debate it with him.

The real area of concern was that to have the Superintendent of Antiquities come storming noisily into town put everything in doubt. What would happen next, Simmilgord wondered, to their project here? The best-case scenario was that Hawid Zakayil would simply prowl around here for a few days, make a few comments and suggestions, give the work his seal of approval, and go zooming off to his next place of inspection, leaving them in peace to continue the work already begun.

But that was too optimistic an outcome. Very quickly it became apparent that something much worse was going to unfold.

Two days after the meeting with Hawid Zakayil, Simmilgord was at work in the municipal archives when Lutiel came bursting in unexpectedly, looking wild-eyed and flushed. "The most amazing – you have to see – you can't imagine – oh, come, Simmilgord, come with me, come! To the tomb! Hurry!"

Simmilgord had never seen his calm, sober-minded friend looking so flustered. There was no choice but to go with him at once, and off they went, pell-mell across town to the excavation site. With Lutiel in the lead, moving so quickly that Simmilgord could barely keep up with him, they scurried down the staircase, through the passage to the tomb-chamber, beyond it into the newly excavated tunnels, and then made a sudden left turn into a part of the dig that Simmigord had never seen before. Lutiel flashed his torch about frenziedly from one wall to the other.

"We broke through into this about an hour ago. Look at it! *Look* at it!"

Both sides of the new tunnel were covered with murals – most of them faded with age, in some places barely visible, mere ghosts of what once had been painted there, but in other sections still relatively fresh and bright, the colors still apparent. At the far end, where the passage widened into a kind of apse, Simmilgord could see the giant image of a seated man in what must have been robes of great magnificence, occupying the entire wall from floor to ceiling, one hand raised in a gesture of benediction, the other resting on his knee, lying there casually but, even so, in a regal manner. Though the whole upper part of the figure's face was gone, its smile remained, a smile of such warmth and godlike benevolence that this could only be meant as a representation of a great monarch, and what other monarch could it be than Dvorn?

To either side of that great throned figure were other paintings, a long series of them, badly damaged in their upper sections and the colors everywhere weakened by the inroads of time. But Simmilgord, staring in awe from one to the next, found it all too easy to suggest meanings for the scenes he saw: this must be the gathering at Kesmakuran where Dvorn had called upon the people of Alhanroel to unite behind his banner, and this his coronation as Pontifex at Stangard Falls on the river Glayge, at the foot of Castle Mount, and this one, where a lesser but still imposing figure was depicted beside him, surely showed

Dvorn raising his colleague Barhold to the newly devised rank of Coronal Lord. And so on and on for twenty yards or more, though the paintings closest to the point where Lutiel had entered the gallery were reduced to the merest spectral outlines. Simmilgord, moving carefully from one to the next, beheld images of vertically mounted wheels, like the waterwheels that might power a mill, and long processions of blurred and almost undiscernible figures, perhaps celebrants in some forgotten holy rite, and a series of wreath-like decorations inscribed with lettering in the same antique script as on the tablets that Prasilet Sungavon had found.

"The oldest paintings in the world," Lutiel said softly. "Scenes from the life of the Pontifex Dvorn."

"Yes." It was just a husky whisper: Simmilgord was barely able to get the syllable out. "Yes. Yes. Yes!" To his astonishment he found himself fighting back tears. "A marvelous discovery, Lutiel." And indeed it was. Even in that moment of jubilation, though, he felt a sudden sense of dread. This find was *too* marvelous. They were never going to get rid of Hawid Zakayil, now.

He could not bring himself to voice the fears that came rushing in upon him. But Lutiel did.

"And now to show it to the Skandar," he said. "Who will steal it from us."

"We will seal this chamber at once," Hawid Zakayil announced briskly, when he had completed his inspection of the new gallery two hours later. "This is the most amazing discovery in my entire career, and we must take no risks with it, none whatsoever. Exposure to the outside atmosphere could very well destroy these paintings in a matter of days. Therefore no one is to enter without permission from me, and I mean *no one*, until we complete our plan for preservation of the murals."

It was not hard for Simmilgord to imagine the things that were going through Lutiel Vengifrons' mind, but he could not bear to look at his friend's face just now. The swiftness with which the Superintendent of Antiquities had taken possession of the find was breathtaking. The most amazing discovery in *his* entire career, yes! And no one to enter the site, not even Lutiel, without permission from *him*. It was his site, now. His discovery. His *amazing* discovery.

Quite predictably the Superintendent of Antiquities made it clear that he intended to stay right here in Kesmakuran and take personal charge of the work. And over the next few days, without actually saying so explicitly, he let it be known to Mayor Kyvole Gannivad, to the Hjort Prasilet Sungavon, and, lastly, to Simmigord and Lutiel themselves, that this site was too important to be left in the hands of amateurs or novices. And – quite explicitly, this time – he revealed that he had some truly marvelous ideas for capitalizing on the tomb's tremendous historical significance.

"This is humiliating, Simmilgord," Lutiel said, when at last they were alone that evening. "I'm going to resign, and so should you."

"What?"

"Can't you see? He's putting the whole thing in his pocket and reducing us to flunkeys. I'll have to beg to be allowed to go into the tomb. He'll bring his own people in to do the preservation work, and they'll want to continue the dig without me. Whatever you find in the archives will have to be turned over to him, and he'll claim credit for having found it. We'll be lucky even to have our names on the paper when he publishes the find."

Simmilgord shook his head. "You're taking this much too seriously. He's behaving exactly as he always behaves when somebody finds an exciting new site, yes, but in a few weeks he'll lose interest and move on. Something big will turn up on the far side of Castle Mount or maybe even down in Suvrael and off he'll go to muscle in on it. Or there'll be a new museum to dedicate at the back end of Zimroel and he'll head over there for six or seven months. He'll keep his finger in our work here, sure. But he can't be everywhere at once, and sooner or later you'll be back in charge of the dig."

"This is very naive of you."

"I don't think so."

"Then you're actually going to remain here, Simmilgord?"

"Yes. Absolutely. And so should you."

"And be pushed aside – cheated, abused—"

"I tell you it won't be like that. Please, Lutiel. Please."

It took some work, but finally, glumly, Lutiel agreed to stay on for a while. The clinching argument was that for him to resign in high dudgeon now would destroy his career: Hawid Zakayil would understand instantly why he was leaving, no matter what pretext he gave, and would take mortal offense, and no young archaeologist who offended the Superintendent of Antiquities was ever going to do archaeological work on Majipoor again. He might just as well start taking a course in accounting or bookkeeping.

So Lutiel remained in Kesmakuran; and Hawid Zakayil went through the pretense, at least, of sharing responsibility for the project with the two of them. He informed Simmilgord that he was arranging financing so that every document found so far could be copied for the benefit of the archives at the Castle and the Labyrinth, a task that would keep Simmilgord busy for a good many weeks to come. And even though the site remained closed, with no further excavation until further notice, Lutiel himself would be admitted for several hours a day to sort through his discoveries in the outer tunnels and to supervise the work of the technicians who would be dealing with the task of preserving the murals against further decay.

Simmilgord wondered just what the Skandar would be doing during this time. Hawid Zakayil seemed to have allocated no specific aspect of the enterprise to himself, but he was too big and rambunctious and restless a presence to be content for long to sit about quietly in a sleepy place like Kesmakuran while such lesser men as Simmilgord and Lutiel went about their work.

The answer came soon enough. One morning Simmilgord and Lutiel received word that they were summoned to a meeting, and a couple of municipal officials escorted them to a place southeast of town, halfway around the base of the mountains from the site of the tomb. Over here the pinkish-gold stone of the main mountain range was sundered by a huge and formidable mass of black basalt, virtually a mountain unto itself, that must have been thrust up into it by some volcanic eruption long ago. Hawid Zakayil was waiting there for them with Mayor Kyvole Gannivad and Prasilet Sungavon when they arrived.

The Skandar pointed at once to the face of the basalt mass.

"Here is where we will put the monument. What do you think, gentlemen? Is this not a properly dramatic site for it?"

"The monument?" Simmilgord said blankly, feeling as though he had come in very late on something that he really should have known about before this.

"The monument to Dvorn!" the mayor cried. "What else do you think we're talking about? Haven't you seen the sketches?"

"Well, to be completely truthful—"

"We'll dig the entrance to the cavern here –" Kyvole Gannivad swept his stubby arms about with a vigorous sweep to indicate a zone perhaps thirty feet high and forty feet wide – "and there'll be a vestibule that will continue onward and downward for – oh, what did we say, Hawid Zakayil, a hundred feet? Two hundred?"

"Something like that," the Skandar said indifferently.

Simmilgord did not understand. A monument? What monument? He had seen no sketches. This was the first he had heard of any of this. "You mean, a kind of historical site, to bring visitors to town? Aside from the tomb itself, I mean."

"The tomb itself is too fragile to be a proper place of pilgrimage," Prasilet Sungavon said. The Hjort spoke the way he might if he were explaining something to a six-year-old. "That's why the Superintendent closed it so quickly, once the murals were discovered. But we need to build something here as a focus of attention on the greatness of the Pontifex Dvorn and on

Kesmakuran's importance in his career. As you say, a kind of historical site that will bring visitors here."

"Exhibits commemorating the life and achievements of Dvorn," said Hawid Zakayil. "Plaques that tell his story – no mythmaking, everything placed in accurate historical context." The Skandar favored Simmilgord with a gaze of such force that he feared he might be burned to a crisp in its glare. "You will be in charge of this part of it, Simmilgord. We will count on you to provide us with all the data, essentially a biography of the Pontifex that can be recreated in graphic form, and to design the exhibits: all the wonder and magic that was the life of Dvorn, set out here in its full glory. I am well aware that this is your special field of expertise. You are precisely the person for the task."

Simmilgord nodded. What could he say? He was over-whelmed by the power of the Skandar's formidable nature. And what Hawid Zakayil was proposing was so astonishing that in a moment everything was transformed for him. Dvorn had been Simmilgord's special obsession since his undergraduate days. There was no way he could refuse this assignment. Already he saw the monument taking shape in his imagination, to expand, to flower and grow – the murals, the statuary, the displays of documents and artifacts – the Museum of Dvorn! The *shrine* of Dvorn! *You will be in charge, Simmilgord*. Hawid Zakayil was handing him the project of his dreams. Once more he heard that magical soaring music that he had heard atop those little hills in the Vale of Gloyn and again in the archives of Kesmakura, the grand swelling sounds of the symphony of Majipoor. To build a commemorative shrine in honor of the first Pontifex – not just a shrine, though, nor even just a museum, but a research center, a place of study, over which he himself would preside—

"Of course, sir," he said hoarsely. "What a superb idea!"

He might as well have been talking to himself. Simmilgord realized that the Skandar had already moved on, turning his attention to Lutiel: "And we will want a replica of the tomb chamber, everything in one-to-one correlation, though some-what restored, of course, for the benefit of the laymen who will want to see it as it was in Dvorn's time. Those wonderful murals, reproduced exactly, with the colors enhanced and the missing portions carefully reconstructed – who better to supervise the work than you, Lutiel? Who, indeed?"

Hawid Zakayil paused, plainly waiting for Lutiel to reply. But no reply was forthcoming, and after a long moment of silence the Skandar simply looked away, his frenetic spirit already moving along to the next consideration, the hotel facilities that the town would need to provide here, and some highway expansion, and similar matters of municipal concern.

The glory and wonder of it all remained with Simmilgord after they had returned to their lodgings. Already he could see the long lines of visitors shuffling reverently past the great replica of the mural of the smiling Dvorn enthroned, pausing to study the historical plaques on the walls, the murmured discussions amongst them of the visionary brilliance of the first Pontifex, even the multitudes of eager readers for the book on Dvorn that he intended to write.

Then he noticed the furious, glowering expression on Lutiel's face.

Lutiel was fuming. He was pacing angrily about. And finally his anger broke into words.

"How absolutely awful! A phony ruin – replicas of the murals, very nicely prettied up for the tourists – !"

It was like being hit with a bucket of cold water.

With some difficulty Simmilgord brought himself down from the lofty fantasies that had engaged his mind. "What's so terrible about that, Lutiel? You can't expect to let them have access to the originals!"

Lutiel turned on him. "Why do they have to see them at all? What do we need this silly cave for? This shiny fraudulent showplace, this phony historical site? And why should *we* be involved? I told you right at the start, before we even came here, I wasn't going to hire on as a paid publicist for the town of Kesmakuran."

"But—"

"You know yourself that most people have no serious interest in what that Skandar wants to put in his museum. They might come and look for five minutes, and move onward, and buy a souvenir or two, maybe a little statuette of Dvorn to put on the mantel, and then start wondering about where to have lunch—"

Simmilgord began to feel his own anger rising. It was true, no denying it, that from the very beginning, from the time the head of the department back at the University had broached the Kesmakuran journey, Lutiel had opposed their getting involved. A "career detour," he had called it then, something irrelevant to the work of two serious young scholars. Yes, Simmilgord had argued him out of that, and had managed to overcome Lutiel's later doubts about the legitimacy of the project on a dozen occasions, and eventually Lutiel had made the discovery of a lifetime, that gallery of murals that any archaeologist would give his right arm to have found, or maybe *both* arms, and even so he went on grumbling and fretting about the issues of integrity that seemed to trouble him so much. Evidently he had never reconciled himself to the project in the first place. And never would.

As calmly as he could Simmilgord said, "You're being absurd, Lutiel. Are you telling me that we do all our work purely for ourselves, that we're like priests of some arcane cult who go through rites and rituals that have no relevance whatever to the real world and the lives of real people in it?"

Lutiel laughed harshly. "And you, Simmilgord? What are you telling *me*? Not a shred of integrity in you, is that it? Ready to sell yourself to the first bidder who comes along?"

Simmilgord gasped. Perhaps, he thought, Lutiel *was* some sort of monk at heart, too pure for this world. But this was going too far.

"When did I ever say—"

"I saw the way you lit up when the Skandar told you you were just the man for the job of putting together the historical side of the new monument."

"Of course I did. Why shouldn't I? It's a tremendous opportunity to put the story of Dvorn across to thousands, even millions of people. And you – when he told you essentially the same thing as he put you in charge of supervising the reconstruction of the murals, the creation of replica that look better than the originals – what did you feel?"

"What I felt was disgust," Lutiel said. "Indignation. I kept my mouth shut, because I couldn't bring myself to stand up to Hawid Zakayil to his face, any more than anyone else can. I told you I'm no publicist, Simmilgord, and certainly I'm not a showman either. Or some sort of theatrical impresario. What I am is a scientist. And so are you, whether you want to believe it or not. You're an historian. History is a science, or should be, anyway. And scientists have no business getting involved in anything as sordid as this."

Sordid?

Simmilgord's head was beginning to ache. He wanted to slide away from this discussion somehow. He was ashamed to face Lutiel.

That stinging charge of hypocrisy – of whoring, even – hurt him deeply. Lutiel was his closest friend. For Lutiel to see him as a hypocrite and a whore was painful. But there was a certain truth in it. A flamboyant character like Hawid Zakayil, who was both a scientist and a manufacturer of public entertainments, and probably somewhat more of the one than of the other, would dismiss such an accusation without a thought. Simmilgord, though, was shaken by it. One part of him thought Lutiel might just be right, that they had no business getting involved in something as far from genuine scholarship as this "monument" promised to be. But another part – the part that remembered the boy who had climbed those mountains and tried to cast his gaze from sea to sea – was wholly caught up in its spell.

They managed after a while to disengage themselves from the quarrel yet again. Simmilgord slept badly that night, profoundly disturbed by all that had been said. In the morning he went early to the archives, with Lutiel still asleep, and spent the day digging feverishly through a section of old municipal documents he had never examined before. There proved to be nothing of the slightest interest in them, but the work itself was soothing, the mechanical selecting of documents and setting them up in the reader and scanning. Dull work, even pointless work, but it was comforting to be focusing his full attention on it.

The ugly words kept coming back nonetheless. *Hypocrite.* *Whore.*

But on the way back from the archives building to his house Simmilgord's thoughts turned back to yesterday's meeting with Hawid Zakayil, toward the monument that he proposed to build in that cavern in the mountain of black basalt. Almost against his will, ideas for its design kept bursting into his mind, until he was dizzy and trembling with excitement. It all came together in the most wondrous way. He could see the layout of the vestibule, the arrangement of the inner rooms, the route that led to the replica of the tomb-chamber, which would be the climax of the experience for the visitor—

He had to smile. Maybe Lutiel was right: maybe he had failed to understand his true vocation all along, that he was not really a scholar at all, that he had actually been destined, even as a small boy atop those rocky hillocks, to be a kind of showman, someone who converts history into the stuff of romance. Perhaps, he told himself, it was quite permissible for him to rise up out of the dusty archives of the world and devote his life to bringing the story of the founding of the Pontificate to a world yearning to know more about it. And he had a bleak vision of Lutiel's future, seeing him endlessly digging and sifting through sandy wastelands, getting nowhere, the great achievement of his life already behind him and the primary credit for it taken from him by someone else. Simmilgord did not want any such fate as that for himself, a lifetime of puttering with ancient documents in cloistered halls and writing papers that no one but his few colleagues would ever read. He could see a new role, a better role, for himself: the man who rediscovered Dvorn, who turned his name into a household word.

When he reached the house he shared with Lutiel he found a note pinned to his pillow:

> *Have handed in my resignation. Setting out for Sisivondal this afternoon. When he publishes my excavation, make sure that my name is on the paper somewhere.*
> *Best of luck, old friend. You'll need it.*
> *L.*

Hawid Zakayil said, "And are you going to resign also?"

The Superintendent of Antiquities spoke in what was for him a surprisingly mild, non-confrontational tone. He sounded merely curious, not in any way angry or menacing.

"No," Simmilgord replied at once, before anything to the contrary could escape his lips. "Of course not. This is strictly Lutiel's decision. I don't happen to share his philosophical outlook."

"His philosophical outlook on *what*?" asked the Skandar, in not quite so mild a way.

Evasively Simmilgord said, "Ends. Means. Ultimate purposes. Lutiel takes everything very seriously, you know. Sometimes *too* seriously." And then he went on, quickly, to keep Hawid Zakayil from continuing this line of inquiry, "Sir, I've had some interesting thoughts since yesterday about how we might handle certain features of the monument. If I might share them with you—"

"Go ahead," said the Skandar gruffly.

"Those wheel-like structures shown in the murals, with a line of what look like celebrants approaching them: they must surely have had some sort of ritual purpose in the days when Dvorn's tomb was an active center of worship. Perhaps we could recreate that ritual in the monument – every hour, let's say, stage a kind of reenactment of what we think it might have been like—"

"Good! Very good!"

"Or even hire people to keep the wheels in constant motion – revolving steadily, powered by some sort of primitive arrangement of pedals – to symbolize the eternal cycle of history, the ongoing continuity of the world through all its millions of years—"

Hawid Zakayil smiled a shrewd Skandar smile.

"I like it, Simmilgord. I like it very much."

And so it came to pass that Simmilgord of Gloyn became the first administrator of the Tomb of Dvorn, as the monument in the black basalt mountain came to be called after a while, and looked after it in the blossoming of its first growth until it became known as the most sacred site of western Alhanroel, where every Coronal would make a point of stopping to pay homage when he made one of his long processional journeys across the world.

4

The Sorcerer's Apprentice

Gannin Thidrich was nearing the age of thirty and had come to Triggoin to study the art of sorcery, a profession for which he thought he had some aptitude, after failing at several for which he had none. He was a native of the Free City of Stee, that splendid metropolis on the slopes of Castle Mount, and at the suggestion of his father, a wealthy merchant of that great city, he had gone first into meat-jobbing, and then, through the good offices of an uncle from Dundilmir, he had become a dealer in used leather. In neither of these occupations had he distinguished himself, nor in the desultory projects he had undertaken afterward. But from childhood on he had pursued sorcery in an amateur way, first as a boyish hobby, and then as a young man's consolation for shortcomings in most of the other aspects of his life – helping out friends even unluckier than he with an uplifting spell or two, conjuring at parties, earning a little by reading palms in the marketplace – and at last, eager to attain more arcane skills, he had taken himself to Triggoin, the capital city of sorcerers, hoping to apprentice himself to some master in that craft.

Triggoin came as a jolt, after Stee. That great city, spreading out magnificently along both banks of the river of the same name, was distinguished for its huge parks and game preserves, its palatial homes, its towering riverfront buildings of reflective gray-pink marble. But Triggoin, far up in the north beyond the grim Valmambra Desert, was a closed, claustrophobic place, dark and unwelcoming, where Gannin Thidrich found himself confronted with a bewildering tangle of winding medieval streets lined by ancient mustard-colored buildings with blank facades and gabled roofs. It was winter here. The trees were leafless and the air was cold. That was a new thing for him, winter: Stee was seasonless, favored all the year round by the eternal springtime of Castle Mount. The sharp-edged air was harsh with the odors of stale cooking-oil and unfamiliar spices; the faces of the few people he encountered in the streets just within the gate were guarded and unfriendly.

He spent his first night there in a public dormitory for way-farers, where in a smoky, dimly lit room he slept, very poorly, on a tick-infested straw mat among fifty other footstore travel-ers. In the morning, waiting on a long line for the chance to rinse his face in icy water, he passed the time by scanning the announcements on a bulletin board in the corridor and saw this:

APPRENTICE WANTED

Fifth-level adept offers instruction for serious student, plus lodging. Ten crowns per week for room and lessons. Some household work required, and assistance in professional tasks. Apply to V. Halabant, 7 Gapeligo Boulevard, West Triggoin.

That sounded promising. Gannin Thidrich gathered up his suitcases and hired a street-carter to take him to West Triggoin. The carter made a sour face when Gannin Thidrich gave him the address, but it was illegal to refuse a fare, and off they went. Soon Gannin Thidrich understood the sourness, for West Triggoin appeared to be very far from the center of the city, a suburb, in fact, perhaps even a slum, where the buildings were so old and dilapidated they might well have dated from Lord Stiamot's time and a cold, dusty wind blew constantly down out of a row of low, jagged hills. Number 7 Gapeligo Boulevard proved to be a ramshackle lopsided structure, three asymmetrical floors behind a weatherbeaten stone wall that showed sad signs of flaking and spalling. The ground floor housed what seemed to be a tavern, not open at this early hour; the floor above it greeted him with a padlocked door; Gannin Thidrich struggled upward with his luggage and at the topmost landing was met with folded arms and hostile glance by a tall, slender woman of about his own age, auburn-haired, dusky-skinned, with keen unwavering eyes and thin, savage-looking lips. Evidently she had heard his bumpings and thumpings on the staircase and had come out to inspect the source of the commotion. He was struck at once, despite her chilly and even forbidding aspect, with the despairing realization that he found her immensely attractive.

"I'm looking for V. Halabant," Gannin Thidrich said, gasping a little for breath after his climb.

"I am V. Halabant."

That stunned him. Sorcery was not a trade commonly practiced by women, though evidently there were some who did go in for it. "The apprenticeship—?" he managed to say.

"Still available," she said. "Give me these." In the manner of a porter she swiftly separated his bags from his grasp, hefting them as though they were weightless, and led him inside. Her chambers were dark, cheerless, cluttered, and untidy. The small room to the left of the entrance was jammed with the apparatus and paraphernalia of the professional sorcerer: astrolabes and ammatepilas, alembics and crucibles, hexaphores, ambivials, rohillas and verilistias, an armillary sphere, beakers and retorts, trays and metal boxes holding blue powders and pink ointments and strange seeds, a collection of flasks containing mysterious colored fluids, and much more that he was unable to identify. A second room adjacent to it held an overflowing bookcase, a couple of chairs, and a swaybacked couch. No doubt this room was for consultations. There were cobwebs on the window and he saw dust beneath the couch, and even a few sandroaches, those ubiquitous nasty scuttering insects that infested the parched Valmambra and all territories adjacent to it, were roaming about. Down the hallway lay a small dirty kitchen, a tiny room with a toilet and tub in it, storeroom piled high with more books and pamphlets, and beyond it the closed door of what he supposed – correctly, as it turned out – to be her own bedroom. What he did not see was any space for a lodger.

"I can offer one hour of formal instruction per day, every day of the week, plus access to my library for your independent studies, and two hours a week of discussion growing out of your own investigations," V. Halabant announced. "All of this in the morning; I will require you to be out of here for three hours every afternoon, because I have private pupils during that time. How you spend those hours is unimportant to me, except that I will need you to go to the marketplace for me two or three times a week, and you may as well do that then. You'll also do sweeping, washing, and other household chores, which, as you surely have seen, I have very little time to deal with. And you'll help me in my own work as required, assuming, of course, your skills are up to it. Is this agreeable to you?"

"Absolutely," said Gannin Thidrich. He was lost in admiration of her lustrous auburn hair, her finest feature, which fell in a sparkling cascade to her shoulders.

"The fee is payable four weeks in advance. If you leave after the first week the rest is refundable, afterwards not." He knew already that he was not going to leave. She held out her hand. "Sixty crowns, that will be."

"The notice I saw said it was ten crowns a week."

Her eyes were steely. "You must have seen an old notice. I raised my rates last year."

He would not quibble. As he gave her the money he said, "And where am I going to be sleeping?"

She gestured indifferently toward a rolled-up mat in a corner of the room that contained all the apparatus. He realized that that was going to be his bed. "You decide that. The laboratory, the study, the hallway, even. Wherever you like."

His own choice would have been her bedroom, with her, but he was wise enough not to say that, even as a joke. He told her that he would sleep in the study, as she seemed to call the room with the couch and books. While he was unrolling the mat she asked him what level of instruction in the arts he had attained, and he replied that he was a self-educated sorcerer, strictly a novice, but with some apparent gift for the craft. She appeared untroubled by that. Perhaps all that mattered to her was the rent; she would instruct anyone, even a novice, so long as he paid on time.

"Oh," he said, as she turned away. "I am Gannin Thidrich. And your name is—?"

"Halabant," she said, disappearing down the hallway.

Her first name, he discovered from a diploma in the study, was Vinala, a lovely name to him, but if she wanted to be called "Halabant," then "Halabant" was what he would call her. He would not take the risk of offending her in any way, not only because he very much craved the instruction that she could offer him, but also because of the troublesome and unwanted physical attraction that she held for him.

He could see right away that that attraction was in no way reciprocated. That disappointed him. One of the few areas of his life where he had generally met with success was in his dealings with women. But he knew that romance was inappropriate, anyway, between master and pupil, even if they were of differing sexes. Nor had he asked for it: it had simply smitten him at first glance, as had happened to him two or three times earlier in his life. Usually such smitings led only to messy difficulties, he had discovered. He wanted no such messes here. If these feelings of his for Halabant became a problem, he supposed, he could go into town and purchase whatever the opposite of a love-charm was called. If they sold love-charms here, and he had no doubt that they did, surely they would sell antidotes for love as well. But he wanted to remain here, and so he would do whatever she asked of him, call her by whatever name she requested, and so forth, obeying her in all things. In this ugly, unfriendly city she was the one spot of brightness and warmth for him, regardless of the complexities of the situation.

But his desire for her did not cause any problems, at first, aside from the effort he had to make in suppressing it, which was considerable but not insuperable.

On the first day he unpacked, spent the afternoon wandering around the unprepossessing streets of West Triggoin during the stipulated three hours for her other pupils, and, finding himself alone in the flat when he returned, he occupied himself by browsing through her extensive collection of texts on sorcery until dinnertime. Halabant had told him that he was free to use her little kitchen, and so he had purchased a few things at the corner market to cook for himself. Afterward, suddenly very weary, he lay down on his mat in the study and fell instantly asleep. He was vaguely aware, sometime later in the night, that she had come home and had gone down the hallway to her room.

In the morning, after they had eaten, she began his course of instruction in the mantic arts.

Briskly she interrogated him about the existing state of his knowledge. He explained what he could and could not do, a little surprised himself at how much he knew, and she did not seem displeased by it either. Still, after ten minutes or so she interrupted him and set about an introductory discourse of the most elementary sort, beginning with a lecture on the three classes of demons, the untamable valisteroi, the frequently useful kalisteroi, and the dangerous and unpredictable irgalisteroi. Gannin Thidrich had long ago encompassed the knowledge of the invisible beings, or at least thought he had; but he listened intently, taking copious notes, exactly as though all this were new to him, and after a while he discovered that what he thought he knew was shallow indeed, that it touched only on the superficialities.

Each day's lesson was different. One day it dealt with amulets and talismans, another with mechanical conjuring devices, another with herbal remedies and the making of potions, another with interpreting the movements of the stars and how to cast spells. His mind was awhirl with new knowledge. Gannin Thidrich drank it all in greedily, memorizing dozens of spells a day. ("To establish a relationship with the demon Ginitiis: *Iimea abrasax iabe iarbatha chramne*" ... "To invoke protection against aquatic creatures: *Loma zath aioin acthase balamaon*" ... "Request for knowledge of the Red Lamp: *Imantou lantou anchomach*" ...) After each hour-long lesson he flung himself into avid exploration of her library, searching out additional aspects of what he had just been taught. He saw, ruefully, that while he had wasted his life in foolish and abortive business ventures, she had devoted her years, approximately the same number as his, to a profound and comprehensive study of the magical arts, and he admired the breadth and depth of her mastery.

On the other hand, Halabant did not have much in the way of a paying practice, skillful though she obviously was. During Gannin Thidrich's first week with her she gave just two brief consultations, one to a shopkeeper who had been put under a geas by a commercial rival, one to an elderly man who lusted after a youthful niece and wished to be cured of his obsession. He assisted her in both instances, fetching equipment from the laboratory as requested. The fees she received in both cases, he noticed, were minimal: a mere handful of coppers. No wonder she lived in such dismal quarters and was reduced to taking in private pupils like himself, and whoever it was who came to see her in the afternoons while he was away. It puzzled him that she remained here in Triggoin, where sorcerers swarmed everywhere by the hundreds or the thousands and competition had to be brutal, when she plainly would be much better off setting up in business for herself in one of the prosperous cities of the Mount where a handsome young sorceress with skill in the art would quickly build a large clientele.

It was an exciting time for him. Gannin Thidrich felt his mind opening outward day by day, new knowledge flooding in, the mastery of the mysteries beginning to come within his grasp.

His days were so full that it did not bother him at all to pass his nights on a thin mat on the floor of a room crammed with ancient acrid-smelling books. He needed only to close his eyes and sleep would come up and seize him as though he had been drugged. The winter wind howled outside, and cold drafts broke through into his room, and sandroaches danced all around him, making sandroach music with their little scraping claws, but nothing broke his sleep until dawn's first blast of light came through the library's uncovered window. Halabant was always awake, washed and dressed, when he emerged from his room. It was as if she did not need sleep at all. In these early hours of the morning she would hold her consultations with her clients in the study, if she had any that day, or else retire to her laboratory and putter about with her mechanisms and her potions. He would breakfast alone – Halabant never touched food before noon – and set about his household chores, the dusting and scrubbing and all the rest, and then would come his morning lesson and after that, until lunch, his time to prowl in the library. Often he and she took lunch at the same time, though she maintained silence throughout, and ignored him when he stole the occasional quick glance at her across the table from him.

The afternoons were the worst part, when the private pupils came and he was forced to wander the streets. He begrudged them, whoever they were, the time they had with her, and he hated the grimy taverns and bleak gaming-halls where he spent these winter days when the weather was too grim to allow him simply to walk about. But then he would return to the flat, and if he found her there, which was not always the case, she would allow him an hour or so of free discourse about matters magical, not a lesson but simply a conversation, in which he brought up issues that fascinated or perplexed him and she helped him toward an understanding of them. These were wonderful hours, during which Gannin Thidrich was constantly conscious not just of her knowledge of the arts but of Halabant's physical presence, her strange off-center beauty, the warmth of her body, the oddly pleasing fragrance of it. He kept himself in check, of course. But inwardly he imagined himself taking her in his arms, touching his lips to hers, running his fingertips down her lean, lithe back, drawing her down to his miserable thin mat on the library floor, and all the while some other part of his mind was concentrating on the technical arcana of sorcery that she was offering him.

In the evenings she was usually out again – he had no idea where – and he studied until sleep overtook him, or, if his head was throbbing too fiercely with newly acquired knowledge, he would apply himself to the unending backlog of housekeeping tasks, gathering up what seemed like the dust of decades from under the furniture, beating the rugs, oiling the kitchen pots, tidying the books, scrubbing the stained porcelain of the sink, and on and on, all for her, for her, for love of her.

It was a wonderful time.

But then in the second week came the catastrophic moment when he awoke too early, went out into the hallway, and blundered upon her as she was heading into the bathroom for her morning bath. She was naked. He saw her from the rear, first, the long lean back and the narrow waist and the flat, almost boyish buttocks, and then, as a gasp of shock escaped his lips and she became aware that he was there, she turned and faced him squarely, staring at him as coolly and unconcernedly as though he were a cat, or a piece of furniture. He was overwhelmed by the sight of her breasts, so full and close-set that they almost seemed out of proportion on such a slender frame, and of her flaring sharp-boned hips, and of the startlingly fire-hued triangle between them, tapering down to the slim thighs. She remained that way just long enough for the imprint of her nakedness to burn its way fiercely into Gannin Thidrich's soul, setting loose a conflagration that he knew it would be impossible for him to douse. Hastily he shut his eyes as though he had accidentally stared into the sun; and when he opened them again, a desperate moment later, she was gone and the bathroom door was closed.

The last time Gannin Thidrich had experienced such an impact he had been fourteen. The circumstances had been somewhat similar. Now, dizzied and dazed as a tremendous swirl of adolescent emotion roared through his adult mind, he braced himself against the hallway wall and gulped for breath like a drowning man.

For two days, though neither of them referred to the incident at all, he remained in its grip. He could hardly believe that something as trivial as a momentary glimpse of a naked woman, at his age, could affect him so deeply. But of course there were other factors, the instantaneous attraction to her that had afflicted him at the moment of meeting her, and their proximity in this little flat, where her bedroom door was only twenty paces from his, and the whole potent master–pupil entanglement that had given her such a powerful role in his lonely life here in the city of the sorcerers. He began to wonder whether she had worked some sorcery on him herself as a sort of amusement, capriciously casting a little lust-spell over him so that she could watch him squirm, and then deliberately flaunting her nakedness at him that way. He doubted it, but, then, he knew very little about what she was really like, and perhaps – how could he say? – there was some component of malice in her character, something in her that drew pleasure from tormenting a poor fish like Gannin Thidrich who had been cast up on her shore. He doubted it, but he had encountered such women before, and the possibility always was there.

He was making great progress in his studies. He had learned now how to summon minor demons, how to prepare tinctures that enhanced virility, how to employ the eyebrow of the sun, how to test for the purity of gold and silver by the laying on of hands, how to interpret weather omens, and much more. His head was swimming with his new knowledge. But also he remained dazzled by the curious sort of beauty that he saw in her, by the closeness in which they lived in the little flat, by the memory of that one luminous encounter in the dawn. And when in the fourth week it seemed to him that her usual coolness toward him was softening – she smiled at him once in a while, now, she showed obvious delight at his growing skill in the art, she even asked him a thing or two about his life before coming to Triggoin – he finally mistook diminished indifference for actual warmth and, at the end of one morning's lesson, abruptly blurted out a confession of his love for her.

An ominous red glow appeared on her pale cheeks. Her dark eyes flashed tempestuously. "Don't ruin everything," she warned him. "It is all going very well as it is. I advise you to forget that you ever said such a thing to me."

"How can I? Thoughts of you possess me day and night!"

"Control them, then. I don't want to hear any more about them. And if you try to lay a finger on me I'll turn you into a sandroach, believe me."

He doubted that she really meant that. But he abided by her warning for the next eight days, not wanting to jeopardize the continuation of his course of studies. Then, in the course of carrying out an assignment she had given him in the casting of auguries, Gannin Thidrich inscribed her name and his in the proper places in the spell, inquired as to the likelihood of a satisfactory consummation of desire, and received what he understood to be a positive prognostication. This inflamed him so intensely with joy that when Halabant came into the room a moment later Gannin Thidrich impulsively seized her and pulled her close to him, pressed his cheek against hers, and frantically fondled her from shoulder to thigh.

She muttered six brief, harsh words of a spell unknown to him in his ear and bit his earlobe. In an instant he found himself scrabbling around amidst gigantic dust-grains on the floor. Jagged glittering motes floated about him like planets in the void. His vision had become eerily precise down almost to the microscopic level, but all color had drained from the world.

When he put his hand to his cheek in shock he discovered it to be an insect's feathery claw, and the cheek itself was a hard thing of chitin. She had indeed transformed him into a sandroach.

Numb, he considered his situation. From this perspective he could no longer see her – she was somewhere miles above him, in the upper reaches of the atmosphere – nor could he make out the geography of the room, the familiar chairs and the couch, or anything else except the terrifyingly amplified details of the immensely small. Perhaps in another moment her foot would come down on him, and that would be that for Gannin Thidrich. Yet he did not truly believe that he had become a sandroach. He had mastered enough sorcery by this time to understand that that was technically impossible, that one could not pack all the neurons and synapses, the total intelligence of a human mind, into the tiny compass of an insect's head. And all those things were here with him inside the sandroach, his entire human personality, the hopes and fears and memories and fantasies of Gannin Thidrich of the Free City of Stee, who had come to Triggoin to study sorcery and was a pupil of the woman V. Halabant. So this was all an illusion. He was not really a sandroach; she had merely made him *believe* that he was. He was certain of that. That certainty was all that preserved his sanity in those first appalling moments.

Still, on an operational level there was no effective difference between thinking you were a six-legged chitin-covered creature one finger-joint in length and actually *being* such a creature. Either way, it was a horrifying condition. Gannin Thidrich could not speak out to protest against her treatment of him. He could not restore himself to human shape and height. He could not do anything at all except the things that sandroaches did. The best he could manage was to scutter in his new six-legged fashion to the safety to be found underneath the couch, where he discovered other sandroaches already in residence. He glared at them balefully, warning them to keep their distance, but their only response was an incomprehensible twitching of their feelers. Whether that was a gesture of sympathy or one of animosity, he could not tell.

The least she could have done for me, he thought, was to provide me with some way of communicating with the others of my kind, if this is to be my kind from now on.

He had never known such terror and misery. But the transformation was only temporary. Two hours later – it seemed like decades to him, sandroach time, all of it spent hiding under the couch and contemplating how he was going to pursue the purposes of his life as an insect – Gannin Thidrich was swept by a nauseating burst of dizziness and a sense that he was exploding from the thorax outward, and then he found himself restored to his previous form, lying in a clumsy sprawl in the middle of the floor. Halabant was nowhere to be seen. Cautiously he rose and moved about the room, reawakening in himself the technique of two-legged locomotion, holding his outspread fingers up before his eyes for the delight of seeing fingers again, prodding his cheeks and arms and abdomen to confirm that he was once again a creature of flesh. He was. He felt chastened and immensely relieved, even grateful to her for having relented.

They did not discuss the episode the next day, and all reverted to as it had been between them, distant, formal, a relationship of pure pedagogy and nothing more. He remained wary of her. When, now and then, his hand would brush against hers in the course of handling some piece of apparatus, he would pull it back as if he had touched a glowing coal.

Spring now began to arrive in Triggoin. The air was softer; the trees grew green. Gannin Thidrich's desire for his instructor did not subside, in truth grew more maddeningly acute with the warming of the season, but he permitted himself no expression of it. There were further occasions when he accidentally enountered her going to and fro, naked, in the hall in earliest morning. His response each time was instantly to close his eyes and turn away, but her image lingered on his retinas and burrowed down into his brain. He could not help thinking that there was something intentional about these provocative episodes, something flirtatious, even. But he was too frightened of her to act on that supposition.

A new form of obsession now came over him, that the visitors she received every afternoon while he was away were not private pupils at all, but a lover, rather, or perhaps several lovers. Since she took care not to have her afternoon visitors arrive until he was gone, he had no way of knowing whether this was so, and it plagued him terribly to think that others, in his absence, were caressing her lovely body and enjoying her passionate kisses while he was denied everything on pain of being turned into a sandroach again.

But of course he *did* have a way of knowing what took place during those afternoons of hers. He had progressed far enough in his studies to have acquired some skill with the device known as the Far-Seeing Bowl, which allows an adept to spy from a distance. Over the span of three days he removed from Halabant's flat one of her bowls, a supply of the pink fluid that it required, and a pinch of the grayish activating powder. Also he helped himself to a small undergarment of Halabant's – its fragrance was a torment to him – from the laundry basket. These things he stored in a locker he rented in the nearby marketplace. On the fourth day, after giving himself a refresher course in the five-word spell that operated the bowl, he collected his apparatus from the locker, repaired to a tavern where he knew no one would intrude on him, set the bowl atop the garment, filled it with the pink fluid, sprinkled it with the activating powder, and uttered the five words.

It occurred to him that he might see scenes now that would shatter him forever. No matter: he had to know.

The surface of the fluid in the bowl rippled, stirred, cleared. The image of V. Halabant appeared. Gannin Thidrich caught his breath. A visitor was indeed with her: a young man, a boy, even, no more than twelve or fifteen years old. They sat chastely apart in the study. Together they pored over one of Halabant's books of sorcery. It was an utterly innocent hour. The second student came soon after: a short, squat fellow wearing coarse clothing of a provincial cut. For half an hour Halabant delivered what was probably a lecture – the bowl did not provide Gannin Thidrich with sound – while the pupil, constantly biting his lip, scribbled notes as quickly as he could. Then he left, and after a time was replaced by a sad, dreamy-looking fellow with long shaggy hair, who had brought some sort of essay or thesis for Halabant to examine. She leafed quickly through it, frequently offering what no doubt were pungent comments.

No lovers, then. Legitimate pupils, all three. Gannin Thidrich felt bitterly ashamed of having spied on her, and aghast at the possibility that she might have perceived, by means of some household surveillance spell of whose existence he knew nothing, that he had done so. But she betrayed no sign of that when he returned to the flat.

A week later, desperate once again, he purchased a love-potion in the sorcerers' marketplace – not a spell to free himself from desire, though he knew that was what he should be getting, but one that would deliver her into his arms. Halabant had sent him to the marketplace with a long list of professional supplies to buy for her – such things as elecamp, golden rue, quicksilver, brimstone, goblin-sugar, mastic, and thekka ammoniaca. The last item on the list was maltabar, and the same dealer, he knew, offered potions for the lovelorn. Rashly Gannin Thidrich purchased one. He hid it among his bundles and tried to smuggle it into the flat, but Halabant, under the pretext of offering to help him unpack, went straight to the sack that contained it, and pulled it forth. "This was nothing that I requested," she said.

"True," he said, chagrined.

"Is it what I think it is?"

Hanging his head, he admitted that it was. She tossed it angrily aside. "I'll be merciful and let myself believe that you bought this to use on someone else. But if I was the one you had in mind for it—"

"No. Never."

"Liar. Idiot."

"What can I do, Halabant? Love strikes like a thunderbolt."

"I don't remember advertising for a lover. Only for an apprentice, an assistant, a tenant."

"It's not my fault that I feel this way about you."

"Nor mine," said Halabant. "Put all such thoughts out of your mind, if you want to continue here." Then, softening, obviously moved by the dumbly adoring way in which he was staring at her, she smiled and pulled him toward her and brushed his cheek lightly with her lips. "Idiot," she said again. "Poor hopeless fool." But it seemed to him that she said it with affection.

Matters stayed strictly business between them. He hung upon every word of her lessons as though his continued survival depended on committing every syllable of her teachings to memory, filled notebook after notebook with details of spells, talismans, conjurations, and illusions, and spent endless hours rummaging through her books for amplifying detail, sometimes staying up far into the night to pursue some course of study that an incidental word or two from her had touched off. He was becoming so adept, now, that he was able to be of great service to her with her outside clientele, the perfect assistant, always knowing which devices or potions to bring her for the circumstances at hand; and he noticed that clients were coming to her more frequently now, too. He hoped that Halabant gave him at least a little credit for that too.

He was still aflame with yearning for her, of course – there was no reason for that to go away – but he tried to burn it off with heroic outpourings of energy in his role as her housekeeper. Before coming to Triggoin, Gannin Thidrich had bothered himself no more about household work than any normal bachelor did, doing simply enough to fend off utter squalor and not going beyond that, but he cared for her little flat as he had never cared for any dwelling of his own, polishing and dusting and sweeping and scrubbing, until the place took on an astonishing glow of charm and comfort. Even the sandroaches were intimidated by his work and fled to some other apartment. It was his goal to exhaust himself so thoroughly between the intensity of his studies and the intensity of his housework that he would have no shred of vitality left over for further lustful fantasies. This did not prove to be so. Often, curling up on his mat at night after a day of virtually unending toil, he would be assailed by dazzling visions of V. Halabant, entering his weary mind like an intruding incubus, capering wantonly in his throbbing brain, gesturing lewdly to him, beckoning, offering herself, and Gannin Thidrich would lie there sobbing, soaked in sweat, praying to every demon whose invocations he knew that he be spared such agonizing visitations.

The pain became so great that he thought of seeking another teacher. He thought occasionally of suicide, too, for he knew that this was the great love of his life, doomed never to be fulfilled, and that if he went away from Halabant he was destined to roam forever celibate through the vastness of the world, finding all other women unsatisfactory after her. Some segment of his mind recognized this to be puerile romantic nonsense, but he was not able to make that the dominant segment, and he began to fear that he might actually be capable of taking his own life in some feverish attack of nonsensical frustration.

The worst of it was that she had become intermittently quite friendly toward him by this time, giving him, intentionally or otherwise, encouragement that he had become too timid to accept as genuine. Perhaps his pathetic gesture of buying that love potion had touched something in her spirit. She smiled at him frequently now, even winked, or poked him playfully in the shoulder with a finger to underscore some point in her lesson. She was shockingly casual, sometimes, about how she dressed, often choosing revealingly flimsy gowns that drove him into paroxysms of throttled desire. And yet at other times she was as cold and aloof as she had been at the beginning, criticizing him cruelly when he bungled a spell or spilled an alembic, skewering him with icy glances when he said something that struck her as foolish, reminding him over and over that he was still just a blundering novice who had years to go before he attained anything like the threshold of mastery.

So there always were limits. He was her prisoner. She could touch him whenever she chose but he feared becoming a sandroach again should he touch her, even accidentally. She could smile and wink at him but he dared not do the same. In no way did she grant him any substantial status. When he asked her to instruct him in the great spell known as the Sublime Arcanum, which held the key to many gates, her reply was simply, "That is not something for fools to play with."

There was one truly miraculous day when, after he had recited an intricate series of spells with complete accuracy and had brought off one of the most difficult effects she had ever asked him to attempt, she seized him in a sudden joyful congratulatory embrace and levitated them both to the rafters of the study. There they hovered, face to face, bosom against bosom, her eyes flashing jubilantly before him. "That was wonderful!" she cried. "How marvelously you did that! How proud I am of you!"

This is it, he thought, the delirious moment of surrender at last, and slipped his hand between their bodies to clasp her firm round breast, and pressed his lips against hers and drove his tongue deep into her mouth. Instantly she voided the spell of levitation and sent him crashing miserably to the floor, where he landed in a crumpled heap with his left leg folded up beneath him in a way that sent the fiercest pain through his entire body.

She floated gently down beside him.

"You will always be an idiot," she said, and spat, and strode out of the room.

*

Gannin Thidrich was determined now to put an end to his life. He understood completely that to do such a thing would be a preposterous overreaction to his situation, but he was determined not to allow mere rationality to have a voice in the decision. His existence had become unbearable and he saw no other way of winning his freedom from this impossible woman.

He brooded for days about how to go about it, whether to swallow some potion from her storeroom or to split himself open with one of the kitchen knives or simply to fling himself from the study window, but all of these seemed disagreeable to him on the esthetic level and fraught with drawbacks besides. Mainly what troubled him was the possibility that he might not fully succeed in his aim with any of them, which seemed even worse than succeeding would be.

In the end he decided to cast himself into the dark, turbulent river that ran past the edge of West Triggoin on its northern flank. He had often explored it, now that winter was over, in the course of his afternoon walks. It was wide and probably fairly deep, its flow during this period of springtime spate was rapid, and an examination of a map revealed that it would carry his body northward and westward into the grim uninhabited lands that sloped toward the distant sea. Since he was unable to swim – one did not swim in the gigantic River Stee of his native city, whose swift current swept everything and everyone willy-nilly downstream along the mighty slopes of Castle Mount – Gannin Thidrich supposed that he would sink quickly and could expect a relatively painless death.

Just to be certain, he borrowed a rope from Halabant's storeroom to tie around his legs before he threw himself in. Slinging it over his shoulder, he set out along the footpath that bordered the river's course, searching for a likely place from which to jump. The day was warm, the air sweet, the new leaves yellowish-green on every tree, springtime at its finest: what better season for saying farewell to the world?

He came to an overlook where no one else seemed to be

around, knotted the rope about his ankles, and without a moment's pause for regret, sentimental thoughts, or final statements of any sort, hurled himself down headlong into the water.

It was colder than he expected it to be, even on this mild day. His plummeting body cut sharply below the surface, so that his mouth and nostrils filled with water and he felt himself in the imminent presence of death, but then the natural buoyancy of the body asserted itself and despite his wishes Gannin Thidrich turned upward again, breaching the surface, emerging into the air, spluttering and gagging. An instant later he heard a splashing sound close beside him and realized that someone else had jumped in, a would-be rescuer, perhaps.

"Lunatic! Moron! What do you think you're doing?"

He knew that voice, of course. Apparently V. Halabant had followed him as he made his doleful way along the riverbank and was determined not to let him die. That realization filled him with a confused mixture of ecstasy and fury.

She was bobbing beside him. She caught him by the shoulder, spun him around to face her. There was a kind of madness in her eyes, Gannin Thidrich thought. The woman leaned close and in a tone of voice that stung like vitriol she said, "*Iaho ariaha ... aho ariaha ... bakaksikhekh! Ianian! Thatlat! Hish!*"

Gannin Thidrich felt a sense of sudden forward movement and became aware that he was swimming, actually swimming, moving downstream with powerful strokes of his entire body. Of course that was impossible. Not only were his legs tied together, but he had no idea of how to swim. And yet he was definitely in motion: he could see the riverbank changing from moment to moment, the trees lining the footpath traveling upstream as he went the other way.

There was a river otter swimming beside him, a smooth sleek beautiful creature, graceful and sinuous and strong. It took Gannin Thidrich another moment to realize that the animal was V. Halabant, and that in fact he was an otter also, that she had worked a spell on them both when she had jumped in beside them, and had turned them into a pair of magnificent aquatic beasts. His legs were gone – he had only flippers down there now, culminating in small webbed feet – and gone too was the rope with which he had hobbled himself. And he could swim. He could swim like an otter.

Ask no questions, Gannin Thidrich told himself. Swim! Swim!

Side by side they swam for what must have been miles, spurting along splendidly on the breast of the current. He had never known such joy. As a human he would have drowned long ago, but as an otter he was a superb swimmer, tireless, wondrously strong. And with Halabant next to him he was willing to swim forever: to the sea itself, even. Head down, nose foremost, narrow body fully extended, he drilled his way through the water like some animate projectile. And the otter who had been V. Halabant kept pace with him as he moved along.

Time passed and he lost all sense of who or what he was, or where, or what he was doing. He even ceased to perceive the presence of his companion. His universe was only motion, constant forward motion. He was truly a river otter now, nothing but a river otter, joyously hurling himself through the cosmos.

But then his otter senses detected a sound to his left that no otter would be concerned with, and whatever was still human in him registered the fact that it was a cry of panic, a sharp little gasp of fear, coming from a member of his former species. He pivoted to look and saw that V. Halabant had reverted to human form and was thrashing about in what seemed to be the last stages of exhaustion. Her arms beat the air, her head tossed wildly, her eyes were rolled back in her head. She was trying to make her way to the riverbank, but she did not appear to have the strength to do it.

Gannin Thidrich understood that in his jubilant onward progress he had led her too far down the river, pulling her along beyond her endurance, that as an otter he was far stronger than she and by following him she had exceeded her otter abilities and could go no farther. Perhaps she was in danger of drowning, even. Could an otter drown? But she was no longer an otter. He knew that he had to get her ashore. He swam to her side and pushed futilely against her with his river-otter nose, trying in vain to clasp her with the tiny otter flippers that had replaced his arms. Her eyes fluttered open and she stared into his, and smiled, and spoke two words, the counterspell, and Gannin Thidrich discovered that he too was in human form again. They were both naked. He found that they were close enough now to the shore that his feet were able to touch the bottom. Slipping his arm around her, just below her breasts, he tugged her along, steadily, easily, toward the nearby riverbank. He scrambled ashore, pulling her with him, and they dropped down gasping for breath at the river's edge under the warm spring sunshine.

They were far out of town, he realized, all alone in the empty but not desolate countryside. The bank was soft with mosses. Gannin Thidrich recovered his breath almost at once; Halabant took longer, but before long she too was breathing normally. Her face was flushed and mottled with signs of strain, though, and she was biting down on her lip as though trying to hold something back, something which Gannin Thidrich understood, a moment later, to be tears. Abruptly she was furiously sobbing. He held her, tried to comfort her, but she shook him off. She would not or could not look at him.

"To be so weak—" she muttered. "I was going under. I almost drowned. And to have you see it – you – *you*—"

So she was angry with herself for having shown herself, at least in this, to be inferior to him. That was ridiculous, he thought. She might be a master sorcerer and he only a novice, yes, but he was a man, nevertheless, and she a woman, and men tended to be physically stronger than women, on the average, and probably that was true among otters too. If she had displayed weakness during their wild swim, it was a forgivable weakness, which only exacerbated his love for her. He murmured words of comfort to her, and was so bold to put his arm about her shoulders, and then, suddenly, astonishingly, everything changed, she pressed her bare body against him, she clung to him, she sought his lips with a hunger that was almost frightening, she opened her legs to him, she opened everything to him, she drew him down into her body and her soul.

Afterward, when it seemed appropriate to return to the city, it was necessary to call on her resources of sorcery once more. They both were naked, and many miles downstream from where they needed to be. She seemed not to want to risk returning to the otter form again, but there were other spells of transportation at her command, and she used one that brought them instantly back to West Triggoin, where their clothing and even the rope with which Gannin Thidrich had bound himself were lying in damp heaps near the place where he had thrown himself into the river. They dressed in silence and in silence they made their way, walking several feet apart, back to her flat.

He had no idea what would happen now. Already she appeared to be retreating behind that wall of untouchability that had surrounded her since the beginning. What had taken place between them on the riverbank was irreversible, but it would not transform their strange relationship unless she permitted it to, Gannin Thidrich knew, and he wondered whether she would. He did not intend to make any new aggressive moves without some sort of guidance from her.

And indeed it appeared that she intended to pretend that nothing had occurred at all, neither his absurd suicide attempt nor her foiling of it by following him to the river and turning them into otters nor the frenzied, frenetic, almost insane coupling that had been the unexpected climax of their long swim. All was back to normal between them as soon as they were at the flat: she was the master, he was the drudge, they slept in their separate rooms, and when during the following day's lessons he bungled a spell, as even now he still sometimes did, she berated him in the usual cruel, cutting way that was the verbal equivalent of transforming him once again into a sandroach. What, then, was he left with? The taste of her on his lips, the sound of her passionate outcries in his ears, the feel of the firm ripe swells of her breasts against the palms of his hands?

On occasions over the next few days, though, he caught sight of her studying him surreptitiously out of the corner of her eye, and he was the recipient of a few not so surreptitious smiles that struck him as having genuine warmth in them, and when he ventured a smile of his own in her direction it was met with another smile instead of a scowl. But he hesitated to try any sort of follow-up maneuver. Matters still struck him as too precariously balanced between them.

Then, a week later, during their morning lesson, she said briskly, "Take down these words: *Psakerba enphnoun orgogorgoniotrian phorbai*. Do you recognize them?"

"No," said Gannin Thidrich, baffled.

"They are the opening incantation of the spell known as the Sublime Arcanum," said Halabant.

A thrill rocketed down his spine. The Sublime Arcanum at last! So she had decided to trust him with the master spell, finally, the great opener of so many gates! She no longer thought of him as a fool who could not be permitted knowledge of it.

It was a good sign, he thought. Something was changing.

Perhaps she was still trying to pretend even now that none of it had ever happened, the event by the riverbank. But it had, it had, and it was having its effect on her, however hard she might be battling against it, and he knew now that he would go on searching, forever if necessary, for the key that would unlock her a second time.

5

Dark Times at the Midnight Market

Business was slow nowadays for the spellmongers of Bombifale's famed Midnight Market, and getting slower all the time. No one regretted that more than Ghambivole Zwoll, licensed dealer in potions and spells: a person of the Vroonish race, a small many-tentacled creature with a jutting beak and fiery yellow eyes, who represented the fourth generation of his line to hold the fifth stall in the leftmost rank of the back room of the Midnight Market of Bombifale.

Oh, the glorious times he could remember! The crowds of eager buyers for the wizardry he had for sale! The challenges triumphantly met, the wonders of conjuring that he had performed! In those great days of yore he had moved without fear through the strangest of realms, journeying among the cockatrices and gorgons, the flame-spitting basilisks and winged serpents, the universes beyond the universe, to bring back the secrets needed to meet the demands of his insatiable clients.

But now – but now – !

Popular interest in the various thaumaturgic arts, which had begun to sprout on Majipoor in the reign of the Coronal Lord Prankipin, had grown into a wild planetwide craze in the days of his glorious successor Lord Confalume. That king's personal dabblings in sorcery had done much to spur the mode for it. But it had been gradually waning during the reigns of the more skeptical monarchs who had followed him, Lord Prestimion and then Lord Dekkeret, and now, a century and more after

Dekkeret's time, sorcery had become a mere minor commodity, neither more nor less in demand than pepper, wine, dishware, or any other commonly used good. When one had need, one consulted the appropriate sort of wizard; but the era when a magus would be besieged by importunate patrons all through the hours of the clock was long over.

In those days the sorcerers' section of the market was open only on the first and third Seadays of the month, creating pent-up demand that helped to spur a sense of urgency among the purchasers. But for the past decade the wizards had of necessity kept their shops open night after night to make themselves readily available to such few customers as did appear, and even so their trade seemed to be waning steadily year after year.

Even a dozen years ago Ghambivole Zwoll had had more work than he could handle. But two years back he had been forced to take in a partner, Shostik-Willeron of the Su-Suheris race, and together they barely managed to eke out a modest living in this era of diminishing fascination with all forms of magecraft. Their coffers were dipping ever lower, their debts were mounting to an uncomfortable level, and they were near the point where they might have to discharge their one employee, the stolid, husky Skandar woman who swept and tidied for them every evening before the shop opened. So it was a matter of some excitement one night, three hours past midnight, when a tall, swaggering young man clad in the flamboyant garb of an aristocrat, close-fitting blue coat with ruffled sleeves trimmed with gold, flaring skirts, wide-brimmed hat trimmed with leather of some costly sort, came sweeping into their shop.

He was red-haired, blue-eyed, handsome, energetic. He had the look of wealth about him. But there was something else about him, or so it seemed to Ghambivole Zwoll, the smirking set of his mouth, the overly rakish slant of his hat, that cried, *scoundrel, wastrel, idler*.

No matter. Ghambivole Zwoll had dealt with plenty of those

in his time. So long as they paid their bills on time, Ghambivole Zwoll had no concern with his clients' moral failings.

The proud lordling struck a lofty pose, his hand resting on the gleaming hilt of the sword that hung from a broad beribboned baldrick at his side, and boomed, "I will have a love potion, if you please. To snare the heart of a lady of the highest birth! And I mean to spare no expense."

Ghambivole Zwoll masked his joy with a calm businesslike demeanor. He stared up – and up and up and up, for the new client was very tall indeed and Vroons are diminutive beings, knee-high at best to humans – and said judiciously, "Yes, yes, of course. We offer such compounds at every level of efficacy and potency." He reached for a writing tablet. "Your name, please?"

He expected some fanciful pseudonym. Instead his visitor said grandly, "I am the Marquis Mirl Meldelleran, fourth son of the third son of the Count of Canzilaine."

"Indeed," said Ghambivole Zwoll, a little stunned, for the Count of Canzilaine was one of the wealthiest and most influential men of Castle Mount. He looked across the room toward the towering figure of Shostik-Willeron, standing against the far wall. The Su-Suheris appeared to be displaying mixed emotions, his optimistic right-hand head glittering with pleasure at the prospect of a hefty fee but the left-hand head, which disliked such high-born fops as this, glowering in distaste. The Vroon shot him a quick bright-eyed glance to let him know that he would handle this client without interference. "I'll need to know the details of your requirements, of course."

"Details?"

"The goal you hope to achieve – whether it be only a seduction and light romance, or something deeper, leading, even, perhaps to a marriage. And some information about the lady's age and physical appearance, her approximate height and weight, you understand, so that we may calculate the proper dosage." He risked letting the intense blaze of his yellow eyes meet the blander gaze of the marquis. As tactfully as he could he said,

"You will, I hope, be forthcoming about these matters, or it may be difficult to fulfill your needs. She is young, I take it?"

"Of course. Eighteen."

"Ah. Eighteen." The Vroon delicately looked away. "And of limited sexual experience, perhaps? I have no wish to pry, you understand, but in order to calculate—"

"Yes," said the Marquis Mirl Meldelleran. "I hold nothing back from you. She is a virgin of the purest purity."

"Ah," said Ghambivole Zwoll.

"And moves in the highest circles at court. She is in fact the Lady Alesarda of Muldemar, of whose beauty and wit you undoubtedly have heard report."

That was jolting news. Ghambivole Zwoll fought to hide any show of the concern that that lady's name had awakened in him, but he was unable to fight back a complex, anguished writhing of his innumerable tentacles. "The Lady – Alesarda – of Muldemar," the Vroon said slowly. "Ah. Ah." His partner was glaring furiously at him now from his station in the corner shadows, the wary left-hand head glowering with wrath and even the normally cheerful right one showing alarm. "I have heard the name. She is, I believe, of royal lineage?"

"Sixth in descent from the Pontifex Prestimion himself."

"Ah. Ah. Ah." Ghambivole Zwoll saw that they were getting into exceedingly deep waters. He wished the marquis had kept the lady's identity to himself. But business was business, and the shop's exchequer was distressingly low. To mask his uncertainties he scribbled notes for quite some time; and then, looking up at last, said with a cheeriness he certainly did not feel, "We will have what you need in one week's time. The fee will be – ah—" Quickly, almost desperately, he reckoned the highest price he thought the traffic would bear, and then doubled it, expecting to be haggled with. "Twenty royals."

"Twenty," said the marquis impassively. "So be it."

Ghambivole wondered what the response would have been if he had said thirty. Or fifty. It had been so long since he had had a client of the marquis's station that he had forgotten that such people were utterly indifferent to cost. Well, too late now.

"Will a deposit of five cause any difficulties, do you think?'

"Hardly." Mirl Meldelleran drew a thick, glossy coin from his purse and dropped it on Ghambivole Zwoll's desk. The Vroon swept it quickly toward him with a trembling tentacle. "One week," said the Marquis Mirl Meldelleran. "The results, I assume, are guaranteed?"

"Of course," said Ghambivole Zwoll.

"This is madness," said Shostik-Willeron, the moment the door of the stall had closed behind the Marquis Mirl Meldelleran and they were alone again. "We will be ruined! A virgin princess of Prestimion's line, one who moves in the highest circles at court, and you propose to fling her into the bed of the fourth son of a third son?"

"Twenty royals," Ghambivole Zwoll said. "Do you know what our gross revenue for the past three months has been? Hardly one third as much. I expected him to bargain me down, and I would have settled for ten, or even five. Or three or two. But twenty – *twenty*!—"

"The risk is tremendous. The sellers of the potion will be traced."

"What of it? We are not the ones who will debauch the young princess."

"But it's an abomination, Ghambivole!" The words were coming from the right-hand head, and that gave Ghambivole Zwoll pause, for the right-hand head always brimmed with enthusiasm and exuberance, while it was the other, the dominant left head, that was ever urging caution. "We'll be whipped! We'll be flayed!"

"We are only purveyors, nothing more. We are protected by the mercantile laws. What we sell is legal, and what he plans to use it for is legal too, however deplorable. The girl is of age."

"So he says."

"If he's lied to me about it, the sin is his. Do you think I would dare to ask the grandson of the Count of Canzilaine for an affidavit?"

"But even so, Ghambivole—"

"Twenty royals, Shostik-Willeron."

They argued over it another fifteen minutes. But in the end the Vroon won, as he knew he would. He was the senior partner; this was his shop, and had been in his family four generations; and he was the only one of the two who had any real skill at wizardry. Shostik-Willeron's sole contribution to the partnership had been capital, not any great knowledge of the art; and if the shop failed, the Su-Suheris would lose that capital. They were in no position to turn away such lucrative business, chancy though it might be.

The partners were an oddly assorted pair. Like all the Su-Suheris race, Shostik-Willeron was tall and slender, with a pallid body tapering upward to a narrow forking neck a foot in length, atop which sprouted a pair of hairless, vastly elongated heads, each of which had an independent mind and identity. Ghambivole Zwoll could hardly have looked more different: a tiny person, barely reaching as high as his partner's shins, fragile and insubstantial of body, with a host of flexible rubbery limbs and a small head out of which jutted a sharp hook of a beak, above which were two huge yellow eyes with horizontal black strips to serve as pupils. There were times when the Vroon barely avoided being trampled by Shostik-Willerson as they moved about their cramped little emporium.

But Ghambivole Zwoll was accustomed to moving in a world of oversized creatures. Vroons were the dominant beings on their own home planet, but giant Majipoor was Ghambivole Zwoll's native world, his ancestors having arrived in the great wave of Vroon immigration during the reign of Lord Prankipin, and like all his kind he wove his way easily and lithely through throngs of heedless entities of much greater size than he, three and four and even five times his height, not only humans but also the reptilian Ghayrogs and the lofty Su-Suheris and the various other peoples of Majipoor, going on up to the gigantic shaggy four-armed Skandars, who stood eight feet tall and taller. Not even the presence of the ponderous slow-witted Skandar cleaning-woman, Hendaya Zanzan, who moved slowly and clumsily about the shop as she dusted and fussed with its displays, intimidated him with her dangerous bulk.

"A love potion," Ghambivole Zwoll said, setting about his task. "One that is suitable to win the heart of a highborn maiden, slender, delicate—"

The job called for no little forethought. At Ghambivole Zwoll's request, the Su-Suheris began taking books of reference down from the high shelves, the reliable old book of incantations that Ghambivole Zwoll had kept by his side since his student days in the sorcerers' city of Triggoin, and the ever-useful Great Grimoire of Hadin Vakkimorin, and Thalimiod Gur's Book of Specifics, and many another volume, more, in fact, than would possibly be needed. Ghambivole Zwoll suspected that he could compound the potion that the marquis had commissioned out of his own fund of accumulated skills, without recourse to any of these books. But he wanted to take no unnecessary risks; he had a whole week to complete what he could probably deal with in a morning; but any miscalculation due to overconfidence would surely have ugly consequences, and that stupefying fee of twenty royals more than amply compensated him for any unnecessary time that he expended on the task. It was not as though he had a great many other things to do this week, after all.

Besides, he loved to burrow in the great array of wizardly materials with which his forefathers had crammed the small shop. These two centuries of professional magicking had made the place a virtual museum of the magus's art. It was not an easy shop to find, tucked away as it was in a far back corner of the huge marketplace, but in happier days it had enjoyed great acclaim, and throngs of impatient clients had jostled elbow-to-elbow in the hall just outside, peering in at the racks of arcane powders and oils, bearing the awesome labels *Scamion* and *Thekka Ammoniaca* and *Elecamp* and *Golden Rue*, and the rows of leather-bound books of great antiquity, and the mysterious devices that sorcerers used, the ammatepilas and rohillas, the ambivials and verilistias, and much more apparatus of that sort, impressive to laymen and useful to practitioners. Even now, in this dreary materialistic era, the patrons of the Midnight Market who had come there to purchase such ordinary things as brooms and baskets, bangles and beads, spices, dried meats, cheese and wine and honey, often took the trouble to wend their way this deep into the building – for the Midnight Market was a huge subterranean vault, long and low, divided into a myriad narrow aisles, with the sorcerers' booths tucked away in the hindmost quarter – to stare through the dusty window of Ghambivole Zwoll's shop. That was all that most of them did, though: stare. The Marquis Mirl Meldelleran had been the first patron to step through the doorway in many days.

He drew the work out for nearly the full week, sequestered in the constricted little Vroon-sized laboratory behind the main showroom, jotting recipes, calculating quantities, measuring, weighing, mixing: the fine brandy of Gimkandale as a base, and then dried ghumba root, and a pinch of fermented hingamort, and some drops of tincture of vejloo, and just a bit of powdered sea-dragon hide, not strictly necessary, but always useful in speeding the effects of such potions. Allow it all to set a little while; then would come the heating, the cooling, the filtering, the titration, the spectral analysis. Meanwhile Shostik-Willeron remained out front, handling a surprising amount of walk-in trade, a Ghayrog who stopped by for a couple of amulets, two tourists from Ni-moya who came in out of nothing more than curiosity and stayed long enough to purchase a dozen of the black candles of divination, and a grain merchant from one of the downslope cities who sought a spell that would cast a blight on the fields of a supplier whom he had come to loathe. Three sales the same week, and also the potion for the marquis!

Ghambivole Zwoll allowed himself to think that perhaps a return to the prosperity of old might be in its early stages.

By the end of the week the job was done. There was one moment of near catastrophe on the evening when Ghambivole Zwoll arrived to begin his night's work and found the massive Skandar charwoman Hendaya Zanzan bashing around with her mop in his rear workroom, where he had left the vials of ingredients that would go into the marquis' potion sitting atop his desk in a carefully arranged row. In disbelief he watched the gigantic woman, who was far too large actually to enter the room, standing at the entrance to the room energetically swinging the mop from side to side and thereby placing everything within in great jeopardy.

"No!" he cried. "What are you doing, idiot? How many times have I told you – Stop! Stop!"

She halted and swung about uncertainly, looming above him like a mountain as she shifted the handle of the mop from one to another of her four arms. "But it has been so many weeks, master, since I last cleaned that room—"

"I've told you *never* to clean that room. Never! Never! And especially not now, when I have work in progress?"

"Never, master?"

"Oh, what a great stupid thing you are. Never: it means Not Ever. Not at any time. Keep your big idiotic mop out of there! Do you understand me, Hendaya Zanzan?"

It seemed to take her quite a while to process the instruction. She stood with all four burly arms drooping, the slow workings of her mind manifesting themselves meanwhile by a series of odd twitchings and clampings of her lips. Ghambivole Zwoll waited, struggling with his temper. He knew it did very little good to get angry with Hendaya Zanzan. The woman was a moron, a great furry clod of a moron, a dull-witted shaggy mass of a creature eight feet high and nearly as wide, hardly more than an animal. Not only stupid but ugly besides, even as Skandars went, flat-faced, empty-eyed, slack-jawed, covered from head to toe with a bestial coarse gray pelt that had the stale stink of some dead creature's hide left too long to fester in the sun. He had no idea why he had hired her – out of pity, probably – nor why he had kept her on so long. The shop did need to be cleaned once in a while, he supposed, but it had been madness to hire anyone as bulky as a Skandar to do the sweeping in such a small, cluttered space, and in any case Shostik-Willeron had little enough to occupy his time and could easily take care of the chore. But for the grace of the Marquis Mirl Meldelleran's twenty-royal job Ghambivole Zwoll would have let her go in another week or two. Now it seemed that he could afford to keep her on a little longer, and he would, for discharging her would be an unpleasant task and he tended to postpone all such things; but if business were to slacken once again—

"I am never to go into this little room," she said finally. "Is that so, master?"

"Very good, Hendaya Zanzan! Very good. Say it once again! Never. Never."

"Never to go into. The little room. Never."

"And never means – ?"

"Not ever?"

He didn't care for the interrogative tone of her reply; but he saw that it was the best he was going to get out of the poor thing, and, sending her on her way, he went into his workshop and closed the door behind him. It took him no more than an hour to complete the final titration for the marquis's potion. While he worked he heard the Su-Suheris moving about in the outer room, talking to someone, then pointlessly shifting furniture about, then whistling to himself in that maddening double-headed counterpoint his species so greatly cherished. What a useless fool the man was! Not a dolt like the Skandar woman, of course, but certainly he had little of the clear-eyed wisdom and cunning that the Su-Suheris, with the benefit of their double brain, were reputed to possess. Ghambivole Zwoll had badly needed an injection of fresh capital to meet the on-going expenses of his shop or he would never have taken him on as a partner, an act that unquestionably would have brought fiery condemnation upon him from his forebears. If only business would pick up a little, he would surely buy Shostik-Willeron out and return to running the place as a sole proprietorship. But he knew what a futile fantasy that was.

Scowling in annoyance, Ghambivole Zwoll poured his completed potion into an elegant flask worthy of the twenty-royal price, inscribed the accompanying spell on a sheet of vellum. On the appointed day the Marquis Mirl Meldelleran returned, clad even more grandly than before, high-waisted doublet of orange velvet, long-legged golden breeches bedecked with loops of braid and buttons, slender dress sword fastened to a wide silk sash tied in a huge bow. "Is this it?" he asked, holding the flask up to a glowglobe above his head and studying it intently.

"Be certain that you are the object of her gaze when she drinks it," said the Vroon. "And here," he said, handing him the vellum scroll, "are the words you must speak as she consumes the potion."

The marquis's brow furrowed. "*Sathis pephoouth mouraph anour*? What nonsense is this?"

"Not nonsense at all. It is a powerful spell. The meaning is, 'Let her be well disposed to me, let her fall in love with me, let her yield to me.' And the third word is pronounced *mouroph*; take care that you get it right, or the effect may be lost. Even worse: you may achieve the opposite of what you desire. Again: *Sathis pephoouth mouroph anour*."

"*Sathis pephoouth mouroph anour*."

"Excellent! But rehearse it many times before you approach her. She will fall helplessly into your arms. I guarantee it, your grace."

"Well, then. *Sathis pephoouth mouraph anour*."

"*Mouroph*, your grace."

"*Mouroph. Sathis pephoouth mouroph anour*."

"She is yours, your grace."

"Let us hope so. And this is yours." The marquis produced his bulging purse and casually tossed two coins, a fine fat ten-royal piece and a glossy fiver, onto Ghambivole Zwoll's desk. "Good day to you. And may the Divine protect you if you have played me false! *Sathis pephoouth mouraph anour. Mouroph. Mouroph.*' He spun neatly on his heel and was gone.

Three days passed quietly. Ghambivole Zwoll made two small sales, one for one crown fifty weights, one for slightly less. Otherwise the shop did no business. Creditors devoured most of the Marquis Mirl Meldelleran's twenty royals almost at once. The Vroon returned to the state of gloom that had occupied him before the arrival of his aristocratic client.

On the second of those three evenings Shostik-Willeron was late coming to the shop; and when he did both his long pallid faces were tightly drawn in the Su-Suheris expression of uneasiness verging on despair.

"I warned you we were making a great mistake," he said at once. "And now I'm sure of it!" It was the right-hand head that spoke: the cheerful, optimistic one, usually.

Ghambivole Zwoll sighed. "What now, Shostik-Willeron?"

"I have been speaking with my kinsman Sagamorn-Endik, who is in service at the Castle. Do you know that the Lady Alesarda of Muldemar, whom you have delivered so blithely into the clutches of that ridiculous dandy with your drug, is spoken of widely at court as the promised bride of the Coronal's son? That by interfering in those nuptials, by despoiling this precious princess, your marquis runs perilously close to treason? And you and I, as abettors of his crime—"

"It is no crime."

"To sleep with a simple scullery maid or some illiterate juggler girl, no. But for the fourth son of the third son of a provincial count to seduce a noblewoman destined for a royal marriage, to interpose his sweaty lusts in such high and delicate negotiations, or simply to be the ones who enable him to carry out such a thing, to be the agents who help him to have his way with her – oh, Ghambivole Zwoll, Ghambivole Zwoll, let us hope that that little potion of yours was a worthless draught! Otherwise your marquis is destroyed, and we are destroyed with him."

"If the potion worked," said the Vroon in the calmest tone he was capable of mustering, "there is no certainty that what took place between the marquis and the princess will become known to anyone else. And if it does, the marquis will have to look to the consequences of his deed on his own. We are mere merchants, protected by law. But if the potion has failed – and how can it have failed, unless he blundered with the spell? – we owe him twenty royals, to fulfill my guarantee. Where will we get twenty royals, Shostik-Willeron? Conjure them out of the air? Look here." He opened the cash drawer of his desk. "This is what's left of it. Three royals, two crowns, and sixty – no, seventy weights. The rest is gone. Let us pray that the potion has done its work, for our own sakes, if nothing else."

"A princess of Muldemar – a descendant of the great Prestimion – a beautiful lass, innocent, pure, betrothed to the son of the Coronal—"

"Stop it, Shostik-Willeron. For all we know, she's no more innocent and pure than that ox of a Skandar who works for us, and everybody at the Castle from the Coronal on down knows it and doesn't care. And even if this tale of royal betrothals should be true – but do we know that it is? Only this kinsman of yours says so – we are in no danger ourselves. We are here to serve the public by making use of our skills, and so we have. We bear no responsibility for our client's interference in other people's arrangements. In any case, this blubbering of yours achieves nothing. What's done is done." Ghambivole Zwoll made shooing gestures with his outermost ring of tentacles. "Go. Go. If you keep this up you will jangle my nerves tonight to no useful purpose."

The Vroon's nerves were indeed already thoroughly jangled,

however much he tried to put a good face on the matter. He wished most profoundly that Mirl Meldelleran had never shared with him the identity of his inamorata. It would have been sufficient to know her age, her approximate height and weight, and, perhaps, some inkling of her degree of experience in the wars of love. But no, no, the braggart Mirl Meldelleran had had to go and name her, besides; and if this rumor of a royal marriage truly had any substance to it, and the marquis's seduction of the princess caused any disruption of that marriage, and the tale of how the marquis had managed to achieve his triumph came out, Shostik-Willeron quite possibly was correct: the magus who had compounded the dastardly potion might very well be made a scapegoat in the hubbub that ensued. Ghambivole Zwoll felt sure that the law would be on his side in any action against him, but a lawyer's fee for defending him against an outraged Prince of Muldemar or, even worse, the Coronal's son would be something more than trifling pocket-change, and he was on the verge of bankruptcy as it was.

Still, there was nothing he could do about any of this now. The potion had been made and delivered and, in all likelihood, used, and, as he had said, whatever had happened after that had happened, and he could only wait and see what consequences befell. He mixed himself a mild calming elixir, and after a time it took effect, and he went about his business without giving the matter further thought.

The next evening, half an hour or so before the official opening time of the Midnight Market, Ghambivole Zwoll was moodily going over his accounts when he heard a disturbance in the hall outside, shouting and clatter, and then came the hammering of a fist on the door of his shop; and, looking up, he beheld the gaudy figure of the Marquis Mirl Meldelleran gesturing at him through the time-dimmed glass.

The marquis looked furious, and he was brandishing his bared sword in his right hand, swishing it angrily back and forth. Ghambivole Zwoll had never seen anyone brandishing a drawn sword before, let alone one that was being waved threateningly in front of his own beak. It was a dress sword, ornate and absurd, intended only an ornamental appurtenance – the fad for swordplay in daily life had long ago ended on Majipoor – but its edge looked quite keen, all the same, and Ghambivole Zwoll had no doubt of the damage it could work on the frail tissues of his small body.

He was alone in the shop. The Skandar woman had already finished her nightly chores and gone, and Shostik-Willeron had not yet arrived. What to do? Darken the room, hide under the desk? No. The marquis had already seen him. He would only smash his way in. That would entail even more expense.

"We are not yet open for business, your grace," said the Vroon through the closed door.

"I know that. I have no time to wait! Let me in."

Sadly Ghambivole Zwoll said, "As you wish, sir."

The Marquis Mirl Meldelleran strode into the shop and took up a stance just inside the door. Everything about him radiated anger, anger, anger. The Vroon looked upward at the figure that rose high above him and made a mild gesture to indicate that he found the bared sword disconcerting.

"The potion," he said mildly. "It was satisfactory, I trust?"

"Up to a point, yes. But only up to a point."

The tale came spilling out quickly enough. The lady had trustingly sipped the drink the marquis had put before her, and the marquis had managed even to recite the spell in proper fashion, and the potion had performed its function most admirably: the Lady Alesarda had instantly fallen into a heated passion, the Marquis Mirl Meldelleran had swept her off to bed, and they had passed such a night together as the marquis had never imagined in his most torrid dreams.

Ghambivole Zwoll sensed that there had to be more to the story than that, and indeed there was; for the next night the marquis had returned to Muldemar House, anticipating a renewal of the erotic joys so gloriously inaugurated the night before, only to find himself abruptly, coolly dismissed. The Lady Alesarda had no wish to see him again, not this evening, not the next evening, not any evening at all between now and the end of the universe. The Lady Alesarda requested, via an intermediary, that the Marquis Mirl Meldelleran never so much as look in her direction, should they find themselves ever again in the same social gathering, which was, unfortunately for her, all too likely, considering that they both moved in the same lofty circles among the younger nobility of Castle Mount.

"It was," said the marquis, smouldering with barely suppressed rage, "the most humiliating experience of my life!"

Ghambivole Zwoll said mildly, "But you came to me seeking, so you said, a night of pleasure with the woman you most desired in all the world. By your own account, my skills have provided you with exactly that."

"I sought a continuing relationship. I certainly didn't seek to be spurned after a single night. What am I to think: that when she looked back on our night together, she thought of my embrace as something vile, something loathsome, something that had left her with nothing but black memories that she longed to purge from her mind?"

"I have heard tell that the lady is betrothed to a great prince of Castle Mount," said the Vroon. "Can it be that when she returned to her proper senses she was smitten by a sense of obligation to her prince? By guilt, by shame, by terrible remorse?"

"I had hoped that her night with me would leave her with no further interest in that other person."

"As well you might, your grace. But the potion was specifically designed to obtain her surrender on that one occasion when it was administered, and so it did. It would not necessarily have a lingering effect after it had left her body."

As he spoke the door opened behind the marquis and Shostik-Willeron, arriving for the night, stepped into the shop. The eyes of the Su-Suheris flickered quickly from Ghambivole Zwoll to the Marquis Mirl Meldelleran to the marquis's unsheathed sword, and a look of terrible dismay crossed his faces. The Vroon signalled to him to be still.

"Literature is full of examples of similar cases," Ghambivole Zwoll said. "The tale of Lisinamond and Prince Ghorn, for example, in which the prince, after at long last consummating the great desire of his life, discovers that she—"

"Spare me the poetic quotations," the marquis said. "I don't regard a single night's success, followed by icy repudiation the next day, as in any way a fulfillment of your guarantee. I require fuller satisfaction."

Satisfaction? What did he mean by that? A duel, perhaps? Ghambivole Zwoll, appalled, did not immediately reply. In that moment of silence Shostik-Willeron stepped forward. "If you will pardon me, your grace," said the Su-Suheris, "I must point out to you that my partner did not stipulate anything more than the assurance that the potion would secure you the lady's favors, and it does appear that this was—"

The Marquis Mirl Meldelleran whirled to face him and flicked his sword savagely through the air from side to side before him. "Be quiet, monster, or I'll cut off your head. Just *one* of them, you understand. As a special favor I'll allow you the choice of which it is to be."

Shostik-Willeron moved into the shadows and said nothing further.

The marquis went on, "To continue: I regard the terms of our agreement as having been breached."

"A refund, milord, would be very difficult for us to—"

"I'm not interested in a refund. Make me a second potion. A stronger one, much stronger, one that will obliterate all other affections from her mind and bind her to me forever. You make it and I'll find some way to get it to her and all will be well, and my account with you will be quits. What do you say, wizard? Can you do that?"

The Vroon pondered the question a moment. Shostik-Willeron was right, he knew: Shostik-Willeron had been right all along. They never should have had anything to do with this grimy business. And they should refuse now to continue with it. Like all his kind, he had some slight power of foretelling the future, and the images that came to him by way of such second sight were not encouraging ones. Whether or not the law was on their side, the great lords of Castle Mount certainly were unlikely to be, and if this slippery marquis continued his pursuit of the Lady Alesandra he would sooner or later bring down the vengeance of those mighty ones not only upon him but upon those who had aided and abetted him in his quest.

On the other hand, that consideration was a relatively abstract one, at least when compared with the sharp and gleaming reality of the sword in the Marquis Mirl Meldelleran's hand. The great lords of Castle Mount were far away; the sword of the marquis was right here and very close. That alone was incentive enough for the Vroon to plunge ahead with this new task that the marquis required of him, regardless of the obvious riskiness of it.

The hard blue eyes were bright with menace. "Well, little magus? Will you do it or won't you?"

In a low, weak voice the Vroon said, "I suppose so, your grace."

"Good. How soon?"

Again Ghambivole Zwoll hesitated. "Eight days? Perhaps nine? The task will not be an easy one, and I realize that you will accept nothing less than complete success. I'll need to consult many sources. And beyond doubt a great many rare ingredients must be obtained, which will take some little while."

"Eight days," said the Marquis Mirl Meldelleran. "Not an hour more."

Compounding such a powerful potion, far more intense than the one he had given the marquis, would be perfectly feasible, of course. It was years since he had made such a thing, but he had not forgotten the art of it. It would call for the utmost in technical skill, Ghambivole Zwoll knew, and would require, just as he had asserted, some rare and costly ingredients: they would have to go back to the moneylenders once again to cover the expense.

But he had no choice. Doubtless Shostik-Willeron was right that there was great peril in meddling in the romantic affairs of the aristocracy; the marriage of a Coronal's son to a princess of Muldemar must surely be a matter not just of romance but of high political intrigue, and woe betide anyone who sought to undo such a match for his own sordid purposes. Still, Ghambivole Zwoll wanted to believe, even now, that whatever consequences might befall such meddling would fall upon the Marquis Mirl Meldelleran, not on the lowly proprietors of some unimportant sorcerers' shop in the Midnight Market. The real peril he and Shostik-Willeron faced, he told himself again and again, was not from so remote a thing as the displeasure of the great lords of the Castle, but rather from the uncontrolled anger of the rash, reckless, and frustrated marquis.

Gloomily Shostik-Willeron concurred in this reasoning. And so they floated a new loan, which left them almost as deep in debt as they had been before the marquis and his twenty-royal commission had come to plague their lives. Ghambivole Zwoll sent orders far and wide to suppliers of precious herbs and elixirs and powders, the bone of this creature and the blood of that one, the sap of this tree, the seed of another, potations of a dozen sort, galliuc and ravenswort, spider lettuce and bloodleaf, wolf-parsley and viperbane and black fennel, and waited, fidgeting, until they began to arrive, and began, once the proper ingredients for the basis of the drug were in his hands, to mix and measure and weigh and test. He doubted very much that he would have the stuff ready by the eighth day, and in truth he had never regarded that as a realistic goal; but the marquis had insisted. The Vroon hoped that when the marquis did return on the eighth day and found the potion still incomplete, he would see that the magus was toiling in good faith and did indeed hope to have the job done in another day or two, or three, and would be patient until then.

The eighth day came and midnight tolled, and the market was thrown open for business. As Ghambivole Zwoll had expected, the drug was not quite ready. But, to his surprise, the Marquis Mirl Meldelleran did not appear to claim it. He was hardly likely to have forgotten; but something pressing must have cropped up to keep him from making the short journey downslope to Bombifale to pick up his merchandise tonight. Just as well, the Vroon thought.

Nor did the marquis show up on the ninth night either, though Ghambivole Zwoll had brought the stuff to the verge of completion by then. The following afternoon, by dint of having worked all through a difficult sleepless day, the Vroon tipped a few drops of the final reagent into the flask, saw the mixture turn to a rewarding amber hue shimmering with highlights of scarlet and green, and knew that the job was finished. If the marquis came here at last this evening to claim his potion, Ghambivole Zwoll would be ready to make delivery. And the marquis would have no complaints this time. The new potion did not even require the recitation of a spell, so powerful was its effect. So the poor highborn simpleton would be spared the effort of memorizing five or six strange words. Ghambivole Zwoll hoped he would be grateful for that.

With midnight still a few hours away, the market had not yet opened for business. Ghambivole Zwoll waited, alone in the shop, tense, eager to have this hazardous transaction done with at last.

A little while later he heard the sounds of some commotion in the hall: an outcry from the warders, someone's angry response, a further protest from one of the warders. In all likelihood, the Vroon thought, the Marquis Mirl Meldelleran had finally come, and in his usual blustering way was trying to force his way into the market before regular hours.

But the noise outside was none of the marquis's doing this time. Abruptly the door of Ghambivole Zwoll's shop burst open and two sturdy-looking men in fine velvet livery brightly emblazoned across the left shoulder with the image of the Muldemar Ruby, the huge red stone that was the well-known emblem of that great princely house, came thundering in. They were armed with formidable swords: no foppish dress swords these, but great gleaming grim-looking military sabers.

Ghambivole Zwoll understood at once what must have happened. Some Muldemar House maid had confessed, or had been made to confess, that her lady had had an illicit nocturnal visitation. One question had led to another, the whole story had come out, the identity of the sorcerer in question had somehow been revealed, and now these thugs had come on their princely master's behalf to take revenge.

The way they were glaring at him seemed to leave no doubt of that. But from the manner in which they held themselves, not merely threatening but at the same time wary, ill at ease, it appeared likely that they feared he would use some dark mantic power against them. As if he could! He cursed them for their stupidity, their great useless height and bulk, their mere presence in his shop. What madness it had been, Ghambivole Zwoll thought, for his forebears to have settled on this world of oafish oversized clods!

"Are you the magus Ghambivole Zwoll?" the bigger of the two demanded, in a voice like rolling boulders. And he slid his great sword a short way into view.

Ghambivole Zwoll, swept now with a terror greater than any he had ever known in his life, shrank back against his desk. If only he could have used some magical power to thrust them out the door, he would have done so. If only. But his powers were gentle ones and these two were huge bulky ruffians, and he did not dare make even the slightest move.

"I am," he murmured, and did what he could to prepare himself for death.

"The Prince of Muldemar will speak with you," the big man said ominously.

The Prince of Muldemar? Here in the marketplace, in

Ghambivole Zwoll's own shop? The fifth or sixth highest noble of the realm?

Incredible. Unthinkable. The man might just as well have said, *The Coronal is here to see you. The Pontifex. The Lady of the Isle.*

The two huge footmen stepped aside. Into the shop came now a golden-haired man of fifty or so, short of stature and slender but broad-shouldered and regal of bearing. His lips were thin and tightly compressed, his face was narrow. It could almost have been the face Ghambivole Zwoll had often seen on coins of long ago, the face of this prince's royal ancestor five generations removed, the great monarch Prestimion.

There was no mistaking the searing anger in the prince's keen, intense greenish-blue eyes.

"You have supplied a potion to a certain unimportant lordling of Castle Mount," the prince said.

Not a question. A statement of fact.

Ghambivole Zwoll's vision wavered. His tentacles trembled.

"I am licensed, sir, to provide my services to the public as they may be required."

"Within discretion. Are you aware that you went far beyond the bounds of discretion?"

"I was asked to fulfill a need. The Marquis Mirl Meldelleran requested—"

"You will not name him. Speak of him only as your client. You should know that your client, who committed a foul act with the aid of your skills, has taken himself at our request this very day into exile in Suvrael."

Ghambivole Zwoll shivered. Suvrael? That terrible place, the sun-blasted, demon-haunted desert continent far to the south? Death would be a more desirable punishment than exile to Suvrael.

In a hoarse croak Ghambivole Zwoll said, "My client asked me to fulfill a need, your grace. I did not think it was my responsibility to—"

"You did not think. You did not think."

"No, your grace. I did not think."

There was no possibility of success in disputing the matter with the Prince of Muldemar. Ghambivole Zwoll bowed his head and waited to hear his sentence.

The Prince said sternly, "You will forget that you ever had dealings with that client. You will forget his very name. You will forget the purpose for which he came to you. You will forget everything connected with him and with the task you carried out on his behalf. Your client has ceased to exist on Castle Mount. If you keep records, Vroon, you will expunge from them all indication of the so-called service you performed for him. Is that understood?"

Seeing that he evidently was going to be allowed to live, Ghambivole Zwoll bowed his head and said in a husky whisper, "I understand and obey, your grace."

"Good."

Was that all? So it seemed. The Vroon gave inward thanks to the half-forgotten gods of his forefathers' ancestral world.

But then the prince, turning, took a long glance around the cluttered shop. His gaze came to rest on the handsome flask on Ghambivole Zwoll's desk, the flask containing the new and potent elixir that the Vroon had prepared for the Marquis Mirl Meldelleran.

"What is that?"

"A potion, your grace."

"Another love potion, is it?"

"Merely a potion, sir." Then, in agony, when the prince gave him a terrible glare: "Yes. One could call it a love potion,"

"For the same client as before? So that he might compound the damage he has already done?"

"I must reply that I am bound by the laws of confidentiality, sir, not to reveal—"

The Prince of Muldemar responded with a somber laugh. "Yes. Yes! Of course. What a law-abiding thing you are, wizard!

Very well. Pick up the flask and drink the stuff yourself."

"Sir?"

"Drink it!"

Aghast, Ghambivole Zwoll cried, "Sir, I must object!"

The prince nodded to one of the footmen. From the corner of his eye Ghambivole Zwoll saw the ugly glint of a saber's blade coming once more into view.

"Sir?" he murmured. "Sir?"

"Drink it, or you'll join your former client in Suvrael, and you'll count yourself lucky that your fate is no worse."

"Yes. Yes. I understand and obey."

There could be no refusing the prince's command. Ghambivole Zwoll reached for the flask and shakily lifted it to his beak.

Dimly the Vroon watched the Prince of Muldemar and his two footmen leaving the shop, a moment later, slamming the door behind them. It was all he could do to cling to consciousness. His head was whirling. A bright crimson haze whirled about him. He was scarcely able to think coherently.

Then through the fog that engulfed his brain he saw the shop door open again, and the huge Skandar woman Hendaya Zanzan entered to begin her evening's work of tidying and sweeping. Ghambivole Zwoll stared at her in awe and wonder. Instantly a sudden all-consuming passion overwhelmed him. She was radiant; she was glorious; she glowed before him like a dazzling flame. He had never seen anyone more beautiful.

He ran to her, reached up, clasped his tentacles tightly around her enormous calf. His heart pounded with a great surge of desperate love. His vision blurred as tears of joy dimmed his blazing yellow eyes.

"Oh, beloved – beloved – !"

6

The Way They Wove the Spells in Sippulgar

I had always yearned to visit Sippulgar, that golden city of the southern coast. Every schoolchild hears tales of its extraordinary beauty. But there are many places on Majipoor I yearn to visit – the Fifty Cities of Castle Mount, or at least a few of them, and marvelous Dulorn, the shining city of crystalline stone that the Ghayrog folk built in far-off Zimroel, and mighty Ni-moya on that same distant continent, and many another. Our world is a huge one, though, and life is short. I am a man of business, an expediter of merchandise, and business has kept me close to my native city of Sisivondal for most of my days.

It was the strange disappearance and presumed death of Melifont Ambithorn, my wife Thuwayne's elder brother, that finally brought me to Sippulgar. I had hardly known Melifont at all, you understand: I had met him just twice, once at my wedding and once perhaps ten years later, when one of his many unsuccessful business ventures brought him to Sisivondal for a few days. He was fifteen years older than my wife and she seemed to regard him more as an uncle than as a brother; but when word came to her that he was thought to have perished in some mysterious and unpleasant way, she was deeply affected, far more than I would have thought, asking me to go at once to Sippulgar to see if I could discover what had happened to him, and to lay a memorial wreath on his grave, if he was indeed dead. Thuwayne herself is no traveler; she dislikes the upheavals and discomforts of even the shortest trip most intensely. But she could not bear to leave her brother's death a mystery, and I think she entertained some hope that I would actually find him still alive. She begged me to go, and I knew that I had no choice but to do it.

For all my fascination with the fabled marvels of Sippulgar, it was not an especially good time for me to be setting out on such a long excursion. Sisivondal is the chief mercantile center of western Alhanroel, where all roads that cross the heart of the continent meet, and we were coming now into the busiest season of the year, when caravans travel from all directions to unload their goods into our warehouses and to buy merchandise for their return journeys. But I will refuse Thuwayne nothing. I cherish her beyond all measure. And so, after just a few mild expressions of uneasiness about undertaking such a venture at this time of year, I put my business affairs into the hands of my most trusted assistant and made my arrangements for my visit to Sippulgar. This was in the time of Lord Confalume, who was then about thirty years into his long and glorious reign as Coronal. Prankipin was our Pontifex. In those days, you know, we enjoyed a time of great prosperity; and also it was the period when all sorts of esoteric new philosophies – sorcery, necromancy, prognostication, the worship of supernatural spirits of every kind, the opening of doors into hidden universes populated by gods and demons – were taking hold on Majipoor.

Thuwayne had been informed that her brother had begun dabbling in certain of those philosophies, and possibly had met his death as a result. I am a man of business, a practical man, concerned with shipping costs and bills of lading, not with the propitiation of demons, and I regard all these new philosophies essentially as lunacy. A few little protective amulets and talismans suffice for me, purely on the off chance that they might do some good; I go no farther into any of this occult stuff. Sippulgar was known to be a spawning-ground for the new cults, and that made me apprehensive. But, as I say, I will refuse Thuwayne nothing.

She asked me to go to Sippulgar to investigate her brother's disappearance and probable death; and so to Sippulgar I went.

Cities are far apart on Majipoor and the road from anywhere to anywhere is usually a long one; but Sippulgar is a port city on the southern sea, and Sisivondal is a heartland city set in the midst of a bare featureless plain some thousands of miles across, far to the north, and so I found myself embarking on what I knew would be the great journey of my lifetime.

Plotting my route was easy. A dozen great highways meet in Sisivondal, intersecting like the spokes of a giant wheel: one coming in from the great port of Alaisor in the west, five going eastward toward Castle Mount, three descending from the north, and three connecting us with the south. Sisivondal's boulevards and avenues are laid out in concentric circles that allow easy connection from one highway to another. All along the streets that run between the circular avenues are rows of warehouses where goods destined for transshipment to other zones of the continent are stored. The group of warehouses I control is close by the Great Southern Highway, the one which would carry me toward my goal, and so, after issuing a last set of instructions to my staff, I set out from there early one morning on my journey toward the sea.

Sisivondal has been called "a thousand miles of outskirts." That is unkind, but I suppose it is true. The central sector is devoted entirely to commerce, many miles of warehouses and not much else; then one passes through the suburban residential district, and beyond that lies a zone of customs sheds and repair shops, gradually trickling off into the parched treeless plain beyond. Our climate is an extremely dry one and our only vegetation is of necessity sturdy: huge lumma-lummas that look like big gray rocks, and prickly garavedas that take a whole century to bring forth their black flower-spikes, and purple-leaved camaganda palms that can go years without a drop of water. Beyond town there is no vegetation at all, only a barren, dusty plain. Not a pretty place, I suppose, but essential to the economy of our continent; and in any case I am used to it.

Gradually, as I left central Alhanroel behind, the world grew more gracious. I spent a day or two in lovely Bailemoona, which I had visited years before, a city famous for its subtle cuisine and its swarms of shining bees, large as small birds and nearly as intelligent. There I hired a carriage to take me southward through the Sulfur Desert, that region of surpassing yellowness, where amidst fantastic eroded spires of soft cream-colored stone the bizarre city of Ketheron was set, a place of twisted yellow towers that could have been the pointed caps of witches. I had been there once before too. Beyond, though, everything was new to me. The air very shortly took on a tropic moistness, becoming soft as velvet, and rain-showers fell frequently. Our caravan rode past the Cliff of Eyes, a white mountain pockmarked with hundreds of dark shining boulders that stared down at us like disapproving orbs, and then we were at the Pillars of Dvorn, two sharp-tipped blue-gray rocks set athwart the highway to mark the boundary between central and southern Alhanroel. On the far side lay Arvyanda of the golden hills: here the slopes were covered by stubby trees whose stiff oval leaves had a metallic texture and yielded a brilliant glint in the strong tropical sunlight. Already I felt very far from Sisivondal, almost on another world entirely.

Gradually the sky grew dark with a thick cover of clouds. We were coming into the jungles of Kajith Kajulon, a green empire where rain falls constantly, more rain in a week than I had seen in the past ten years, and the trunks of the trees were bright with the red and yellow splashes of enormous fungi. There was no end to the rain, nor to the clouds of insects that swarmed around us, and we were besieged by armies of scarlet lizards and loud flat-headed toads. Long chains of blue spiders hung down from every branch, eyeing us in a sinister way. We rode through Kajith Kajulon for many days. I thought my bones would melt in the humid air.

But at last we left that dense forest and emerged into the coastal province of Aruachosia, of which Sippulgar is the capital. Now we were just a few hundred miles from the sea, and the air, though warm and moist and heavy, was tempered by salty breezes out of the south. Just ahead lay the breathtaking wonder that is Sippulgar.

Everyone always calls it *golden* Sippulgar. Now I saw why. Its buildings, which are no more than two and three stories high, are made from a golden sandstone, flecked with bits of mica, that gleams with a dazzling brightness when the sun comes up out of the southern sea. I was amazed by the intensity of that brightness, and by the lushness of the decorative plantings that lined the streets: a hundred different kinds of tropical shrubs, all of them unknown to me, whose blossoms blazed forth in orange and green and scarlet and blue and gold, with darker ones in maroon and even jet-black interspersed among them for contrast. They exuded such a wealth of fragrance that the air itself seemed perfumed. Small wonder this district is known as the Incense Coast. I could not tell one plant from another, but I knew from a lifetime spent among bills of lading and customs forms that the region around Sippulgar was rich in cinnamon and khazil, the balsam called hinnam, thanibong trees and scarlet fhiiis, and many another scented plant, from which were produced a host of aromatic oils and gums.

I had booked a room in a hotel close to the city center, so that it would be easy for me to consult the official documents and records I needed in my quest. It was situated just a couple of blocks from the waterfront; and on my way there it was my bad luck to become entangled in a religious procession, of a sort that I soon learned was ubiquitous here. And so I stood for an hour and a half waiting amidst my baggage before I was able to cross the street and continue on to my lodgings.

Even in this era of multitudinous cults and sorceries, Sippulgar stands out for its abundance of strange creeds. Perhaps it is the heavy tropical air that spawns such credulity. At home in

Sisivondal only one of these superstitions holds sway, the cult of the Beholders. All too frequently I have seen its worshippers dancing ecstatically down Grand Alaisor Avenue, strewing costly imported flower-petals everywhere and blowing on pipes and flutes as the grotesque statuettes that are their seven sacred artifacts are carried on high, preceding the great box that they call the Ark of the Mysteries and the ebony cart that carries their high priest, who wears a mask with the visage of a terrifying yellow-eyed hound. What it is that the Beholders seek, and what they find, I will never know; but at least we have only that one cult to interrupt the smooth flow of commerce with its antics. In Sippulgar, I soon would learn, there were dozens.

From a distance I heard the shrill shriek of bellhorns, the crashing of cymbals, the tremendous uproar of a platoon of kettle-drums. When I drew nearer I saw my route blocked by a horde of marchers wearing nothing but loincloths and sandals, striding along with their heads upraised to the sky. There seemed to be millions of them. The people of Sippulgar are dark-skinned, mostly, no doubt some adaptation to the intense sunlight, but the sweat-shiny bodies of the marchers were streaked with bright splotches of red and green and purple that echoed the gaudiness of the shrubs in bloom all about them. There was no hope of crossing the street. I stood and waited. Eventually a group of weeping, chanting worshippers came down the boulevard pulling a massive platform on which stood the wooden image of a winged serpent that had the frightening toothy-snouted blazing-eyed face of a jakkabole, that ravenous, angry beast of the eastern highlands. I turned to the man who stood beside me. "I am a stranger here," I said. "What god is that they worship?"

"It is Time," he told me. "The devourer of all."

Yes. The winged serpent that flies ever onward, jaws agape, engulfing everything in its path, as even the maddened jakkaboles do when they descend on the farms of the Vrambikat Valley in their ravening hunger. I watched the good folk of

Sippulgar, lost in their madness, march on and on and on until at last the boulevard was clear, and I went across to my hotel and sank down gratefully on the softest of beds.

What I knew about my brother-in-law Melifont's life, and of his supposed fate, was this:

He was one of those unhappy men fated to fail at every enterprise he turned his hand to, despite the advantages of intelligence, zeal, and energy. At an early age he had left Sisivondal for the southlands to seek his fortune. He involved himself first in a mining project in the lava country back of the port of Glystrintal, where since time immemorial bold fools had sought for rumored mines of silver and gold. Melifont found neither silver nor gold, and when he moved on to search for the equally fabulous iron mines of Skakkenoir of the red soil, he returned so damaged from his adventures that his recovery took over a year. Hoping then for a quieter life, he settled next on the Stoienzar Peninsula, where he worked for a time as a tavernkeeper but appears also to have helped to found a bank that prospered greatly for a time, though ultimately it came to grief in a spectacular way. It was during his period of prosperity that I married his younger sister, and he returned to Sisivondal for the first time in many years to attend the ceremony. He was then about forty, a tall, handsome man with a florid face and sleek black hair, who limped a little, a souvenir of his mining project in Skakkenoir. I found him charming – magnetic, even – and Thuwayne, who had not seen her swaggering brother since she was a little girl, looked at him constantly in wonder and fascination. He presented us with a wedding gift of surprising generosity, which I put to good use in the expansion of my warehousing business.

Next we heard of him, his bank had failed – the malfeasance of a conniving partner, we were told – and he was off to Zimroel to sell rope to the Shapeshifters, or some such thing. Very little news travels from remotest Zimroel to our part of the world, and I have no idea how Melifont occupied himself for the decade that followed; but then he turned up in Sisivondal once again, looking very much older, his hair now gray and sparse, his limp more pronounced, but he was still charismatic, still full of ambition and optimism. His new endeavor was a shipping company that proposed to run a ferry service across the Inner Sea between Piliplok in Zimroel and the port of Tolaghai in our sun-blasted southern continent of Suvrael. I thought it was a crazy idea myself – Suvrael is a terrible place, and produces almost nothing useful – but in my relief at not being asked to finance his company out of my own pocket I gladly introduced him to several bankers of my acquaintance, whom he charmed into putting up a huge sum to underwrite his shipping operation. That was the last I saw of my brother-in-law Melifont. Now and again I asked my friends in shipping circles what they had heard of his ferry company, and in time I learned that it, too, had gone bankrupt. We heard from him only once more: a letter, three years back, that let us know that he had settled now in Sippulgar and had some interesting ideas for capitalizing on business conditions there. After that, only silence, until the puzzling next-of-kin letter from the Prefecture of Sippulgar inviting my sister to collect her brother's effects.

The letter did not actually say he was dead. He was simply "no longer in Sippulgar," she was told, and there was unclaimed property which would revert to the province if not collected by a member of his family. Certainly the implication of death was there, but not the certainty. I made inquiries in official circles and learned, after much patient probing, that Melifont Ambithorn had vanished under mysterious circumstances, was not expected to return, and his property in Sippulgar, such as it might be – undescribed – was formally considered to have been abandoned by him. Further inquiry yielded me nothing. "Mysterious circumstances," was all anyone would say, and though I used my best political and commercial connections to get some more detailed explanation, the mystery remained a mystery. He had disappeared, and so far as the Prefecture of

Sippulgar was concerned there was no likelihood of his turning up again, but no one would say explicitly that he was dead. Thuwayne could not accept such vagueness. Thus my journey to Sippulgar.

My first call was at the Prefecture. I bore documents establishing my family connection with Melithorn and informing me of the procedure I was supposed to follow when in Sippulgar, but even so it took me two hours to reach any official with authority to assist me in the case. He was, of course, a Hjort, puffy-faced and rough-skinned, with an enormous toadlike head. I do not like those officious creatures – who does? – but Hjorts populate our bureaucracy to such a degree that it is impossible for me to avoid frequent contact with them, and I have learned to be patient with their superciliousness and coarseness. The Hjort spent a long time pondering my papers, muttering to himself and jotting down copious notes, and said, finally, "Why are you here in place of his sister?"

I said with some restraint, "His sister – my wife – is not in a state of health that permits such a long journey. But I believe these documents make it clear that I am her officially designated representative."

The documents I had shown him said so in the very first sentence. I refrained from pointing that out. The Hjort muttered to himself some more and at length, scowling – and when a Hjort scowls, it is with a mouth that stretches from Alhanroel to Zimroel – he scribbled something and applied his stamp of office to it and shoved it across the desk to me. It was a permit to receive the personal effects of Melifont Ambithorn, citizen of Sippulgar, legally presumed to be deceased.

His effects weren't to be had at the Prefecture, of course. I had to cross half the city, a journey that entangled me in two more religious processions, noisy and fervid, before I reached the government storehouse where Melifont's things were being kept. After the predictable official delays I was given three good-sized boxes, which I took back to my hotel to inspect.

One of them contained some clothing, a little cheap jewelry, and a small collection of books. There was nothing useful there. The second box, I was displeased to see, was crammed with what even I could recognize as the apparatus used in the practice of sorcery: ambivials, crucibles, alembics, ammatepilas, an astrolabe, a pair of phalangaria, stoppered flasks containing oils and powders of many colors, and various other instruments whose names I did not know. I sorted through this stuff with mounting distaste. Why had my brother-in-law, that restless, energetic man whose ambitions had driven him into all those ill-fated ventures in mining, banking, and shipping, gathered about himself such a hodgepodge of useless claptrap, such a huge collection of instruments and materials suitable only for exploiting the delusions of a credulous populace?

The answer to my question was right there in the question itself. But – perhaps it was the fatigue of my long day's quest, or some effect of the close, humid air – it was some long while before I saw what should have been instantly obvious.

I opened the third box. In it were papers, arranged in no perceptible order: documents relating to Melifont's many defunct business enterprises of years gone by, travel brochures, extracts from technical books, and so on, everything jumbled hopelessly together. I picked through it and was rewarded, after a time, with a small handwritten journal, practically illegible, the first entry of which was dated just eighteen months before. I leafed through it, but found my brother-in-law's scribbled writing difficult to make out and the entries themselves cryptic to the point of incoherence, and set it aside for further study. Then came another great wad of obsolete commercial records, and, below these, the one useful find in the whole messy mass: a leather binder in which were kept a group of contracts and municipal licenses and other material, all of it just a couple of years old, pertaining to the partnership between Melifont Ambithorn and a certain Nikkon Flurivole, citizen of Sippulgar, with whom Melifont proposed to organize a firm devoted to "the enhancement and furthering of the spiritual welfare of the people of Sippulgar and the entire Aruachosian coast."

And instantly I saw it all. My brother-in-law, having spent thirty years of his life failing at this promising project and that one, had in a desperate moment begun to dabble in sorcery, and very likely had gone on from that to set himself up in the business of starting a new religion.

Locating his partner, this Nikkon Flurivole, was my obvious next step. But there were no Flurivoles listed in the municipal directory, and a visit to the Prefecture got me nowhere, since the civic government was plainly not going to provide information about its citizens merely to gratify the curiosity of strangers from Sisivondal. In vain did I display the writ that allowed me to investigate the fate of Melithon Ambithorn, and the legal papers that showed that this Flurivole had been his partner in the last known commercial undertaking of his life. My writ, I was told, extended to information about Melithon Ambithorn and no one else.

I know how to handle such bureaucratic obfuscation. Bribing Hjorts is a fool's game – they will take your money and report you for attempted bribery – but the city administration was not made up entirely of Hjorts, and after a couple of attempts I found a chatty little undersecretary in the Registry of Names who, for the price of a couple of bowls of good Muldemar wine looked Flurivole up for me and reported that he was, like Melifont, "no longer in Sippulgar," that he was carried in the registry as "disappeared under mysterious circumstances," and that his personal effects were available for claiming by the next of kin, but to date no one had filed a request for them. My jolly new friend even supplied me with Flurivole's last known address; but when I went there – it was a residential hotel in a not very golden corner of the city – I learned that his rooms had been rented to someone else quite some while back, that the rental agent could not or would not tell me anything about Flurivole at all, and that the new tenant knew nothing about his predecessor in the building. Nor did the name of Melifont Ambithorn mean anything to him.

I was stymied. But I am a persistent man.

Often, when desired knowledge is difficult or impossible to find, it is best to stop looking for a time, and give the information a chance to come looking for you instead. I settled down to follow that tactic. I longed to be home, to dine at my own table, to sleep in my own bed, above all to hold my wife in my arms once again. Never had we spent so many days apart, and the separation was a torment to me. But I could not abandon my quest now. I had already missed the heart of the shipping season at home anyway; I did not want to return to Thuwayne with the mystery of her brother's disappearance unsolved; and I was confident that I would sooner or later stumble upon the next clue in the puzzle.

For a week I wandered Sippulgar as a tourist might do. It is, after all, one of our most beautiful cities, well worth seeing. We of Sisivondal have learned to get along without municipal beauty in our lives, but that does not mean we are indifferent to it. So I visited the botanical gardens that Lord Tharamond had founded somewhere in the mists of antiquity, and saw more horticultural wonders in half an hour than I had in all the years of my life. I clambered to the observation deck of the immense Hendighail Tower and peered out over the Inner Sea, imagining I could see all the way to Suvrael. I looked at the masterpieces of art in the prefectorial museum. And one day I drifted down to the waterfront and discovered a street that held, cheek by jowl, half a dozen temples to the gods of alien worlds.

Sippulgar, for some reason, is home to a great many expatriate beings from other worlds. I don't mean Hjorts or Ghayrogs or Skandars or the three or four other non-human species that have dwelled alongside us on Majipoor for thousands of years, and whose populations are thoroughly integrated into our own; I mean later comers whose numbers can be counted in the hundreds at best, scatterings from one world and another who, having come here for some commercial reason, have chosen never to return to their home planets. It may be that the mild humid climate of Sippulgar is appealing to these folk; at any rate, there are plenty of them there, of ten or a dozen different kinds, and that one particular street along the waterfront has been designated as their religious district. They have built a row of temples to their gods there, most of them small buildings, but, I discovered, dramatic and startling in their appearance, since their architecture owes nothing to Majipoori custom but is derived instead from the styles of the worshippers' native worlds. So one building that looks like a collection of interlocking pink bubbles stands precariously close to another that is a cluster of threatening black spikes, an inverted green triangle is neighbor to a set of yellow insectoid legs reaching in suppliant fashion to the sky, and so forth.

I suppose I am more tolerant of alien religions than I am of the home-grown creeds that have sprung up all over Majipoor in the past generation. Aliens are, as hardly needs to be said, *alien*, and it is quite reasonable to think that the strange workings of their minds have given rise to strange beliefs deeply rooted in their ancient civilizations. But belief in the supernatural is something new to us, and, it seems to me, quite extrinsic to our established nature. We acknowledge the existence of what we call the Divine, yes, but we have never backed that acknowledgment with scriptures or rituals; yet suddenly a new credulity has swept the world, a passionate and almost pathetic willingness to believe in the unbelievable, and I for one, dull prosaic businessman that I am, am not comfortable with it. So I feel disdain and even scorn for the frantic processions of the Beholders and the sea-dragon worshippers and the flagellantes and the blood-drinkers, for the installation in the plazas of our cities of huge idols with ten heads and twenty arms, for the believers in omens and prodigies, demons and goblins, for those who fill their homes with amulets and holy images, and all the rest of it; but, standing in front of this row of alien temples, I experienced only a sort of aesthetic pleasure, what one feels whenever one travels through the world and sees something attractive, something altogether different from what one sees at home.

I fall easily into conversations with strangers; and so it was, as I stood across the street watching strange-looking beings coming and going at the outworlders' temples, I found myself discussing – warily, at first, then more openly – my attitude toward our current spate of religiosity with a fellow curiosity-seeker, an on-looker who, by the hue of his skin, was probably a native of this region. He was a small, finely built man with brightly gleaming eyes that shined like beacons out of his purple-black face, and he seemed to know which planet each of the different outworld types we were watching had come from. I complimented him on his knowledge, to which he replied, after telling me that his name was Vundafor Thorb and that his home was in the nearby town of Bekadu, that it was his business to know such things: he was an importer whose specialty was supplying these aliens with the foodstuffs and beverages of their native worlds. He said it in a casual way that told me that he actually disliked the presence of all these outworlders in Sippulgar, but that he saw it as a prime business opportunity.

"My late brother-in-law, I think, took the same attitude to-ward our new religions," I said. "I have reason to think he saw all this feverish piety as nothing more than a good thing suitable for exploitation."

"Oh?" And he gave me a sharp look, as though I had offended him by implying that I thought his own attitude revealed a cyni-cal love of profit, which in fact I did. Not that I saw anything wrong with that. But then he smiled and said, "So he went into the religion business, your brother-in-law?"

"Apparently so." And, bit by bit, I told him what little I could:

the nature of Melifont's character, his repeated failure in a series of grandiose enterprises, and the final letter telling my wife and me that he had embarked on some new project in Sippulgar, followed in time by the official notice of his disappearance. "I've been given three boxes full of his effects," I said. "I found a diary in them that I've barely been able to decipher, but which talks about a partner of his named Nikkon Flurivole, and some legal papers indicating that he and this Flurivole were starting a company that was intended to bring 'spiritual benefits' to the people of Sippulgar. I translate that as meaning that they were going to trump up some lucrative new religion, don't you?"

"Surely that must be it," said my new friend.

"And in another box was a whole sorcerers' shop full of the claptrap devices that wizards use – crucibles and alembics and ambivials and whatnot. You know what I mean."

"Melifont Ambithorn was his name, you said?"

"Yes. And his partner was Nikkon Flurivole."

"Indeed. I knew them, actually. Had some business dealings with them, as a matter of fact. A tall, dramatic-looking man, who walked with a limp? And the other one short, round-faced, sleepy-looking?"

"I don't know anything about the other one. But the tall man with a limp – yes, that was Melifont!" I could have wept with delight. If I had been a believer in any of the new gods, I would have given thanks to him. "What can you tell me about them?" I asked eagerly.

Thorb shrugged. "Not very much. I sold them velvet hangings for their chapel, two, two-and-a-half years ago. And some very fine carpets. They spared no expense, you know."

"That would be like Melifont," I said. "So they had a chapel. What sort of religion were they running?"

"I don't know much about it. I even forget the name of their creed. There are so many nowadays, you know. I think it was one of the wonder-working ones: predict the future, cure the ailing, maybe even raise the dead. They had quite a following for a while. It all ended badly for them, of course."

"Tell me!"

"Well, now, I don't really know. They both disappeared, is all I can say. Loud noises were heard. Outcries in the night. Some say they were carried off by their own demons, creatures they had summoned themselves." He grinned, flashing teeth white as ivory. "Not that I give much credence to that, of course. Nor, I suspect, would you. But they vanished. Leaving me, I might add, with unpaid invoices to the amount of close to four hundred royals. I recovered what I could from their cult, but I assure you that I'm still out of pocket to the tune of no small sum."

"You can have that whole box of wizards' equipment if you like," I heard myself saying. My offer, the generosity of which took me by surprise, was an indication of the rush of joy I felt just then at actually having through great good luck come across a clue to this mystery. "Some magus might want to purchase it, and that will help you recover the rest of your loss. Carried off by their own demons, is that the story? Well, hardly likely. Skipping out on their own creditors, I suspect! But at least you've provided me with something to start on. I wonder where I could find some members of their cult to talk to."

"I can't help you with that," he said. "But you might try hunting up their high priest. He's still around, you know. Macola Endrago is the name. He'll tell you a thing or two!"

Macola Endrago.

I hurried back to my hotel and pounced on Melifont's journal, which had been becoming gradually less impenetrable to me as I grew more familiar with the idiosyncrasies of his handwriting. Endrago? Endrago? Yes! "M.E. suggests increase in payments." Could that be anyone else? Their employee, their hired high priest, wanting his salary raised. Then I found the entire name, *Endrago*, followed by an irritated-looking squiggle. Six pages later, "Macola very difficult today." My heart was pounding.

Again, again, again: M.E., M.E. "A troublesome man. These damned fanatics!" I think the word was *fanatics*. Another entry: "He is impossible. I cannot cope with his … " The last word of the sentence was unreadable. Scarcely anything in the journal that had to do with Endrago was legible, and what there was was maddeningly incomplete – perhaps the journal was mostly in code, or perhaps Melifont was simply one of those untidy men who could not be bothered to write with care. But I knew that my fortuitous encounter with Vundafor Thorb of Bekadu had set me on the right trail. Already I was beginning to form a hypothesis: this Endrago, this priest, obviously had been an annoyingly contentious man, ever hungry for a greater share in the profits from the fraudulent cult that my wife's brother and his equally shifty friend had put together for the sake of exploiting the naive and easily gulled people of this overly trusting city. Knowing that he was essential to the operation, Endrago must have been forever demanding higher wages for his services, and the two harried partners, perhaps already behind on their bills, had stalled him with one prevarication after another until he had boiled over with rage and murdered them. It would not have seemed implausible, in Sippulgar's present climate of superstition and gullibility, for the priest to claim that he had seen or heard them being torn to pieces by demons who had carried their bodies off to some other sphere. And now the income from the chapel would be all his to keep.

Vundafor Thorb had taken my offer of Melifont's magical equipment seriously. I suppose I would have done the same if I had been in his position. The next day he came to call for it. I would rather have kept those things to sell on my own behalf, since the costs of my journey to Sippulgar were beginning to mount. But there was no help for it: I had offered, I must make good. And he had brought me the address of the priest Macola Endrago, so I was able, in my mind, to write off the loss of the equipment as the price of this valuable information.

I knew better than to approach this Endrago immediately

and directly. One does not leap hastily upon a murder suspect and shower him with unsupported accusations. Instead I went to the address Thorb had given me – it was in a district in the dreary northeastern part of the city, where the sea breezes did not often reach and the air seemed stale and thick – and carried out some preliminary reconaissance.

At a tavern on a back street I invested a couple of crowns in a pot of beer and a plate of sausages, and quickly began to draw the innkeeper, a cheerful, easy sort of man, into conversation. I was, I told him, a traveler from Sisivondal – I saw no use in trying to disguise my northern accent – who had suffered some unspecified family tragedy and had come to Sippulgar to recover from his loss under the warm tropical sunlight. But I was lonely, terribly lonely, I said, and I felt in need of spiritual counselling. "In Sisivondal," I said, "we have the creed of the Beholders, and I derive much consolation from their rites. But there is no outpost of that faith here." I beckoned for a second pot of beer and asked him if he could recommend any place of worship, especially one in this quarter of town, where I might find the solace I needed.

He offered me five such places. There was the conventicle of this and the sanctuary of that, and the tabernacle of something else, the shrine of yet one more, and, of course, the drum-banging cult of Time the Devourer that was the special favorite of the citizens of golden Sippulgar. I carefully wrote all these down, but I allowed that I was seeking something quieter and more personal, something other than a cult that was built around loud public processions.

"Well, then, my friend, you should have said so straightaway! What you need is the Temple of Eternal Comfort, where even the sorest heart will find some ease. It's a quiet place, and not as popular as it used to be, but I can vouch for it. Macola Endrago is high priest there, and a kinder, more understanding man you will never hope to find from one end of the world to another."

Macola Endrago! All roads seemed to lead to Macola Endrago!

I felt as though I had reached into my purse and come forth with the winning ticket for the Sisivondal municipal lottery.

I found the Temple of Eternal Comfort without much difficulty: it was a ten-minute walk from the tavern. Despite its resonant name, it was drab and unprepossessing: a long, bare, narrow room, probably a converted shop, with a simple painted sign above its door. I saw none of the carpets and velvet hangings of which Vundafor Thorb had spoken, only some rows of wooden benches. He must have repossessed his merchandise. No one was there but a haggard, weary-looking man in shabby clothes, who was slowly sweeping the chapel floor.

I said that I wanted to speak with the priest Macola Endrago.

"He comes toward evening," the man said. "What sort of business do you have with him?"

Once again I explained that I was a stranger in Sippulgar, lonely and in need of healing, and told him that a sympathetic innkeeper had suggested I come here.

The man, who identified himself as the sexton of the chapel, Graimon Sten by name, looked surprised at that. "We get very few new communicants these days," he said. "We have had certain difficulties, you know. Because of what happened here. But that ought not to discourage you. Macola Endrago will give you the help you need."

I maintained my guise of ignorance. "Because of what happened here? And what was that?"

The sexton Graimon Sten hesitated a moment. Then he said, with a slight twitch of his lips, "Our founders have left us, and no one knows where they are. That shouldn't be of any real concern: we still have our Macola Endrago, who is the heart and soul of our faith. But of course, when there's the least hint of scandal about a chapel, or even what is *suspected* to be scandal—"

"Yes, the innkeeper I mentioned did speak highly of this Endrago. But what's this about a scandal? The founders – what about them? They've left you, you say?" Trying to sound merely casually curious, I said, "Left you to go where? And why did they go?"

Plainly the entire topic was distressing to him. He looked downward, concentrating pointedly on his sweeping. But I persevered.

"They disappeared. Not a trace." He paused, still avoiding my glance. Then he said, almost under his breath, "One story has it that they were murdered by a member of the congregation who held a grudge against them. His wife had died, and he was sick with grief and asked them to bring her back from the dead. He was willing to pay a huge sum of money if they would. They promised to do it, so it's said. But they couldn't."

"So he went insane and killed them? You think that's what happened to them?"

"I don't think anything," the sexton said. He looked up and let his eyes meet mine, but only for a moment. "Nobody pays me to think. I told you because you asked. Listen, it's just something that I heard someone say."

"Someone reliable?"

"How would I know. It sounds pretty wild to me. The man is still a communicant here. He doesn't have the look of a murderer about him."

I risked pressing him a little harder. "Even so: is it possible that the story's true?"

"It's possible that anything's true. Life is full of disappointments; anger may rise up in the most surprising people. And restoring the dead was never any part of our creed here. If that was what he expected, he didn't have any chance of getting it, did he? And that could have upset him. But what does it matter? The men are gone. We struggle on without them. Macola Endrago will be here in two hours, and I know he will give your soul the ease it needs."

Now I had three theories: that Macola Endrago had murdered Ambithorn and Flurivole in a dispute over money, that one of their own communicants had killed them in rage because they had failed to perform a miracle for him, or that they had indulged in some rash conjuring-up of demons and had been destroyed by the very spirits they had summoned. The Endrago theory was supported to some extent by my brother-in-law's own journal. The sexton had not put forth the angry-communicant theory with much conviction, in fact did not seem really to believe it at all. And the third, the carried-off-by-demons notion, I rejected out of hand, of course. Which left the Endrago theory as the only likely one.

But five minutes in the presence of Macola Endrago and I knew that all my conjectures about him were wrong. The man was a saint.

He was very tall, very thin, almost frail, a spidery, fleshless figure of a man, older than I had expected. His dark Sippulgaru skin seemed to have faded with the years to a light pale violet. He had a long rectangular face from which emanated the kindest of smiles and a gaze of the utmost gentleness and benevolence, and he was surrounded by such an aura of love and warmth and purity that at the mere sight of him I felt a crazy yearning to drop to my knees before him and kiss the hem of his threadbare robe. There was no mistaking his goodness: that sort of thing can't be counterfeited. He held out both his hands to me and clasped them about mine, and murmured some sort of blessing in the softest, most whispery of voices. The Temple of Eternal Comfort might have been the shameless concoction of two callous entrepreneurs in quest of easy money, but this man Endrago, I knew at once, was the embodiment of true holiness, sincere in his beliefs, genuinely good. How my brother-in-law must have hated him! In every aspect of his character, by word and deed, this Endrago had displayed the greatest possible contrast to his employers' crass materialistic ways.

I trust such flashes of insight when they come to me. Confronted with such incontrovertible sanctity, I was unable to spin any false stories about my visit to Sippulgar. I simply told him that my wife had asked me to come here to learn the details of her brother Melifont's fate.

"Ah," said Macola Endrago softly, softly: a mere faint gust of breath. "How sad it was! They summoned the irgalisteroi, your Melifont and his friend; and the irgalisteroi destroyed them. I had warned them, again and again: these spirits are real, they are dangerous. They would not listen. They thought they could use the irgalisteroi for their private profit. But they wove the spells better than they knew, and they were punished terribly for their greed and their impetuousness. As a man of your sort is surely aware, it is hard to protect fools from their own folly."

"The irgalisteroi?"

"Yes. Proiarchis, it may have been whom they invoked. Or Remmer, more likely. I came in just as it was ending. I heard the screams: the most terrible cries of agony, they were, and there was the sound of the atmosphere collapsing around them – it is like thunder, you know, thunder right there in the room. The air grows dark. The whole world seems to shake. The sky itself is split apart. I opened the door and found that the two men had already been carried off. If I had arrived any sooner, I would have died with them."

"You will pardon me, father," I said, "but I am only a merchant of Sisivondal, a plain worldly man, and I know nothing of supernatural matters. Proiarchis, Remmer, irgalisteroi – these names are only names to me."

"Ah," he said again. "Of course."

And he told me. There are, he explained, three classes of demons. That was the word he used, demons, and what he meant by it was the inhabitants of the invisible world, a concept that seemed not to have any fantastical connotations for him: he accepted without the least hint of skepticism the presence of unknown and unknowable worlds immediately adjacent to our own. These demons were the original prehistoric inhabitants of our planet, before even the Shapeshifters had come here. In ancient times the Shapeshifters had mastered them, though, confining them under powerful spells. The valisteroi, he said, were a group that had somehow escaped those spells and live now beyond the sphere of the sun, invulnerable to all conjuring. The kallisteroi, who dwell between the sky and the Great Moon and have a certain degree of freedom of action, are sympathetic to us and will sometimes agree to do services for us when properly asked by the adept; in any case they never do harm. And then there are the irgalisteroi, the demons of the subterranean world, who can be compelled to perform many duties, but who are angry, dangerous beings entirely capable of turning on an unskillful summoner and destroying him.

It says much for the spiritual force that lay behind this saintly man's mild demeanor and the incantatory power of his gentle voice that I was able to accept as factual data, for the moment, all that he was telling me about these various categories of nonexistent phantoms. As he spoke I went leaping ahead of him to the conclusion that Ambithorn and Flurivole, perhaps as a drunken irresponsible prank or possibly with the wild hope of discovering that the irgalisteroi actually were real and could be commanded to heap them with riches, had incautiously brought some potent demon out of the land of the invisible, using a borrowed spell, but had not been able to control it. Not only didn't I doubt his belief in such entities, I think I felt, just for the moment, under the irresistible strength of his incandescent sincerity, some belief in them myself.

"I can give you a glimpse of them," he said. "I would prefer not to meddle with Remmer or Proiarchis myself, though if I brought them here they might confirm what I have told you of your brother-in-law's end. But I can call up for you some of the less dangerous spirits, if you are curious about such things: Minim, say, who restores lost knowledge, or Ruhid, who brings relief from fever. Theddim, if you wish, who can control the coursing of the blood through our hearts—"

He mentioned several more, each with some highly specialized function. All those imaginary creatures! Such madness to believe in their existence! And yet I could not really scoff. Despite myself I was impressed by how much ingenuity had gone into devising and naming them. And part of me, just a part, began to wonder just how imaginary they actually were. That shook me more than I know how to tell: that I could even begin, for the moment, to believe.

"Thank you, no, father," I said hoarsely. "I'm not ready, I think, for such sights." And I could not tell, just then, whether I was refusing the demonstration to avoid embarrassing the good man when his nonsense failed to produce results, or out of fear that his spells and gestures just might present me with a vision of Minim or Ruhid or Theddim right there in the room before my scornful unbelieving eyes.

That Macola Endrago might be responsible for the deaths of Melithorn and Flurivole in some disagreement over wages now seemed inconceivable to me. Whatever disputes between the three men Melithorn's journal alluded to could much better be accounted for by the fact that Endrago actually believed in the tenets of the Temple of Eternal Comfort, whatever those might be, while his two employers had regarded the chapel merely as a money-making enterprise. Endrago's mere presence there each day would have been a constant silent reproach to them, and they might well at last have let him know in some blunt and mocking way that they had nothing but contempt for his unworldly faith in the creed that they had pasted together out of bits and scraps of other religions. But could that have led him to murder them? No, never. If a murderous impulse lurked anywhere in Macola Endrago's soul, then I am no judge of men.

Which left me nothing to fall back on, then, but the conjecture offered to me by the sexton Graimon Sten that a disgruntled worshipper had killed them, and not even the sexton seemed to take that idea very seriously. Of course there was also the death-at-the-hands-of-angry-demons hypothesis, but of course that was not an idea I was capable of embracing. Endrago apparently was the only witness to that event, and even he had come upon the scene after the demons had done their work. I doubted that he had fashioned the tale out of whole cloth. But a man who can believe in invisible demons in the first place is likely to believe in other theories as well that men of my sort are unable to accept.

My longing to quit this place and return to Thuwayne was all but overwhelming by now. But I knew I could not give up at this point, for I felt a strange certainty that I would have the answer I sought before much longer. So each day I continued to go, toward the middle of the afternoon, to the Temple of Eternal Comfort. There was always a handful of worshippers there, kneeling on the bare floor, eyes closed, deep in meditation. I imitated them. From time to time a deacon in a white robe trimmed with scarlet would appear and ring a little bell, and the congregation would rise and sing a hymn, and participate in a sort of contrapuntal ritual chant, and incense would be burned and mysterious lights would glow in the corners of the long room, and sometimes misty, shimmering apparitions would briefly make themselves visible. At the climax of the ceremony Macola Endrago would emerge from a back room and deliver a brief, sweet sermon, counselling us to let the troubles of the world slide from our shoulders like water, and calling upon this spirit or that one to aid us in that task, and one by one we would approach the altar beside him and drink from a common vessel containing a thick, almost viscous wine.

It all was a bit of a strain on my patience; but I did come every day, I knelt and rose and pretended to chant the chants, and listened to Endrago's sermon and I drank from the cup of communion, and I must say that I would leave the chapel feeling released from the ordinary tensions of the moment. And each day I waited for Jaakon Gameel – that was the name of the man who, so rumor had it, had been responsible for the disappearance of the two founders – to make an appearance at the chapel. Graimon Sten had promised to point him out to me. But four days passed, and five, and six, and I told myself that a murderer never does return to the scene of the crime, whatever the popular belief may be.

Then in the second week of my vigil someone I had not seen before was present in the chapel when I arrived, and Graimon Sten, passing close beside me, murmured, "That's the one."

A great sadness came over me at that. For I am, I do maintain, a capable judge of men; and, I thought, if the plump, placid dumpling of a man who was Jaakon Gameel could have been responsible for the deaths of Melifont Ambithorn and Nikkon Flurivole, then I will be the next Coronal of Majipoor.

I studied him carefully. The people of Sippulgar are generally lean and bony, but this one was round-faced, fat-cheeked, a stubby cabbagy blob of a man with a mild, innocent face. Plainly he was a true believer in the teachings of his faith. When he knelt in prayer he passionately pressed his forehead hard against the floor. Sometimes I heard him sobbing. When the time came to chant, he chanted with a sort of desperate fervor. When Endrago delivered his sermon he responded to each familiar point with a short, sharp nod, like one who has been struck by unarguable revelation. When we went up to the altar for the cup of communion, he held it with both hands and drank deeply. After the ceremony he sat for a long while, as though stunned, and eventually left without a word to anybody.

Day after day I waited and left the chapel when he left; and on the fifth day I hailed him in the street, and told him I was a stranger in town, a lonely visitor who felt the need for company, and in one way and another I was able to persuade him to come with me to that nearby tavern. There I brought forth for him the sad though altogether fictional tale of the tragic events that had befallen my family in Sisivondal and propelled me into this journey southward to Sippulgar. He listened with care and such obvious sympathy for a fellow sufferer that I felt a bit ashamed of my own crafty mendacity.

But he did not respond at once with the story of his own bereavement, as I had expected. He fell silent, as though some dam within him was holding him back. I waited, urging him with my eyes to confide in me, and before long I could see the dam beginning to break.

Quickly, then, his tale came pouring out of him. A young and beautiful wife, apple of his eye, his treasure, his only joy, a paragon among women, a wife far beyond his true deserts, the envy of all his friends – struck down in the second year of their marriage, carried off in a trice by the sting of some venomous tropical insect. Inconsolable, half dead with sorrow, he had gone from one creed's chapel to another, he said, seeking the one that might have the power to restore her to him; but of course there was none that did. Someone had told him of the Temple of Eternal Comfort, and he had made his last attempt there. He had spoken most earnestly with the two founders, and with the high priest Endrago, begging them to work the miracle for him. Each of them had said it could not be done: in our world death is final and there is no coming back from it. Yet he had persisted. He was a man of some means; one day he came to Melifont and Flurivole and offered them half his wealth if they would intercede with the spirit world on his behalf for the return of his wife from the dead.

"And they attempted it, did they?"

He was silent a long moment, looking downward. Then he raised his face to mine and a look of terrible regret bordering on agony came into his eyes. He seemed to be staring past me into the darkest of abysses.

"Yes," he said, barely audibly. "Finally they agreed. They asked the spirits, yes. And – and—"

He faltered. He fell silent.

I prodded him. "Nothing happened, of course."

"Oh, yes, something happened," he said, in that same soft, quavering voice. "But not the return of my wife." And he looked away again, shivering as though in the grip of irremediable guilt and shame, and began to weep.

*

Macola Endrago said to me, when I told him that I was about to take my leave of Sippulgar, "It is for the best, I think. Seek your solace at home. We can give you no help here, for you are a man without belief."

"You see that, do you?"

"I saw it from the first. When I told you how your wife's brother met his death, you looked at me as though I were telling you children's fables. When you pray in the chapel, you hold yourself like a man who wishes he were almost anywhere else. When you come up to take the cup you have no presence of the god about you. None of this is hard to see." His voice came to me as though from far away, gentle, kindly, infinitely sad. "Return to your wife, my friend. You came here to solve a mystery, and I provided you with the information you needed, and you are unable to accept it. So you may as well go."

"I'd be pleased to believe that the men were torn apart by those demons – Remmer, Proiarchis, are those the names? – if only I could. But I can't. I *can't*. There are no such beings."

"No?"

"No," I said. "Everything in my soul tells me that."

He smiled his gentle, loving smile. "I offered to summon Theddim or Minim for you. You refused. Shall I give you another chance? I could bring up Remmer or Proiarchis, even. There would be risks, but I could do it, and then you would know the truth. Shall I? I would do that for you, my friend. I would embrace the risk, so that your eyes might be opened."

For a moment I wavered in the face of the inexorable force of his belief.

Again he smiled – that mild, sweet, saintly smile of his. And in his eyes, which were not mild or sweet or saintly at all, I saw the implacable will, the utter conviction, the invincible strength, that sustained his faith.

"Let me show you what you are so unwilling to see."

I gasped and struggled for breath. Melifont may have been a fraud, but not this Endrago. I was burning in the awful fire of his sincerity. In that moment I felt sure that this man really had walked with demons. And now he will take me by the hand and lead me to them. I shuddered under the inexorable force of his belief. It fell upon me like a hammer. I wanted to run from him, but I was frozen where I stood.

"No," I said once more, even as I stared bewilderedly into the darkness of the chapel.

That shape – that shadowy form with blazing eyes—

At that instant it seemed to me that the dread figure of Proiarchis was rearing up before me to tell me why Melifont Ambithorn and his partner had had to be slain.

I began to tremble. A door was opening. Fiercely I slammed it shut. I slammed it and held it with all my strength. As Macola Endrago reached out toward me I backed away. "Please. No." And I said, though it was a lie and he surely was aware of that, "I know nothing about demons, and I want to know nothing about them. If such things as demons do exist."

The saintly smile yet again. My heart shriveled under the heat of that smile. "If, indeed."

"But let me say that if they do – *if* they do – I would never presume to ask you to take so great a risk on my behalf. If anything went wrong, I could never forgive myself."

He showed no anger, no disappointment, no surprise.

"Very well," he said, and our meeting was over.

The next day I left Sippulgar, hiring an express courier to get me back to Sisivondal as quickly as possible. And when at last I was with my wife Thuwayne again I told her that no one in Sippulgar had any real idea of what had happened to her brother, but that he had vanished and after the appropriate legal period had elapsed he had been declared officially dead, and the most probable explanation was that he had failed in business one last time, failed so completely that he had taken his own life to escape his creditors. More than that, I said, we will never know. And I think that that last part, at least, is the truth.

7

The Seventh Shrine

O ne last steep ridge of the rough, boulder-strewn road lay between the royal party and the descent into Velalisier Plain. Valentine, who was leading the way, rode up over it and came to a halt, looking down with amazement into the valley. The land that lay before him seemed to have undergone a bewildering transformation since his last visit. "Look there," the Pontifex said, bemused. "This place is always full of surprises, and here is ours."

The broad shallow bowl of the arid plain spread out below them. From this vantage point, a little way east of the entrance to the archaeological site, they should easily have been able to see a huge field of sand-swept ruins. There had been a mighty city here once, that notorious Shapeshifter city where, in ancient times, so much dark history had been enacted, such monstrous sacrilege and blasphemy. But – surely it was just an illusion? – the sprawling zone of fallen buildings at the center of the plain was almost completely hidden now by a wondrous rippling body of water, pale pink along its rim and pearly gray at its middle: a great lake where no lake ever had been.

Evidently the other members of the royal party saw it too. But did they understand that it was simply a trick? Some fleeting combination of sunlight and dusty haze and the stifling midday heat must have created a momentary mirage above dead Velalisier, so that it seemed as if a sizable lagoon, of all improbable things, had sprung up in the midst of this harsh desert to engulf the dead city.

It began just a short distance beyond their vantage point and extended as far as the distant gray-blue wall of great stone monoliths that marked the city's western boundary. Nothing of Velalisier could be seen. None of the shattered and time-worn temples and palaces and basilicas, nor the red basalt blocks of the arena, the great expanses of blue stone that had been the sacrificial platforms, the tents of the archaeologists who had been at work here at Valentine's behest since late last year. Only the six steep and narrow pyramids that were the tallest surviving structures of the prehistoric Metamorph capital were visible – their tips, at least, jutting out of the gray heart of the ostensible lake like a line of daggers fixed point-upward in its depths.

"Magic," murmured Tunigorn, the oldest of Valentine's boy-hood friends, who held the post now of Minister of External Affairs at the Pontifical court. He drew a holy symbol in the air. Tunigorn had grown very superstitious, here in his later years.

"I think not," said Valentine, smiling. "Just an oddity of the light, I'd say."

And, just as though the Pontifex had conjured it up with some counter-magic of his own, a lusty gust of wind came up from the north and swiftly peeled the haze away. The lake went with it, vanishing like the phantom it had been. Valentine and his companions found themselves now beneath a bare and merciless iron-blue sky, gazing down at the true Velalisier – that immense dreary field of stony rubble, that barren and incoherent tumble of dun-colored fragments and drab threadbare shards lying in gritty beds of wind-strewn sand, which was all that remained of the abandoned Metamorph metropolis of long ago.

"Well, now," said Tunigorn, "perhaps you were right, majesty. Magic or no, though, I liked it better the other way. It was a pretty lake, and these are ugly stones."

"There's nothing here to like at all, one way or another," said Duke Nascimonte of Ebersinul. He had come all the way from his great estate on the far side of the Labyrinth to take part in this expedition. "This is a sorry place and always has been. If

I were Pontifex in your stead, your majesty, I'd throw a dam across the River Glayge and send a raging torrent this way, that would bury this accursed city and its whole history of abominations under two miles of water for all time to come."

Some part of Valentine could almost see the merit of that. It was easy enough to believe that the somber spells of antiquity still hovered here, that this was a territory where ominous enchantments held sway.

But of course Valentine could hardly take Nascimonte's suggestion seriously. "Drown the Metamorphs' sacred city, yes! By all means, let's do that," he said lightly. "Very fine diplomacy, Nascimonte. What a splendid way of furthering harmony between the races that would be!"

Nascimonte, a lean and hard-bitten man of eighty years, with keen sapphire eyes that blazed like fiery gems in his broad furrowed forehead, said pleasantly, "Your words tell us what we already know, majesty: that it's just as well for the world that you are Pontifex, not I. I lack your benign and merciful nature – especially, I must say, when it comes to the filthy Shapeshifters. I know you love them and would bring them up out of their degradation. But to me, Valentine, they are vermin and nothing but vermin. Dangerous vermin at that."

"Hush," said Valentine. He was still smiling, but he let a little annoyance show as well. "The Rebellion's long over. It's high time we put these old hatreds to rest forever."

Nascimonte's only response was a shrug.

Valentine turned away, looking again toward the ruins. Greater mysteries than that mirage awaited them down there. An event as grim and terrible as anything out of Velalisier's doleful past had lately occurred in this city of long-dead stones: a murder, no less.

Violent death at another's hands was no common thing on Majipoor. It was to investigate that murder that Valentine and his friends had journeyed to ancient Velalisier this day.

"Come," he said. "Let's be on our way."

He spurred his mount forward, and the others followed him down the stony road into the haunted city.

The ruins appeared much less dismal at close range than they had on either of Valentine's previous two visits. This winter's rains must have been heavier than usual, for wildflowers were blooming everywhere amidst the dark, dingy waste of ashen dunes and overturned building-blocks. They dappled the gray gloominess with startling little bursts of yellow and red and blue and white that were almost musical in their emphatic effect. A host of fragile bright-winged kelebekkos flitted about amongst the blossoms, sipping at their nectar, and multitudes of tiny gnat-like ferushas moved about in thick swarms, forming broad misty patches in the air that glistened like silvery dust.

But more was happening here than the unfolding of flowers and the dancing of insects. As he made his descent into Velalisier Valentine's imagination began to teem suddenly with strange-nesses, fantasies, marvels. It seemed to him that inexplicable flickers of sorcery and wonder were arising just beyond the periphery of his vision. Sprites and visitations, singing word-lessly to him of Majipoor's infinite past, drifted upward from the broken edge-tilted slabs and capered temptingly about him, leaping to and fro over the porous, limy soil of the site's surface with frantic energy. A subtle shimmer of delicate jade-green iridescence that had not been apparent at a distance rose above everything, tinting the air: some effect of the hot noontime light striking a luminescent mineral in the rocks, he supposed. It was a wondrous sight all the same, whatever its cause.

These unexpected touches of beauty lifted the Pontifex's mood. Which, ever since the news had reached him the week before of the savage and perplexing death of the distinguished Metamorph archaeologist Huukaminaan amidst these very ruins, had been uncharacteristically bleak. Valentine had had such high hopes for the work that was being done here to uncover and restore the old Shapeshifter capital; and this murder had stained everything.

The tents of his archaeologists came into view now, lofty ones gaily woven from broad strips of green, maroon, and scarlet cloth, billowing atop a low sandy plateau in the distance. Some of the excavators themselves, he saw, were riding toward him down the long rock-ribbed avenues on fat plodding mounts: about half a dozen of them, with chief archaeologist Magadone Sambisa at the head of the group.

"Majesty," she said, dismounting, making the elaborate sign of respect that one would make before a Pontifex. "Welcome to Velalisier."

Valentine hardly recognized her. It was only about a year since Magadone Sambisa had come before him in his chambers at the Labyrinth. He remembered a dynamic, confident, bright-eyed woman, sturdy and strapping, with rounded cheeks florid with life and vigor and glossy cascades of curling red hair tumbling down her back. She seemed oddly diminished now, haggard with fatigue, her shoulders slumped, her eyes dull and sunken, her face sallow and newly lined and no longer full. That great mass of hair had lost its sheen and bounce. He let his amazement show, only for an instant, but long enough for her to see it. She pulled herself upright immediately, trying, it seemed, to project some of her former vigor.

Valentine had intended to introduce her to Duke Nascimonte and Prince Mirigant and the rest of the visiting group. But before he could do it, Tunigorn came officially forward to handle the task.

There had been a time when citizens of Majipoor could not have any sort of direct conversation with the Pontifex. They were required then to channel all intercourse through the court official known as the High Spokesman. Valentine had quickly abolished that custom, and many another stifling bit of imperial etiquette. But Tunigorn, by nature conservative, had never been comfortable with those changes. He did whatever he could to preserve the traditional aura of sanctity in which Pontifexes once had been swathed. Valentine found that amusing and charming and only occasionally irritating.

The welcoming party included none of the Metamorph archaeologists connected with the expedition. Magadone Sambisa had brought just five human archaeologists and a Ghayrog with her. That seemed odd, to have left the Metamorphs elsewhere. Tunigorn formally repeated the archaeologists' names to Valentine, getting nearly every one garbled in the process. Then, and only then, did he step back and allow the Pontifex to have a word with her.

"The excavations," he said. "Tell me, have they been going well?"

"Quite well, majesty. Splendidly, in fact, until – *until*—" She made a despairing gesture: grief, shock, incomprehension, helplessness, all in a single poignant movement of her head and hands.

The murder must have been like a death in the family for her, for all of them here. A sudden and horrifying loss.

"*Until*, yes. I understand."

Valentine questioned her gently but firmly. Had there, he asked, been any important new developments in the investigation? Any clues discovered? Claims of responsibility for the killing? Were there any suspects at all? Had the archaeological party received any threats of further attacks?

But there was nothing new at all. Huukaminaan's murder had been an isolated event, a sudden, jarring, and unfathomable intrusion into the serene progress of work at the site. The slain Metamorph's body had been turned over to his own people for interment, she told him, and a shudder that she made an ineffectual effort to hide ran through the entire upper half of her body as she said it. The excavators were attempting now to put aside their distress over the killing and get on with their tasks.

The whole subject was plainly an uncomfortable one for her. She escaped from it as quickly as she could. "You must be tired from your journey, your majesty. Shall I show you to your quarters?"

Three new tents had been erected to house the Pontifex and his entourage. They had to pass through the excavation zone itself to reach them. Valentine was pleased to see how much progress had been made in clearing away the clusters of pernicious little ropy-stemmed weeds and tangles of woody vines that for so many centuries had been patiently at work pulling the blocks of stone one from another.

Along the way Magadone Sambisa poured forth voluminous streams of information about the city's most conspicuous features as though Valentine were a tourist and she his guide. Over here, the broken but still awesome aqueduct. There, the substantial jagged-sided oval bowl of the arena. And there, the grand ceremonial boulevard, paved with sleek greenish flagstones.

Shapeshifter glyphs were visible on those flagstones even after the lapse of twenty thousand years, mysterious swirling symbols, carved deep into the stone. Not even the Shapeshifters themselves were able to decipher them now.

The rush of archaeological and mythological minutiae came gushing from her with scarcely a pause for breath. There was a certain frantic, even desperate, quality about it all, a sign of the uneasiness she must feel in the presence of the Pontifex of Majipoor. Valentine was accustomed enough to that sort of thing. But this was not his first visit to Velalisier and he was already familiar with much of what she was telling him. And she looked so weary, so depleted, that it troubled him to see her expending her energy in such needless outpourings.

But she would not stop. They were passing, now, a huge and very dilapidated edifice of gray stone that appeared ready to fall down if anyone should sneeze in its vicinity. "This is called the Palace of the Final King," she said. "Probably an erroneous name, but that's what the Piurivars call it, and for lack of a better one we do too."

Valentine noted her careful use of the Metamorphs' own

name for themselves. *Piurivars*, yes. University people tended to be very formal about that, always referring to the aboriginal folk of Majipoor that way, never speaking of them as Metamorphs or Shapeshifters, as ordinary people tended to do. He would try to remember that.

As they came to the ruins of the royal palace she offered a disquisition on the legend of the mythical Final King of Piurivar antiquity, he who had presided over the atrocious act of defilement that had brought about the Metamorphs' ancient abandonment of their city. It was a story with which all of them were familiar. Who did not know that dreadful tale?

But they listened politely as she told of how, those many thousands of years ago, long before the first human settlers had come to live on Majipoor, the Metamorphs of Velalisier had in some fit of blind madness hauled two living sea-dragons from the ocean: intelligent beings of mighty size and extraordinary mental powers, whom the Metamorphs themselves had thought of as gods. Had dumped them down on these platforms, had cut them to pieces with long knives, had burned their flesh on a pyre before the Seventh Pyramid as a crazed offering to some even greater gods in whom the King and his subjects had come to believe.

When the simple folk of the outlying provinces heard of that orgy of horrendous massacre, so the legend ran, they rushed upon Velalisier and demolished the temple at which the sacrificial offering had been made. They put to death the Final King and wrecked his palace, and drove the wicked citizens of the city forth into the wilderness, and smashed its aqueduct and put dams across the rivers that had supplied it with water, so that Velalisier would be thenceforth a deserted and accursed place, abandoned through all eternity to the lizards and spiders and jakkaboles of the fields.

Valentine and his companions moved on in silence when Magadone Sambisa was done with her narrative. The six sharply tapering pyramids that were Velalisier's best-known monuments came now into view, the nearest rising just beyond the court-yard of the Final King's palace, the other five set close together in a straight line stretching to the east. "There was a seventh, once," Magadone Sambisa said. "But the Piurivars themselves destroyed it just before they left here for the last time. Nothing was left but scattered rubble. We were about to start work there early last week, but that was when – when—" She faltered and looked away.

"Yes," said Valentine softly. "Of course."

The road now took them between the two colossal platforms fashioned from gigantic slabs of blue stone that were known to the modern-day Metamorphs as the Tables of the Gods. Even though they were abutted by the accumulated debris of two hundred centuries, they still rose nearly ten feet above the surrounding plain, and the area of their flat-topped surfaces would have been great enough to hold hundreds of people at a time.

In a low sepulchral tone Magadone Sambisa said, "Do you know what these are, your majesty?"

Valentine nodded. "The sacrificial altars, yes. Where the Defilement was carried out."

Magadone Sambisa said, "Indeed. It was also at this site that the murder of Huukaminaan happened. I could show you the place. It would take only a moment."

She indicated a staircase a little way down the road, made of big square blocks of the same blue stone as the platforms themselves. It gave access to the top of the western platform. Magadone Sambisa dismounted and scrambled swiftly up. She paused on the highest step to extend a hand to Valentine as though the Pontifex might be having difficulty in making the ascent, which was not the case. He was still almost as agile as he had been in his younger days. But he reached for her hand for courtesy's sake, just as she – deciding, maybe, that it would be impermissible for a commoner to make contact with the flesh of a Pontifex – began to pull it anxiously back. Valentine, grinning, leaned forward and took the hand anyway, and levered himself upward.

Old Nascimonte came bounding swiftly up just behind him, fol lowed by Valentine's cousin and close counsellor, Prince Mirigant, who had the little Vroonish wizard Autifon Deliamber riding on his shoulder. Tunigorn remained below. Evidently this place of ancient sacrilege and infamous slaughter was not for him.

The surface of the altar, roughened by time and pockmarked everywhere by clumps of scruffy weeds and incrustations of red and green lichen, stretched on and on before them, a stupendous expanse. It was hard to imagine how even a great multitude of Shapeshifters, those slender and seemingly boneless people, could ever have hauled so many tremendous blocks of stone into place.

Magadone Sambisa pointed to a marker of yellow tape in the form of a six-pointed star that was affixed to the stone a dozen feet or so away. "We found him here," she said. "Some of him, at any rate. And some here." There was another marker off to the left, about twenty feet farther on. "And here." A third star of yellow tape.

"They dismembered him?" Valentine said, appalled.

"Indeed. You can see the bloodstains all about." She hesitated for an instant. Valentine noticed that she was trembling now. "All of him was here except his head. We discovered that far away, over in the ruins of the Seventh Pyramid."

"They know no shame," said Nascimonte vehemently. "They are worse than beasts. We should have eradicated them all."

"Who do you mean?" asked Valentine.

"You know who I mean, majesty. You know quite well."

"So you think this was Shapeshifter work, this crime?"

"Oh, no, majesty, no!" Nascimonte said, coloring the words with heavy scorn. "Why would I think such a thing? One of our own archaeologists must have done it, no doubt. Out of professional jealousy, let's say, because the dead Shapeshifter had come upon some important discovery, maybe, and our own people wanted to take credit for it. Is that what you think,

Valentine? Do you believe any human being would be capable of this sort of loathsome butchery?"

"That's what we're here to discover, my friend," said Valentine amiably. "We are not quite ready for arriving at conclusions, I think."

Magadone Sambisa's eyes were bulging from her head, as though Nascimonte's audacity in upbraiding a Pontifex to his face was a spectacle beyond her capacity to absorb. "Perhaps we should continue on to your tents now," she said.

It felt very odd, Valentine thought, as they rode on down the rubble-bordered roadway that led to the place of encampment, to be here in this forlorn and eerie zone of age-old ruins once again. But at least he was not in the Labyrinth. So far as he was concerned, any place at all was better than the Labyrinth.

This was his third visit to Velalisier. The first had been long ago when he had been Coronal, in the strange time of his brief overthrow by the usurper Dominin Barjazid. He had stopped off here with his little handful of supporters – Carabella, Nascimonte, Sleet, Ermanar, Deliamber, and the rest – during the course of his northward march to Castle Mount, where he was to reclaim his throne from the false Coronal in the War of Restoration.

Valentine had still been a young man, then. But he was young no longer. He had been Pontifex of Majipoor, senior monarch of the realm, for nine years now, following upon the fourteen of his service as Coronal Lord. There were a few strands of white in his golden hair, and though he still had an athlete's trim body and easy grace he was starting to feel the first twinges of the advancing years.

He had vowed, that first time at Velalisier, to have the weeds and vines that were strangling the ruins cleared away, and to send in archaeologists to excavate and restore the old toppled buildings. And he had intended to allow the Metamorph leaders to play a role in that work, if they were willing. That was part of his plan for giving those once-despised and persecuted natives of the planet a more significant place in Majipoori life; for he knew that Metamorphs everywhere were smouldering with barely contained wrath, and could no longer be shunted into the remote reservations where his predecessors had forced them to live.

Valentine had kept that vow. And had come back to Velalisier years later to see what progress the archaeologists had made.

But the Metamorphs, bitterly resenting Valentine's intrusion into their holy precincts, had shunned the enterprise entirely. That was something he had not expected.

He was soon to learn that although the Shapeshifters were eager to see Velalisier rebuilt, they meant to do the job themselves – after they had driven the human settlers and all other offworld intruders from Majipoor and taken control of their planet once more. A Shapeshifter uprising, secretly planned for many years, erupted just a few years after Valentine had regained the throne. The first group of archaeologists that Valentine had sent to Velalisier could achieve nothing more at the site than some preliminary clearing and mapping before the War of the Rebellion broke out; and then all work there had had to be halted indefinitely.

The war had ended with victory for Valentine's forces. In designing the peace that followed it he had taken care to alleviate as many of the grievances of the Metamorphs as he could. The Danipiur – that was the title of their queen – was brought into the government as a full Power of the Realm, placing her on an even footing with the Pontifex and the Coronal. Valentine had, by then, himself moved on from the Coronal's throne to that of the Pontifex. And now he had revived the idea of restoring the ruins of Velalisier once more; but he had made certain that it would be with the full cooperation of the Metamorphs, and that Metamorph archaeologists would work side by side with the scholars from the venerable University of Arkilon in the north to whom he had assigned the task.

In the year just past great things had been done toward rescuing the ruins from the oblivion that had been encroaching on them for so long. But he could take little joy in any of that. The ghastly death that had befallen the senior Metamorph archaeologist atop this ancient altar argued that sinister forces still ran deep in this place. The harmony that he thought his reign had brought to the world might be far shallower than he suspected.

Twilight was coming on by the time Valentine was settled in his tent. By a custom that even he was reluctant to set aside, he would stay in it alone, since his consort Carabella had remained behind in the Labyrinth on this trip. Indeed, she had tried very strongly to keep him from going himself. Tunigorn, Mirigant, Nascimonte, and the Vroon would share the second tent; the third was occupied by the security forces that had accompanied the Pontifex to Velalisier.

He stepped out into the gathering dusk. A sprinkling of early stars had begun to sparkle overhead, and the Great Moon's bright glint could be seen close to the horizon. The air was parched and crisp, with a brittle quality to it, as though it could be torn in one's hands like dry paper and crumbled to dust between one's fingers. There was a strange stillness in it, an eerie hush.

But at least he was out of doors, here, gazing up at actual stars, and the air he breathed here, dry as it was, was *real* air, not the manufactured stuff of the Pontifical city. Valentine was grateful for that.

By rights he had no business being out and abroad in the world at all.

As Pontifex, his place was in the Labyrinth, hidden away in his secret imperial lair deep underground beneath all those coiling levels of subterranean settlement, shielded always from the view of ordinary mortals. The Coronal, the junior king who lived in the lofty castle of forty thousand rooms atop the great heaven-piercing peak that was Castle Mount, was meant to be the active figure of governance, the visible representative of royal majesty on Majipoor. But Valentine loathed the dank Labyrinth where his lofty rank obliged him to dwell. He relished every opportunity he could manufacture to escape from it.

And in fact this one had been thrust unavoidably upon him. The killing of Huukaminaan was serious business, requiring an inquiry on the highest levels; and the Coronal Lord Hissune was many months' journey away just now, touring the distant continent of Zimroel. And so the Pontifex was here in the Coronal's stead.

"You love the sight of the open sky, don't you?" said Duke Nascimonte, emerging from the tent across the way and limping over to stand by Valentine's side. A certain tenderness underlay the harshness of his rasping voice. "Ah, I understand, old friend. I do indeed."

"I see the stars so infrequently, Nascimonte, in the place where I must live."

The duke chuckled. "*Must* live! The most powerful man in the world, and yet he's a prisoner! How ironic that is! How sad!"

"I knew from the moment I became Coronal that I'd have to live in the Labyrinth eventually," Valentine said. "I've tried to make my peace with that. But it was never my plan to be Coronal in the first place, you know. If Voriax had lived—"

"Ah, yes, Voriax—" Valentine's brother, the elder son of the High Counsellor Damiandane: the one who had been reared from childhood to occupy the throne of Majipoor. Nascimonte gave Valentine a close look. "It was a Metamorph, was it not, who struck him down in the forest? That has been proven now?"

Uncomfortably Valentine said, "What does it matter now who killed him? He died. And the throne came to me, because I was our father's other son. A crown I had never dreamed of wearing. Everyone knew that Voriax was the one who was destined for it."

"But he had a darker destiny also. Poor Voriax!"

Poor Voriax, yes. Struck down by a bolt out of nowhere while hunting in the forest eight years into his reign as Coronal, a bolt from the bow of some Metamorph assassin skulking in the trees. By accepting of his dead brother's crown, Valentine had doomed himself inevitably to descend into the Labyrinth some day, when the old Pontifex died and it became the Coronal's turn to succeed to the greater title, and to the cheerless obligation of underground residence that went with it.

"As you say, it was the decision of fate," Valentine replied, "and now I am Pontifex. Well, so be it, Nascimonte. But I won't hide down there in the darkness all the time. I can't."

"And why should you? The Pontifex can do as he pleases."

"Yes. Yes. But only within our law and custom."

"You shape law and custom to suit yourself, Valentine. You always have."

Valentine understood what Nascimonte was saying. He had never been a conventional monarch. For much of the time during his exile from power in the period of the usurpation he had wandered the world earning a humble living as an itinerant juggler, kept from awareness of his true rank by the amnesia that the usurping faction had induced in him. Those years had transformed him irreversibly; and after his restoration to the royal heights of Castle Mount he had comported himself in a way that few Coronals ever had before – mingling openly with the populace, spreading a cheerful gospel of peace and love even as the Shapeshifters were making ready to launch their long-cherished campaign of war against the conquerors who had taken their world from them.

And then, when the events of that war made Valentine's succession to the Pontificate unavoidable, he had held back as long as possible before relinquishing the upper world to his protege Lord Hissune, the new Coronal, and descending into the subterranean city that was so alien to his sunny nature.

In his nine years as Pontifex he had found every excuse to emerge from it. No Pontifex in memory had come forth from the Labyrinth more than once a decade or so, and then only to attend high rites at the castle of the Coronal; but Valentine popped out as often as he could, riding hither and thither through the land as though he were still obliged to undertake the formal grand processionals across the countryside that a Coronal must make. Lord Hissune had been very patient with him on each of those occasions, though Valentine had no doubt that the young Coronal was annoyed by the senior monarch's insistence on coming up into public view so frequently.

"I change what I think needs changing," Valentine said. "But I owe it to Lord Hissune to keep myself out of sight as much as possible."

"Well, here you are above ground today, at any rate!"

"It seems that I am. This is one time, though, when I would gladly have forgone the chance to come forth. But with Hissune off in Zimroel—"

"Yes. Clearly you had no choice. You had to lead this investigation yourself." They fell silent. "A nasty mess, this murder," Nascimonte said, after a time. "Pfaugh! Pieces of the poor bastard strewn all over the altar like that!"

"Pieces of the government's Metamorph policy, too, I think," said the Pontifex, with a rueful grin.

"You think there's something political in this, Valentine?"

"Who knows? But I fear the worst."

"You, the eternal optimist!"

"It would be more accurate to call me a realist, Nascimonte. A realist."

The old duke laughed. "As you prefer, majesty." There was another pause, a longer one than before. Then Nascimonte said, more quietly, now, "Valentine, I need to ask your forgiveness for an earlier fault. I spoke too harshly, this afternoon, when I talked of the Shapeshifters as vermin who should be exterminated. You know I don't truly believe that. I'm an old man. Sometimes I speak so bluntly that I amaze even myself."

Valentine nodded, but made no other reply.

"And telling you so dogmatically that it had to be one of his fellow Shapeshifters who killed him, too. As you said, it's out of line for us to be jumping to conclusions that way. We haven't even started to collect evidence yet. At this point we have no justification for assuming—"

"On the contrary. We have *every* reason to assume it, Nascimonte."

The duke stared at Valentine in bewilderment. "Majesty!"

"Let's not play games, old friend. There's no one here right now but you and me. In privacy we're free to speak unvarnished truths, are we not? And you said it truly enough this afternoon. I did tell you then that we mustn't jump to conclusions, yes, but sometimes a conclusion is so obvious that it comes jumping right at us. There's no rational reason why one of the human archaeologists – or one of the Ghayrogs, for that matter – would have murdered one of his colleagues. I don't see why anyone else would have done it, either. Murder is such a very rare crime, Nascimonte. We can hardly even begin to understand the motivations of someone who'd be capable of doing it. But someone did."

"Yes."

"Well, and which race's motivations are hardest for us to understand, eh? To my way of thinking the killer almost certainly would have to be a Shapeshifter – either a member of the archaeological team, or one who came in from outside for the particular purpose of carrying out the assassination."

"So one might assume. But what possible purpose could a Shapeshifter have for killing one of his own kind?"

"I can't imagine. Which is why we're here as investigators," said Valentine. "And I have a nasty feeling that I'm not going to like the answer when we find it."

At dinner that night in the archaeologists' open-air mess hall, under a clear black sky ablaze now with swirling streams of brilliant stars that cast cold dazzling light on the mysterious humps and mounds of the surrounding ruins, Valentine made the acquaintance of Magadone Sambisa's entire scientific team. There were seventeen in all: six other humans, two Ghayrogs, eight Metamorphs. They seemed, every one of them, to be gentle, studious creatures. Not by the greatest leap of the imagination could Valentine picture any of these people slaying and dismembering their venerable colleague Huukaminaan.

"Are these the only persons who have access to the archaeological zone?" he asked Magadone Sambisa.

"There are the day laborers also, of course."

"Ah. And where are they just now?"

"They have a village of their own, over beyond the last pyramid. They go to it at sundown and don't come back until the start of work the next day."

"I see. How many are there altogether? A great many?"

Magadone Sambisa looked across the table toward a pale and long-faced Metamorph with strongly inward-sloping eyes. He was her site supervisor, Kaastisiik by name, responsible for each day's deployment of diggers. "What would you say? About a hundred?"

"One hundred twelve," said Kaastisiik, and clamped his little slit of a mouth in a way that demonstrated great regard for his own precision.

"Mostly Piurivar?" Valentine asked.

"Entirely Piurivar," said Magadone Sambisa. "We thought it was best to use only native workers, considering that we're not only excavating the city but to some extent rebuilding it. They don't appear to have any problem with the presence of non-Piurivar archaeologists, but having humans taking part in the actual reconstruction work would very likely be offensive to them."

"You hired them all locally, did you?"

"There are no settlements of any kind in the immediate vicinity of the ruins, your majesty. Nor are there many Piurivars living anywhere in the surrounding province. We had to bring them in from great distances. A good many from Piurifayne itself, in fact."

Valentine raised an eyebrow at that. From *Piurifayne*?

Piurifayne was a province of far-off Zimroel, an almost unthinkable distance away on the other side of the Inner Sea. Eight thousand years before, the great conqueror Lord Stiamot – he who had ended for all time the Piurivars' hope of remaining independent on their own world – had driven those Metamorphs who had survived his war against them into Piurifayne's humid jungles and had penned them up in a reservation there. Though the old restrictions had long since been lifted and Metamorphs now were permitted to settle wherever they pleased, more of them still lived in Piurifayne than anywhere else; and it was in the subtropical glades of Piurifayne that the revolutionary Faraataa had founded the underground movement that had sent the War of the Rebellion forth upon peaceful Majipoor like a river of seething lava.

Tunigorn said, "You've questioned them all, naturally? Established their comings and goings at the time of the murder?"

Magadone Sambisa seemed taken aback. "You mean, treat them as though they were suspects in the killing?"

"They *are* suspects in the killing," said Tunigorn.

"They are simple diggers and haulers of burdens, nothing more, Prince Tunigorn. There are no murderers among them, that much I know. They *revered* Dr. Huukaminaan. They regarded him as a guardian of their past – almost a sacred figure. It's inconceivable that any one of them could have carried out such a dreadful and hideous crime. Inconceivable!"

"In this very place some twenty thousand years ago," Duke Nascimonte said, looking upward as if he were speaking only to the air, "the King of the Shapeshifters, as you yourself reminded us earlier today, caused two enormous sea-dragons to be butchered alive atop those huge stone platforms back there. It was clear from your words this afternoon that the Shapeshifters of those days must have regarded sea-dragons with even more reverence than you say your laborers had for Dr. Huukaminaan. They called them 'water-kings,' am I not right, and gave them names, and thought of them as holy elder brothers, and addressed prayers to them? Yet the bloody sacrifice took place here in Velalisier even so, the thing that to this very day the Shapeshifters themselves speak of as the Defilement. Is this not true? Permit me to suggest, then, that if the King of the Shapeshifters could have done such a thing back then, it isn't all that inconceivable that one of your own hired Metamorphs here could have found some reason to perpetrate a similar atrocity last week upon the unfortunate Dr. Huukaminaan on the very same altar."

Magadone Sambisa appeared stunned, as though Nascimonte had struck her in the face. For a moment she could make no reply. Then she said hoarsely, "How can you use an ancient myth, a fantastic legend, to cast suspicion on a group of harmless, innocent—"

"Ah, so it's a myth and a legend when you want to protect these harmless and innocent diggers and haulers of yours, and absolute historical truth when you want us to shiver with rapture over the significance of these piles of old jumbled stones?"

"Please," Valentine said, glaring at Nascimonte. "*Please*." To Magadone Sambisa he said, "What time of day did the murder take place?"

"Late at night. Past midnight, it must have been."

"I was the last to see Dr. Huukaminaan," said one of the Metamorph archaeologists, a frail-looking Piurivar whose skin had an elegant emerald hue. Vo-Siimifon was his name; Magadone Sambisa had introduced him as an authority on ancient Piurivar script. "We sat up late in our tent, he and I, discussing an inscription that had been found the day before. The lettering was extremely minute; Dr. Huukaminaan complained of a headache, and said finally that he was going out for a walk. I went to sleep. Dr. Huukaminaan did not return."

"It's a long way," Mirigant observed, "from here to the sacrificial platforms. *Quite* a long way. It would take at least half an hour to walk there, I'd guess. Perhaps more, for someone his age. He was an old man, I understand."

"But if someone happened to encounter him just outside the camp, though," Tunigorn suggested, "and *forced* him to go all the way down to the platform area—"

Valentine said, "Is a guard posted here at the encampment at night?"

"No. There seemed to be no purpose in doing that."

"And the dig site itself? It's not fenced off, or protected in any way?"

"No."

"Then anyone at all could have left the day-laborers' village as soon as it grew dark," Valentine said, "and waited out there in the road for Dr. Huukaminaan to come out." He glanced toward Vo-Siimifon. "Was Dr. Huukaminaan in the habit of taking a walk before bedtime?"

"Not that I recall."

"And if he *had* chosen to go out late at night for some reason, would he have been likely to take so long a walk?"

"He was quite a robust man, for his age," said the Piurivar. "But even so that would have been an unusual distance to go just for a stroll before bedtime."

"Yes. So it would seem." Valentine turned again to Magadone Sambisa. "It'll be necessary, I'm afraid, for us to question your laborers. And each member of your expedition, too. You understand that at this point we can't arbitrarily rule anyone out."

Her eyes flashed. "Am I under suspicion too, your majesty?"

"At this point," said Valentine, "nobody here is under suspicion. And everyone is. Unless you want me to believe that Dr. Huukaminaan committed suicide by dismembering himself and distributing parts of himself all over the top of that platform."

*

The night had been cool, but the sun sprang into the morning sky with incredible swiftness. Almost at once, early as it was in the day, the air began to throb with desert warmth. It was necessary to get a quick start at the site, Magadone Sambisa had told them, since by midday the intense heat would make work very difficult.

Valentine was ready for her when she called for him soon after dawn. At her request he would be accompanied only by some members of his security detachment, not by any of his fellow lords. Tunigorn grumbled about this, as did Mirigant. But she said – and would not yield on the point – that she preferred that the Pontifex alone come with her today, and after he had seen what she had to show him he could make his own decisions about sharing the information with the others.

She was taking him to the Seventh Pyramid. Or what was left of it, rather, for nothing now remained except the truncated base, a square structure about twenty feet long on each side and five or six feet high, constructed from the same reddish basalt from which the great arena and some of the other public buildings had been made. East of that stump the fragments of the pyramid's upper section, smallish broken blocks of the same reddish stone, lay strewn in the most random way across a wide area. It was as though some angry colossus had contemptuously given the western face of the pyramid one furious slap with the back of his ponderous hand and sent it flying into a thousand pieces. On the side of the stump away from the debris Valentine could make out the pointed summit of the still-intact Sixth Pyramid about five hundred feet away, rising above a copse of little contorted trees, and beyond it were the other five, running onward one after another to the edge of the royal palace itself.

"According to Piurivar lore," Magadone Sambisa said, "the people of Velalisier held a great festival every thousand years, and constructed a pyramid to commemorate each one. So far as we've been able to confirm by examining and dating the six undamaged ones, that's correct. This one, we know, was the last in the series. If we can believe the legend" – and she gave Valentine a meaningful look – "it was built to mark the very festival at which the Defilement took place. And had just been completed when the city was invaded and destroyed by those who had come here to punish its inhabitants for what they had done."

She beckoned to him, leading him around toward the northern side of the shattered pyramid. They walked perhaps fifty feet onward from the stump. Then she halted. The ground had been carefully cut away here. Valentine saw a rectangular opening just large enough for a man to enter, and the beginning of a passageway leading underground and heading back toward the foundations of the pyramid.

A star-shaped marker of bright yellow tape was fastened to a good-sized boulder just to the left of the excavation.

"That's where you found the head, is it?" he asked.

"Not there. Below." She pointed into the opening. "Will you follow me, your majesty?"

Six members of Valentine's security force had gone with Valentine to the pyramid site that morning: the giant warrior-woman Lisamon Hultin, his personal bodyguard, who had accompanied him on all his travels since his juggling days; two shaggy hulking Skandars; a couple of Pontifical officials whom he had inherited from his predecessor's staff; and even a Metamorph, one Aarisiim, who had defected to Valentine's forces from the service of the arch-rebel Faraataa in the final hours of the War of the Rebellion and had been with the Pontifex ever since. All six stepped forward now as if they meant to go down into the excavation with him, though the Skandars and Lisamon Hultin were plainly too big to fit into the entrance. But Magadone Sambisa shook her head fiercely; and Valentine, smiling, signalled to them all to wait for him above.

The archaeologist, lighting a hand-torch, entered the opening in the ground. The descent was steep, via a series of precisely chiseled earthen steps that took them downward nine or ten feet. Then, abruptly, the subterranean passageway leveled off. Here there was a flagstone floor made of broad slabs hewn from some glossy green rock. Magadone Sambisa flashed her light at one and Valentine saw that it bore carved glyphs, runes of some kind, reminiscent of those he had seen in the paving of the grand ceremonial boulevard that ran past the royal palace.

"This is our great discovery," she said. "There are shrines, previously unknown and unsuspected, under each of the seven pyramids. We were working near the Third Pyramid about six months ago, trying to stabilize its foundation, when we stumbled on the first one. It had been plundered, very probably in antiquity. But it was an exciting find all the same, and immediately we went looking for similar shrines beneath the other five intact pyramids. And found them: also plundered. For the time being we didn't bother to go digging for the shrine of the Seventh Pyramid. We assumed that there was no hope of finding anything interesting there, that it must have been looted at the time the pyramid was destroyed. But then Huukaminaan and I decided that we might as well check it out too, and we put down this trench that we've been walking through. Within a day or so we reached this flagstone paving. Come."

They went deeper in, entering a carefully constructed tunnel just about wide enough for four people to stand in it abreast. Its walls were fashioned of thin slabs of black stone laid sideways like so many stacked books, leading upward to a vaulted roof of the same stone that tapered into a series of pointed arches. The craftsmanship was very fine, and distinctly archaic in appearance. The air in the tunnel was hot and musty and dry, ancient air, lifeless air. It had a stale, dead taste in Valentine's nostrils.

"We call this kind of underground vault a processional hypogeum," Magadone Sambisa explained. "Probably it was used by priests carrying offerings to the shrine of the pyramid."

Her torch cast a spreading circlet of pallid light that allowed Valentine to perceive a wall of finely dressed white stone blocking the path just ahead of them. "Is that the foundation of the pyramid we're looking at?" he asked.

"No. What we see here is the wall of the shrine, nestling against the pyramid's base. The pyramid itself is on the far side of it. The other shrines were located right up against their pyramids in the same way. The difference is that all the others had been smashed open. This one has apparently never been breached."

Valentine whistled softly. "And what do you think is inside it?"

"We don't have any idea. We were putting off opening it, waiting for Lord Hissune to return from his processional in Zimroel, so that you and he could be on hand when we broke through the wall. But then – the murder—"

"Yes," Valentine said soberly. And, after a moment: "How strange that the destroyers of the city demolished the seventh pyramid so thoroughly, but left the shrine beneath it intact! You'd think they would have made a clean sweep of the place."

"Perhaps there was something walled up in the shrine that they didn't want to go near, eh? It's a thought, anyway. We may never know the truth, even after we open it. *If* we open it."

"If?"

"There may be problems about that, majesty. Political problems, I mean. We need to discuss them. But this isn't the moment for that."

Valentine nodded. He indicated a row of small indented apertures, perhaps nine inches deep and about a foot high, that had been chiseled in the wall some eighteen inches above ground level. "Were those for putting offerings in?"

"Exactly." Magadone Sambisa flashed the torch across the row from right to left. "We found microscopic traces of dried flowers in several of them, and potsherds and colored pebbles in others – you can still see them there, actually. And some animal remains." She hesitated. "And then, in the alcove on the far left—"

Her torchlight came to rest on a star of yellow tape attached to the shallow alcove's back wall.

Valentine gasped in shock. *"There?"*

"Huukaminaan's head, yes. Placed very neatly in the center of the alcove, facing outward. An offering of some sort, I suppose."

"To whom? To what?"

The archaeologist shrugged and shook her head.

Then, abruptly, she said, "We should go back up now, your majesty. The air down here isn't good to spend a lot of time in. I simply wanted you to see where the shrine was situated. And where we found the missing part of Dr. Huukaminaan's body."

Later in the day, with Nascimonte and Tunigorn and the rest now joining him, Magadone Sambisa showed Valentine the site of the expedition's other significant discovery: the bizarre cemetery, previously unsuspected, where the ancient inhabitants of Velalisier had buried their dead.

Or, more precisely, had buried certain fragments of their dead. "There doesn't appear to be a complete body anywhere in the whole graveyard. In every interment we've opened, what we've found is mere tiny bits – a finger here, an ear there, a lip, a toe. Or some internal organ, even. Each item carefully embalmed, and placed in a beautiful stone casket and buried beneath one of these gravestones. The part for the whole: a kind of metaphorical burial."

Valentine stared in wonder and astonishment.

The twenty-thousand-year-old Metamorph cemetery was one of the strangest sights he had seen in all his years of exploring the myriad wondrous strangenesses that Majipoor had to offer.

It covered an area hardly more than a hundred feet long and sixty feet wide, off in a lonely zone of dunes and weeds a short way beyond the end of one of the north-south flagstone boulevards. In that small plot of land there might have been ten thousand graves, all jammed together. A small stela of brown sandstone, a hand's-width broad and about fifteen inches high, jutted upward from each of the grave plots. And each of them crowded in upon the ones adjacent to it in a higgledy-piggledy fashion so that the cemetery was a dense agglomeration of slender close-set gravestones, tilting this way and that in a manner that utterly befuddled the eye.

At one time every stone must have lovingly been set in a vertical position above the casket containing the bit of the departed that had been chosen for interment here. But the Metamorphs of Velalisier had evidently gone on jamming more and more burials into this little funereal zone over the course of centuries, until each grave overlapped the next in the most chaotic manner. Dozens of them were packed into every square yard of terrain.

As the headstones continued to be crammed one against another without heed for the damage that each new burial was doing to the tombs already in place, the older ones were pushed out of perpendicular by their new neighbors. The slender stones all leaned precariously one way and another, looking the way a forest might after some monstrous storm had passed through, or after the ground beneath it had been bent and buckled by the force of some terrible earthquake. They all stood at crazy angles now, no two slanting in the same direction.

On each of these narrow headstones a single elegant glyph was carved precisely one-third of the way from the top, an intricately patterned whorl of the sort found in other zones of the city. No symbol seemed like any other one. Did they represent the names of the deceased? Prayers to some long-forgotten god?

"We hadn't any idea that this was here," Magadone Sambisa said. "This is the first burial site that's ever been discovered in Velalisier."

"I'll testify to that," Nascimonte said, with a great jovial wink. "I did a little digging here myself, you know, long ago. Tomb-hunting, looking for buried treasure that I might be able to sell somewhere, during the time I was forced from my land in the reign of the false Lord Valentine and living like a bandit in this desert. But not a single grave did any of us come upon then. Not one."

"Nor did we detect any, though we tried," said Magadone Sambisa. "When we found this place it was only by sheer luck. It was hidden deep under the dunes, ten, twelve, twenty feet below the surface of the sand. No one suspected it was here. But one day last winter a terrific whirlwind swept across the valley and hovered right up over this part of the city for half an hour, and by the time it was done whirling the whole dune had been picked up and tossed elsewhere and this amazing collection of gravestones lay exposed. Here. Look."

She knelt and brushed a thin coating of sand away from the base of a gravestone just in front of her. In moments the upper lid of a small box made of polished gray stone came into view. She pried it free and set it to one side.

Tunigorn made a sound of disgust. Valentine, peering down, saw a thing like a curling scrap of dark leather lying within the box.

"They're all like this," said Magadone Sambisa. "Symbolic burial, taking up a minimum of space. An efficient system, considering what a huge population Velalisier must have had in its prime. One tiny bit of the dead person's body buried here, preserved so artfully that it's still in pretty good condition even after all these thousands of years. The rest of it exposed on the hills outside town, for all we know, to be consumed by natural processes of decay. A Piurivar corpse would decay very swiftly. We'd find no traces, after all this time."

"How does that compare with present-day Shapeshifter burial practices?" Mirigant asked.

Magadone Sambisa looked at him oddly. "We know next to nothing about present-day Piurivar burial practices. They're a pretty secretive race, you know. They've never chosen to tell us anything about such things and evidently we've been too polite to ask, because there's hardly a thing on record about it. Hardly a thing."

"You have Shapeshifter scientists on your own staff," Tunigorn said. "Surely it wouldn't be impolite to consult your own associates about something like that. What's the point of training Shapeshifters to be archaeologists if you're going to be too sensitive of their feelings to make any use of their knowledge of their own people's ways?"

"As a matter of fact," said Magadone Sambisa, "I did discuss this find with Dr. Huukaminaan not long after it was uncovered. The layout of the place, the density of the burials, seemed pretty startling to him. But he didn't seem at all surprised by the concept of burial of body parts instead of entire bodies. He gave me to understand what had been done here wasn't all that different in some aspects from things the Piurivars still do today. There wasn't time just then for him to go into further details, though, and we both let the subject slip. And now – now—"

Once more she displayed that look of stunned helplessness, of futility and confusion in the face of violent death, that came over her whenever the topic of the murder of Huukaminaan arose.

Not all that different in some aspects from things the Piurivars still do today, Valentine repeated silently.

He considered the way Huukaminaan's body had been cut apart, the sundered pieces left in various places atop the sacrificial platform, the head carried down into the tunnel beneath the Seventh Pyramid and carefully laid to rest in one of the alcoves of the underground shrine.

There was something implacably alien about that grisly act of dismemberment that brought Valentine once again to the conclusion, mystifying and distasteful but seemingly inescapable, that had been facing him since his arrival here. *The murderer of the Metamorph archaeologiist must have been a Metamorph himself.* As Nascimonte had suggested earlier, there seemed to be a ritual aspect to the butchery that had all the hallmarks of Metamorph work.

But still it made no sense. Valentine had difficulty believing that the old man could have been killed by one of his own people.

"What was Huukaminaan like?" he asked Magadone Sambisa. "I never met him, you know. Was he contentious? Cantankerous?"

"Not in the slightest. A sweet, gentle person. A brilliant scholar. There was no one, Piurivar or human, who didn't love and admire him."

"There must have been one person, at least," said Nascimonte wryly.

Perhaps Nascimonte's theory was worth exploring. Valentine said, "Could there have been some sort of bitter professional disagreement? A dispute over the credit for a discovery, a battle over some piece of theory?"

Magadone Sambisa stared at the Pontifex as though he had gone out of his mind. "Do you think we kill each other over such things, your majesty?"

"It was a foolish suggestion," Valentine said, with a smile. "Well, then," he went on, "suppose Huukaminaan had come into possession of some valuable artifact in the course of his work here, some priceless treasure that would fetch a huge sum in the antiquities market. Might that not have been sufficient cause for murdering him?"

Again the incredulous stare. "The artifacts we find here, majesty, are of the nature of simple sandstone statuettes, and bricks bearing inscriptions, not golden tiaras and emeralds the size of gihorna eggs. Everything worth looting was looted a long, long time ago. And we would no more dream of trying to make a private sale of the little things that we find here than we would – would – than, well, than we would of murdering each other. Our finds are divided equally between the university museum in Arkilon and the Piurivar treasury at Ilirivoyne. In any case – no, no, it's not even worth discussing. The idea's completely absurd." Instantly her cheeks turned flame-red. "Forgive me, majesty, I meant no disrespect."

Valentine brushed the apology aside. "What I'm doing, you

see, is groping for some plausible explanation of the crime. A place to begin our investigation, at least."

"*I'll* give you one, Valentine," Tunigorn said suddenly. His normally open and genial face was tightly drawn in a splenetic scowl that brought his heavy eyebrows together into a single dark line. "The basic thing that we need to keep in mind all the time is that there's a curse on this place. You know that, Valentine. A *curse*. The Shapeshifters themselves put the dark word on the city, the Divine knows how many thousands of years ago, when they smashed it up to punish those who had chopped up those two sea-dragons. They intended the place to be shunned forever. Only ghosts have lived here ever since. By sending these archaeologists of yours in here, Valentine, you're disturbing those ghosts. Making them angry. And so they're striking back. Killing old Huukaminaan was the first step. There'll be more, mark my words!"

"And you think, do you, that ghosts are capable of cutting someone into five or six pieces and scattering the parts far and wide?"

Tunigorn was not amused. "I don't know what sorts of things ghosts may or may not be capable of doing," he said staunchly. "I'm just telling you what has crossed my mind."

"Thank you, my good old friend," said Valentine pleasantly. "We'll give the thought the examination it deserves." And to Magadone Sambisa he said, "I must tell you what has crossed *my* mind, based on what you've shown me today, here and at the pyramid shrine. Which is that the killing of Huukaminaan strikes me as a ritual murder, and the ritual involved is some kind of Piurivar ritual. I don't say that that's what it was; I just say that it certainly looks that way."

"And if it does?"

"Then we have our starting point. It's time now to move to the next phase of our work, I think. Please have the kindness to call your entire group of Piurivar archaeologists together this afternoon. I want to speak with them."

"One by one, or all together?"

"All of them together at first," said Valentine. "After that, we'll see."

But Magadone Sambisa's people were scattered all over the huge archaeological zone, each one involved with some special project, and she begged Valentine not to have them called in until the working day was over. It would take so long to reach them all, she said, that the worst of the heat would have descended by the time they began their return to camp, and they would be compelled to trek across the ruins in the full blaze of noon, instead of settling in some dark cavern to await the cooler hours that lay ahead. Meet with them at sundown, she implored him. Let them finish their day's tasks.

That seemed only reasonable. He said that he would.

But Valentine himself was unable to sit patiently by until dusk. The murder had jarred him deeply. It was one more symptom of the strange new darkness that had come over the world in his lifetime. Huge as it was, Majipoor had long been a peaceful place where there was comfort and plenty for all, and crime of any sort was an extraordinary rarity. But, even so, just in this present generation there had been the assassination of the Coronal Lord Voriax, and then the diabolically contrived usurpation that had pushed Voriax's successor – Valentine – from his throne for a time.

The Metamorphs, everyone knew now, had been behind both of those dire acts.

And after Valentine's recovery of the throne had come the War of the Rebellion, organized by the embittered Metamorph Faraataa, bringing with it plagues, famines, riots, a worldwide panic, great destruction everywhere. Valentine had ended that uprising, finally, by reaching out himself to take Faraataa's life – a deed that the gentle Valentine had regarded with horror, but which he had carried out all the same, because it had to be done.

Now, in this new era of worldwide peace and harmony that

Valentine, reigning as Pontifex, had inaugurated, an admirable and beloved old Metamorph scholar had been murdered in the most brutal way. Murdered here in the holy city of the Metamorphs themselves, while he was in the midst of archaeological work that Valentine had instituted as one way of demonstrating the newfound respect of the human people of Majipoor for the aboriginal people they had displaced. And there was every indication, at least at this point, that the murderer was himself a Metamorph.

But that seemed insane.

Perhaps Tunigorn was right, that all of this was merely the working out of some ancient curse. That was a hard thing for Valentine to swallow. He had little belief in such things as curses. And yet – yet—

Restlessly he stalked the ruined city all through the worst heat of the day, heedless of the discomfort, pulling his hapless companions along. The sun's great golden-green eye stared unrelentingly down. Heat-shimmers danced in the air. The leathery-leaved little shrubs that grew all over the ruins seemed to fold in upon themselves to hide from those torrid blasts of light. Even the innumerable skittering lizards that infested these rocks grew reticent as the temperature climbed.

"I would almost think we had been transported to Suvrael," said Tunigorn, panting in the heat as he dutifully labored along beside the Pontifex. "This is the climate of the miserable southland, not of our pleasant Alhanroel."

Nascimonte gave him a sardonic squinting smirk. "Just one more example of the malevolence of the Shapeshifters, my lord Tunigorn. In the days when the city was alive there were green forests all about this place, and the air was cool and mild. But then the river was turned aside, and the forests died, and nothing was left here but the bare rock that you see, which soaks up the heat of noon and holds it like a sponge. Ask the archaeologist lady, if you don't believe me. This province was deliberately turned into a desert, for the sake of punishing those who had committed great sins in it."

"All the more reason for us to be somewhere else," Tunigorn muttered. "But no, no, this is our place, here with Valentine, now and ever."

Valentine scarcely paid attention to what they were saying. He wandered aimlessly onward, down one weedy byway and another, past fallen columns and shattered facades, past the empty shells of what might once have been shops and taverns, past the ghostly outlines marking the foundation of vanished dwellings that must once have been palatial in their grandeur. Nothing was labeled, and Magadone Sambisa was not with him, now, to bend his ear with endless disquisitions about the former identities of these places. They were bits and pieces of lost Velalisier, that was all he knew: skeletonic remnants of this ancient metropolis.

It was easy enough, even for him, to imagine this place as the lair of ancient phantoms. A glassy glimmer of light shining out of some tumbled mass of broken columns – odd scratchy sounds that might have been those of creatures crawling about where no creatures could be seen – the occasional hiss and slither of shifting sand, sand that moved, so it would appear, of its own volition—

"Every time I visit these ruins," he said to Mirigant, who was walking closest to him now, "I'm astounded by the antiquity of it all. The weight of history that presses down on it."

"History that no one remembers," Mirigant said.

"But its weight remains."

"Not our history, though."

Valentine shot his cousin a scornful look. "So you may believe. But it's Majipoor's history, and what is that if not ours?"

Mirigant shrugged and made no answer.

Was there any meaning, Valentine wondered, in what he had just said? Or was the heat addling his brain?

He pondered it. Into his mind there came, with a force almost like that of an explosion, a vision of the totality of vast

253

Majipoor. Its great continents and overwhelming rivers and immense shining seas, its dense moist jungles and great deserts, its forests of towering trees and mountains rich with strange and wonderful creatures, its multitude of sprawling cities with their populations of many millions. His soul was flooded with an overload of sensation, the perfume of a thousand kinds of flowers, the aromas of a thousand spices, the savory tang of a thousand wondrous meats, the bouquet of a thousand wines. It was a world of infinite richness and variety, this Majipoor of his.

And by a fluke of descent and his brother's bad luck he had come first to be Coronal and now Pontifex of that world. Twenty billion people hailed him as their emperor. His face was on the coinage; the world resounded with his praises; his name would be inscribed forever on the roster of monarchs in the House of Records, an imperishable part of the history of this world.

But once there had been a time when there were no Pontifexes and Coronals here. When such wondrous cities as Ni-Moya and Alaisor and the fifty great urban centers of Castle Mount did not exist. And in that time before human settlement had begun on Majipoor, this city of Velalisier already was.

What right did he have to appropriate this city, already thousands of years dead and desolate when the first colonists arrived from space, into the flow of human history here? In truth there was a discontinuity so deep between *their* Majipoor and *our* Majipoor, he thought, that it might never be bridged.

In any case he could not rid himself of the feeling that this place's great legion of ghosts, in whom he did not even believe, were lurking all around him, and that their fury was still unappeased. Somehow he would have to deal with that fury, which had broken out now, so it seemed, in the form of a terrible act that had cost the life of a studious and inoffensive old man. The logic that infused every aspect of Valentine's soul balked at any comprehension of such a thing. But his own fate, he knew, and perhaps the fate of the world, might depend on his finding a solution to the mystery that had exploded here.

"You will pardon me, good majesty," said Tunigorn, breaking in on Valentine's broodings just as a new maze of ruined streets opened out before them. "But if I take another step in this heat, I will fall down gibbering like a madman. My very brain is melting."

"Why, then, Tunigorn, you should certainly seek refuge quickly, and cool it off! You can ill afford to damage what's left of it, can you, old friend?" Valentine pointed in the direction of the camp. "Go back. Go. But I will continue, I think."

He was not sure why. But something drove him grimly forward across this immense bedraggled sprawl of sand-choked sun-blasted ruins, seeking he knew not what. One by one his other companions dropped away from him, with this apology or that, until only the indefatigable Lisamon Hultin remained. The giantess was ever-faithful. She had protected him from the dangers of Mazadone Forest in the days before his restoration to the Coronal's throne. She had been his guardian in the belly of the sea-dragon that had swallowed them both in the sea off Piliplok, that time when they were shipwrecked sailing from Zimroel to Alhanroel, and she had cut him free and carried him up to safety. She would not leave him now. Indeed she seemed willing to walk on and on with him through the day and the night and the day that followed as well, if that was what here-quired of her.

But eventually even Valentine had had enough. The sun had long since moved beyond its noon height. Sharp-edged pools of shadow, rose and purple and deepest obsidian, were beginning to reach out all about him. He was feeling a little light-headed now, his head swimming a little and his vision wavering from the prolonged strain of coping with the unyielding glare of that blazing sun, and each street of tumbled-down buildings had come to look exactly like its predecessor. It was time to go back. Whatever penance he had been imposing on himself by such an exhausting journey through this dominion of death and destruction must surely have been fulfilled by now. He leaned on Lisamon Hultin's arm now and again as they made their way toward the tents of the encampment.

Magadone Sambisa had assembled her eight Metamorph archaeologists. Valentine, having bathed and rested and had a little to eat, met with them just after sundown in his own tent, accompanied only by the little Vroon, Autifon Deliamber. He wanted to form his opinions of the Metamorphs undistracted by the presence of Nascimonte and the rest; but Deliamber had certain Vroonish wizardly skills that Valentine prized highly, and the small many-tentacled being might well be able to perceive things with those huge and keen golden eyes of his that would elude Valentine's own human vision.

The Shapeshifters sat in a semicircle with Valentine facing them and the tiny wizened old Vroon at his left hand. The Pontifex ran his glance down the group, from the site-boss Kaastisiik at one end to the paleographer Vo-Siimifon on the other. They looked back at him calmly, almost indifferently, these seven rubbery-faced slope-eyed Piurivars, as he told them of the things he had seen this day, the cemetery and the shattered pyramid and the shrine beneath it, and the alcove where Huukaminaan's severed head had been so carefully placed by his murderer.

"There was, wouldn't you say, a certain formal aspect to the murder?" Valentine said. "The cutting of the body into pieces? The carrying of the head down to the shrine, the placement in the alcove of offerings?" His gaze fastened on Thiuurinen, the ceramics expert, a lithe, diminutive Metamorph woman with lovely jade-green skin. "What's your reading on that?" he asked her.

Her expression was wholly impassive. "As a ceramicist I have no opinion at all."

"I don't want your opinion as a ceramicist, just as a member of the expedition. A colleague of Dr. Huukaminaan's. Does it seem to you that putting the head there meant that some kind of offering was being made?"

"It is only conjecture that those alcoves were places of offering," said Thiuurinen primly. "I am not in a position to speculate."

Nor would she. Nor would any of them. Not Kaastisiik, not Vo-Siimifon, not the stratigrapher Pamikuuk, not Hieekraad, the custodian of material artifacts, nor Driismiil, the architectural specialist, nor Klelliin, the authority on Piurivar paleo-technology, nor Viitaal-Twuu, the specialist in metallurgy.

Politely, mildly, firmly, unshakably, they brushed aside Valentine's hypotheses about ritual murder. Was the gruesome dismemberment of Dr. Huukaminaan a hearkening-back to the funereal practices of ancient Velalisier? Was the placing of his head in that alcove likely to have been any kind of propitiation of some supernatural being? Was there anything in Piurivar tradition that might countenance killing someone in that particular fashion? They could not say. They would not say. Nor, when he inquired as to whether their late colleague might have had an enemy here at the site, did they provide him with any information.

And they merely gave him the Piurivar equivalent of a shrug when he wondered out loud whether there could have been some struggle over the discovery of a valuable artifact that might have led to Huukaminaan's murder; or even a quarrel of a more abstract kind, a fierce disagreement over the findings or goals of the expedition. Nobody showed any sign of outrage at his implication that one of them might have killed old Huukaminaan over such a matter. They behaved as though the whole notion of doing such a thing were beyond their comprehension, a concept too alien even to consider.

During the course of the interview Valentine took the opportunity to aim at least one direct question at each of them. But the result was always the same. They were unhelpful without seeming particularly evasive. They were unforthcoming without appearing unusually sly or secretive. There was nothing overtly suspicious about their refusal to cooperate. They seemed to be precisely what they claimed to be: scientists, studious scholars, devoted to uncovering the buried mysteries of their race's remote past, who knew nothing at all about the mystery that had erupted right here in their midst. He did not feel himself to be in the presence of murderers here.

And yet – and yet—

They were Shapeshifters. He was the Pontifex, the emperor of the race that had conquered them, the successor across eight thousand years of the half-legendary soldier-king Lord Stiamot who had deprived them of their independence for all time. Mild and scholarly though they might be, these eight Piurivars before him surely could not help but feel anger, on some level of their souls, toward their human masters. They had no reason to cooperate with him. They would not see themselves under any obligation to tell him the truth. And – was this only his innate and inescapable racial prejudices speaking, Valentine wondered? – intuition told him to take nothing at face value among these people. Could he really trust the impression of apparent innocence that they gave? Was it possible ever for a human to read the things that lay hidden behind a Metamorph's cool impenetrable features?

"What do you think?" he asked Deliamber, when the seven Shapeshifters had gone. "Murderers or not?"

"Probably not," the Vroon replied. "Not these. Too soft, too citified. But they were holding something back. I'm certain of that."

"You felt it too, then?"

"Beyond any doubt. What I sensed, your majesty – do you know what the Vroon word *hsirthiir* means?"

"Not really."

"It isn't easy to translate. But it has to do with questioning someone who doesn't intend to tell you any lies but isn't necessarily going to tell you the truth, either, unless you know exactly how to call it forth. You pick up a powerful perception that there's an important layer of meaning hidden somewhere beneath the surface of what you're being told, but that you aren't going to be allowed to elicit that hidden meaning unless you ask precisely the right question to unlock it. Which means, essentially, that you already have to know the information that you're looking for before you can ask the question that would reveal it. It's a very frustrating sensation, *hsirthiir*: almost painful, in fact. It is like hitting one's beak against a stone wall. I felt myself placed in a state of *hsirthiir* just now. Evidently so did you, your majesty."

"Evidently I did," said Valentine.

There was one more visit to make, though. It had been a long day and a terrible weariness was coming over Valentine now. But he felt some inner need to cover all the basic territory in a single sweep; and so, once darkness had fallen, he asked Magadone Sambisa to conduct him to the village of the Metamorph laborers.

She was unhappy about that. "We don't usually like to intrude on them after they've finished their day's work and gone back there, your majesty."

"You don't usually have murders here, either. Or visits from the Pontifex. I'd rather speak with them tonight than disrupt tomorrow's digging, if you don't mind."

Deliamber accompanied him once again. At her own insistence, so did Lisamon Hultin. Tunigorn was too tired to go – his hike through the ruins at midday had done him in – and Mirigant was feeling feverish from a touch of sunstroke; but formidable old Duke Nascimonte readily agreed to ride with the Pontifex, despite his great age. The final member of the party was Aarisiim, the Metamorph member of Valentine's security staff, whom Valentine brought with him not so much for protection – Lisamon Hultin would look after that – as for the *hsirthiir* problem.

Aarisiim, turncoat though he once had been, seemed to Valentine to be as trustworthy as any Piurivar was likely to be: he had risked his own life to betray his master Faraataa to Valentine in the time of the Rebellion, when he had felt that Faraataa had gone beyond all decency by threatening to slay the Metamorph queen. He could be helpful now, perhaps, detecting things that eluded even Deliamber's powerful perceptions.

The laborers' village was a gaggle of meager wickerwork huts outside the central sector of the dig. In its flimsy makeshift look it reminded Valentine of Ilirivoyne, the Shapeshifter capital in the jungle of Zimroel, which he had visited so many years before. But this place was even sadder and more disheartening than Ilirivoyne. There, at least, the Metamorphs had had an abundance of tall straight saplings and jungle vines with which to build their ramshackle huts, whereas the only construction materials available to them here were the gnarled and twisted desert shrubs that dotted the Velalisier plain. And so their huts were miserable little things, dismally warped and contorted.

They had had advance word, somehow, that the Pontifex was coming. Valentine found them arrayed in groups of eight or ten in front of their shacks, clearly waiting for his arrival. They were a pitiful starved-looking bunch, gaunt and shabby and ragged, very different from the urbane and cultivated Metamorphs of Magadone Sambisa's archaelogical team. Valentine wondered where they found the strength to do the digging that was required of them in this inhospitable climate.

As the Pontifex came into view they shuffled forward to meet him, quickly surrounding him and the rest of his party in a way that caused Lisamon Hultin to hiss sharply and put her hand to the hilt of her vibration-sword.

But they did not appear to mean any harm. They clustered excitedly around him and to his amazement offered homage in the most obsequious way, jostling among themselves for a chance to kiss the hem of his tunic, kneeling in the sand before him, even prostrating themselves. "No," Valentine cried, dismayed. "This isn't necessary. It isn't right." Already Magadone Sambisa was ordering them brusquely to get back, and Lisamon Hultin and

Nascimonte were shoving the ones closest to Valentine away from him. The giantess was doing it calmly, unhurriedly, efficiently, but Nascimonte was prodding them more truculently, with real detestation apparent in his fiery eyes. Others came pressing forward as fast as the first wave retreated, though, pushing in upon him in frantic determination.

So eager were these weary toil-worn people to show their obeisance to the Pontifex, in fact, that he could not help regarding their enthusiasm as blatantly false, an ostentatious overdoing of whatever might have been appropriate. How likely was it, he wondered, that any group of Piurivars, however lowly and simple, would feel great unalloyed joy at the sight of the Pontifex of Majipoor? Or would, of their own accord, stage such a spontaneous demonstration of delight?

Some, men and women both, were even allowing themselves to mimic the forms of the visitors by way of compliment, so that half a dozen blurry distorted Valentines stood before him, and a couple of Nascimontes, and a grotesque half-sized imitation of Lisamon Hultin. Valentine had experienced that peculiar kind of honor before, in his Ilirivoyne visit, and he had found it disturbing and even chilling then. It distressed him again now. Let them shift shapes if they wished – they had that capacity, to use as they pleased – but there was something almost sinister about this appropriation of the visages of their visitors.

And the jostling began to grow even wilder and more frenzied. Despite himself Valentine started to feel some alarm. There were more than a hundred villagers, and the visitors numbered only a handful. There could be real trouble if things got out of control.

Then in the midst of the hubbub a powerful voice called out,"Back! Back!" And at once the whole ragged band of Shapeshifters shrank away from Valentine as though they had been struck by whips. There was a sudden stillness and silence. Out of the now motionless throng there stepped a tall Metamorph of unusually muscular and powerful build. He made a deep gesticulation and announced, in a dark rumbling tone quite unlike that of any Metamorph voice Valentine had ever heard before, "I am Vathiimeraak, the foreman of these workers. I beg you to feel welcome here among us, Pontifex. We are your servants."

But there was nothing servile about him. He was plainly a man of presence and authority. Briskly he apologized for the uncouth behavior of his people, explaining that they were simple peasants astounded by the presence of a Power of the Realm among them, and this was merely their way of showing respect.

"I know this man," murmured Aarisiim into Valentine's left ear.

But there was no opportunity just then to find out more; for Vathiimeraak, turning away, made a signal with one upraised hand and instantly the scene became one of confusion and noise once again. The villagers went running off in a dozen different directions, some returning almost at once with platters of sausages and bowls of wine for their guests, others hauling lopsided tables and benches from the huts. Platoons of them came crowding in once more on Valentine and his companions, this time urging them to sample the delicacies they had to offer.

"They're giving us their own dinners!" Magadone Sambisa protested. And she ordered Vathiimeraak to call off the feast. But the foreman replied smoothly that it would offend the villagers to refuse their hospitality, and in the end there was no help for it: they must sit down at table and partake of all that the villagers brought for them.

"If you will, majesty," said Nascimonte, as Valentine reached for a bowl of wine. The duke took it from him and sipped it first; and only after a moment did he return it. He insisted also on tasting Valentine's sausages for him, and the scraps of boiled vegetables that went with them.

It had not occurred to Valentine that the villagers would try to poison him. But he allowed old Nascimonte to enact his charming little rite of medieval chivalry without objection. He was too fond of the old man to want to spoil his gesture.

Vathiimeraak said, when the feasting had gone on for some time, "You are here, your majesty, about the death of Dr. Huukaminaan, I assume?"

The foreman's bluntness was startling. "Could it not be," Valentine said good-humoredly, "that I just wanted to observe the progress being made at the excavations?"

Vathiimeraak would have none of that. "I will do whatever you may require of me in your search for the murderer," he said, rapping the table sharply to underscore his words. For an instant the outlines of his broad, heavy-jowled face rippled and wavered as if he were on the verge of undergoing an involuntary metamorphosis. Among the Piurivar, Valentine knew, that was a sign of being swept by some powerful emotion. "I had the greatest respect for Dr. Huukaminaan. It was a privilege to work beside him. I often dug for him myself, when I felt the site was too delicate to entrust to less skillful hands. He thought that that was improper, at first, that the foreman should dig, but I said, No, no, Dr. Huukaminaan, I beg you to allow me this glory, and he understood, and permitted me. How may I help you to find the perpetrator of this dreadful crime?"

He seemed so solemn and straightforward and open that Valentine could not help but find himself immediately on guard. Vathiimeraak's strong, booming voice and overly formal choice of phrase had an overly theatrical quality. His elaborate sincerity seemed much like the extreme effusiveness of the villagers' demonstration, all that kneeling and kissing of his hem: unconvincing because it was so excessive.

You are too suspicious of these people, he told himself. This man is simply speaking as he thinks a Pontifex should be spoken to. And in any case I think he can be useful.

He said, "How much do you know of how the murder was committed?"

Vathiimeraak responded without hesitation, as if he had been holding a well-rehearsed reply in readiness. "I know that it happened late at night, the week before this, somewhere between the Hour of the Gihorna and the Hour of the Jackal. A person or persons lured Dr. Huukaminaan from his tent and led him to the Tables of the Gods, where he was killed and cut into pieces. We found the various segments of his body the next morning atop the western platform, all but his head. Which we discovered later that day in one of the alcoves along the base of the Shrine of the Downfall."

Pretty much the standard account, Valentine thought. Except for one small detail.

"The Shrine of the Downfall? I haven't heard that term before."

"The shrine of the Seventh Pyramid is what I mean," said Vathiimeraak. "The unopened shrine that Dr. Magadone Sambisa found. The name that I used is what we call it among ourselves. You notice that I do not say she 'discovered' it. We have always known that it was there, adjacent to the broken pyramid. But no one ever asked us, and so we never spoke of it."

Valentine glanced across at Deliamber, who nodded ever so minutely. *Hsirthiir* again, yes.

Something was not quite right, though. Valentine said, "Dr. Magadone Sambisa told me that she and Dr. Huukaminaan came upon the seventh shrine jointly, I think. She indicated that he was just as surprised at finding it there as she had been. Are you claiming that you knew of its existence, but he didn't?"

"There is no Piurivar who does not know of the existence of the Shrine of the Downfall," said Vathiimeraak stolidly. "It was sealed at the time of the Defilement and contains, we believe, evidence of the Defilement itself. If Dr. Magadone Sambisa formed the impression that Dr. Huukaminaan was unaware that it was there, that was an incorrect impression." Once again the edges of the foreman's face flickered and wavered. He looked worriedly toward Magadone Sambisa and said, "I mean no offense in contradicting you, Dr. Magadone Sambisa."

"None taken," she said, a little stiffly. "But if Huukaminaan knew of the shrine before the day we found it, he never said a thing about it to me."

"Perhaps he had hoped it would not be found," Vathiimeraak replied.

This brought a show of barely concealed consternation from Magadone Sambisa; and Valentine himself sensed that there was something here that needed to be followed up. But they were drifting away from the main issue.

"What I need you to do," said Valentine to the foreman, "is to determine the whereabouts of every single one of your people during the hours when the murder was committed." He saw Vathiimeraak's reaction beginning to take form, and added quickly, "I'm not suggesting that we believe at this point that anyone from the village killed Dr. Huukaminaan. No one at all is under suspicion at this point. But we do need to account for everybody who was present in or around the excavation zone that night."

"I will do what I can to find out."

"Your help will be invaluable, I know," Valentine said.

"You will also want to enlist the aid of our khivanivod," Vathiimeraak said. "He is not among us tonight. He has gone off on a spiritual retreat into the farthest zone of the city to pray for the purification of the soul of the killer of Dr. Huukaminaan, whoever that may be. I will send him to you when he returns."

Another little surprise.

A khivanivod was a Piurivar holy man, something midway between a priest and a wizard. They were relatively uncommon in modern Metamorph life, and it was remarkable that there should be one in residence at this scruffy out-of-the-way village. Unless, of course, the high religious leaders of the Piurivars had decided that it was best to install one at Velalisier for the duration of the dig, to insure that everything was done with the proper respect for the holy places. It was odd that Magadone Sambisa hadn't mentioned to him that a khivanivod was present here.

"Yes," said Valentine, a little uneasily. "Send him to me, yes. By all means."

As they rode away from the laborers' village Nascimonte said, "Well, Valentine, I'm pained to confess that I find myself once again forced to question your judgment."

"You do suffer much pain on my behalf," said Valentine, with a twinkling smile. "Tell me, Nascimonte: where have I gone amiss this time?"

"You enlisted that man Vathiimeraak as your ally in the investigation. You treated him, in fact, as though he were a trusted constable of police."

"He seems steady enough to me. And the villagers are terrified of him. What harm is there in asking him to question them for us? If we interrogate them ourselves, they'll just shut up like clams – or at best they'll tell us all kinds of fantastic stories. Whereas Vathiimeraak might just be able to bully the truth out of them. Some useful fraction of it, anyway."

"Not if he's the murderer himself," said Nascimonte.

"Ah, is that it? You've solved the crime, my friend? Vathiimeraak did it?"

"That could very well be."

"Explain, if you will, then."

Nascimonte gestured to Aarisiim. "Tell him."

The Metamorph said, "Majesty, I remarked to you when I first saw Vathiimeraak that I thought I knew that man from somewhere. And indeed I do, though it took me a little while more to place him. He is a kinsman of the rebel Faraataa. In the days when I was with Faraataa in Piurivayne, this Vathiimeraak was often by our side."

That was unexpected. But Valentine kept his reaction to himself. Calmly he said, "Does that matter? What of our amnesty, Aarisiim? All rebels who agreed to keep the peace after the collapse of Faraataa's campaign have been forgiven and restored to full civil rights. I should hardly need to remind you, of all people, of that."

"It doesn't mean they all turned into good citizens overnight, does it, Valentine?" Nascimonte demanded. "Surely it's possible that this Vathiimeraak, a man of Faraataa's own blood, still harbors powerful feelings of—"

Valentine looked toward Magadone Sambisa. "Did you know he was related to Faraataa when you hired him as foreman?"

She seemed embarrassed. "No, majesty, I certainly did not. But I was aware that he had been in the Rebellion and had accepted the amnesty. And he came with the highest recommendation. We're supposed to believe that the amnesty has some meaning, doesn't it? That the Rebellion's over and done with, that those who took part in it and repented deserve to be allowed—"

"And has he truly repented, do you think?" Nascimonte asked. "Can anyone know, really? I say he's a fraud from top to toe. That big booming voice! That high-flown style of speaking! Those expressions of profound reverence for the Pontifex! Phony, every bit of it. And as for killing Huukaminaan, just look at him! Do you think it could have been easy to cut the poor man up in pieces that way? But Vathiimeraak's built like a bull-bidlak. In that village of thin flimsy folk he stands out the way a dwikka tree would in a flat meadow."

"Because he has the strength for the crime doesn't yet prove that he's guilty of it," said Valentine in some annoyance. "And this other business, of his being related to Faraataa – what possible motive does that give him for slaughtering that harmless old Piurivar archaeologist? No, Nascimonte. No. No. No. You and Tunigorn between you, I know, would take about five minutes to decree that the man should be locked away for life in the Sangamor vaults that lie deep under the Castle. But we need a little evidence before we proclaim anyone a murderer." To Magadone Sambisa he said, "What about this khivanivod, now? Why weren't we told that there's a khivanivod living in this village?"

"He's been away since the day after the murder, your majesty," she said, looking at Valentine apprehensively. "To be perfectly truthful, I forgot all about him."

"What kind of person is he? Describe him for me."

A shrug. "Old. Dirty. A miserable superstition-monger, like all these tribal shamans. What can I say? I dislike having him around. But it's the price we pay for permission to dig here, I suppose."

"Has he caused any trouble for you?"

"A little. Constantly sniffing into things, worrying that we'll commit some sort of sacrilege. *Sacrilege*, in a city that the Piurivars themselves destroyed and put a curse on! What possible harm could we do here, after what they've already inflicted on it?"

"This was their capital," said Valentine. "They were free to do with it as they pleased. That doesn't mean they're glad to have us come in here and root around in its ruins. But has he actually tried to halt any part of your work, this khivanivod?"

"He objects to our unsealing the Shrine of the Downfall."

"Ah. You did say there was some political problem about that. He's filed a formal protest, has he?" The understanding by which Valentine had negotiated the right to send archaeologists into Velalisier included a veto power for the Piurivars over any aspect of the work that was not to their liking.

"So far he's simply told us he doesn't want us to open the shrine," said Magadone Sambisa. "He and I and Dr. Huuka-minaan were supposed to have a meeting about it last week and try to work out a compromise, although what kind of middle ground there can be between opening the shrine and *not* opening it is hard for me to imagine. In any event the meeting never happened, for obvious tragic reasons. Now that you're here, perhaps you'll adjudicate the dispute for us when Torkkinuuminaad gets back from wherever he's gone off to."

"Torkkinuuminaad?" Valentine said. "Is that the khivanivod's name?"

"Torkkinuuminaad, yes."

"These jawbreaking Shapeshifter names," Nascimonte said grumpily. "Torkkinuuminaad! Vathiimeraak! Huukaminaan!"

He glowered at Aarisiim. "By the Divine, fellow, was it absolutely necessary for you people to give yourself names that are so utterly impossible to pronounce, when you could just as easily have—"

"The system is very logical," Aarisiim replied serenely. "The doubling of the vowels in the first part of a name implies—"

"Save this discussion for some other time, if you will," said Valentine, making a chopping gesture with his hand. To Magadone Sambisa he said, "Just out of curiosity, what was the khivanivod's relationship with Dr. Huukaminaan like? Difficult? Tense? Did he think it was sacrilegious to pull the weeds off these ruins and set some of the buildings upright again?"

"Not at all," Magadone Sambisa said. "They worked hand in glove. They had the highest respect for each other, though the Divine only knows why Dr. Huukaminaan tolerated that filthy old savage for half a minute. Why? Are you suggesting that *Torkkinuuminaad* could have been the murderer?"

"Is that so unlikely? You haven't had a single good thing to say about him yourself."

"He's an irritating nuisance and in the matter of the shrine, at least, he's certainly made himself a serious obstacle to our work. But a murderer? Even I wouldn't go that far, your majesty. Anyone could see that he and Huukaminaan had great affection for each other."

"We should question him, all the same," said Nascimonte.

"Indeed," said Valentine. "Tomorrow, I want messengers sent out through the archaeological zone in search of him. He's somewhere around the ruins, right? Let's find him and bring him in. If that interrupts his spiritual retreat, so be it. Tell him that the Pontifex commands his presence."

"I'll see to it," said Magadone Sambisa.

"The Pontifex is very tired, now," said Valentine. "The Pontifex is going to go to sleep."

*

Alone in his grand royal tent at last after the interminable exertions of the busy day, he found himself missing Carabella with surprising intensity: that small and sinewy woman who had shared his destiny almost from the beginning of the strange time when he had found himself at Pidruid, at the other continent's edge, bereft of all memory, all knowledge of self. It was she, loving him only for himself, all unknowing that he was in fact a Coronal in baffled exile from his true identity, who had helped him join the juggling troupe of Zalzan Kavol; and gradually their lives had merged; and when he had commenced his astounding return to the heights of power she had followed him to the summit of the world.

He wished she were with him now. To sit beside him, to talk with him as they always talked before bedtime. To go over with him the twisting ramifications of all that had been set before him this day. To help him make sense out of the tangled mysteries this dead city posed for him. And simply to *be* with him.

But Carabella had not followed him here to Velalisier. It was a foolish waste of his time, she had argued, for him to go in person to investigate this murder. Send Tunigorn; send Mirigant; send Sleet; send any one of a number of high Pontifical officials. But why go yourself?

"Because I must," Valentine had replied. "Because I've made myself responsible for integrating the Metamorphs into the life of this world. The excavations at Velalisier are an essential part of that enterprise. And the murder of the old archaeologist leads me to think that conspirators are trying to interfere with those excavations."

"This is very far-fetched," said Carabella, then.

"And if it is, so be it. But you know how I long for a chance to free myself of the Labyrinth, if only for a week or two. So I will go to Velalisier."

"And I will not. I loathe that place, Valentine. It's a horrid place of death and destruction. I've seen it twice, and its charm isn't growing on me. If you go, you'll go without me."

"I mean to go, Carabella."

"Go, then. If you must." And she kissed him on the tip of the nose, for they were not in the custom of quarreling, or even of disagreeing greatly. But when he went, it was indeed without her. She was in their royal chambers in the Labyrinth tonight, and he was here, in his grand but solitary tent, in this parched and broken city of ancient ghosts.

They came to him that night in his dreams, those ghosts.

They came to him with such intensity that he thought he was having a sending – a lucid and purposeful direct communication in the form of a dream.

But this was like no sending he had ever had. Hardly had he closed his eyes but he found himself wandering in his sleep among the cracked and splintered buildings of dead Velalisier. Eerie ghost-light, mystery-light, came dancing up out of every shattered stone. The city glowed lime-green and lemon-yellow, pulsating with inner luminescence. Glowing faces, ghost-faces, grinned mockingly at him out of the air. The sun itself swirled and leaped in wild loops across the sky.

A dark hole leading into the ground lay open before him, and unquestioningly he entered it, descending a long flight of massive lichen-encrusted stone steps with archaic twining runes carved in them. Every movement was arduous for him. Though he was going steadily lower, the effort was like that of climbing. Struggling all the way, he made his way ever deeper, but he felt constantly as though he were traveling upward against a powerful pull, ascending some inverted pyramid, not a slender one like those above ground in this city, but one of unthinkable mass and diameter. He imagined himself to be fighting his way up the side of a mountain; but it was a mountain that pointed downward, deep into the world's bowels. And the path was carrying him down, he knew, into some labyrinth far more frightful than the one in which he dwelled in daily life.

The whirling ghost-faces flashed dizzyingly by him and went spinning away. Cackling laughter floated backward to him out of the darkness. The air was moist and hot and rank. The pull of gravity was oppressive. As he descended, traveling through level after endless level, momentary flares of dizzying yellow light showed him caverns twisting away from him on all sides, radiating outward at incomprehensible angles that were both concave and convex.

And now there was sudden numbing brightness. The throbbing fire of an underground sun streamed upward toward him from the depths ahead of him, a harsh, menacing glare.

Valentine found himself drawn helplessly toward that terrible light; and then, without perceptible transition, he was no longer underground at all, but out in the vastness of Velalisier Plain, standing atop one of the great platforms of blue stone known as the Tables of the Gods.

There was a long knife in his hand, a curving scimitar that flashed like lightning in the brilliance of the noon sun.

And as he looked out across the plain he saw a mighty procession coming toward him from the east, from the direction of the distant sea: thousands of people, hundreds of thousands, like an army of ants on the march. No, two armies; for the marchers were divided into two great parallel columns. Valentine could see, at the end of each column far off near the horizon, two enormous wooden wagons mounted on titanic wheels. Great hawsers were fastened to them, and the marchers, with mighty groaning tugs, were hauling the wagons slowly forward, a foot or two with each pull, into the center of the city.

Atop each of the wagons a colossal water-king lay trussed, a sea-dragon of monstrous size. The great creatures were glaring furiously at their captors but were unable, even with a sea-dragon's prodigious strength, to free themselves from their bonds, strain as they might. And with each tug on the hawsers the wagons bearing them carried them closer to the twin platforms called the Tables of the Gods.

The place of the sacrifice.

The place where the terrible madness of the Defilement was

to happen. Where Valentine the Pontifex of Majipoor waited with the long gleaming blade in his hand.

"Majesty? Majesty?"

Valentine blinked and came groggily awake. A Shapeshifter stood above him, extremely tall and greatly attenuated of form, his eyes so sharply slanted and narrowed that it seemed at first glance that he had none at all. Valentine began to jump up in alarm; and then, recognizing the intruder after a moment as Aarisiim, he relaxed.

"You cried out," the Metamorph said. "I was on my way to you to tell you some strange news I have learned, and when I was outside your tent I heard your voice. Are you all right, your majesty?"

"A dream, only. A very nasty dream." Which still lingered disagreeably at the edges of his mind. Valentine shivered and tried to shake himself free of its grasp. "What time is it, Aarisiim?"

"The Hour of the Haigus, majesty."

Past the middle of the night, that was. Well along toward dawn.

Valentine forced himself the rest of the way into wakefulness. Eyes fully open now, he stared up into the practically featureless face. "There's news, you say? What news?"

The Metamorph's color deepened from pale green to a rich chart reuse, and his eye-slits fluttered swiftly three or four times. "I have had a conversation this night with one of the archaeologists, the woman Hieekraad, she who keeps the records of the discovered artifacts. The foreman of the diggers brought her to me, the man Vathiimeraak, from the village. He and this Hieekraad are lovers, it seems."

Valentine stirred impatiently. "Get to the point, Aarisiim."

"I approach it, sir. The woman Hieekraad, it seems, has revealed things to the man Vathiimeraak about the excavations that a mere foreman might otherwise not have known. He has told those things to me this evening."

"Well?"

"They have been lying to us, majesty – all the archaeologists, the whole pack of them, deliberately concealing something important. Something *quite* important, a major discovery. Vathiimeraak, when he learned from this Hieekraad that we had been deceived in this way, made the woman come with him to me, and compelled her to reveal the whole story to me."

"Go on."

"It was this," said Aarisiim. He paused a moment, swaying a little as though he were about to plunge into a fathomless abyss. "Dr. Huukaminaan, two weeks before he died, uncovered a burial site that had never been detected before. This was in an otherwise desolate region out at the western edge of the city. Magadone Sambisa was with him. It was a post-abandonment site, dating from the historic era. From a time not long after Lord Stiamot, actually."

"But how could that be?" said Valentine, frowning. "Completely aside from the little matter that there was a curse on this place and no Piurivar would have dared to set foot in it after it was destroyed, there weren't any Piurivars living on this continent at that time anyway. Stiamot had sent them all into the reservations on Zimroel. You know that very well, Aarisiim. Something's wrong here."

"This was not a Piurivar burial, your majesty."

"What?"

"It was the tomb of a human," Aarisiim said. "The tomb of a *Pontifex*, according to the woman Hieekraad."

Valentine would not have been more surprised if Aarisiim had set off an explosive charge. "A Pontifex?" he repeated numbly. "The tomb of a Pontifex, here in Velalisier?"

"So did this Hieekraad say. A definite identification. The symbols on the wall of the tomb – the Labyrinth sign, and other things of that sort – the ceremonial objects found lying next to the body – inscriptions – everything indicated that this was a Pontifex's grave, thousands of years old. So she said; and I think she was telling the truth. Vathiimeraak was standing over her, scowling, as she spoke. She was too frightened of him to have uttered any falsehoods just then."

Valentine rose and paced fiercely about the tent. "By the Divine, Aarisiim! If this is true, it's something that should have been brought to my attention as soon as it came to light. Or at least mentioned to me upon my arrival here. The tomb of some ancient Pontifex, and they hide it from me? Unbelievable. Unbelievable!"

"It was Magadone Sambisa herself who ordered that all news of the discovery was to be suppressed. There would be no public announcement whatever. Not even the diggers were told what had been uncovered. It was to be a secret known to the archaeologists of the dig, only."

"This according to Hieekraad also?"

"Yes, majesty. She said that Magadone Sambisa gave those orders the very day the tomb was found. This Hieekraad furthermore told me that Dr. Huukaminaan disagreed strenuously with Magadone Sambisa's decision, that indeed they had a major quarrel over it. But in the end he gave in. And when the murder happened, and word came that you were going to visit Velalisier, Magadone Sambisa called a meeting of the staff and reiterated that nothing was to be said to you about it. Everyone involved with the dig was specifically told to keep all knowledge of it from you."

"Absolutely incredible," Valentine muttered.

Earnestly Aarisiim said, "You must protect the woman Hieekraad, majesty, as you investigate this thing. She will be in great trouble if Magadone Sambisa learns that she's the one who let the story of the tomb get out."

"Hieekraad's not the only one who's going to be in trouble," Valentine said. He slipped from his nightclothes and started to dress.

"One more thing, majesty. The khivanivod – Torkkinuuminaad? He's at the tomb site right now. That's where he went to make his prayer retreat. I have this information from the foreman Vathiimeraak."

"Splendid," Valentine said. His head was whirling. "The village khivanivod mumbling Piurivar prayers in the tomb of a Pontifex! Beautiful! Wonderful! –Get me Magadone Sambisa, right away, Aarisiim."

"Majesty, the hour is very early, and—"

"Did you hear me, Aarisiim?"

"Majesty," said the Shapeshifter, more subserviently this time. He bowed deeply. And went out to fetch Magadone Sambisa.

"An ancient Pontifex's tomb, Magadone Sambisa, and no announcement is made? An ancient Pontifex's tomb, and when the current Pontifex comes to inspect your dig, you go out of your way to keep him from learning about it? This is all extremely difficult for me to believe, let me assure you."

Dawn was still an hour away. Magadone Sambisa, called from her bed for this interview, looked even paler and more and haggard than she had yesterday, and now there might have been a glint of fear in her eyes as well. But for all that, she still was capable of summoning some of the unrelenting strength that had propelled her to the forefront of her profession: there was even a steely touch of defiance in her voice as she said, "Who told you about this tomb, your majesty?"

Valentine ignored the sally. "It was at your order, was it, that the story was suppressed?"

"Yes."

"Over Dr. Huukaminaan's strong objections, so I understand."

Now fury flashed across her features. "They've told you everything, haven't they? Who was it? Who?"

"Let me remind you, lady, that I am the one asking the questions here. It's true, then, that Huukaminaan disagreed with you about concealing the discovery?"

"Yes." In a very small voice.

"Why was that?"

"He saw it as a crime against the truth," Magadone Sambisa said, still speaking very quietly now. "You have to understand, majesty, that Dr. Huukaminaan was utterly dedicated to his work. Which was, as it is for us all, the recovery of the lost aspects of our past through rigorous application of formal archaeological disciplines. He was totally committed to this, a true and pure scientist."

"Whereas you are not committed quite so totally?"

Magadone Sambisa reddened and glanced shamefacedly to one side. "I admit that my actions may make it seem that way. But sometimes even the pursuit of truth has to give way, at least for a time, before tactical realities. Surely you, a Pontifex, would not deny that. And I had reasons, reasons that seemed valid enough to me, for not wanting to let news of this tomb reach the public. Dr. Huukaminaan didn't agree with my position; and he and I battled long and hard over it. It was the only occasion in our time as co-leaders of this expedition that we disagreed over anything."

"And finally it became necessary, then, for you to have him murdered? Because he yielded to you only grudgingly, and you weren't sure he really would keep quiet?"

"*Majesty!*" It was a cry of almost inexpressible shock.

"A motive for the killing can be seen there. Isn't that so?"

She looked stunned. She waved her arms helplessly about, the palms of her hands turned outward in appeal. A long moment passed before she could bring herself to speak. But she had recovered much of her composure when she did.

"Majesty, what you have just suggested is greatly offensive to me. I am guilty of hiding the tomb discovery, yes. But I swear to you that I had nothing to do with Dr. Huukaminaan's death. I can't possibly tell you how much I admired that man. We had our professional differences, but—" She shook her head. She looked drained. Very quietly she said, "I didn't kill him. I have no idea who did."

Valentine chose to accept that, for now. It was hard for him to believe that she was merely play-acting her distress.

"Very well, Magadone Sambisa. But now tell me why you decided to conceal the finding of that tomb."

"I would have to to tell you, first, an old Piurivar legend, a tale out of their mythology, one that I heard from the khivanivod Torkkinuuminaad on the day that we found the tomb."

"Must you?"

"I must, yes."

Valentine sighed. "Go ahead, then."

Magadone Sambisa moistened her lips and drew a deep breath.

"There once was a Pontifex, so the story goes," she said, "who lived in the years soon after the conquest of the Piurivars by Lord Stiamot. This Pontifex had fought in the War of the Conquest himself when he was a young man, and had had charge over a camp of Piurivar prisoners, and had listened to some of their campfire tales. Among which was the story of the Defilement at Velalisier – the sacrifice by the Final King of the two sea-dragons, and the destruction of the city that followed it. They told him also of the broken Seventh Pyramid, and of the shrine beneath it, the Shrine of the Downfall, as they called it. In which, they said, certain artifacts dating from the day of the Defilement had been buried – artifacts that would, when properly used, grant their wielder god-like power over all the forces of space and time. This story stayed with him, and many years later when he had become Pontifex he came to Velalisier with the intention of locating the shrine of the Seventh Pyramid, the Shrine of the Downfall, and opening it."

"For the purpose of bringing forth these magical artifacts, and using them to gain god-like power over the forces of space and time?"

"Exactly," said Magadone Sambisa.

"I think I see where this is heading."

"Perhaps you do, majesty. We are told that he went to the site of the shattered pyramid. He drove a tunnel into the ground; he came upon the stone passageway that leads to the wall of the shrine. He found the wall and made preparations for breaking through it."

"But the seventh shrine, you told me, is intact. Since the time of the abandonment of the city no one has ever entered it. Or so you believe."

"No one ever has. I'm sure of that."

"This Pontifex, then – ?"

"Was just at the moment of breaching the shrine wall when a Piurivar who had hidden himself in the tunnel overnight rose up out of the darkness and put a sword through his heart."

"Wait a moment," said Valentine. Exasperation began to stir in him. "A Piurivar popped out of nowhere and killed him, you say? A *Piurivar?* I've just gone through this same thing with Aarisiim. Not only weren't there any Piurivars anywhere in Alhanroel at that time, because Stiamot had locked them all up in reservations over in Zimroel, but there was supposed to be a curse on this place that would have prevented members of their race from going near it."

"Except for the guardians of the shrine, who were exempted from the curse," said Magadone Sambisa.

"Guardians?" Valentine said. "What guardians? I've never heard anything about Piurivar guardians here."

"Nor had I, until Torkkinuuminaad told me this story. But at the time of the city's destruction and abandonment, evidently, a decision was made to post a small band of watchmen here, so that nobody would be able to break into the seventh shrine and gain access to whatever's in there. And that guard force remained on duty here throughout the centuries. There were still guardians here when the Pontifex came to loot the shrine. One of them tucked himself away in the tunnel and killed the Pontifex just as he was about to chop through the wall."

"And his people buried him *here?* Why in the world would they do that?"

Magadone Sambisa smiled. "To hush things up, of course. Consider, majesty: A Pontifex comes to Velalisier in search of forbidden mystical knowledge, and is assassinated by a Piurivar who has been sneaking around undetected in the supposedly abandoned city. If word of that got around, it would make everyone look bad."

"I suppose that it would."

"The Pontifical officials certainly wouldn't have wanted to let it be known that their master had been struck down right under their noses. Nor would they be eager to advertise the story of the secret shrine, which might lead others to come here looking for it too. And surely they'd never want anyone to know that the Pontifex had died at the hand of a Piurivar, something that could reopen all the wounds of the War of the Conquest and perhaps touch off some very nasty reprisals."

"And so they covered everything up," said Valentine.

"Exactly. They dug a tomb off in a remote corner of the ruins and buried the Pontifex in it with some sort of appropriate ritual, and went back to the Labyrinth with the news that his majesty had very suddenly been stricken down at the ruins by an unknown disease and it had seemed unwise to bring his body back from Velalisier for the usual kind of state funeral. Ghorban, was his name. There's an inscription in the tomb that names him. Ghorban Pontifex, three Pontifexes after Stiamot. He really existed. I did research in the House of Records. You'll see him listed there"

"I'm not familiar with the name."

"No. He's not exactly one of the famous ones. But who can remember them all, anyway? Hundreds and hundreds of them, across all those thousands of years. Ghorban was Pontifex only a short while, and the only event of any importance that occurred during his reign was something that was carefully obliterated from the records. I'm speaking of his visit to Velalisier."

Valentine nodded. He had paused by the great screen outside the Labyrinth's House of Records often enough, and many times had stared at that long list of his predecessors, marveling at the names of all-but-forgotten monarchs, Meyk and Spurifon and Heslaine and Kandibal and dozens more. Who must have been great men in their day, but their day was thousands of years in the past. No doubt there was a Ghorban on the list, if Magadone Sambisa said there had been: who had reigned in regal grandeur for a time as the Coronal Lord Ghorban atop Castle Mount, and then had succeeded to the Pontificate in the fullness of his years, and for some reason had paid a visit to this accursed city of Velalisier, where he died, and was buried, and fell into oblivion.

"A curious tale," Valentine said. "But what is there in it that would have made you want to suppress the discovery of this Ghorban's tomb?"

"The same thing that made those ancient Pontifical officials suppress the real circumstances of his death," replied Magadone Sambisa. "You surely know that most ordinary people already are sufficiently afraid of this city. The horrible story of the Defilement, the curse, all the talk of ghosts lurking in the ruins, the general spookiness of the place – well, you know what people are like, your majesty. How timid they can be in the face of the unknown. And I was afraid that if the Ghorban story came out – the secret shrine, the search for mysterious magical lore by some obscure ancient Pontifex, the murder of that Pontifex by a Piurivar – there'd be such public revulsion against the whole idea of excavating Velalisier that the dig would be shut down. I didn't want that to happen. That's all it was, your majesty. I was trying to preserve my own job, I suppose. Nothing more than that."

It was a humiliating confession. Her tone, which had been vigorous enough during the telling of the tale, now was flat, weary, almost lifeless. To Valentine it had the sound of complete sincerity.

"And Dr. Huukaminaan didn't agree with you that revealing the discovery of the tomb could be a threat to the continuation of your work here?"

"He saw the risk. He didn't care. For him the truth came first and foremost, always. If public opinion forced the dig to be shut down, and nobody worked here again for fifty or a hundred or five hundred years, that was all right with him. His integrity wouldn't permit hiding a startling piece of history like that, not for any reason. So we had a big battle and finally I pushed him into giving in. You've seen how stubborn I can be. But I didn't kill him. If I had wanted to kill anybody, it wouldn't have been Dr. Huukaminaan. It would have been the khivanivod, who actually *does* want the dig shut down."

"He does? You said he and Huukaminaan worked hand in glove."

"In general, yes. As I told you yesterday, there was one area where he and Huukaminaan diverged: the issue of opening the shrine. Huukaminaan and I, you know, were planning to open it as soon as we could arrange for you and Lord Hissune to be present at the work. But the khivanivod was passionately opposed. The rest of our work here was acceptable to him, but not that. The Shrine of the Downfall, he kept saying, is the holy of holies, the most sacred Piurivar place."

"He might just have a point there," Valentine said.

"You also don't think we should look inside that shrine?"

"I think that there are certain important Piurivar leaders who might very much not want that to happen."

"But the Danipiur herself has given us permission to work here! Not only that, but she and all the rest of the Piurivar leaders understand that we've come here to restore the city – that we hope to undo as much as we can of the harm that thousands of years of neglect have caused. They have no quarrel with that. But just to be completely certain that our work would give no offense to the Piurivar community, we all agreed that the expedition would consist of equal numbers of Piurivar and non-Piurivar archaeologists, and that Dr. Huukaminaan and I would share the leadership on a co-equal basis."

"Although you turned out to be somewhat more co-equal

than he was when there happened to be a significant disagreement between the two of you, didn't you?"

"In that one instance of the Ghorban tomb, yes," said Magadone Sambisa, looking just a little out of countenance. "But only that one. He and I were in complete agreement at all times on everything else. On the issue of opening the shrine, for example."

"A decision which the khivanivod then vetoed."

"The khivanivod has no power to veto anything, majesty. The understanding we had was that any Piurivar who objected to some aspect of our work on religious grounds could appeal to the Danipiur, who would then adjudicate the matter in consultation with you and Lord Hissune."

"Yes. I wrote that decree myself, actually."

Valentine closed his eyes a moment and pressed the tips of his fingers against them. He should have realized, he told himself, that problems like these would inevitably crop up. This city had too much tragic history. Terrible things had happened here. The mysterious aura of Piurivar sorcery still hovered over the place, thousands of years after its destruction.

He had hoped to dispel some of that aura by sending in these scientists. Instead he had only enmeshed himself in its dark folds.

After a time he looked up and said, "I understand from Aarisiim that where your khivanivod has gone to make his spiritual retreat is in fact the Ghorban tomb that you've taken such pains to hide from me, and that he's there at this very moment. Is that true?"

"I believe it is."

The Pontifex walked to the tent entrance and peered outside. The first bronze streaks of the desert dawn were arching across the great vault of the sky.

"Last night," he said, "I asked you to send messengers out looking for him, and you said that you would. You didn't, of course, tell me that you knew where he was. But since you do know, get your messengers moving. I want to speak with him first thing this morning."

"And if he refuses to come, your majesty?"

"Then have him brought."

The khivanivod Torkkinuuminaad was every bit as disagreeable as Magadone Sambisa had led Valentine to expect, although the fact that it had been necessary for Valentine's security people to threaten to drag him bodily from the Ghorban tomb must not have improved his temper. Lisamon Hultin was the one who had ordered him out of there, heedless of his threats and curses. Piurivar witcheries and spells held little dread for her, and she let him know that if he didn't go to Valentine more or less willingly on his own two feet, she would carry him to the Pontifex herself.

The Shapeshifter shaman was an ancient, emaciated man, naked but for some wisps of dried grass around his waist and a nasty-looking amulet, fashioned of interwoven insect legs and other such things, that dangled from a frayed cord about his neck. He was so old that his green skin had faded to a faint gray, and his slitted eyes, bright with rage, glared balefully at Valentine out of sagging folds of rubbery skin.

Valentine began on a conciliatory note. "I ask your pardon for interrupting your meditations. But certain urgent matters must be dealt with before I return to the Labyrinth, and your presence was needed for that."

Torkkinuuminaad said nothing.

Valentine proceeded regardless. "For one thing, a serious crime has been committed in the archaeological zone. The killing of Dr. Huukaminaan is an offense not only against justice but against knowledge itself. I'm here to see that the murderer is identified and punished."

"What does this have to do with me?" asked the khivanivod, glowering sullenly. "If there has been a murder, you should find the murderer and punish him, yes, if that is what you feel you must do. But why must a servant of the Gods That Are be compelled by force to break off his sacred communion like this? Because the Pontifex of Majipoor commands it?" Torkkinuuminaad laughed harshly. "The Pontifex! Why should the commands of the Pontifex mean anything to me? I serve only the Gods That Are."

"You also serve the Danipiur," said Valentine in a calm, quiet tone. "And the Danipiur and I are colleagues in the government of Majipoor." He indicated Magadone Sambisa and the other archaeologists, both human and Metamorph, who stood nearby. "These people are at work in Velalisier this day because the Danipiur has granted her permission for them to be here. You yourself are here at the Danipiur's request, I believe. To serve as spiritual counsellor for those of your people who are involved in the work."

"I am here because the Gods That Are require me to be here, and for no other reason."

"Be that as it may, your Pontifex stands before you, and he has questions to ask you, and you will answer."

The shaman's only response was a sour glare.

"A shrine has been discovered near the ruins of the Seventh Pyramid," Valentine went on. "I understand that the late Dr. Huukaminaan intended to open that shrine. You had strong objections to that, am I correct?"

"You are."

"Objections on what grounds?"

"That the shrine is a sacred place not to be disturbed by profane hands."

"How can there be a sacred place," asked Valentine, "in a city that had a curse pronounced on it?"

"The shrine is sacred nevertheless," the khivanivod said obdurately.

"Even though no one knows what may be inside it?"

"I know what is inside it," said the khivanivod.

"You? How?"

"I am the guardian of the shrine. The knowledge is handed down from guardian to guardian."

Valentine felt a chill traveling along his spine. "Ah," he said. "The guardian. Of the shrine." He was silent a moment. "As the officially designated successor, I suppose, of the guardian who murdered a Pontifex here once thousands of years ago. The place where you were found praying just now, so I've been told, was the tomb of that very Pontifex. Is that so?"

"It is."

"In that case," said Valentine, allowing a little smile to appear at the corners of his mouth, "I need to ask my guards to keep very careful watch on you. Because the next thing I'm going to do, my friend, is to instruct Magadone Sambisa and her people to proceed at once with the opening of the seventh shrine. And I see now that that might place me in some danger at your hands."

Torkkinuuminaad looked astounded. Abruptly the Metamorph shaman began to go through a whole repertoire of violent changes of form, contracting and elongating wildly, the borders of his body blurring and recomposing with bewildering speed.

But the archaeologists too, both the human ones and the two Ghayrogs and the little tight-knit group of Shapeshifters, were staring at Valentine as though he had just said something beyond all comprehension. Even Tunigorn and Mirigant and Nascimonte were flabbergasted. Tunigorn turned to Mirigant and said something, to which Mirigant replied only with a shrug, and Nascimonte, standing near them, shrugged also in complete bafflement.

Magadone Sambisa said in hoarse choking tones, "Majesty? Do you mean that? I thought you said only a little while ago that the best thing would be to leave the shrine unopened!"

"I said that? I?" Valentine shook his head. "Oh, no. No. How long will it take you to get started on the job?"

"Why – let me see—" He heard her murmur, "The recording devices, the lighting equipment, the masonry drills—" She grew quiet, as if counting additional things off in her mind. Then she said, "We could be ready to begin in half an hour."

"Good. Let's get going, then."

"No! This will not be!" cried Torkkinuumaad, a wild screech of rage.

"It will," said Valentine. "And you'll be there to watch it. As will I." He beckoned toward Lisamon Hultin. "Speak with him, Lisamon. Tell him in a persuasive way that it'll be much better for him if he remains calm."

Magadone Sambisa said, wonderingly, "Are you serious about all this, Pontifex?"

"Oh, yes. Yes. Very serious indeed."

The day seemed a hundred hours long.

Opening any sealed site for the first time would ordinarily have been a painstaking process. But this one was so important, so freighted with symbolic significance, so potentially explosive in its political implications, that every task was done with triple care.

Valentine himself waited at surface level during the early stages of the work. What they were doing down there had all been explained to him – running cables for illumination and ventilating pipes for the excavators; carefully checking with sonic probes to make sure that opening the shrine wall would not cause the ceiling of the vault to collapse; sonic testing of the interior of the shrine itself to see if there was anything important immediately behind the wall that might be imperiled by the drilling operation.

All that took hours. Finally they were ready to start cutting into the wall.

"Would you like to watch, majesty?" Magadone Sambisa asked.

Despite the ventilation equipment, Valentine found it hard work to breathe inside the tunnel. The air had been hot and stale enough on his earlier visit; but now, with all these people crowded into it, it was thin, feeble stuff, and he had to strain his lungs to keep from growing dizzy.

The close-packed archaeologists parted ranks to let him come forward. Bright lights cast a brilliant glare on the white stone facade of the shrine. Five people were gathered there, three Piurivars, two humans. The actual drilling seemed to be the responsibility of the burly foreman Vaathimeraak. Kaastisiik, the Piurivar archaeologist who was the site boss, was assisting. just behind them was Driismiil, the Piurivar architectural expert, and a human woman named Shimrayne Gelvoin, who also was an architect, evidently. Magadone Sambisa stood to the rear, quietly issuing orders.

They were peeling the wall back stone by stone. Already an area of the facade perhaps three feet square had been cleared just above the row of offering-alcoves. Behind it lay rough brickwork, no more than one course thick. Vaathimeraak, muttering to himself in Piurivar as he worked, now was chiseling away at one of the bricks. It came loose in a crumbling mass, revealing an inner wall made of the same fine black stone slabs as the tunnel wall itself.

A long pause, now, while the several layers of the wall were measured and photographed. Then Vaathimerak resumed the inward probing. Valentine was at the edge of queasiness in this foul, acrid atmosphere, but he forced it back.

Vaathimeraak cut deeper, halting to allow Kaastisiik to remove some broken pieces of the black stone. The two architects came forward and inspected the opening, conferring first with each other, then with Magadone Sambisa; and then Vaathimeraak stepped toward the breach once again with his drilling tool.

"We need a torch," Magadone Sambisa said suddenly. "Give me a torch, someone!"

A hand-torch was passed up the line from the crowd in the rear of the tunnel. Magadone Sambisa thrust it into the opening, peered, gasped.

"Majesty? Majesty, would you come and look?"

By that single shaft of light Valentine made out a large rectangular room, which appeared to be completely empty except for a large square block of dark stone. It was very much like the glossy block of black opal, streaked with veins of scarlet ruby, from which the glorious Confalume Throne at the castle of the Coronal had been carved.

There were things lying on that block. But what they were was impossible to tell at this distance.

"How long will it take to make an opening big enough for someone to enter the room?" Valentine asked.

"Three hours, maybe."

"Do it in two. I'll wait above ground. You call me when the opening is made. Be certain that no one enters it before me."

"You have my word, majesty."

Even the dry desert air was a delight after an hour or so of breathing the dank stuff below. Valentine could see by the lengthening shadows creeping across the deep sockets of the distant dunes that the afternoon was well along. Tunigorn, Mirigant, and Nascimonte were pacing about amidst the rubble of the fallen pyramid. The Vroon Deliamber stood a little distance apart.

"Well?" Tunigorn asked.

"They've got a little bit of the wall open. There's something inside, but we don't know what, yet."

"Treasure?" Tunigorn asked, with a lascivious grin. "Mounds of emeralds and diamonds and jade?"

"Yes," said Valentine. "All that and more. Treasure. An enormous treasure, Tunigorn." He chuckled and turned away. "Do you have any wine with you, Nascimonte?"

"As ever, my friend. A fine Muldemar vintage."

He handed his flask to the Pontifex, who drank deep, not pausing to savor the bouquet at all, guzzling as though the wine were water.

The shadows deepened. One of the lesser moons crept into the margin of the sky.

"Majesty? Would you come below?"

It was the archaeologist Vo-Siimifon. Valentine followed him into the tunnel.

The opening in the wall was large enough now to admit one person. Magadone Sambisa, her hand trembling, handed Valentine the torch.

"I must ask you, your majesty, to touch nothing, to make no disturbance whatever. We will not deny you the privilege of first entry, but you must bear in mind that this is a scientific enterprise. We have to record everything just as we find it before anything, however trivial, can be moved."

"I understand," said Valentine.

He stepped carefully over the section of the wall below the opening and clambered in.

The shrine's floor was of some smooth glistening stone, perhaps rosy quartz. A fine layer of dust covered it. No one has walked across this floor for twenty thousand years, Valentine thought. No human foot has ever come in contact with it at all.

He approached the broad block of black stone in the center of the room and turned the torch full on it. Yes, a single dark mass of ruby-streaked opal, just like the Confalume throne. Atop it, with only the faintest tracery of dust concealing its brilliance, lay a flat sheet of gold, engraved with intricate Piurivar glyphs and inlaid with cabochons of what looked like beryl and carnelian and lapis lazuli. Two long, slender objects that could have been daggers carved from some white stone lay precisely in the center of the gold sheet, side by side.

Valentine felt a tremor of the deepest awe. He knew what those two things were.

"Majesty? Majesty?" Magadone Sambisa called. "Tell us what you see! Tell us, please!"

But Valentine did not reply. It was as though Magadone Sambisa had not spoken. He was deep in memory, traveling back eight years to the climactic hour of the War of the Rebellion.

He had, in that hour, held in his hand a dagger-like thing much like these two, and had felt the strange coolness of it, a coolness that gave a hint of a fiery core within, and had heard a complex far-off music emanating from it into his mind, a turbulent rush of dizzying sound.

It had been the tooth of a sea-dragon that he had been grasping then. Some mystery within that tooth had placed his mind in communion with the mind of the mighty water-king Maazmoorn, a dragon of the distant Inner Sea. And with the aid of the mind of Maazmoorn had Valentine Pontifex reached across the world to strike down the unrepentent rebel Faraataa and bring that sorry uprising to an end.

Whose teeth were these, now?

He thought he knew. This was the Shrine of the Downfall, the Place of the Defilement. Not far from here, long ago, two water-kings had been brought from the sea to be sacrificed on platforms of blue stone. That was no myth. It had actually happened. Valentine had no doubt of that, for the sea-dragon Mazmoorn had shown it to him with the full communion of his mind, in a manner that admitted of no question. He knew their names, even: one was the water-king Niznorn and the other the water-king Domsitor. Was this tooth here Niznorn's, and this one Domsitor's?

Twenty thousand years.

"Majesty? Majesty?"

"One moment," Valentine said, speaking as though from halfway around the world.

He picked up the left-hand tooth. Grasped it tightly. Hissed as its fiery chill stung the palm of his hand. Closed his eyes, allowed his mind to be pervaded by its magic. Felt his spirit beginning to soar outward and outward and outward, toward some waiting dragon of the sea – Maazmoorn again, for all he could know, or perhaps some other one of the giants who swam in those waters out there – while all the time he heard the sounding bells, the tolling music of that sea-dragon's mind.

And was granted a vision of the ancient sacrifice of the two water-kings, the event known as the Defilement.

He already knew, from Mazmoorn in that meeting of minds

years ago, that that traditional name was a misnomer. There had been no defilement whatever. It had been a voluntary sacrifice; it had been the formal acceptance by the sea-dragons of the power of That Which Is, which is the highest of all the forces of the universe.

The water-kings had given themselves gladly to those Piurivars of long-ago Velalisier to be slain. The slayers themselves had understood what they were doing, perhaps, but the simple Piurivars of the outlying provinces had not; and so those simpler Piurivars had called it a Defilement, and had put the Final King of Velalisier to death and smashed the Seventh Pyramid and then had wrecked all the rest of this great capital, and had laid a curse on the city forever. But the shrine of these teeth they had not dared to touch.

Valentine, holding the tooth, beheld the sacrifice once more. Not with the bound sea-dragons writhing in fury as they were brought to the knife, the way he had seen it in his nightmare of the previous night. No. He saw it now as a serene and holy ceremony, a benign yielding up of the living flesh. And as the knives flashed, as the great sea-creatures died, as their dark flesh was carried to the pyres for burning, a resounding wave of triumphant harmony went rolling out to the boundaries of the universe.

He put the tooth down and picked up the other one. Grasped. Felt. Surrendered himself to its power.

This time the music was more discordant. The vision that came to him was that of some unknown man of middle years, garbed in a rich costume of antique design, clothing befitting to a Pontifex. He was moving cautiously by the smoky light of a flickering torch down the very passageway outside this room where Magadone Sambisa and her archaeologists now clustered. Valentine watched that Pontifex of long ago approaching the white unsullied wall of the shrine. Saw him press the flat of his hand against it, pushing as though he hoped to penetrate it by his own strength alone. Turning from it, then, beckoning to workmen with picks and spades, indicating that they should start hacking their way through it.

And a figure uncoiling out of the darkness, a Shapeshifter, long and lean and grim-faced, taking one great step forward and in a swift unstoppable lunge driving a knife upward and inward beneath the heart of the man in the brocaded Pontifical robes

"Majesty, I beg you!"

Magadone Sambisa's voice, ripe with anguish.

"Yes," said Valentine, in the distant tone of one who has been lost in a dream. "I'm coming."

He had had enough visions, for the moment. He set the torch down on the floor, aiming it toward the opening in the wall to light his way. Carefully he picked up the two dragon-teeth – letting them rest easily on the palms of his hands, taking care not to touch them so tightly as to activate their powers, for he did not want now to open his mind to them – and made his way back out of the shrine.

Magadone Sambisa stared at him in horror. "I asked you, your majesty, not to touch the objects in the vault, not to cause any disturbance to—"

"Yes. I know that. You will pardon me for what I have done."

It was not a request.

The archaeologists melted back out of his way as he strode through their midst, heading for the exit to the upper world. Every eye was turned to the things that rested on Valentine's upturned hands.

"Bring the khivanivod to me here," he said quietly to Aarisiim. The light of day was nearly gone now, and the ruins were taking on the greater mysteriousness that came over them by night, when moonlight's cool gleam danced across the shattered city's ancient stones.

The Shapeshifter went rushing away. Valentine had not wanted the khivanivod anywhere near the shrine while the opening of the wall was taking place; and so, over his violent objections,

Torkkinuuminaad had been bundled off to the archaeologists' headquarters in the custody of some of Valentine's security people. The two immense woolly Skandars brought him forth now, holding him by the arms.

Anger and hatred were bubbling up from the shaman like black gas rising from a churning marsh. And, staring into that jagged green wedge of a face, Valentine had a powerful sense of the ancient magic of this world, of mysteries reaching toward him out of the timeless misty Majipoor dawn, when Shapeshifters had moved alone and unhindered through this great planet of marvels and splendors.

The Pontifex held the two sea-dragon teeth aloft.

"Do you know what these are, Torkkinuuminaad?"

The rubbery eye-folds drew back. The narrow eyes were yellow with rage. "You have committed the most terrible of all sacrileges, and you will die in the most terrible of agonies."

"So you do know what they are, eh?"

"They are the holiest of holies! You must return them to the shrine at once!"

"Why did you have Dr. Huukaminaan killed, Torkkinu-uminaad?"

The khivanivod's only answer was an even more furiously defiant glare.

He would kill me with his magic, if he could, thought Valentine. And why not? I know what I represent to Torkkanuuminaad. For I am Majipoor's emperor and therefore I am Majipoor itself, and if one thrust would send us all to our doom he would strike that thrust.

Yes. Valentine was in his own person the embodiment of the enemy: of those who had come out of the sky and taken the world away from the Piurivars, who had built their own gigantic sprawling cities over virgin forests and glades, had intruded themselves by the billions into the fragile fabric of the Piurivars' trembling web of life. And so Torkkinuuminad would kill him, if he could, and by killing the Pontifex kill, by the symbolism of magic, all of human-dominated Majipoor

But magic can be fought with magic, Valentine thought.

"Yes, look at me," he told the shaman. "Look right into my eyes, Torkkinuuminaad."

And let his fingers close tightly about the two talismans he had taken from the shrine.

The double force of the teeth struck into Valentine with a staggering impact as he closed the mental circuit. He felt the full range of the sensations all at once, not simply doubled, but multiplied many times over. He held himself upright nevertheless; he focused his concentration with the keenest intensity; he aimed his mind directly at that of the khivanivod.

Looked. Entered. Penetrated the khivanivod's memories and quickly found what he was seeking.

Midnight darkness. A sliver of moonlight. The sky ablaze with stars. The billowing tent of the archaeologists. Someone coming out of it, a Piurivar, very thin, moving with the caution of age.

Dr. Huukaminaan, surely.

A slender figure stands in the road, waiting: another Metamorph, also old, just as gaunt, raggedly and strangely dressed.

The khivanivod, that one is. Viewing himself in his own mind's eye.

Shadowy figures moving about behind him, five, six, seven of them. Shapeshifters all. Villagers, from the looks of them. The old archaeologist does not appear to see them. He speaks with the khivanivod; the shaman gestures, points. There is a discussion of some sort. Dr. Huukaminaan shakes his head. More pointing. More discussion. Gestures of agreement. Everything seems to be resolved.

As Valentine watches, the khivanivod and Huukaminaan start off together down the road that leads to the heart of the ruins.

The villagers, now, emerging from the shadows that have concealed them. Surrounding the old man; seizing him; covering his mouth to keep him from crying out. The khivanivod approaches him.

The khivanivod has a knife.

Valentine did not need to see the rest of the scene. Did not *want* to see that monstrous ceremony of dismemberment at the stone platform, nor the weird ritual afterward in the excavation leading to the Shrine of the Downfall, the placing of the dead man's head in that alcove.

He released his grasp on the two sea-dragon teeth and set them down with great care beside him on the ground.

"Now," he said to the khivanivod, whose expression had changed from one of barely controllable wrath to one that might almost have been resignation. "There's no need for further pretending here, I think. Why did you kill Dr. Huukaminaan?"

"Because he would have opened the shrine." The khivanivod's tone was completely flat, no emotion in it at all.

"Yes. Of course. But Magadone Sambisa also was in favor of opening it. Why not kill her instead?"

"He was one of us, and a traitor," said Torkkinuuminaad. "She did not matter. And he was more dangerous to our cause. We know that she might have been prevented from opening the shrine, if we objected strongly enough. But nothing would stop him."

"The shrine was opened anyway, though," Valentine said.

"Yes, but only because you came here. Otherwise the excavations would have been closed down. The outcry over Huukaminaan's death would demonstrate to the whole world that the curse of this place still had power. You came, and you opened the shrine; but the curse will strike you just as it struck the Pontifex Ghorban long ago."

"There is no curse," Valentine said calmly. "This is a city that has seen much tragedy, but there is no curse, only misunderstanding piled on misunderstanding."

"The Defilement—"

"There was no Defilement either, only a sacrifice. The destruction of the city by the people of the provinces was a vast mistake."

"So you understand our history better than we do, Pontifex?"

"Yes," said Valentine. "Yes. I do." He turned away from the shaman and said, glancing toward the village foreman, "Vathiimeraak, there are murderers living in your settlement. I know who they are. Go to the village now and announce to everyone that if the guilty ones will come forward and confess their crime, they'll be pardoned after they undergo a full cleansing of their souls."

Turning next to Lisamon Hultin, he said, "As for the khivanivod, I want him handed over to the Danipiur's officials to be tried in her own courts. This falls within her area of responsibility. And then—"

"Majesty!" someone called. "Beware!"

Valentine swung around. The Skandar guards had stepped back from the khivanivod and were staring at their own trembling hands as though they had been burned in a fiery furnace. Torkinuuminaad, freed of their grasp, thrust his face up into Valentine's. His expression was one of diabolical intensity.

"Pontifex!" he whispered. "Look at me, Pontifex! Look at me!"

Taken by surprise, Valentine had no way of defending himself. Already a strange numbness had come over him. The dragon-teeth went tumbling from his helpless hands. Torkinuuminaad was shifting shape, now, running through a series of grotesque changes at a frenzied rate, so that he appeared to have a dozen arms and legs at once, and half a dozen bodies; and he was casting some sort of spell. Valentine was caught in it like a moth in a spider's cunningly woven strands. The air seemed thick and blurred before him, and a wind had come up out of nowhere. Valentine stood perplexed, trying to force his gaze away from the khivanivod's fiery eyes, but he could not. Nor could he find the strength to reach down and seize hold of the two dragon-teeth that lay at his feet. He stood as though frozen, muddled, dazed, tottering. There was a burning sensation in his breast and it was a struggle simply to draw breath.

There seemed to be phantoms all around him.

A dozen Shapeshifters – a hundred, a thousand—

Grimacing faces. Glowering eyes. Teeth; claws; knives. A horde of wildly cavorting assassins surrounded him, dancing, bobbing, gyrating, hissing, mocking him, calling his name derisively—

He was lost in a whirlwind of ancient sorceries.

"Lisamon?" Valentine cried, baffled. "Deliamber? Help me – help—" But he was not sure that the words had actually escaped his lips.

Then he saw that his guardians had indeed perceived his danger. Deliamber, the first to react, came rushing forward, flinging his own many tentacles up hastily in a counter-spell, a set of gesticulations and thrusts of mental force intended to neutralize whatever was emanating from Torkkinuuminaad. And then, as the little Vroon began to wrap the Piurivar shaman in his web of Vroonish wizardry, Vathiimeraak advanced on Torkinuuminaad from the opposite side, boldly seizing the shaman in complete indifference to his spells, forcing him down to the ground, bending him until his forehead was pressing against the soil at Valentine's feet.

Valentine felt the grip of the shaman's wizardry beginning to ebb, then easing further, finally losing its last remaining hold on his soul. The contact between Torkinuuminaad's mind and his gave way with an almost audible snap.

Vathiimeraak released the khivanivod and stepped back. Lisamon Hultin now came to the shaman's side and stood menacingly over him. But the episode was over. The shaman remained where he was, absolutely still now, staring at the ground, scowling bitterly in defeat.

"Thank you," Valentine said simply to Deliamber and Vathiimeraak. And, with a dismissive gesture: "Take him away."

Lisamon Hultin threw Torkinuuminaad over her shoulder like a sack of calimbots and went striding off down the road.

*

A long stunned silence followed. Magadone Sambisa broke it, finally. In a hushed voice she said, "Your majesty, are you all right?"

He answered only with a nod.

"And the excavations," she said anxiously, after another moment. "What will happen to them? Will they continue?"

"Why not?" Valentine replied. "There's still much work to be done." He took a step or two away from her. He touched his hands to his chest, to his throat. He could still almost feel the pressure of those relentless invisible hands.

Magadone Sambisa was not finished with him, though.

"And these?" she asked, indicating the sea-dragon teeth. She spoke more aggressively now, taking charge of things once again, beginning to recover her vigor and poise. "If I may have them now, majesty—"

Angrily Valentine said, "Take them, yes. But put them back in the shrine. And then seal up the hole you made today."

The archaeologist stared at him as though he had turned into a Piurivar himself. With a note of undisguised asperity in her voice she said, "What, your majesty? What? Dr. Huukaminaan died for those teeth! Finding that shrine was the pinnacle of his work. If we seal it up now—"

"Dr. Huukaminaan was the perfect scientist," Valentine said, not troubling to conceal his great weariness now. "His love of the truth cost him his life. Your own love of truth, I think, is less than perfect, and therefore you will obey me in this."

"I beg you, majesty—"

"No. Enough begging. I don't pretend to be a scientist at all, but I understand my own responsibilities. Some things should remain buried. These teeth are not things for us to handle and study and put on display at a museum. The shrine is a holy place to the Piurivars, even if they don't understand its own holiness. It's a sad business for us all that it ever was uncovered. The dig itself can continue, in other parts of the city. But put these back. Seal that shrine and stay away from it. Understood?"

She looked at him numbly, and nodded.

"Good. Good."

The full descent of darkness was settling upon the desert now. Valentine could feel the myriad ghosts of Velalisier hovering around him. It seemed that bony fingers were plucking at his tunic, that eerie whispering voices were murmuring perilous magics in his ears.

Most heartily he yearned to be quit of these ruins. He had had all he cared to have of them for one lifetime.

To Tunigorn he said, "Come, old friend, give the orders, make things ready for our immediate departure."

"Now, Valentine? At this late hour?"

"Now, Tunigorn. Now." He smiled. "Do you know, this place has made the Labyrinth seem almost appealing to me! I feel a great desire to return to its familiar comforts. Come: get everything organized for leaving. We've been here quite long enough."